D1472395

SWEETSIR

Helen Yglesias

SIMON AND SCHUSTER • NEW YORK

FOR JOSE

PART ONE

1

SHE WANTED TO WIN this fight. She would win it at any cost. She
had had enough. From now on she meant to give as good as she
got. He wanted a fight, she'd give him a good fight. Hadn't she always wanted to please him?

He had shoved her against the kitchen cabinets, cornering her
between the open drawers and the refrigerator. She struggled to
get away from his punishing, slapping open hand hitting her on the
side of her head.

She said, "You can't do this to me, Sweets. If you hit me again,
I'll get you, I will." Her voice was shockingly loud.

His voice stayed low, almost a whisper. "Shut up, shut up, shut
up," he said and punctuated each with a whack.

A leaping roar of fire ignited behind her eyes and ears. It was
like making love, this fight. Hatred, like love, could become a
charged entity building into a living presence between them. He
loved hatred? She'd give him hatred. From the open kitchen
drawer she grabbed a long carving knife. That would scare him.
Maddeningly, instead of backing off, he closed in, hitting her with
one hand, clinging with the other to the wrist of the hand that held
the knife. They locked into a powerful embrace. Her breathing
stripped her throat dry; his breathing sang in her face. They were
one body, dancing, shaking, lifting off the floor, pulling backward
across the kitchen floor. Now he was backed up against the wall.
She had him now, she had him, she had stopped him, everything
had come to a stop. They faced each other, she and her husband, in
a bewitched space of extraordinary calm, looking into each other's

eyes more directly than they ever had, his seemingly astounded by what he saw. She had him now, she had him, she had stopped him, everything had come to a stop. Had she won the fight then?

Yes. There was that split of a moment, now past, when she had felt the knife go in and come out—so easily—in and out with no effort at all. Was that what had happened?

She heard a drawling good-little-girl voice saturated with meekness. "Oh, did I hit you? Did the knife hit you?"

This ludicrously false voice was hers? The other raging voice still looped the room—"I'll get you, Sweets, if you hit me again, I will, I'll get you"—crowding the apologetic "Oh, did I hit you?"—too confused to be separated.

Now something terrible was happening to Sweets, making him grow larger, slower, blacker, paler, all the rich color of his bright skin sucked out into his black, black hair, while time and sound and motion were being sucked out of the room.

"Oh, did I hit you?" she repeated, and corrected herself. "Did the knife hit you?"

The knife was innocent, the knife was without intention. It had entered so easily and emerged so effortlessly, what harm could it have done other than a little cut, the innocent knife?

Their fight had lifted them to a charmed, stopped space so like the exhilarated elation of love it seemed to her that she had the power to shape time and space to her demand that this moment be stayed forever, or better still, retreat, go backward, be the moment before she grabbed the kitchen knife. Yet out of her reach, Sweets lurched beyond the charmed, held space she commanded—as if his body were the vehicle of the accident, not the victim. Then it was his own fault? Had he been the driver?

Her husband danced away from her, attached himself to a kitchen chair as his partner, floated with it, half sat on it, now foolishly hugged it, his face turned always to hers, his astounded eyes fixed on hers, his mouth open and loose, working at the message conveyed by his eyes, a message demanding more energy than he had available for communication by way of speech while concentrating on his slow waltz with the chair. He gave up then, let the chair fall, and started on a dragging collapse that beached him gently wrecked at her feet, flat out on the floor at her feet, his eyes still fixed on hers, at rest.

She needed to make Sweets comfortable on the floor. She wanted time to think about her feet being bare. She wondered why Johnny was screaming about somebody being shot. It was taking a long, long time for her to think about these matters in an orderly fashion before deciding what she must do.

"What's the matter, Sweets?" She spoke very calmly, to reassure him. After all, it was only one of their fights.

She saw now a little blood on the sleeve of his undershirt. A little cut on the inner, upper arm, not bleeding heavily. Her husband was acting just like a man, scaring himself to death because the knife had cut him a little.

Why was all the bright, bright color fleeing his face? Stay, bright color that I love, she commanded.

"Oh, did I hit you? Did the knife hit you?"

Inane repetition, drawled in the good-little-girl voice impossible for her to quiet.

His head fell to the side in a gesture unlike him, but keeping his eyes intently fixed on her, he answered in words so perfectly and naturally his that they burst the enchantment in which she had been locked, and let reality rush in.

"Yeah, ya stupid shit," he said, "ya hit me all right."

2

Tourist brochures described Eatonville as "nestled" in a broad, peaceful New England valley surrounded by commanding peaks. "Nestled" wouldn't have been everybody's word, though there were those who cuddled into Eatonville as into the arms of a nurturing mother, clinging to her before any others, and particularly if they had little experience of different areas of the world.

"Squeezed" was another word. Squeezed into a frozen mold in winter, thawing into the heavy mistiness of summer. For those who favored "squeezed," there was a pervasive sense of overbearing weather, of dark pines against submissive white birches. In the winter there was the constant snow and ice, cold and wind; in the summer, humid heat, persistent fog and rain. It took lots of rain to keep that valley so green.

"Cowered" was a good word. The town cowered against the wilderness just beyond. It clung to the edge of the country. The great rough sea claimed the shore; to the north foreigners took over, not even English-speaking. Bleak New England sister states hung at the other borders—a sisterhood disowned, divided by their insistence on their own uniqueness—stubborn against invaders, out-of-staters, flatlanders messing up Eatonville's private, superior ways of being.

The best in the world, yet always bitterly inadequate, both to the "nestled" and the "squeezed." Population 63,000. There was a post office, a library, a handsome town hall and a court building, churches and church spires, public schools (grade and high school), one private academy and a state university campus. Any-

thing anybody could think to need was laid out for sale on the strip
—car wash, supermarkets, McDonald's, seven different brands of
gas, Holiday Inn, Chuck Wagon, Zayre's and the rest of them.
There was a roller-skating rink, a disco, barbershops and beauty
parlors, two bowling alleys, fairgrounds, a big-shot Romanian de-
fector living back in the woods, indoor tennis courts and an Olym-
pic-size swimming pool over at the Holiday Inn. There were cemeteries, restaurants, bars and a Cinema 1, 2, 3 (even if 3 was mostly
closed), excellent ski runs right outside of town, top-notch locally
produced cheese and very good local chickens. A lot of the fish
catch went down to Boston. On the capitol dome, real gold
gleamed, eating up taxpayer money as if money was as easy to find
as syrup rising through the sugar-maple taps in March.

There was work to be had in the paper mills, the marble and
granite quarries, on the fishing boats or on the dairy farms and
chicken farms; women worked in the hospital, the supermarkets,
the five-and-tens, the fine shops in the ski area or the restaurants
and bars and motels, serving the tourists. There wasn't anything to
stop anybody from becoming a lawyer or a doctor, a dentist, a vet-
erinarian, a travel agent, a documentary filmmaker or a banker, and
some did.

Gossip was a big local industry.

The morning after the Sweetsir family fight, Eatonville woke up
glad to see the early news reports enlivened by a local murder. It
had been an oppressively hot summer, and though that morning
there was a temperature drop of ten degrees, a heavy cloud cover
masked the sun and topped the enclosing green hills with a saturat-
ing silver dampness. Enervating. Lots of complaints. Headaches,
pain in the joints, difficulty in breathing. Relieved a person of one's
intimate troubles to read in the morning paper while eating breakfast how Mrs. Sally Sweetsir killed her husband. Some heard it on
the radio, leaning over the kitchen sink doing the dishes, or behind
the wheel of the car waiting for the traffic light on Center Street
Bridge, or from the TV newscaster, half watching, half listening
while tidying the living room.

AP, UP, WCAF, WFKV, WNTN, WILL all carried identical ac-
counts.

Mrs. Sally Sweetsir, age 32, of Eatonville, was arrested by the State Police last night for the murder of her husband. Morgan Beauchamp Sweetsir, age 34, was taken to Central Hartshead Hospital by ambulance shortly after 9 P.M. last night, as a result of a stab wound. Emergency treatment was administered. Mr. Sweetsir expired at approximately 10:30 P.M. Mrs. Sweetsir will be arraigned in Hartshead Superior Court later today.

Early risers and insomniacs who owned CBs had heard the news much earlier, reported as a shooting. The student-run University radio station compounded the error, picking up "shooting" and mishearing the name of the dead man as "Switzer," pinning the victim as Professor Max Switzer, whose violent death at the hands of his frail, soft-spoken wife electrified the academic community. The campus station broadcast corrections and apologies all day. It was a good thing for the student running the show that his passing grade in Media Arts 101 was already on record or the Dean of the Arts School would have flunked him.

3

OFFICER HARDING LEVEEN, the investigating and arresting officer on the Sweetsir case, easily located a motive for the murder. Filling in that slot in his report form, he typed: "Anger, resulting from a family quarrel."

Hardy LeVeen liked doing reports. At headquarters he was regarded as unusual in that skill, and he had been complimented so often he daydreamed of writing a novel someday, after he took his early retirement. He had enough stories under his belt to fill more than one volume, and a lot more interesting stuff than the junk they sold in paperback these days. There was nothing like the real thing, when you came right down to it, no substitute for real life, for what he experienced every day on the job, day after day.

He squirmed to settle more comfortably in a chair a bit too small for his big frame. He seemed also a little swollen with excitement about this case. Something to do with the woman who had done it, something about her. He'd have to keep a check on himself. Public Defender lawyers were quicker than a spaniel on a rabbit. Couldn't give those smartass New York Jews a chink to crawl into or they'd be all over you.

He completed the top boxes in no time: date, initial report, county, town, that junk. Under Status of Investigation he typed CLOSED. It was an open-and-shut case if there ever was one. Under Subject of Investigation he typed HOMICIDE. He halted when he reached Complaint Received.

All the early complaints had come in as a shooting, because of that damn kid, the victim's son, going around yelling his head off about his father being shot. The defense could make that youngster look like a 100 percent idiot. Just the kind of handle they grabbed for. The boy had to be protected. He was the one witness to the crime. He could be important to the prosecution. Officer LeVeen hesitated, his huge curved fists hovering over the typewriter keys, then he typed:

September 4 at 2100 hours a telephone call from the Eatonville Security in Eatonville advised of a report of a stabbing at the Beauchamp residence on the so-called River End Road in Eatonville and that the Hartshead Ambulance was responding.

No sense muddying up the waters.

He filled in date of crime and name and address of the victim, dob/pob and SS#, copying the string of numbers carefully. Thirty-four years old, poor bastard. Wiped out at age thirty-four. He heard the woman babbling, "I didn't mean it, Sweets, I love you, Sweets, breathe, honey, breathe, breathe for me, I love you, Sweets." Yeah, sure.

His notes for Description of Scene were extensive and he copied them intact:

The scene is an unpainted two-story building comprising a multiple dwelling unit of two apartments located on the so-called River End Road in the town of Eatonville. The building under description is one of four away from the highway, this particular building being the last, the other three setting in front of it along the dirt road in the direction of the highway. The driveway to the lot is approximately two tenths of a mile from the junction of Town Road #60 and State Road #6. Proceeding north on Town Road #60, one would take a right turn into the dirt road or driveway which leads by the three buildings situated in front of it and come to the fourth building which is the scene.

A queer setup. He would have had trouble finding the place except that neighbors were bunched up at the entrance to the alley like ravens at a compost heap. An ambulance and another police car had parked so sloppily there was hardly enough room for Le-Veen's car. That started his anger rising and he was in a rage when he hit the kitchen doorway. The Beauchamp residence? What Beauchamp would live in such a dump?

Morgan Beauchamp Sweetsir, laid out on the floor, more dead than alive.

Officer LeVeen stood on the rotting porch, wondering if it could stand up to a man's weight. Porch littered with leaves, a stash of cut and split wood, piled any old way along with some junk for the dog—a feeding dish and water bowl. A big dog lay in a corner, head up, alert but quiet. Officer LeVeen noted a heavy stick, longer and thicker than a baseball bat, leaning against the house front next to the entrance door, and he entered that detail on his pad. Nothing had come of that. A meaningless detail.

Inside, total wreckage. Couldn't blame it all on the fight either or on the mess of the body on the floor. It was clear that it hadn't ever been a really decent home, in spite of a couple of pitiful decorative touches. One hanging plant was still intact.

Dirty dishes in the sink. Nobody bothered to turn off the TV blasting away in the living room. Officer LeVeen had to think of it, go in and turn it off.

And getting in the way, wailing like a sick cat, that woman weeping and moaning over what she had done.

Another woman in the room told her right. "Ya shoulda thoughta that before ya done it."

The poor bastard laying on the floor was as much to blame. Officer LeVeen didn't put it all on the wife. It was the man who should call the shots in a marriage, set the style of living for the whole family. What kind of a man had Sweets become anyway, covering his body with tattoos like that? Sweets hadn't had his body marred by colored snakes and birds when they were at school together. When the hell had he done that to himself?

Morgan Beauchamp Sweetsir—what a la-de-dah name for a fellow like Sweets. A regular guy, just like all the other guys. Little bit wilder, little bit handsomer, drank a little more than most, even at school. Everybody liked Sweets. There was some talk that he beat up on his women, but when it came to that, if you went after all the guys who clobbered their dames, there'd be nobody left at the Hilltop drinking beer of a Friday night. And then you'd only have gathered the ones who bragged about it.

Officer LeVeen had never hit a woman in his life and never would if he could help it. But that didn't make him a stranger to the notion. Some women needed straightening out by that method. In his own case he wasn't attracted to the type of woman who needed straightening out, as anybody could see by the woman he had married. Just compare the *neatness* of his house to that mess he had walked into—making allowances, naturally, for an event having occurred. The two were so far apart there wasn't any way to compare them. Perfect orderliness in his house. Wall-to-wall, drapes closed, needlepoint cushions placed just so, nothing cluttering the side tables but lamps and pretty ashtrays, clean and gleaming; on the coffee table a centerpiece of dried flowers she had been taught to arrange at a course she took, and next to the bouquet a book on antique American furniture lying sideways, as if someone had just put it down after looking it over. No TV roaring away in his living room. He put his entertainment unit in the family room where the door could be shut on the three kids. The mess family living created had to be controlled; a woman had to subdue a household, like a general running his troops, or chaos reigned. *His* wife knew how to keep a house because she damn well knew that's how her husband demanded she keep it. He had to put some blame on Morgan Sweetsir right there. Whatever kind of slut he married, he should have trained her better.

Too busy puttin the wood to her, no doubt.

Unbidden, he had a momentary vision of the hospital orderliness of the kitchen his wife kept. On the wall, a teakettle clock ticked, and the healthy hanging plants swung gently as if recently handled. On the gleaming floor a naked man lay, stabbed and bleeding to death, himself, on his immaculate kitchen floor.

Officer LeVeen consulted his notes and proceeded, immersing himself in the detail that offered security:

The peak of the structure runs from east to west. The doors are situated on the north side facing the river; there are two doors located at either end of the porch, the east end and the west end: one leads to each apartment. On the first floor, facing north, there are two windows in the center of the building and one window on each side of each door; on the second floor, there are . . .

He was content working up this description, delighting in the precision of his observation, his use of words and of the colon and semicolon. He would have liked to let himself go and use words like "wretched" and "dilapidated," inappropriate words for a police report, story-teller words, to be put aside until the moment of early retirement when he'd really have a go at writing.

He typed:

A detailed description of the inside of the scene by the Mobile Crime Lab is attached.

Now he was up to a description of the accused. He typed: "Described as a white female, age 32, 5–6, 123 lbs., blue eyes," then backtracked and corrected "blue" to "bluish-green. Blond hair, appears to be bleached or tinted; slender build, fair complexion."

When he had first seen her at the scene he had thought her a plain slut. Plain, a slut, and hysterical. Period. His mother had always said, "A woman should look as if she just stepped out of a bandbox." He had no idea what that literally meant, but he knew it didn't apply to barefoot Sally Sweetsir sitting on the kitchen floor crying, her breasts practially hanging out of her soiled low-cut T-shirt. No bra, of course. He had a momentary revolting flash of his wife's elongated slack breasts with large, flat, dirt-colored nipples. Sally Sweetsir's nipples would be the color of roses, he knew it.

He typed: "The accused holds operator's license # . . ." and painstakingly copied a long string of letters and numbers. "The accused's occupation is as Executive Secretary of Eatonville Associates in the town of Eatonville. The accused is widowed."

It galled him that a woman could kill her husband and be called a widow. There should be another word for a murdering wife.

He pressed on to Modus Operandi.

During the hours of approximately 1730 hours and 2100 hours, apparently the ACCUSED and the VICTIM had been arguing. These were apparently a series of arguments about family arrangements, supper, doctor visits, baby-sitting, etc. According to the ACCUSED, she had advised the VICTIM that the doctor had informed her that she had a positive Pap smear, and that there was a possibility of cancer. According to the ACCUSED, the VICTIM, upon hearing this, called her a liar and hit her. The VICTIM apparently then threatened to leave. The ACCUSED apparently asked him not to leave and apparently attempted to restrain him. According to the ACCUSED, the VICTIM hit her again, knocking her to the floor. According to the ACCUSED, she got up, and when the VICTIM raised his hand again the ACCUSED opened a kitchen drawer and removed a knife, saying, "If you hit me, I'll get you." Apparently the VICTIM backed away from the ACCUSED. Apparently the ACCUSED followed and struck the VICTIM with the knife, which apparently went through the left arm and into the chest cavity.

It was then that Officer Harding LeVeen typed his explanation for MOTIVE: "Anger, resulting from a family quarrel."

He hurried now, eager to finish. It was an open-and-shut case. The woman had admitted it. The boy had witnessed it. He typed: "DISCOVERED BY: SWEETSIR, Matthew, son of the VICTIM, present during the event" before realizing he was copying from early, incorrect notes. The boy's name wasn't Sweetsir, it was John Matthews, and he wasn't legally anybody's son, it seemed. Wearily, he corrected the form: "DISCOVERED BY: MATTHEWS, John, member of the household, present during the event."

It had taken him hours getting the relationships figured out. Damn mess.

The woman had turned to him before getting into the ambulance. It was then he noticed the unusual prettiness of her eyes, how they seemed to be smiling, even in her anguish. She had asked him to call the little girl's mother. "Kay Sweetsir," she said, "4832. She should be with her mother tonight." So the little girl wasn't hers either. Just the teenage girl was hers, the foul-mouthed one.

He listed under EXHIBITS:

Personal belongings of the VICTIM collected from Central
Hartshead Hospital personnel:
1 small jackknife
1 ivory toothpick
1 set standard fingernail clippers
1 Taylor key #T8oR on key ring attached to leather strip
32 cents in change
1 torn black wallet, initialed MBS, containing driver's li-
    cense, ID, dentist appointment card and a one-dollar bill
These are in custody of the Evidence Room.
The clothing worn by the VICTIM was placed in plastic garbage bags by hospital employees and signed over by this
writer to the State Police lab. Other exhibits will be listed by
the State Police Crime Lab personnel who checked the scene
of the crime.

Now he was up to the tricky parts. The woman had shot her
mouth off and hung herself right there under his nose in the hospital corridor. Weeping, hysterical, babbling, her anguished, smiling
eyes riveted to the emergency-room door, she had cooked her own
goose. But he had to cover his ass even so.
She refused to move from the floor of the hospital corridor, her
strangely smiling, weeping eyes glued to the closed emergency-
room door where they were working on Morgan Sweetsir. In sloppy
jeans and a loose top, her bare feet dirty, one of them bloodied, the
stringy hair giving her a sluttish, plain look, her vulnerability
worked on him like a seduction. One leg of her jeans had hiked up,
and he saw a bare, slender, smooth ankle swelling into the rich
curve of her calf and followed through satisfactorily in the way her
ass filled her jeans.
He typed:

At this time this writer proceeded to complete a State Police
Officer's Arrest Report on Mrs. SWEETSIR, first taking a MIRANDA
WARNING and a PUBLIC DEFENDER RIGHTS form and advising Mrs.

SWEETSIR that I was going to read it to her. I began the reading of the MIRANDA FORM at 2216 hours.

She had thrown him a wild glance, and let out a crazy laugh. "You can save yourself the bother. I know all about that rights shit."

He reread what he had written. Something wrong with the way he was capitalizing some things and not others. Have to correct that when he gave it to the girl for final typing. He continued, concentrating hard.

While this writer was reading the MIRANDA WARNING to Mrs. SWEETSIR, Dr. Warren Brett from the emergency room approached us and spoke to Mrs. SWEETSIR, informing her that medical efforts to save MORGAN SWEETSIR had failed and advising her of the DEATH OF HER HUSBAND. After a few moments passed, I resumed reading the MIRANDA WARNING and I completed it. I then asked the ACCUSED, SALLY SWEETSIR, if she understood and she stated that she did understand, and she signed the acknowledgment of the receipt of RIGHTS. The reading of the RIGHTS and the SIGNING were witnessed by Jeanine Southby, a Hartshead County Mental Health Worker. The time of the SIGNING was 2228 hours.

This writer then proceeded to read the WAIVER OF RIGHTS to the ACCUSED. Upon completion, the ACCUSED said she believed that she wanted to talk to a former boss who was a lawyer. This writer advised SALLY SWEETSIR that she was entitled to this RIGHT, but she immediately altered her statement, stating, "No, I don't want to talk to an attorney. I don't want to talk to anybody. I did it. I know that I did it." I then asked the ACCUSED if she wished to sign the WAIVER OF RIGHTS and she agreed. . . .

The woman was done for. She babbled out the whole story, telling about the day-long fight, and the nonsmoking setting their nerves on edge and the baby-sitting complications and the doctor visit and her fear of cancer, then the fight about that and throwing the wedding rings around and his threatening to leave and clobbering her to get free of her hanging on and her threatening to get him, and then doing it, stabbing him. She was nailed by her own admission. He had her nailed. Nothing left to do but get it all down carefully and properly on the form.

Her grief was so acute, it pervaded the air of the closed room in which he interrogated her like the perfume of sex in a bedroom. Well she had made a horrible mess, hadn't she? It was only right that he force her to lick some of it up.

4

SHE WAS BLABBING away her life. She was talking her throat raw. She signed whatever they put before her.

"I know all about that rights shit," she said to the tall good-looking cop, and she signed the paper.

She had always aimed to please men.

She and Sweets had been fighting, one of their regular bad fights. She had had one awful day trying to please him, trying to stave off the fight.

She had grabbed the knife from the kitchen drawer to stop him hitting her, to scare him. Had she grabbed the knife from the kitchen drawer to kill him? Had she wanted to kill him to stop his ugly mouth and his punishing hand? No, she had only meant to scare him. The knife slid in and out very easily. Yes, she had been aware of the knife sliding in and out with no effort. She figured it had cut his arm a little. That's what she thought had happened.

Then Sweets began that long crazy dance with the chair. Then he slid on his back at her feet, his head fallen sideways, as if to turn away not only from her but from the whole weary effort of being. All his color was running out, all the color was leaving his lips, all the bright dark color she loved in his bright dark skin was draining away, incredibly draining out in a moment. He kept his eyes strangely fixed on her face. His mouth worked. To speak? To spit?

"Oh, did I hit you?"

She heard herself saying, "Oh, did I hit you?" over and over.

Then Sweets said, "Yeah, ya stupid shit, ya hit me all right."

He spoke quietly, concentrating his energy elsewhere. Then he closed his eyes. He was dying. How could he be dying in a moment? She would forcibly, sensibly stop him dying. She would hold him afloat, staunch the oozing away of his being before her eyes. She would do this thing for him, as she did so many other things for him.

She heard Johnny: "She's gone crazy. She shot Sweets. She shot my daddy. Get out of her way, get upstairs. She's crazy. C'mon, c'mon, we gotta get away from her, get upstairs."

He was fighting with the girls, he was herding Judy and Laura up the staircase. She could hear the TV, very loud. Judy was screaming. She wouldn't go. She clung to the banister screaming that she wouldn't go, she wanted to watch the program, Johnny had promised she could watch the program. The three kids locked into a mad jig on the stairs.

She yelled, "Get help, call Ty, call an ambulance."

Still the lunatic fuss continued on the stairs. She forced her voice, made it very commanding, very mother-voice.

"Fuck it, Johnny, let go of the girls and get the fuck next door for help. Tell Ty to call an ambulance. What are you doing? Move. Move."

Now she saw a wound on Sweets's arm, and a little blood, not much blood. The knife must have hit an artery, she decided. The knife was an instrument that had devised its own plans—nothing to do with her. "Artery" evoked "tourniquet," a mechanical association out of first aid instructions, out of stories of accidents that happened to other people. Something should be tied around Sweets's arm, a dish towel. What had happened to the dish towel? The kitchen was in an awful mess.

The girls stood at the foot of the stairs in the doorway, staring and silent.

Incomprehensibly to her, she heard Laura asking, "Are you all right, Mom? Mom, are you all right?" She couldn't make any sense of the question. As if the use of the name others called her mother might return a better response, Laura said, "Sally? Sally, are you all right? Your foot's bleeding," and returned to childhood with an almost whimpering, "Mom? Mom?"

"You're driving me crazy," Sally yelled, and saw the tears start in her daughter's terrified round liquid-black eyes. "Oh, baby, Laura baby, help me, help me save him. Help me put a towel around his arm."

Laura came straight to her side to help her.

Now Ty Parsons and his wife, Helen, were also in the room, pushing Laura aside. She understood in that instant that what she had done had split her life wide open for anybody to enter it now. She lost herself, lost the practical, good-sense side of herself, lost the thread of what must be done to save Sweets. She heard herself gasping and crying, talking uncontrollably, endlessly endlessly talking, talking.

"Breathe, Sweets, breathe, breathe, baby, you're all right, you're all right, honey, don't be scared, oh Sweets baby, don't scare yourself to death, just breathe, you can do it, do it for me, I love you, honey, I love you, I love you, I didn't mean to do this, I didn't mean to, breathe, honey, breathe, breathe."

"Ya shoulda thoughta that sooner, before ya done what ya done," Helen Parsons said.

For one miraculous beat, Sweets opened his eyes. Milky and glazed, they rolled upward in his head. Mercifully, the lids closed again.

Ty would help her. He was the man in the room among the women and the kids. He must understand the need to get Sweets to the hospital fast. She pleaded with him to help her get Sweets to the car, but she couldn't seem to make Ty understand.

Now she wanted everybody out. There were too many people around. Others were an interference, breaking her connection with Sweets, the deep pulse between herself and Sweets that would will him to stay alive. She wanted everybody out now—the kids and Ty and especially Helen Parsons, lording it in her officious, critical, next-door-neighbor, sour-self way. She had never had any use for Ty and Helen Parsons, so what were they doing here? Out. Clear everybody out. Leave her alone with Sweets so that she could do what had to be done to save him.

She remembered the rings then. She had to find them where they had been flung during the fight, had to put one wedding band back on Sweets's finger and the other on her own, where they belonged, charms to make him all better, to turn their situation backward where they were before the fight when the knife was safely in the kitchen drawer and there wasn't any little cut on Sweets's arm.

No, better get him to the hospital first. Again she pleaded with Ty to help her.

"Ya not supposed to move a person hurt bad like he is," Ty said. He had planted himself between her and Sweets's body. She smelled sweat and beer. His big belly in its soiled undershirt bulged over the imbedded belt of his dark-green work pants.

"Where's the gun?" he said, holding out a hand. "The police are gonna be askin for the gun."

She pushed and pulled, struggling to raise Sweets to a position where she could help him walk to the car.

"Now quit, Sally," Ty yelled at her. "Ya tryin to make sure ya kill im good? Ya not supposed to touch im, not supposed to move im, not supposed to do nothin. Now ya quit and wait for the ambulance."

"It's taking too long to get here," she said. "It's taking too long."

"Now quit," Ty said, "or I'll hafta get rough with ya."

"Ya shoulda thoughta what ya was doin before ya done it," Helen Parsons said.

Sally concentrated on Sweets, only Sweets mattered.

And heard herself babbling, "Breathe, breathe, baby, you can breathe, you can do it. You're the strongest man in the world, you know you are, you can beat it, do it for me. I love you, baby, breathe, baby, breathe, Sweets, just breathe until the ambulance gets here."

"Stop tellin im to breathe," Ty said. "Ya can see he's breathin too hard. Ya don't know what the hell ya doin, so just be quiet and don't do nothin, will ya?"

"Ya done enough already," Helen Parsons said.

She hadn't done enough. She hadn't found the rings. The rings would work their magic. Busy searching the floor for the rings she missed the moment when the ambulance arrived. She was half aware of sirens and of the room jamming up with people and equipment, but she concentrated on her search until she found the rings where they had been flung close together near the wood stove. She pushed in among the medics and the gear, tugging and working away to inch the ring down on Sweets's finger. His hand wasn't like itself. There wasn't any tension in it. She could hear herself sobbing and chattering until she had the rings on, his on his hand and hers on her hand, and then felt better, felt quieter, felt stilled inside for a split second.

She saw now that the ambulance crew weren't all men. One was a woman. In a frenzy again she appealed to the woman to hurry, hurry, they were taking too long, what were they doing anyway, why weren't they getting him right to the hospital? They had ripped open Sweets's undershirt. What had happened to the little arm wound? There was a different wound, an evil rip on the side of Sweets's chest. Even the little arm wound wasn't just a little arm wound but two openings on the inner flesh of his arm, and these two with the larger one entering the chest made three red, hungry mouths among the colored birds and snakes. It was as if she had never seen these tattoos before, they appeared so lurid against the plaster no-color of his skin.

She lost all control. She was babbling, sobbing, yelling at the medics to hurry, hurry, they were dawdling, taking too long to get Sweets on the stretcher, why were they bothering with a stretcher, why were they bothering with all those tubes and paraphernalia, why weren't they just putting him in the ambulance and getting him to the hospital fast, fast?

They tried to keep her away from Sweets, but she wouldn't let them shove her back from him. It was the polite voice of a young male attendant that got through to her.

"Ma'am, could you please move back and give us some room, please?"

"Can't you see that I'm responsible for this?" she said.

It was important to her to make herself clear to this polite young man, and the beat of time in which she held his eyes and he seemed to be listening, nodding at her understandingly, was a momentary solace.

"Can't you see that I have to help?" she said.

"Ma'am," he repeated, "could you please move back? Please stop fiddling with the patient's hand? We need more room, ma'am."

She hated him then. They didn't know what they were doing, shoving all this junk at Sweets, handling him so roughly they were probably doing more harm than good. The room was jammed with people. Outside she heard more sirens, was aware of more flashing, revolving lights.

She heard meaningless words.

"EMT."

"CPR."

"Get an airway in."

"O Two mask."

"He's vomiting, suction him."

"Goddam."

The polite young man said, "You're in the way of our taking the vitals, ma'am," and he pushed her aside.

She heard herself, "Don't let him die, don't let him die, don't let him die."

If she could catch the eye of the woman paramedic she knew the woman would listen to her and answer her.

"Will he be all right? Will he be all right?"

The woman's tiny dark eyes slid away from contact. She said, "You're in the way, ma'am. Step further back. We need more room here." Fat hunk, no better than a man, with a deep, dark, cold voice of an angry man.

She heard more gibberish.

"Get the oxygen equipment outta the way."

"Set up the EOR for a Code Ninety-nine."

"Tubing airline outta the way."

"Ma'am, will you please step back? We need more room for the backboard, we have to put him on a gurney."

She yelled, "Hurry, hurry, you don't need that stuff, just hurry."

Someone yelled, "Jesus Christ, ya want him to fall off the backboard on us? We know what we're doin, ma'am. We know what we're doin. Ya want him to fall off the backboard, that what ya want, the patient slippin off the backboard?"

A new cop arrived.

"This the shooting incident?" he said. "This the Beauchamp residence?"

She knew this cop. She'd seen him around. He and Sweets always stopped to talk.

"Knifing. Stabbing." The polite crew member, polite again, talking to the cop. "Code Ninety-nine," he said.

An older man she hadn't noticed before said, almost gently, "Ya can ride in the ambulance with us, ma'am."

There was still another cop arriving as they moved out.

"This the shooting accident?" he said.

The confusion of noise and flashing lights blinded, deafened, numbed her. Yet, as if no other sounds existed, she clearly heard little Judy whimpering.

"Listen," she said, turning at the door of the ambulance. "Could you do me a big favor?" She had stretched out an arm toward the tall good-looking cop who knew Sweets. "Could you please put in a call to the little girl's mother? Judy's mother. Kay Sweetsir, 4832. Tell her to come get her daughter. The kid should be with her mother tonight."

"Goddam it, ma'am!" It was the polite medic, closing the door of the ambulance, asking his puzzling question. "Y'know what's holding us up now, ma'am? Y'know what's holding us up getting to the hospital now? You are, ma'am."

"What?" she said, and started crying and babbling again, "I'm sorry, I'm sorry, I'm sorry. I didn't mean to. I didn't mean to," and heard herself unable to stop, repeating and repeating, "I'm sorry, I didn't mean to," unable to stop babbling, babbling, babbling.

5

IT ASTOUNDED Laura how freely Johnny and Judy were blabbing to the cops, ripping all the family secrets wide open, explaining, or trying to, that none of the kids were related really, making everybody look bad, themselves, Sally, even their own daddy, well, Judy's own daddy anyway, and while he was dying too.

Laura knew Sweets would die. His death was sealed for her by the awful color his skin had turned and by the milky, rolling eyes. What was unreal and dreamlike was that her mother had done it to him.

In the yard, in the confusion and the excitement of the lights and the noise, they waited for Kay to arrive to pick up Judy. The ambulance had just left, carrying away Sweets and her mother. She felt miserably abandoned. She envied little Judy in a way. Judy would be out of the whole mess soon.

She was deadly sleepy. She would have given a lot to be allowed to go to sleep, excuse herself, "G'night, everybody, see ya later," run upstairs to the room she shared with Judy. Turn her back on the whole scene. Yet along with the dulled sleepiness there was an intense cutting awareness, and between the heaviness and the quickness of her heightened senses she felt totally unlike herself. That was scary.

She wished she could turn off the blah, blah, blah. *Shut up, everybody. Everybody quiet now.* The cop who was encouraging Judy and Johnny to talk, taking notes of every little thing they told him, had a look on his face as he listened that made her sick to her stomach—cold, wiped off, guarded against any attempt to figure out what he was thinking.

They kept on and on about how none of them were related, Johnny and Judy and herself, because the cop couldn't seem to get it straight. Then Judy got off about Sally and Sweets fighting all the time.

"Alla time. Always fightin. And Sally fights back. Sally don't take nothin from nobody. They were havin this big fight a coupla weeks ago or months, it was back in the big house, the nice house we were livin in then, and Sally made a regular dinner but when my daddy come to the table he pushed his plate away, just shoved it away like my daddy would when he was in a certain mood, y'know. He made some remark about the food bein real rotten and pushed the whole plate of food away from him that Sally had been workin on at the stove for a couple hours. So then, *blam, blam,* Sally picks up her plate and his plate and throws them right at him full of spaghetti and meatballs."

She burst out laughing, just the way she had when it happened.

"I had to go to my room to laugh so he wouldn't hit me."

She studied her stubby little nails that she had covered with Laura's Revlon Icy Pink nail polish.

The cop was writing it all down.

Judy said, "Sally's a really neat fighter. When my daddy went after her, she hit him back. My mama never did that. My mama sits and takes it. I never told nobody but I really like that about Sally. It's neat."

The cop said, "How old are you, sis?"

"Eight, going on nine."

"Did you hear your stepmother say anything to your daddy during the quarrel, during the fight tonight?"

"Who?" Judy said.

"Your stepmother. Your daddy's wife."

"Y'mean Sally?"

The cop nodded.

"I just call her Sally," Judy said.

"Well, okay," the cop said. "Did you hear her say anything?"

"I was watchin a program on TV," Judy said.

"How come you don't live with your own mother?" There wasn't any way the cop would ever get it straight.

"I told ya before," Judy said. "My daddy wanted me and

Johnny. He just took Johnny, but he had to get the court to say he could take me to live with him and Sally, y'know to be with the other kids, Johnny and Laurie. The court said it was okay because they had a better house. Better setup. We lived over the other end of town then in a nice house, didn't we?" She turned to Laura and then to Johnny for confirmation.

"We had a more stable environment," Laura said. It was a phrase she didn't know she knew. The cop barely glanced at her.

The cop asked Johnny, "You hear anything during the fight?"

"I came in the room, in the kitchen when she was stabbin him. She was sayin, 'I'll get you,' and he was like pleadin with her, my daddy, he was sayin 'Honey, what are you doin, I love you, y'know I love you, stop, stop, please stop.'"

"I could hear them fightin," Laura said. "Sounded like he was knockin her around. I could hear him callin her a fuckin asshole. I didn't hear no honey, love ya stuff."

The cop looked at Laura with his scary no-expression.

Laura said, "We all of us were watchin the TV show, me and Johnny and Judy."

Ty Parsons, hanging around like a leech instead of going away and leaving them alone, had to put in his bit.

"I rushed right over, the minute the boy called me, right after I called the ambulance. She was cryin and beggin forgiveness. She was sayin, 'I'm sorry I did it, honey, please forgive me,' and right then Sweets opened his eyes and said, 'Too late, honey. Too late to be sorry. Ya shoulda thoughta that before, honey. Ya shoulda thoughta that sooner.'"

"Sweets never said nothin like that," Laura said. "I was there all the time *he* was and Sweets never said nothin."

Ty Parsons shot her an outraged glance. Her throat was as parched as if she were being forced to recite in school before the entire class. Her mother had mounted the step and the ambulance doors had closed on her. She had left without a word of guidance for Laura, left her daughter to deal alone with cops and their questions, with Judy and Johnny babbling, and now Ty Parsons shooting his mouth off. She wasn't going to stand around like a lump and let them get away with telling everything wrong.

Johnny whispered, "Quit doin that, Laurie."

"I can talk like everybody else does," she said.

He grabbed her hand. "Quit pullin ya top down flat like that," he said. "And stop that jumpin and bouncin up and down."

She didn't know what he was talking about, but she made an effort to stand still. She locked her hands behind her back.

Kay Sweetsir pulled up in her new Subaru. She didn't greet anybody. She stayed in the car with the motor running, leaning her head out to identify herself to the cops as Judy's mother. Judy ran to her, calling out "Bye" to them, with a little wave of her fingers in the air. Kay opened the car door and Judy hopped in and Kay drove right out the driveway without a word to anybody. Without a word to Johnny, who she practically brought up. Laura thought, *Just like Sally did, too, leaving me without a word.*

The short, ordinary-looking cop said, "You kids can ride to the hospital with us." He spoke as if he was trying to be kind, but what emerged sounded tired and disgusted with life. "Y'like, one can ride with me and the other with Officer LeVeen."

"Can we ride together, me and him?" Laura said.

She wanted to stay as far as possible from the other cop, the tall, good-looking one. Johnny grabbed her arm and clung to it.

"Can we ride together, with you?" she said to the short cop.

Johnny squeezed her arm, moved down to capture her hand. She clung to his fingers gratefully.

They kept their hands locked, bunched up in the front seat of the police car, even when their palms became uncomfortably sweaty. The revolving lights and the speed of the car made familiar territory strange. The trip over Denby Hill into Hartshead seemed endlessly long. It was as if she had never passed over this ground before, as if these roads and their darkened homes were alien places, housing alien creatures. It took an immense effort to concentrate on the conversation between the cop and Johnny, about the wonders of modern medical practice and how they'd fix up Morgan, how Morgan would be okay.

Laura knew that Morgan wouldn't be okay.

She and Johnny entered the emergency section together, still holding hands. Her mother was sitting smack in the center of the corridor floor, carrying on, crying and babbling, "I told him if he hit me again I'd get him, oh, God, I didn't mean to do this, I didn't mean it," looking a mess in bare feet, one foot cut up and bloodied, her makeup all smeared, looking the way she did when she was cleaning house and was mad at the world, sloppy-discontented, and her hair hanging greasy and stringy—and at the same time looking totally unlike herself, not like Laura's mother at all but some stranger Laura didn't feel a thing for, didn't even like. Laura pulled her hand out of Johnny's sweaty grip, wiped it dry on the back of her jeans. She was aware that Johnny gave her a funny glance, but she couldn't read it.

The tall, scary cop was directly behind them. He told the nice cop to take the kids into the waiting room. "Tell them to sit there and stay put," he said, as if they weren't right there listening to him.

"I want to be with my mother," Laura said. Her statement was a surprise to herself. "I should be with my mother."

The tall cop didn't even acknowledge that she had spoken. He motioned with his head for them to get moving. Laura did what she was told. The room they entered was small, with a couch, armchairs, some little tables. They were the only people in it. A TV, high on the wall, was switched on to a movie in color. She couldn't hear properly, couldn't locate herself in what was going on in the movie. She sat astride the arm of the couch. She could keep her mother in view from that spot, hear her babbling and crying, see her legs sprawled on the floor, her body rocking. She could even see Sally's smeared mascara.

The short cop said, "You kids rest here awhile. Stay put, now," and went out into the corridor.

Johnny came to stand directly in front of her, blocking her vision. His blue eyes seemed to swim in a red, heated liquid.

"Quit it, Laura," he said. "Quit pullin on ya goddam top."

She unhooked her thumbs from the hem of her T-shirt.

"Don't even know when I'm doin it," she said.

"Ya bet ya don't know what ya doin," he said.

"Didn't say *that*," she said.

"And quit boppin ya goddam crotch up and down. What if somebody was here lookin at ya?"

"Don't ya tell me nothin like that," she yelled. "Who ya think ya are? And get the fuck outta m'way. Can't see m'Mom, with ya hulk in the way."

The short cop turned to check them out, started toward the little waiting room, but was interrupted by a group of people coming in with a kid, a man carrying the child like a drape of cloth over his arms. In a couple of minutes most of them were herded into the room with her and Johnny.

She was violently upset, as if Johnny's dumb comment was the worst thing that had happened on this bad night. It took a strong effort not to cry. She concentrated on sitting still, on listening to what was happening outside the room.

Now the tall cop was at the center desk where a skinny man with a huge Adam's apple kept his bugged-out eyes on Sally as if Sally were some kind of snake.

"Did you hear the woman say, 'I stabbed him. I told him if he hit me again I'd get him and I did'?" the cop said without any expression.

The man behind the desk came to attention slowly. He composed his face into a no-expression before he looked at the cop. They looked at one another with the same no-expression.

He said, "What?"

The cop repeated, "Did you hear the woman, the woman sitting on the floor, did you hear her make a statement to the effect that she stabbed her husband?" The cop glanced at his note pad. "To the effect that 'I told him if he hit me again I'd get him and I did'?" He looked up at the man behind the desk. "Did you hear the woman make a statement to that effect?"

"She's hysterical," the man at the desk said. His Adam's apple bobbed up and down like a target in a shooting booth. "She doesn't know what she's saying. She's hysterical."

"Not askin for an opinion," the cop said. His voice stayed flat, but it pushed. "Officer Grant says you mentioned to him you heard the woman make a statement to the effect that she stabbed her husband."

The man drew in his breath. "I heard her," he said, blowing the breath out. "Everybody heard her. She isn't watching what she's saying."

"Okay," the cop said. "All I wanted to know."

The cop walked by the door of the emergency room. Laura appealed to him. "I wanna sit with my mother. Why can't I go sit with my mother?" She was appalled that she had spoken. She sounded like a dumb kid. *I want my mommy.* It was painful to endure the attention turning toward her.

To her amazement, the boss cop stopped. He pointed out a woman who had been hovering around Sally.

"That lady's Mrs. Southby. She's a mental-health worker assigned special to this kind of work," he said, like a teacher who was going to tell a thing—once.

She didn't dare ask, "What kind of work?"

He said, "Me and Mrs. Southby have been trying to persuade Mrs. Sweetsir to get up off the floor and come sit down in the waiting room. She almost started to do it once, but no, she changed her mind and sat right down on the floor again." He paused. "Ya mother said she couldn't bear to be near you kids right now. She said she only wants to be near her husband. All she cares about is how her husband's doing in there."

He said, "Understand?"

She nodded. She understood the part about Morgan, she could stand to put up with that part. What she couldn't bear to hear was "you kids," as if she counted for no more with her mother than Johnny did, Johnny who wasn't even Sweets's kid. At least Judy was Morgan's own kid, and if Sally had been more concerned with Judy than she had been with her own daughter, she could bear that. She began to cry but halted herself at once, acutely conscious of curious strangers watching, studying her and Sally and Johnny, wondering about them and judging them by their dirty torn jeans. Not fair. If she had had any warning she would have washed her hair that morning. Sally should have washed her hair, and it was about time her mother got up off the floor and stopped her crying and wailing, and stopped smearing her makeup.

Time itself had gone crazy. It stood still for long stretches. Then suddenly it rushed forward too fast for her to catch what was happening. At that moment everybody was moving at once, the two cops and the mental-health worker, and a bunch of people in and out of the operating room—even Sally had been raised up off the floor, not toward Laura and the waiting room but down the corridor into some little room whose door remained open and where Laura could see her mother crying and hear her talking her head off.

Johnny came to her side. "What'd the cop say?"

"I dunno. Some crazy stuff. See that creepy-lookin woman? He said she's a mental-health worker. Y'think they think my mom's crazy?"

"I got this awful feelin he told ya Sweets was dyin."

Did he believe that Sweets wasn't dying?

She said, "He's gotta be dyin, Johnny."

He grabbed for her as for something to hold on to and pressed his body against hers. She knew that the effort he was concentrating on was to keep from crying, but right there in the public waiting room, in front of all those strangers, what she clearly felt happen was his sex grow big and hard against her thigh.

"He can't," he said. "What'll I do without him?" and pressed harder against her thigh.

She felt a mix of revulsion and attraction—a flush of heat, followed by a chilling shudder, like a fever. Maybe she was getting her period too soon. Secret fantasies of Johnny's love for her had occupied her for such a long time that to be receiving his confusing message at this inappropriate moment was wildly irritating to her. If the pressure of his rising flesh wasn't exactly the acting out of her complicated dreams of Johnny as her slave-worshipper and master-lover, still, surely *something* was happening even if it was happening in a public emergency waiting room of Central Hartshead Hospital.

She knew Johnny Matthews better than any other boy. In some ways she knew him to be perfect. His looks were perfect, and the way he handled his body was perfect, moving all of a piece, controlled but easy at the same time, jumping on his bike in one fluid leap, like a dancer, just the way Morgan did.

There were other things about him that she hated, even if she felt sorry for him. She hated his being an orphan and brooding about who his parents were. She hated his devotion to Morgan—as if Morgan was Johnny's master-God and Johnny was some kind of little puppy who was eternally grateful to Morgan just because Morgan had taken him in when he was a baby and treated him like his own son. Treated him like shit. He never adopted him, and he'd beat up on him for nothing—for keeping his head down when Sweets fancied he should lift it, or for lifting his head when Sweets decided he should keep it lowered. And Johnny took it all and stayed grateful, as if Sweets was giving him something valuable instead of plain, hard *nothing*. It was Johnny who was giving more than he was getting, that was for sure, giving Morgan respect and worship and love.

But what she most resented was Johnny's beautiful fair strength because it was so much like Sally's. Everybody took Johnny Matthews for Laura's brother. He went around saying he was, for one thing, and for another, he looked so much like Sally, everybody assumed he was Laura Ciomei's brother. Mixed-up names didn't mean much in Eatonville. The whole thing gave her a headache. Because if he was her brother, why was he kneading her hand, flushing her loins with heat, and how was she supposed to react, goddam it? As if he was her brother—or what?

People kept coming out of the emergency operating room. Johnny was gripping her so hard, she couldn't stand it. She pulled free of him. A man in a surgeon's outfit came out of the emergency room and with big, swift steps walked to the little room where Sally was with the cop and the mental-health worker. She knew from the terrible wail Sally let loose that the doctor had told Sally that Morgan was dead.

Now a woman in a blue uniform with a no-expression face and voice was telling Johnny and Laura that Morgan was dead. Not that Laura heard a clear word that the woman was saying, but she knew what she was saying. Were those people given lessons, she wondered, in fixing their voices and faces in that no-expression attitude? The way the TV newscasters were all taught to talk the same way?

Then she lost track of where she was and what was happening, as if the world had died, momentarily, with Sweets; and Laura was left totally alone.

When she came back to herself, she heard Johnny babbling. He was telling not lies exactly but not the truth either. Not what Laura would call the truth. He was babbling to the cop who had driven them to the hospital and the cop was taking notes of what Johnny was saying. Saying that Sally was always on top of Morgan, never left him alone, was always after him.

"If she hadn't kept afta him like she did, it never woulda happened. She was always afta him," he said.

The truth was they were always on top of one another. That was the way they liked it, Sally and Sweets, together all the time, just the two of them. Why wasn't Johnny telling that?

Now Johnny was blabbing about the different parts of the fight, about Sally baby-sitting for her boss's son and having to go see the doctor and wanting Morgan to help with the kid, and about Sally slamming in and out of the house, and about the hollering and about her smashing the chair. The way he told it, the fight was all Sally's fault.

Laura forced herself to speak. "He was ugly-actin from the minute he woke up this mornin," Laura said. "This afternoon, I mean."

"Who?" the cop said.

"Morgan, Sweets," she said. "He was in one of his moods where he was set on bein ugly no matter what."

The cop looked at her, surprised, then altered his face to no-expression.

"When he woke up about one o'clock, all I did was ask him if I could go up to Penny's house, my friend's house, and Sweets said, 'I don't give a fuck what ya do.'"

"C'mon," Johnny said. "Just Sweets's way a talkin, y'know it, Laurie."

"And afta Mom went out to see if she could find him because he left the house mad, he came back while she was still out and he opens up the frigerator and he sees that Mom had some wine and he goes, 'She start drinkin a ready?' and I said, 'Yes, Mom had a little wine' and he goes, 'Don't get smart or I'll knock ya fuckin head off.' And then he goes, 'Ask Johnny what I'll do.' Didn't he, Johnny, didn't he?"

"Didn't mean nothin when my daddy talked like that," Johnny said. "Y'know it, Laurie. Just my daddy's way a talkin. If she hadn't kept afta him like she did it never woulda happened. She was always afta him. Once they were havin a fight and she smashed two plates a food against the side a his head. She'd break glasses and things in the kitchen. She broke that chair."

"Sweets broke more stuff n she did," Laura interrupted. "He hurt her wrist and he broke her other wristwatch."

"Tonight?" the cop said.

"Other time," Laura said. "Today he was real ugly from the minute he woke up. When Mom came home with that weird kid, her boss's kid, before her appointment to see about that cancer test, and she was upset cause Sweets wouldn't let the kid stay in the house with him, Sweets said he was too busy to bother with that asshole of a kid, and then Mom asked if we had gotten dog food because we were out of dog food, if anybody had thought to get some dog food and nobody answered her except me and she said, 'Thank you for answering, Laura, since Morgan isn't speaking to me, apparently. . . .'"

Laura was lost. She was floundering in a swamp of Sally's guilt that threatened to ooze into her own bones. Was it her fault that her mother had killed Sweets? She should have been a better daughter, should have helped Sally, offered to take care of that stupid kid, offered sincerely. She should have bought the dog food even if Blackie wasn't her dog. She should have made the supper herself instead of waiting until Sally came home. There was a pot roast all cooked, she could have thought to take it out of the freezer. She should have prepared some frozen mashed potatoes or some minute rice. That would have made a supper.

Johnny said, "It neva woulda happened if she didn't keep afta him like she does."

"Naggin a lot?" the cop said.

"She was callin him all day from work. All day long, callin him from work."

But why wasn't he telling that that was the way Sally and Sweets liked it? They liked to talk to each other on the phone three four times a day when they were both working, checking in with each other three four times a day.

"She called up maybe four five times. A coupla times he really wasn't in, but a coupla times he really was in even though he told me to say he wasn't in. Then she called up one last time and asked if he was in the house, and he was, but he told me to say no because he didn't wanta talk to her and I said 'No' and she said, 'I know he's there, Johnny, but forget it, don't bother him.'"

"Ya see?" Laura said. "Ya see?"

The cop didn't look at her, so how could he see?

"Your daddy works nights?" the cop asked Johnny.

"No," Johnny said. "He's on that road crew. Buildin the spur on the interstate."

He choked and cleared his throat in a queer sound. "I mean he was," he said.

"Not working that day?" the cop asked.

"What?" Johnny said, and rushed on as if the cop had asked a different question. "They were fightin hot and heavy all day. It was hangin in the air all day. Ya could cut it with a knife."

They were in a little room with a desk and a couple of chairs and the door closed, Laura and Johnny and the cop. Laura had no memory of having gotten there from the waiting room.

"You heard them fighting?" the cop said.

"It was gettin hot and heavy when that movie come on the TV," Johnny said. "About the Ku Klux Klan and the FBI."

"You heard it?" the cop said.

"Just the first part, until the station break," Johnny said.

"No," the cop said. "I meant the fight. You heard them fighting?"

"Oh," Johnny said. "She never knew when to quit. She kept afta him. 'You don't care, you don't care.' That's all I heard her sayin. And my daddy comin back at her with 'Shut up. Shut up. Shut up.' That's all I heard that I remember. 'Shut up' and 'You don't care.' 'You don't care' and 'Shut up.'"

"They were quarrelin about the cancer and the doctor, goin to the doctor," Laura rushed in. "Sweets thought she was lyin about the cancer thing. He was callin her a fuckin liar. He said, 'I'm callin that doctor n showin ya up, ya fuckin liar. I'm sick a ya tricks.' He didn't believe her—that anythin was wrong—he was actin like she only wanted pity or somethin and was lyin to get it. Then they'd like quiet down between the yellin. Between the yellin, other stuff happened. Like she was growlin to herself in the kitchen and knockin the pots around, slammin things, y'know. Sweets jumps up and says, 'Shut your fuckin mouth, quit that fuckin commotion.' She musta gotten mad cause she got in the car and took off. Maybe two

seconds cause she come right back and they started fightin again.
He was hittin her and callin her a fuckin asshole and stuff and I
heard Mom yellin, 'You can't do this to me, Morgan.'"

Laura stopped. She meant what she was saying to clear her
mother, to help the cop understand her mother, but what if she was
blabbing like the others and doing nothing but harm?

"How old are you?" the cop said.

"Sixteen," Laura said.

The cop studied her coldly, apparently finding something to dislike in what he saw. He examined his notes.

"You're Judy Sweetsir, the daughter?"

"Laura," she said. "Ciomei," pronouncing it "Syomy," as it was
pronounced in her school. "Laura Ciomei. I'm Sally's daughter."

The cop looked very tired.

"You adopted too?"

"What?" she said.

"Okay, okay," the cop said. "You part of the family, living in the
house?"

She took a deep breath. "Sally's my mother. Sally Sweetsir. My
father's Vin Ciomei. They divorced, but I got my father's name."

Shame, fear, anger flooded her at the confusion in her life.

"Ya know my father?"

She needed to win this cop back to his kindlier feelings about
her; it was too dangerous to have both cops disliking her. "Vin
Ciomei? He used to work over to the quarry, but he ain't workin
much these days."

"Talian fellow?" the cop said.

"My father's American," Laura said.

"Dunno him," the cop said.

"What happened neva woulda happened if she hadn't kept afta
him," Johnny said. "She killed him. She stabbed him."

"You were in the room," the cop said. "You saw it happen?"

"I was watchin the show and at the break I started for the
kitchen but I saw my daddy backin away from her, they were like
locked together and I saw a big knife in her hand and it went in
and come out and then my daddy started collapsin and then he fell
on the floor."

"You hear him say anything?"

Johnny looked at the cop with tears in his eyes. "He said, 'What are ya doin, honey, I love ya, stop, stop. Please stop.'"

"He never said that," Laura said.

"Did she stop then?" the cop asked Johnny.

"I guess," Johnny said. After a pause, he said, "She got in the way of the ambulance crew. They had to keep pushin her outta the way."

"She was tryin to help," Laura said. "The ambulance was takin so long she said we should take him to the hospital in the car cause the ambulance was takin so long but we couldn't lift him, we tried, and anyway Ty was stoppin us, Ty Parsons, our neighbor, Sweets's best friend next door, he was right, I guess we shoulda left him, left him on the floor it woulda been better but anyway we couldn't lift him so we didn't do no harm. Then they came rushin in with their boxes of stuff, the paramedics, and they wrapped somethin around his arm, sort of a gauze thing and they had all that other stuff, tubes and things and a microfying glass. . . ." She stumbled over the unfamiliar word, humiliated by the conviction that she had mispronounced it. "Mom was tryin to help and to hurry them up and she was tryin to encourage Sweets to breathe. She kept tellin him to breathe and tellin him that she loved him and she didn't mean to do it."

"She kept crowdin in and gettin in the way of the medics," Johnny said.

"Y'know she was tryin to help," Laura said.

The woman in the blue uniform opened the door. The cop held up his hand for them to shush and conferred with her at the door. Then the cop returned to them. He didn't look directly at either Laura or Johnny, but, fixing on an indeterminate spot in between and with his face even more carefully composed into no-expression, he told them that Sally had been arrested.

It was as if the news were a hot black wind sucking her into a vibrating hole. The floor heaved. She was overwhelmed by a bad smell she couldn't identify but was sure it was coming from her own body. Her vision blurred. Again she lost touch with what was around her.

Now her father was in the room and Johnny was holding her against him, his arm firmly around her shoulders. She was aware of shame at her father's small, dark, fumbling, silent presence—and of joy at Johnny's golden closeness, again miraculously hers.

"Laurie and me'll be okay, long as we stay together. Why can't we just go back to our own house?" Johnny, arguing, not very convincingly.

Where were they being sent? Were they being arrested too?

"Okay, okay," the cop said. "C'mon, c'mon, you can't go back there till the crime lab winds up, I told you before. Little cooperation here now would help y'know. Do what her mother said to do. The woman said to call the girl's father and go with him."

"Go where?" Laura said.

"C'mon, c'mon," the cop said, "get them going here, will you?"

"Yessir," her father said. "I'll take care of them, officer, I'll take care . . ." trailing away as if he couldn't take care of anything.

She and Johnny followed Vin hand in hand to the parking lot. It tore her insides, like a violent indigestion, that they were leaving Sally behind, yet it wasn't until the car was moving through town and she had settled into her father's familiar beat-up VW smelling of rotting fruit and her old dog that she absorbed the satisfying realization that her mother had been concerned about her. At a terrible moment, Sally had thought of her, had asked the cop to call Vin to take care of her. If it was satisfying, why had she begun to shake and sob convulsively? She hardly had time to warn Vin that she was going to be sick and to make it out of the car before she vomited up all the spaghetti and stuff she had had for supper, fighting off Johnny's offer to help, desperate to hide from him the slobbiness of her weakness.

"Ya better sit up front," Johnny said. He put his hands on her shoulders as if to steady her.

Her father barely glanced at her.

"Ya been drinkin?" he said.

She said, "Oh, Jesus, lemme alone."

He said, "Ya okay now? Should I start to move?"

"Let's go," she said. "I'm okay."

They moved through the streets of the quiet, darkened, shut-up town as through an alien place. Out on the state road a menacing fog rolled in heavy patches, mysteriously clearing to reveal the blacktop surface and a brilliant newly painted white center line.

She wanted to be the one doing the driving. Drive the damn car into the nearest tree and end the whole mess.

Entering the dank, soiled boredom of her father's house was an admission of overwhelming failure. So was the foul odor of her sick old dog. Biff lay on a filthy blanket, unable to rise on all fours to greet her. He wasn't any older than she was and there he was dying on her. She forced herself to hug him. He wagged his tail once, then again, panting. His breath was so bad-smelling she had to turn away.

Her father stood in the middle of the kitchen, bent and embarrassed. He didn't know what to say to her and Johnny, or what to do with them.

He mumbled, "I dunno where ya gonna sleep. No clean sheets. Needa do a laundry."

"We'll be okay," Johnny said.

Laura was violently awake now. "I ain't sleepy," she said.

Her father stood, hesitant and vague, then he half turned as if heading somewhere. The back of his pants hung disgustingly loose and wrinkled. Why couldn't he fill his pants the way a man should —the way Johnny filled his jeans? Sickness rose in her throat.

Johnny said, "Listen, Mr. Ciomei, ya go on to sleep." He pronounced it "Syomy." She hated that name of hers. "Ya get yaself some sleep. We'll be okay. I ain't sleepy either."

Her father remained half turned away, indecisive.

"Ya go on to bed," Johnny said. "And thanks for comin to get us, Mr. Ciomei."

"Ya call me Vin," Vin said. "Least I c'd do."

He moved toward the stairs, paused then on the first step.

"Ya sure I can't get ya nothin? Sure ya'll be okay?"

He looked at his daughter sadly, yearningly. Was there something he should be doing that he wasn't doing?

She smiled and waved him ahead, watched stupidly as he climbed the stairs laboriously. A worn-out old man supposed to be her father. Let him go. She wished Johnny would go too. She would have preferred to be left alone, free to give way to whatever it was she was holding off so fiercely. At that moment she almost loathed Johnny Matthews, standing there looking at her, planted on the tile floor, his torso firmly settled on his hips, one leg slightly forward and bent, his crotch bulging in his tight jeans, strength flowing upward into his powerful arms and shoulders and into the enticing column of his neck crowned by the fair, fair head.

Something must have showed on her face.

He said, "What's the matter? Somethin the matter?"

She said, "I don't believe ya said that. Ya seriously askin me what's the matter? If somethin's the matter?"

They stared at one another in a dramatic pause.

"How bout some little somethin like maybe I'll never see my mother again. Would ya call that somethin the matter?"

A part of her enjoyed the drama of her outburst. Another part rejected it as a falsehood, as though none of what had happened had indeed happened but had been fabricated by her for excitement. Like an actor responding to her cues, Johnny nodded solemnly, holding his strong-man pose.

"Like in 'Hawaii Five O,'" he said. "*Book her*. They done that to Sally."

"What, what is it they done?"

The notion stabbed her that he was glad Sally had been arrested. She was crying now.

"Could she get the electric chair?"

"I guess," he said. "Or a life sentence."

"I can't stand it," she howled. "How'm I supposed to stand all this happenin to me?"

"What about to me?" he yelled.

The edifice of his posture crumpled. He sat abruptly, propping his head between his hands, leaning on the kitchen table. He seemed attacked by a bad case of shuddering hiccups, but she realized it was his way of crying. Her own tears were effectually stopped by outrage at Johnny having stolen her moment of drama. Nobody was giving her an inch in what was going on. They were intent on wiping her out of the event, as if she didn't exist.

Yet, astounded by Johnny's collapse, she almost forgot about herself. She had never seen this Johnny before. Even with Sweets all over him and Johnny buckling under, Johnny still managed a certain defiance, but now he had dwindled to a little boy, with a little boy's body scrunched on the ladderback chair that was too small for him, its worn-out rush seat hanging in shreds under his bulging ass. She could have kicked him right in the butt, the way Sweets would have, for making such a fuss. Acting like a goddam baby.

Sally would have known what to do to return Johnny to his manhood, and with that thought she was besieged by an image of Sally in a cell. Damp walls. Rats scampering across a stone-cold floor.

She was shaking again. She couldn't bear Johnny crying. She'd really kick him in the ass if he didn't stop. She felt bad enough. She had never felt so bad in her life. Her skin crawled; it was coming loose, separating from her bones, lifting away from her frame. She flung her arms around her middle to hold herself together. To hell with Johnny. He was nothing to her; he was nobody to her.

This kitchen was very upsetting too. It didn't look anything like she remembered it from the years she and Sally had lived here. They had never lived in this stale, foul odor. She remembered good, warm smells, peace and quiet, cleanliness and comfort; she remembered her large, loving grandfather. Sure, and being ashamed of him before her friends because he couldn't speak English. And hardly a single vivid memory of her daddy. How could she have lived with Vin all those years and not have any memories of him?

"Why'd ya leave my daddy, Mom?"

She had dared to ask the question after an awful fight between Sweets and Sally. "I never remember fightin. Y'know. Nothin like that. Maybe I just didn't understand what was goin on, but I can't remember nothin bad between ya, Mom."

She was dismayed that Sally turned to her with the terrific smile she used to charm strangers.

"Your daddy is a real nice, kind man. Always was and always will be. Our marriage died of boredom, honey, that's the true reason I left him."

There was no way to understand that statement. Sally could have put up with boredom, if not for the sake of the marriage, then for the sake of her daughter—couldn't she? If her mother really loved her, she would have endured a little boredom. The fact was, nobody was willing to endure anything for Laura's sake. Johnny Matthews wouldn't even shut up, though he was driving her crazy.

Food. Food always made everything better.

"C'mon," she said. "Stop it now, c'mon, c'mon. I bet ya hungry."

He probably hadn't heard her over his crying. She raised her voice.

"I'm hungry. Would ya believe I'm hungry?"

She kept talking. Talk would get him out of his fit of crying and it would save her too.

"Will ya look at this fridge? There ain't a goddam thing in it."

Scattered on the stained shelves was a disarray of beer, milk, Pepsis, bread, ricotta covered with green mold, a half-filled can of dog food, eggs.

"See what's in the freezer," she said.

"Not much," she said.

The freezer held bags of french fries, packages of peas, cans of orange juice, a ruined thin spread of vanilla ice cream at the bottom of a gallon container.

"I'm gonna make us some french fries," she said. "Okay? Okay, Johnny?"

The sounds coming from him altered slightly. She was getting somewhere.

"Will ya look at this stove?" she said. "Just look at this tray. We'll be eatin more dirt n potatoes."

"Ya hungry?" she said. "Johnny? Ya hungry?"

All noises had now stopped. Though she knew he was shaking his head *no*, she pretended she didn't, and raised her voice.

"Johnny, answer me, ya hungry?"

There was a mumbled response.

"How bout a beer?" she said. "There's beer. Ya wanna beer?"

"Okay," he said in a thick voice.

"Here's ya beer," she said.

"That is one grungy-lookin table," she said.

"So's ya face," she said. Then, "Here's some paper towel. Bounty. Mops up more."

"Broke the fuckin holder," she said. "This place is a mess. It's a wreck. Everythin ya touch breaks. Touch it and ya break it. It's gross."

Johnny was blowing his nose, grunting, clearing his throat.

"Maybe there's something more interesting to eat out in the pantry," she said, and from out there inventoried for him, "Soup, peanut butter, spaghetti, artichoke hearts, lentils. No spaghetti," she said. "Never wanna eat spaghetti again."

"Ya think it's dirty in there, ya should see it out here," she said.

"Hey, how bout some soup?" she said.

"I ain't hungry," he said, almost clearly.

"Manhandlers," she said. "They're good."

"I dunno. If ya gonna have some," he said.

"Here's a Chunky. I like Chunkys."

He had pulled himself together, wiped up his face. She gestured with the can of soup in his direction.

"Trick is to find a can opener."

She rummaged through drawers, her back to him.

"Where the fuck is a can opener?" she said.

His voice normal now, but subdued, Johnny said, "I thought ya father lives with ya uncle."

"Correct," she said.

She had intended her answer to be funny, but it just seemed stupid.

"Well, where is he?" Johnny said.

"Who?"

"Ya daddy's uncle."

"I dunno. Asleep upstairs, I guess. Or out back. How should I know? Listen," she said, "ya got any idea where they'd keep a fuckin can opener in this fuckin house?"

"Hey," he said. "Ya want ya daddy to hear ya talkin like that?"

She said, "A lot he cares."

"Boo-hoo," Johnny said.

"Fuck off," she said.

He shook his head as if she were hopeless.

"Ain't he ya uncle too?" he persisted.

Irritated, she considered the question. Didn't her father's uncle have to be her uncle?

"I guess so," she said. "My great-uncle, I guess."

"Ya like him?" Johnny said.

"Jesus Christ, who?"

"Ya uncle, ya great-uncle, whatever he is."

She abandoned the search for the can opener to study Johnny.

What was he getting at? His face crumpled, as if he were going to bawl again.

"They could make ya live here, y'know."

"Who?" she said. "No way, uh, uh."

"He's ya father, and the other's ya uncle."

"No way," she said.

"Don't ya like ya uncle?" he said.

"He's a crazy old man who can't talk English. All he says in English is 'hot dog' and 'yessiree.' Besides, he's ancient. He could die any minute."

Johnny said, "Sh, sh, he'll hear ya."

She had been yelling. He was driving her crazy with this talk of being forced to live with her daddy and old Uncle Arturo.

"I don't understand ya, Johnny. Ya really puzzle me. How come ya so fuckin interested in my Uncle Arturo all of a sudden?"

"That his name?" he said.

She turned her back on him, locking the soup can between her knees, crouching a bit to secure it. With both hands she rummaged through the mess of the kitchen drawers. She was pleasantly aware of the tension of her buttocks in the tight jeans. She knew that Johnny was responding to the provocation her ass offered. She glanced back at him. He dropped his arms to his lap, flushing deeply. His bloodshot blue eyes looked straight into hers in angry yearning.

"Ya know somethin," she attacked him. She was the one who should be angry. "Ya know somethin. I'm on to ya. Ya just tryin to make me feel bad. That's all ya doin, talkin about my Great-Uncle Arturo. As if I ain't feelin bad enough. Ya tryin to get to me, tryin to break me down."

"That really his name?" he said. And then, "Wall opener. Right behind ya," pointing, grinning. The grin made him wonderfully handsome again.

"Goddam," she said. "Ya seen it all along while I been friggin with those drawers?"

"Dee–cent," she said, using the opener. "Somethin finally works in this house."

She bumped the open can down hard on the counter top. A little gusher of soup leaped upward, splashing on the tiles. They both began to laugh. In a gesture that defied him she pulled her T-shirt down over her thighs, flattening the thin cloth against her breasts. She waved the bottom of the shirt to allow air under it, then let it ride back into position.

"It's *hot*," she said.

He laughed out loud. She joined him.

"Want another beer?" she said.

"Ya gonna have one?"

"Sure. I'm gonna get drunk."

She pretended drunkenness, staggering, sticking out her ass.

"Ya been drinkin, little girl?" She was mimicking her father's earlier comment.

"I got myself drunk on one fuckin beer," Johnny said. "What's in this beer, anyhow?"

"Cube of sugar, dash of hash," she said, snapping her fingers and moving her hips. "Hey, I'm a poet and I don't know it."

"Y'know," Johnny said, "y'look a lot like ya daddy."

She had started the soup heating and was checking the french fries in the oven. Without turning toward him, she sing-songed her response.

"Ya just tryin to get to me, ya just tryin to get to me."

"What's wrong with lookin like ya daddy?"

"Nothin if ya like a green complexion and this kinda hair," she said, pulling at her heavy black hair.

He loved the way her hair hung and moved of a piece, like cloth or the ripple of a muscle.

"Lot prettier than mine," he said, tugging at his blond flyaway stuff. "And ya got ya black eyes from him, they're pretty."

Was he kidding her? She concentrated on putting out the food: two bowls of soup, crackers with peanut butter, french fries with lots of salt and ketchup, two beers. They ate at the kitchen table like an old married couple.

"Maybe they'll let us live together," Johnny said, when they were through and she had begun to clear the table.

"Ya serious?" she said.

"Sure," he said. "Ya care to?"

She said, "They'll never let us. Sixteen and seventeen. And not really related." She burst into sobs. "What'll they do to Sally? What'll they do to her? What'll they do to my mom?"

He shushed her. "Ya wanna wake them up?" His voice was breaking again.

She forced herself to stop crying, brushing the gush of wetness across her cheeks into her long heavy hair with the flat of her palms. He pushed his chair back from the table, partly knocking it over but recovering it with a graceful forward movement of his long arm. It started him circling in a wild gyration that ended with him flinging himself on the floor on his back. It scared her to suspect he had lost all control. He lay still, one arm shielding his eyes, the other limp on the floor while in perfect harmony one leg splayed outward, the other rested taut, bent at the knee. Between his widely spread thighs he offered his groin in a sweet, forbidden invitation.

She crouched next to him on the cool, tile floor. The smell of her sick old dog was wicked strong down here. The dog was asleep, breathing noisily, as if each rattling gasp might be his last.

With his arm covering his eyes, Johnny said, "Ya didn't like Sweets much, did ya, Laurie?"

"Sure," she said, "sure I liked Sweets. Course I liked Sweets."

"Why should ya?" he said. "Always talkin rough to ya, talkin ugly. Ya picked up some rough ways a talkin, I guess from Sweets."

Was he criticizing her?

"Sally's always been good with me," he said. "I ain't sayin nothin against Sally's treatment . . . but . . ." He stopped.

After a while he said, "She shouldn't a done it."

"Course she shouldn't a done it," Laura said and began to cry.

"Don't," he said. "Don't start cryin, we'll never stop. When we started livin together like a family I made believe to myself, y'know, that Sally was my real mother and Sweets my real daddy. That'd make us brother and sister, y'know."

"Y'think Sweets was ya real daddy?" she said.

"It don't matter now, I guess. Funny," he said. "Sweets never took me places with him. And just today, he took me with him— with him and Ty.

"Seems like a million years ago," he said.

"Where to?" she said.

"Over to Hale's Road to work on fixin his dune buggy."

The truth was he hadn't enjoyed the outing. It was only now that he rearranged the flat, uncomfortable time into an idyllic last contact with Sweets.

It had been unbearably hot. He had been pretty much ignored by the two men except for the moments he was needed to help lift. He stood around watching, bored out of his mind, most of the day. After the dune buggy was fixed, it was the two men who had all the fun of test driving it while he waited in the hot field doing nothing. They needed him again to help load it into the big truck. Then they all started home, dropping in at the Hilltop on the way. Sweets launched a first-class riot because Gil wouldn't let Johnny sit at the bar. It was embarrassing for Johnny. What was Sweets kicking up such a fuss for? He knew there was no way Gil could allow an underage boy to sit at the bar. Sweets was carrying on just for the hell of it, buying a beer and hauling it outside for Johnny to drink, daring anybody to stop him. Gil was disgusted. He gave up and looked the other way. Sweets was hollering, "Gettin so bad in this country they'll be regulatin our dreams next, they'll be regulatin how many times a day a man's allowed to piss."

That wasn't what he wanted to remember. He wanted some glowing precious memory he didn't possess.

In a thick unsteady voice he said, "Well, at least we spent his last day together, me n Sweets."

She extended a finger to the base of Johnny's fair, strong, smooth throat, and felt a sob start under her touch as if she had pressed a button to release it. He pulled her to him and locked his legs and arms around her.

6

Now THAT SHE had been arrested and locked up, she could shut up. There was nobody in any of the other cells but a teenage kid, pale and slim, very neat in permanent-press pants and a light-yellow zipper jacket. It was very cool in the cells. Air conditioning?

She insulated herself against the young man's interest in her. She'd better start learning how to do that well. She could have used some insulation against those strangers in the emergency rooms, against the cops and the goddam mental-health woman. Supposed to be helping her. About as much help as a hangover on a rainy Sunday with a houseful of kids.

It was behind her now, the interrogations and signing of papers and the fingerprinting and picture-taking, the humiliation of the matron's search. More ahead, worse ahead.

Was she doing everything wrong? She didn't care. Let them give her what she deserved.

"I know all about that rights shit," she had said to the tall, good-looking cop, and she signed the paper. She'd gambled on him liking her. She waived her right to call in a lawyer. She had thought about Jack Winters. She had worked for him a couple of years back. Had a bit of a winging with him. Nothing much. She knew what his reaction would be. *Sally's being a pain in the ass.* Acting as if he owed her something. She'd be okay. She didn't need anybody's help. She'd be all right.

Tomorrow there'd be an arraignment.

Something was thrown into her cell.

"Have a cigarette," the kid said. "It helps. Stops you from crying."

She saw a box of cigarettes with matches tucked into the wrapper. So she was still crying. She hadn't realized that.

The youngster seemed older, now that he had spoken. Maybe he was one of those thirty-to-forty-year-olds who look like kids until they're sixty. She could tell from his speech that he was from away.

She forced her voice to steady itself. "Thanks," she said. She picked the box up from the floor. She and Sweets had pledged themselves to stop smoking. None of that mattered now; all that was meaningless now.

"No need to thank me," the fellow said. "Glad to be able to help."

She was having trouble handling the cigarette.

"The thing about it is," the fellow said, "you have to take a deep breath to light up, and that does it, that stops the crying."

Striking the match was particularly difficult. She gave it three tries. The fellow kept encouraging her.

"There you go, now. Oops. Try again. There you go. Now you've got it. Oops. Okay, now you've got it, this time you're right on target, you're home safe," like some kind of cheerleader-type minister.

She inhaled deeply. He was right. She had stopped crying. She felt better, too, toughened, more in command. As soon as she exhaled, she inhaled again.

"It's a very simple theory," the fellow said. "It's impossible to cry and inhale at the same time. You'd choke. It works like a charm. Some people whistle, sing, talk—that blocks off the crying mechanism too."

She nodded.

"You latch on to these techniques after you've been around a bit," he said.

She inhaled again and pressed down on the bridge of her nose in a habitual gesture, before she released the smoke. She really was feeling better. From a supply of tissues that the mental-health worker had given her, she drew one and blew her nose, then another to wipe away some of the wet on her face. She must look a real mess. She turned from the fellow a bit.

"I've been in and out of a lot of jails," he said. "In my time."

She knew that the correct response was to display some interest in his hard-luck story, but she didn't want to know. She wasn't up

to a buddy-buddy scene. She was grateful he had given her cigarettes. She'd be more grateful if he shut up now.

"Would you like these back?" she said.

She waved the pack in the air, the matches tucked in where he
had placed them.

"No, you keep those," he said. "I have another pack. I always
carry two, three. Just in case."

"Thanks," she said. "I can use them. I can use any help I can
get."

It disgusted her that she had said that. She wanted to snatch
back her words from the cool, antiseptic space of the brightly
lighted cell. A sob pushed up into her throat. She took another deep
drag.

"What time is it?" she said.

He pointed to a large clock in the corridor. It was a little before
two o'clock. The information assumed no workable shape for her.
Times of night had to do with mornings, but this night had cut off
all connection to her habitual mornings. Mornings had to do, first,
with determining what kind of mood Sweets was in. That would
never be necessary again.

"Is that clock right?" she said.

"Think so," he said.

She reached automatically for her wristwatch, but it had been
broken in the fight. It was somewhere on the kitchen floor. Her
hands reminded her that her ring had been taken from her—the
wedding ring that was going to make everything all right.

"Time drags in jail," the fellow said. "I know. I've been in the
best and the worst of them."

He was pushing her to ask why he had been in all those jails, but
she wouldn't. That line of conversation would inevitably lead to her
own arrest.

The jail was very like the hospital—brightly lit, spacious, clean—
with the same kind of vinyl walls and floors. There were hard
benches around three sides of the cell she was in, padded with a
kind of thin mattress. In a corner, sheltered from view but not
closed off by a door, was a very clean flush toilet. She'd let her
bladder burst before she'd empty it where this guy could listen to
her. Whatever this fellow was, young or middle-aged, some kind of

creepy criminal or one of those civil-rights-protester saints, she didn't want him listening to her pee.

"Are you feeling better now?" he said.

He had worked up a reassuring smile that enraged her with its falseness.

"Feeling better?" he repeated.

"What about?"

He obviously thought her some kind of amateur dumb-dumb whore who had been picked up on the streets of Eatonville. Was he planning to be her savior? She had a surprise in store for him. Let his question come; she'd give him a run for his money.

"You get picked up right here in town?" he said.

She took a long drag and expelled the smoke with deliberation before she replied—like an actress on a TV show, thrusting out one hip, tilting her head, playing out a provocative delivery to shock.

"Well, no," she said. "They came out to the house. Because I stabbed my husband in our kitchen, with a kitchen knife."

His smile wavered, held, in disbelief. He laughed as if she were kidding.

"They didn't actually arrest me until he died in the hospital."

There was a momentary satisfaction in watching his assurance crumple into an astonishment and respect, tinged by fear.

"With a kitchen knife," she repeated.

His smile persisted but it had become so falsely wooden, she could imagine it would need to be hacked from his face. Then gratification drained away and she wanted only to get beyond his vision.

"I'm dead sleepy, really dead. I'm dead," she said and moved to the farthest end of the cell.

She threw herself on the narrow pad, flat on her back, one hand muffling her irresponsible mouth. How could she have said any of that speech, and especially the last?

She closed her eyes. The bed rose, swam, dipped, circled and swooped. There was a violent, roaring noise. She listened intently for the source and located it in her body, in her head. The sound shot her to her feet to pace. Now her foot burned. She sat on the bench to examine her bare foot and found a long, shallow cut, caked with dried blood and dirt. Good, at least the cut made for a real cause for pain.

Sweets lay on the floor, his head slid to one side, saying, "Yeah, ya stupid shit, ya hit me all right."

There would never be another word from him.

This time, flat on her stomach on the padded bench, she anchored herself in solidity. Still the bed rose, shimmered while she soared and swooped above, seeing another Sally below face down on the narrow pad, one hand trailing on the floor, a howling creature in the worst possible fix in life. Who was that woman?

Now both were joined, striding the cell, crying and babbling.

No longer smiling, the fellow in the other cell reminded her, "Smoke. Light up." His voice was tight with a strained compassion.

She stopped herself from pacing, concentrated on the ritual of the cigarette, took a long therapeutic drag. He was right. She was ashamed of having tried to shock him. Suppose he really was a minister of God. God knew. His minister could forgive her.

"Listen," she said. "I love him. I loved him. Somebody has to forgive me. You understand?"

PART TWO

7

SALLY WAS NOT quite fifteen when she met Vin Ciomei. She and Priscilla Houghton, the girlfriend she hung around with at that time, spent a Saturday night at the State Fair where they picked up a couple of older guys. The men treated them to enough beer to catch a buzz, and to things to eat—hot corn, hamburgers, tacos, cotton candy—and to a bunch of scary rides plus a couple of chances at the firing range. Each fellow had his own car, so when Sally lost track of Priscilla and her pickup, she didn't worry about Priscilla getting home, and as for herself, nobody at home was expecting her until some time the following day. She often slept at Priscilla's place—or the other way around. This man Vin Ciomei was so sweet and polite that she agreed to whatever he suggested. And so the night ended at a motel where more out of a sense of what was owing to her personal vision of a daring self than out of any overpowering passionate need or curosity, she let Vin Ciomei do it to her.

It was her first time and nothing like what she had expected. It was a singularly flat experience. Not even any blood or pain, and certainly no pleasure.

Vin Ciomei immediately decided that she wasn't no virgin. She didn't argue. He had treated her very nicely and he had told her she was as pretty as an angel, and after he finished he had said he was in love with her. No sense starting a big dispute and spoiling the whole evening.

Vin Ciomei was thirty-one, more than double her age. She saw him as a romantic figure, just fading into old age, exotically different from the dumb kids at school.

Something to do with his being part of an Italian family made it essential that their love affair be kept secret. She didn't argue about that either.

Secrecy bothered her. Was he ashamed of her? He spoke as if he was ashamed of himself. Other times he growled that the world was against them, the world was at fault.

She had never heard of statutory rape. Years later, it occurred to her that Vin might have been concerned about statutory rape back then.

Her friend Priscilla covered up the affair for her. She was supposed to tell Sally's father or her sisters that Sally spent the night at her house when Sally and Vin were at the motel. In fact, her daddy never asked, never checked, and her two older sisters were busy acting out their own secrets.

It pleased her that she dazzled Vin Ciomei. She was a dime a dozen in school, yet to Vin she was a wonder—a big, smooth, honey blonde with smiling blue eyes and long mascaraed lashes. She stood on long, solid, shapely legs, blossoming into luscious buttocks, narrowing again to form her elegant waistline. Her breasts were wonderful—firm, high, golden offerings, each ending in a burst of rosy nipple like "a flower in a garden," he said. He marveled that there wasn't a visible hair on her body except for the fluff on her mound of Venus. His expression. Mound of Venus. He had this poetic streak in him.

He was small and thin and covered with silky black hairs like a coat of fur—down to the joints of each finger and toe. When she wore high heels she was taller than he. That wasn't a bother to him or to her because they never went out anywhere except to the motel. The motel was an expensive one located at the other end of Branden Falls. They weren't likely to meet anybody they knew there. It was strictly for people from away—the ski crowd.

She saw a kid she knew from the district high school out there once. She had peeked out from behind the heavy flower-printed drapes to see what the noise was about one late Sunday evening and watched Duane Johnston making an asshole of himself with a crowd from away, all of them laughing at the way he spoke.

She had better things to do than to get mad at Duane Johnston. She could play in the bathroom, set the controls for steam or needle shower, turn on the heat lamp, fool around with the dimmers, watch color TV, order a Coke or even a hamburger from room service; she could walk barefoot on the wall-to-wall carpeting, hop from one big bed to the other. There was even a desk with stationery and postcards of Branden Mountain and the ski slopes. She'd turn on the TV as soon as they were in the door and never turned it off. Vin would do it to her and then while she'd be watching the TV he'd play with her nipples and fool around with her "mound." That seemed to excite him, and it excited her, more than when he went in. There were times that she'd think, yeah, this is it, this time it's gonna happen, he'd get so excited, stroking and licking her while she was watching some show, but then when he'd get on top and really get going inside her somehow the heat would die away and he'd start coming so fast he'd be done before she could start up again. She'd be overcome by a sad, stale, dreary state that she thought highly inappropriate to the motel with its great gadgets, and to Vin, who always told her how much he loved her and how beautiful she was and who was spending a lot of money on her. In gratitude she'd say that she loved him too.

She didn't know whether she did or she didn't. Watching him rub himself down with the big white bath towel, she saw, instead of her glamorous older lover, a puny, middle-aged, hairy-bodied man with a balding head and a long, slack, purple penis. She felt sorry for him and looked away, saying to herself, "Excuse me, excuse me," as if she had accidentally wandered into a stranger's room.

He told her that he worked in the quarry, that it paid good, but that it was work that broke his ass, especially during the winter, when the weather turned colder than a witch's tit. He told her that his father and his uncle were stonecutters, and that he had begun that way too, as an apprentice, but that he wasn't that good at it; he did better working in the quarry. He said that he was the only one in his family who had stayed in Eatonville, that all his brothers and sisters had gotten away from the old man's work and were really doing good elsewhere. He had so many brothers and sisters she couldn't get them straight. He didn't supply details, but he and his family sounded rich. Comfortable, anyway. And he certainly spent money freely once a week at the motel. As freely as he could, just staying put in the room. He said his mother had died that year and that he was in mourning. There was something deeply, deeply sad about him, a buried, quiet sadness that made her pity him.

She told him a little about her mother being dead too, and about her father and her two sisters, but she didn't want to talk about her home and family to Vin. Going to the motel was a visit to fantasy land. She was glamour girl for a night. He made her feel like a heroine in a movie.

After the first couple of times, he brought a fancy gown for her to wear, carrying it and a bottle of red wine in a brown paper bag. She learned to like wine with Vin. He would take the nightgown with him when they left, bringing another the next time, four in all, repeating them in regular order until he showed up with a fifth, an all-white crochet-lace-trimmed gown, like a wedding dress.

That was the night she told him she was pregnant. He put his head down and turned a yellowish green. The way he looked and the way he spoke, as if they were at a funeral, made her pity him, when she should be pitying herself. "Don't worry, Sally," he said. "I'll marry ya. I'll do right by ya. If ya want it, that is, if ya want it. The . . ." trailing away, unfinished.

She had expected to be disappointed in his response. Wasn't it her fault? Yet she couldn't stand that he hadn't been able to say the word "baby" out loud. She certainly did want it—*it*—the baby, the child, he could bet his sweet bippy she wanted the baby, stubbornly, absolutely, no matter what he said or anybody said, her father, her sisters, the school, the whole world. And yes, she wanted him to do right by her. She wasn't going to be stuck with an illegitimate kid at her age. Damn right he'd have to marry her.

"Ya don't hafta think ya hafta," she said to him. "I c'n take care a myself."

"Ain't ya in love with me?" he said.

"Sure," she said. "Sure. What do ya think I am anyway? What ya thinkin about me anyway?"

They stared at one another miserably.

"Ya don't hafta," she said again. "Don't think ya hafta."

"I know I don't hafta," he said.

Half proud, half terrified, she told her father and her sisters the next day that she and Vin were getting married. "Ya don't hafta marry him, y'know," her father said. "What are ya marrying him for? Huh? Huh? Ya don't hafta."

"It's too late," her older sister Dorothy said. "She's too far gone."

"I know it, I know it, I know it," her father said. "She still don't hafta marry him. Huh? We'll help ya take care of the kid, huh? I'll support you the best I c'n, like I been doin. Huh? Huh? Haven't done so bad for ya so far. Huh? Done the best I could, the best any man could, huh? Huh?"

His pale-blue eyes were burned out with anguish. She was supposed to worry about him too, about disappointing him too? Didn't anybody owe *her* anything? She knew she was his favorite among his three daughters, the one "most like a boy," his compensation for fathering no sons, but didn't that work both ways, with more give and take than he was offering? It wasn't *her* fault that his wife died of cancer when his daughters were little; after all, it was her mother that had died on her too, so why did she owe her father anything more than her father owed her?

"I swear," he said, "if it ain't one thing it's another. I'm livin in some kinda goddam soap opera, except it's real, no goddam TV show. Not collectin any big money on it like those actors, by Jesus.

"Couldn't ya watch out for her? Like her mother woulda? Teach her to take care a herself? Huh? Huh?" he said to her sisters. And to Sally, "Never gave ya motha a passin thought did ya, havin ya fun? Huh? Huh?

"I tried to do right by ya," he said. "Did my best, huh? Nothin's good enough. Nothin works. Here ya are, ruinin yaself, ruinin ya chances."

"Well, he's marryin me, ain't he?" she said, miserable now.

It wasn't fair, any of it. Her father had put his need on her to be daring and independent and then when she answered his need, when she acted like he wanted her to, bam, bam, she disappointed him. He wouldn't be creating this fuss if she were a son, would he now?

Except if she were a son, she wouldn't be the one carrying the stigma, some girl like her would be carrying the stigma, catching hell from her dad.

What puzzled her about her situation was why it wasn't being considered a successful foray into doing the right thing? Vin was marrying her, wasn't he? Wasn't it a triumph?

"He's marryin me, ain't he?" she repeated.

"Not much of a choice, huh?" her father said. "Choice between facin the music all alone or marryin that foreign feller? Don't call that a choice."

"Hey," Sally said, "he was born right here in town, born right here in Eatonville."

She looked toward her silent sisters for support. They knew Vin Ciomei's rep; they could assure their father that Vin was a good catch. They remained sullenly silent, not looking at her. Okay, they preferred to act jealous and mean, she'd harden herself against them too.

"Don't you say 'Hey' to me," her father said. "Don't start actin big. Ya still my baby daughter, still under my roof, still in my keepin."

"I know it, Daddy," she said.

Vin had warned her to be sweet and humble. "Ya a kid," he said. "We gotta get ya father's permission. So ask the right way, okay?"

The motel hadn't been a bit of fun this last time. Vin was pale, alarmed, depressed. They didn't do anything, not even watch the TV, just talked around and around the whole thing in a dreary way while they ate burgers he had brought in. No wine. No nightgowns. No room service. He took her back to Priscilla's before nine thirty. She put a big smile on her face before going into Priscilla's. She had already told Priscilla she and Vin were getting married, and even if she no longer knew whether or not she really wanted to marry Vin, she knew he was her ticket out of her troubles. There was no other way to go.

"I know Vin Ciomei," her father said. He pronounced it "Syomy," like everybody in Eatonville did. "I know his father and I know him. I know his uncle too. If they ain't foreign—I don't know what foreign is. Ya ever heard them talkin in that lingo a theirs? Well I heard it plenty. They come inta the market. Get some kinda outta state check they cash on me. I know em bettern anybody. If Vin Ciomei ain't foreign, how come he talks that lingo so good, huh? Huh? Only lingo he talks with his father, y'know that? Ya gonna be his wife, ya won't even understand the lingo they use.

Huh? Huh? He can tell ya what he likes, he can tell ya whatever pops inta his head, tell ya they're talkin about the moon, for all ya know, and them talkin against ya, runnin ya down, by Jesus, and how the hell would ya know, not understandin the lingo and all, huh? Huh?"

She said, "Oh, Daddy."

He said, "Fella calls me on the telephone. Important occasion like this. He scared or somethin? He too friggin busy? Why don't he walk in here like a man? In person? Make a personal appearance, like a man, huh?

"Not even comin to meet ya folks, not even takin ya t'meet his folks. Don't call that right. Ya don't hafta marry him. Just because he put the wood to ya, ya don't hafta smash your life before ya even come to sixteen years of age. When ya come to freshen we'll take care of ya—and the baby. Huh? Huh?"

He glared at his three girls with his burned-out blue eyes. Was she touched by his plea? It would never work. She knew it couldn't work. The three of them would be on her back all the time, making her pay for her mistake. There was no way to go but marriage and Vin.

"I'll be okay, Daddy," she said. "You watch. We're gonna do good, me and Vin."

"By Jesus, he's the one will be doin good," her father said. "Practically a middle-aged man. Practically my age. He's the one'll be havin it good when it's colder than a witch's tit out, huh? Huh? With a young girl to warm 'm up."

"Oh, Daddy," she said, and glanced uncomfortably at her sisters' sullen, no-help faces.

Yet, when she was settled into marriage with Vin, and into motherhood, it was her sisters who came through for her, crazy about baby Laura, helping her, both of them as good as gold, and it was her father who turned sullen, unappreciative of her ranch-style new house, always harping on the fact that it was the Branden Falls bank that owned her house, not Vin Ciomei anyhow. He was obviously sick with disappointment at a grandchild that was still another female. His love for Sally was turned around toward Patsy, the middle sister, and he pinned his hopes on Patsy until Patsy married some flatlander temporarily working in the area and left to live in Lincoln, Nebraska, of all places. And then even Dorothy, the oldest and meekest and mildest, married a fellow from away, though they remained living nearby just outside Hartshead. It was then their father seemed to lose heart in all of them.

"He's give up on us," Dorothy said.

Sally agreed he was right to give up on Dorothy.

Here was Dorothy, fat as a house, barging into Sally's neat-as-a-pin place, dragging along her three stepsons, her husband's boys, part of the marriage package. No bargain, those three—eight, nine and ten—looking like triplets, handsome enough but wilder than a pack of dogs, and hungrier, disrupting the peaceful space of Sally's house with grunts and squabbles and a shared annoying habit each had of shoving his blond-white long hair out of his eyes by swinging his whole upper body in an arc. Between the three it was dizzying, because if one wasn't swinging away, another was.

Their daddy was right to give up on Dorothy the way she was pulling herself down to worse than where they had come from, living in the woods in a shack with no flush and no way to keep warm except for wood stoves and plastic on the windows, running a busted washing machine three times a day, hanging the clothes on the line, carrying them in frozen stiff to dry out all over the furniture, getting filthier than they were before they were washed—if that was possible. Enough to drive any woman mad. No wonder his first wife ended up crackers. Now Dorothy was pregnant with her own kid, pretending to be happy, smiling from ear to ear, pretending that mess in the woods was a farm, calling it "the farm," talking about her chickens and eggs and her goat and pigs, all of them living together worse than animals along with two big dogs and God knows how many cats.

"Ya sister's out to win first prize for the fattest ass in the state," her father said to Sally. "Competin against some real champs, too," he said, indicating the shuddering backside of a huge woman in bright orange stretch pants.

None of that let-yourself-go life for Sally. Sally had put a little weight on with the pregnancy, but she wasn't dreaming away her winters wolfing spaghetti and baked goods and coming out in the spring a fat white worm, all pasty and pimply. She was watching her figure, taking care of her hair, wearing nice clothes.

"Don't be lettin go a yaself like ya sister Dotty. Don't take a leaf from her book," he said. "Wake up one mornin to see yaself fat and old with ya husband run off with another woman. No use to start cryin then."

"Oh, Daddy," she said. "I don't look so bad, do I?"

He didn't give her much satisfaction. "Ya okay," he said. "Fa a kid a sixteen."

He glanced at her. She was struck again by how much hot anguish his cold blue eyes could generate. She felt bitterly defensive against that hot-cold attack.

"It's ya husband I'd be complainin about. I don't give him a hundred percent. Not with that family he come from. Dunno how a daughter a mine expects to raise a family tied to that crew."

For Sally, that kind of talk meant her family had virtually abandoned her to an engulfing, baffling, alien atmosphere. Now there was only herself and Vin and the baby and Vin's family. And while the baby and she generated a closed circuit of pleasure, a vital current that refreshed and delighted, Vin and she generated less and less connection. She had never been much of a talker, but it was strangling to have nobody to talk to. She and Vin never talked. And then, married, with a baby to tend, how could she keep up her friendships with kids still in high school? She never even saw Priscilla Houghton anymore, or any of the rest of the crowd she had helled around with.

In a dreamlike confusion, she lowered herself into the dark maze of Vin's family.

First there was Papa Ciomei, Vin's father. He shared a big old house out on the quarry road with Uncle Arturo. It took a while before Sally got that relationship straight. Uncle Arturo was Vin's mother's brother, so Papa Ciomei and Uncle Arturo were brothers-in-law. She congratulated herself on having cleared up the first puzzle, as if she had passed a major examination. Then there was the house itself, covered with fancy shingling and ornate trim outside. Inside it looked to her like a haunted house in a movie. Little worn-out rugs on top of big worn-out rugs, family pictures and religious pictures covering torn wallpaper, decrepit fancy lamps, and bunches of other stuff falling apart and crowding one on top of the other. There always seemed to be a party going on. Lots of rich, strange food, wine, big bowls of fruit and nuts. Even when it was a family tragedy, someone dying or in the hospital, there was a party going on. Papa Ciomei and Uncle Arturo (and Vin, of course) were the only family members living in the state, but there was a constant stream of visiting relatives from away, paying their respects to the two old men, sharing some good event or some tragedy—a marriage or a kid's graduation, a sickness or a death. Impossible to get the relationships straight. She concentrated on Vin's brothers and sisters and their sons and daughters; that proved hard enough. Everybody else seemed to be sons and daughters of Uncle Arturo, or of other aunts and uncles, or descendants of ancient *paisanos* of the little hometown in Italy that Papa Ciomei and Uncle Arturo had come from.

She found it a full-time job trying to straighten out the question of names. One person could have as many as four different names. Like Uncle Arturo who was also Papa Turo, Papa Conti, Cuco and Pasta. That's the way it went with all of them. Just when she had accustomed herself to Vin disappearing into Vincenzo and Cenzo, a sister arrived from Pittsburgh whose name for Vin was Cho-Cho. It was a relief that nobody pinned a nickname on her or baby Laura, though "Sally" and "Laura" were transformed by the Ciomei open-vowel pronunciation into liquid, exotic-sounding new names that Sally had to admit she really liked, "Sollee" and "Lowra."

What she didn't like was how she was cut out of the conversation. Talk usually started in English, but it inevitably wandered into Italian, leaving her stranded, depressed, disconnected. Even the littlest kids spoke Italian. Added to too much rich food and wine, the sense of estrangement gave her a headache. All that smiling she had to go in for. Smiling and smiling at all the old men and women, at Vin's flashy, loud, exuberant brothers and sisters, smiling at the dark noisy kids rushing about, rattling away in Italian.

She lost Vin at these gatherings. Not that she normally felt she had him solid. He had always faded away on her. At his father's house he fell into separate pieces she couldn't put together into any recognizable pattern at all, crumbling into a stranger she could only observe, a part of a show she had never been properly invited to participate in.

She didn't understand this man she had married. There was in him an endless depth of quietness and sadness that sapped her energy. Even though he was so much older than she, it was like having two babies, baby Laura and baby Vin.

The dark infant at her breast was the more satisfying. She clung to the flow of connection, feeling happiness, love, feeling shame that passion was spurred by a sucking infant, but insisting on her happiness with the child, except for those terrible moments, without warning, when her enclosure became imprisonment and erupted her into uncontrollable rage that wanted only to smash this circle of feedings and naps and shit and diapers and wash and dry and feedings and naps and shit and diapers and wash and dry interspersed with housework and cooking, over and over.

Yet she clung to her life, to her house, making it nice, keeping it perfect, the new little prefab that Vin had bought for them to be a family in. Goddam it, she was going to make a family if it killed her. She reached for styles beyond the limits she knew, learning from magazines and TV how to do things, how to make a dressing-table skirt, how to prepare tuna-fish casserole, learning also by keeping her eyes and ears open, studying the I-own-the-earth walk of the sleek, flat-hipped vacationing out-of-state girls with their toned-down style and simple, clean-hanging hair. She called the Avon lady one rainy November afternoon. She took a lesson in makeup, learned how to do her eyes up right, told the Avon lady how much she hated her pointy-chin witch look and was taught how to square off her face. She bought a mess of stuff from the Avon lady, paying out of her household money. She even bought earrings and a silver necklace. She told Vin her father had bought it for her. She couldn't imagine why he believed her.

Motel time was gone. Motel time had faded into a fantasy that seemed never to have happened. Rules that never existed in the motel governed their marriage bed. Vin was always exhausted, he had to get his sleep, didn't he, if she wanted him to go to work in the morning? He said it was forbidden for him to touch her breasts while she was nursing. She made up a few rules of her own. She was tired; she wasn't interested. She refused to wear the sexy night-gowns while her milk was spilling over. She said he had to help her come. She put his hand on her mound, but he wouldn't, he pulled away. It was a sin, he said, it was prohibited. Okay. When he asked her to take him in her mouth she said No, she didn't like to do it.

She said, "Ain't what ya askin me to do a sin?"

It was a relief that he spent two nights a week away from the house, coming home late.

Those nights she had a love affair with herself. She indulged herself, ate steak, french fries, chocolate Mallomars—or nothing, if that suited her. Laura was asleep in her crib in her little room, and after Sally washed the dishes she went to her own room. She drank wine or beer. She talked aloud, danced, sang, took all her clothes off, acting out the latest variation on a continuous erotic daydream in which a faceless, nameless man did to her what she willed him to do. Sometimes he was horrible and mean. She cried and begged— then he turned wonderful. He bathed her in perfumed bubble stuff bought from the Avon lady. Her lover teased, patting her dry with slow, lingering caresses, powdering and smoothing her silken body with lotion. Aroused as both lover and beloved, her breasts heaving, her groin burning, one part of her coolly purposeful and pushing, the other receptive and yearning, both climbed into the marriage bed of the pretty room she had fashioned for the marriage of Vin and Sally Ciomei. Bringing herself to full satisfaction, she turned her back on Vin's empty side of the bed and fell asleep.

Once, observing herself in the full-length bathroom mirror as she patted and powdered, she saw, not the image of her fantasy, but the reality of a tall, blond young woman with clouded eyes and a flushed, sullen face, handling herself. Poor thing, she thought, nobody loves her—and the magic progression faltered for some seconds before she willed it back into rhythm.

It was Vin and no fantasy lover who made her pregnant again. Yet she clung to loving herself obsessively. Pregnant, she did it to herself so often, she almost stopped bothering with the fantasy part, doing it cold whenever she had a moment—during baby Laura's daytime naps, and not only at night when Vin was out but also nights when Vin was at home, locking herself in the bathroom, and soaking in the tub.

She wanted it so much she could do it thinking of anything, thinking not of sexy, romantic love but of something she wanted to buy for the house, thinking of bills, thinking coldly of Vin's distance, thinking angrily of the haze of the feelings with which he approached fatherhood. It was as if giving herself satisfaction was paying him back for being unable to connect with her and baby Laura, and of remaining so aloof, so untouched by the new pregnancy. He might see them as a family more strongly if the new baby turned out to be a boy, but that thought also made her angrier with him. Then, even while doing it, instead of romantic images, violent visions took over—kicks, blows, smashing fists into a nameless face.

She thought she might be going crazy. She had nobody to talk to about it—or about anything else. She never saw her sister Dorothy, never saw anybody but Vin and the family. On her monthly checkups at the hospital in Hartshead, she dropped into the supermarket to say hello to her father. She would search him out, down the messy aisles or at one of the checkouts, supervising a cashier, or behind the desk in the little partitioned office, or at a distance striding the aisle in the coat he wore like a uniform, proudly displaying the supermarket insignia and his manager identification on the pocket, smiling and greeting people, his eyes hot and anxious, his manner fake-breezy and hearty. Their conversation usually depressed her.

"Ya lookin good."

"Ya lookin good, too, Dad."

"I ain't too bad," he said.

"Little girl lookin good," he said. "Little green though, ain't she? Unhealthy-lookin?"

She knew he hated it that Laura looked so Italian.

"That's her colorin," she said smiling, breezy. "Gets her complexion from her father." She couldn't resist rubbing his nose in it. "She's healthy. Say hello to Grandpa, Laura," she said.

Laura stared at the strange man seriously.

"Not too friendly, huh?"

"Not if she don't know ya," Sally said. "She's friendly if she knows ya."

He looked away, preoccupied.

"Ya hear from Dotty and Patsy?" she said.

"Well, y'know," he said. "Got their problems."

"Sure," she said.

"Like everybody," he said. "Everythin okay over to ya house?"

"Everythin real good. Real good."

"See ya got another comin," he said, nodding at her bulge.

"Sure have," she said.

He called out, "Jess, get some bad boys down front here. We got a bottleneck here. Need some bad boys."

For a second she envisioned her daddy as the ultimate punishing father, ruling supermarket conduct; then the PA system translated his order.

"All bag boys to the front. All bag boys up front, please."

She laughed. "I heard ya wrong and thought ya said *bad* boys," she said.

"What?" he said, puzzled, distracted, his hot eyes sweeping his domain, checking on the bag boys hurrying to the checkout stations.

"Nothin," she said. "Guess ya busy, Dad. Good to see ya."

"Sure," he said. "See ya later, then."

"Sure," she said. "See ya later, Dad."

Toward the end of the pregnancy Vin came with her on her weekly Saturday hospital visits. They stopped at the supermarket together to say hello to her father. It amazed her how friendly the two men were with each other—breezy enough with each other to blow her clean away.

"Hey, how ya doin there?"

"Not bad. How ya doin?"

"Not too bad. Got ya pickup overhauled yet?"

"Well, he says it's fixed but that don't mean it's runnin good."

"Ya can't trust nobody these days on vehicles."

"Ya hear that Jimmy started out on his own? Jimmy Rawlins?"

"The way I hear it is he's only doin body work."

"He'll work on engines."

"None of them foreign makes. Won't work on Subarus and Saabs. Won't work on VWs. He fixed a Toyota I know of. Fixed it perfect. So far."

"Well, y'know the sayin. So far so good."

"Well, if I run into any more trouble—with this lemon I got I'm bound to. I'll try anythin."

"He's on the Ridge Road. Ya make a right turn after the Sears warehouse on Route Seven."

"I know where he's at."

"Well, I hope ya don't need him."

"I sure hope I don't."

"See ya later now."

"See ya later."

"See ya later, Dad. Say bye to Grandpa, Laurie."

Laura only stared.

8

IT WAS at the next checkup at the hospital that the doctor told her the baby was dead. Nobody knew why. She was always hearing about all the great things the medical profession could do, but medicine couldn't say why her baby was dead inside her, or why she had to go on carrying it, waiting for it to be the right time to deliver a dead baby. The doctor didn't look into her eyes when he told her. It made her sick how his eyes wouldn't look straight into hers when he talked to her.

"We don't have the answers to this one," he said. "The important thing is that you're very young and perfectly healthy, you can have another child with no difficulty, you can have as many as you choose. That's the thing to keep your sights on," he said, avoiding her steady, demanding gaze.

Vin was good at avoiding her eyes too.

She was being punished for the sin of having done it to herself so often. She could have harmed something, dislocated something. The baby had stopped moving inside, but hope persisted. She'd will a live baby. She entered the hospital on a set date and an intern rigged up an intravenous flowing into the inside crook of her elbow. Strapped down, she lost her will, but the painful labor started up hope again. There was no way to absorb such cruel pain without some chance for a live child.

They told her the baby was a boy when she insisted on knowing. Apart from her hopes for Vin, she had daydreamed a baby boy, an infant male head at her breast, another closed circle of love for herself, different from the one with Laura.

She had been invaded by death. Death had marked a chalked X in her womb, claiming the territory. She would never trust another life to that desolated place.

"Ya win some, ya lose some," Vin said. He was perched on a high stool beside her hospital bed in the ward she shared with three women who had delivered live babies. He was the only visitor in the room. She could see his discomfort and understood that his fake tough stance was more for the benefit of the other patients than for her. One of them, an older woman who had delivered her seventh child that morning, was asleep. The others, lively and upright in their beds, were young women who now knew each other well enough to ask "How ya doin?" and answer "Doin good." They didn't hide their interest in the oddly matched couple who had lost a child. "Ya think maybe it's because ya husband's too old?" Another refuted that theory. "Only happens if the woman's past her time. Then the kid comes out deformed or retarded."

When Papa Ciomei arrived and Vin was forced to talk to him in Italian, the scene was a real show for them.

"Ya should charge admission," Sally said between her teeth to Vin, sliding her eyes in the direction of the audience.

He took her words as an assault and transformed his rage into irritation at Papa Ciomei's presence, as excessive as Papa Ciomei himself. He wanted Papa Ciomei out of there, quick, quick. Not so easy. Papa Ciomei, loaded with flowers and a basket of incredibly huge ripe peaches, impossible to obtain anywhere in New England at that season, she would have thought, had also arrived with a plan for lightening her heart. It was at that moment, reading his compassion for her loss in his eyes, that she began to love Papa Ciomei. His plan called for her to be led to a window overlooking the parking lot, driven in a wheelchair, he insisted. She asked Vin to reassure the old man. She was perfectly capable of walking.

It took some doing to locate the right window, given Papa Ciomei's no English and Vin's resistance. Finally stationed at the correct spot, he triumphantly displayed Uncle Arturo in his good suit and felt hat, steadying Laura atop the hood of their old Pontiac. Laura waved her arm limply, laughing and gazing vaguely in the wrong direction, resolutely turned again and again by Uncle Arturo to the right window in the blind rows of openings in the long, uniform structure. Sally smiled to see her baby, then she cried. Vin jumped on Papa Ciomei as the cause of her tears, but Vin's papa was righter than Vin. Feeling bad was feeling better.

Papa Ciomei took his time kissing her goodbye. Vin made it plain that the old man couldn't move out fast enough for him. Papa Ciomei held her hands in a strong, dry, warm clasp, leaving a space between them, saving her from any accidentally crushing harm his great size might inflict. He leaned forward and down kissing her with deliberate firmness as if the intent were to implant a solid impression of his sculptured full lips on her forehead. She recognized the gift of a blessing and smiled her thanks into his anguished, comforting face.

Papa Ciomei disposed of, Vin, once again perched on the high stool alongside her bed, self-consciously aware of listeners-in, touched the secret button releasing the regular guy he was supposed to be.

"Well, I betta be goin'," he said. "Don't wanna leave Laurie with the two old characters for longern we hafta, do we now, Motha?"

He smiled slightly, in complicity with the derision he knew he could count on from their audience.

She shut her eyes. She hated being called Motha. She was nineteen, for Christ's sake. Why was this man, almost forty, calling her *Motha?*

She wanted him to go away.

She wanted a husband at her side, but a different man, more like the man his papa was.

She pulled the light covers up to her neck and opened her eyes. "Roll the bed down, will ya, Vin. I'm pooched."

He was nothing like his papa. He was small, thin, sad, quiet, afraid, incompetent. It was astonishing that such a papa had fathered this son. He rolled the bed straight up before he got it to go down.

She tried to trap her husband's frightened, fleeing gaze, nail it to the truth of her despair.

He hung on to his breezy tone. "By Jesus, if it ain't one thing it's anotha. Ain't it now?"

She nodded.

"Just when I need it the most, my car goes and breaks down on me. Ain't that the limit?"

She shut her eyes. "Ya c'n use mine. Sure ya check the oil though. It's been eatin oil."

"I know it," he said. "I know it." And after a pause, "If it wasn't for bad luck, by Jesus, we wouldn't have no luck at all, ain't that right, Motha?"

"Guess so," she said.

He drew in his breath, expelled it, exuding a spurt of calm. Clearly, for him, a trouble spot had been safely navigated to a safe shore.

"See ya later," he said, almost cheerfully. "Don't be worryin about anythin now." He was on his feet, ready to flee. He wanted to be gone as much as she wanted him gone.

"Ya comin to visit again?"

"Ain't ya comin home tomorrow?"

"I dunno. That what the doctor said?"

"What he told me," Vin said.

"Ya pickin me up?"

"Ya kiddin? The old man'd kill me if I let ya come home on ya own. Anyways, we only got the one car now."

"Okay," she said. "See ya later, then."

"See ya later," he said and gave her a quick, scared peck on her cheek before he fled.

9

When Laura started kindergarten, Sally's life changed a little. Her mornings were filled with getting Vin off to work and his lunch pail packed, dressing Laura, setting her off to the bus stop at the end of their road, making the beds, tidying the living room, washing up the bathroom, doing the laundry. Then nothing. A warm, empty, safe quietness in which she drifted without effect. Time passed without event, without markings, becalmed. Then Laura was back home, dropped by the returning school bus, trudging up the road. Soon it was time to prepare supper, bathe Laurie, greet Vin, sit down to a silent meal broken only by the child's chatter. Then Vin went to "the club," or dropped over to see Papa Ciomei and Uncle Arturo, or he retired to the room they called the den, where he fell asleep before the TV. She had no friends, did nothing socially. Watching TV made her restless. She built a fire in the open fireplace, sat before it daydreaming—not the old sex daydreams she had forsworn—but dreams of opening a shop, becoming a doctor, maybe an actress, or just running away one morning from the quiet, empty house, getting in the car and driving off, never coming back, the details of the dream vague, soft and enticing.

She and Vin hardly did it anymore. Fear of the treachery her body might hold? All desire had been damped down, put out. At her twelve-week checkup after the delivery of the dead baby, she told her doctor she wanted "a real good contraceptive." He gave her so many choices, from an operation to all kinds of gadgets stuck in her body, that he made her dizzy. She ended choosing the pill, "almost one hundred percent effective," he said. Now when Vin wanted it, she'd go along with him with more ease of mind, knowing she was protected. At the gynecologist's office she chatted with the women waiting for their appointments. Nobody mentioned desire. Mechanisms were the thing—the loop, the pill, the diaphragm, home remedies.

"My husband yanks it out just before he comes," an older woman said. "Weekly special. He thinks he invented it. Trouble is, it doesn't work. I'm getting me one of them loop things, before I have so many kids I'll be just like the old woman in the shoe. What he don't know don't hurt him."

After a couple of months her periods stopped. The doctor assured her she wasn't pregnant. It was one of the reactions some women developed to the pill. Good enough. Now she was through with everything, sex, childbearing, bleeding. Maybe she'd be the first freak developed by the pill, turn into a man, become the male her father had always wanted.

Remote from time, from everything around her except Laura, she passed her twenty-first birthday. She'd be old before she knew it, fading into nothing, into death; the only mark left behind on the world would be her dark, beautiful, round-eyed child. She daydreamed of going back to school, got as far as the town public library and lost her ambition in the romance of novels, gobbling down stories at the rate of one a day, sometimes two. Mornings, alone in the still house, she wrote poetry, hiding the finished product in the bureau under her panties and the five nightgowns, closet-worn and tacky-looking. She fought against letting her appearance go, kept her weight down, rinsed blond lights into her hair, kept it clean and washed, made up her eyes with the blue eye shadow and black mascara. It was hard to go out, torment to greet people, to smile and smile, to say, "Feelin good," but she forced herself to leave the house to shop for food and for Laura's clothing. She needed little clothing for herself.

On a vividly sunny morning, with a fresh wind scudding dramatic clouds across a brilliantly blue sky and skimming the fallen leaves across the lawns and the roadways, she headed her car toward the shopping mall, but instead drove past it, straight on out of town—out, out, on her way out, enraptured by the prospect, as if in one of her daydreams—until she hit the quarry road, and on a whim halted her flight and pulled into the Hartshead Quarry's visitors' parking. She joined a group of tourists, following the guided tour to a platform where from an immense height she tried to distinguish Vin among the diminished hardhat figures strung out along the scaffolds on the cliffs of the cruelly harsh, stunningly handsome stone pit. She thought she spotted him far below on a narrow ledge, until the figure moved into a stance uncharacteristic of Vin. She made similar false identifications with figure after figure and then gave up trying to locate him. From this spectacular view, all quarry workers were alike, it seemed.

She was swamped by an intense, guilty sorrow for her husband. How little he amounted to in this crushing, oblivious landscape. What did he get out of life, and out of her with her grudging love— if it was love at all that she felt for him? Leaning on the protective railing, exhilarated by the clean strong wind, she daydreamed an accident of toppling monster cranes and crashing boulders below, the delicate ladders and planks of the rigging giving way in a mess of falling bodies that would kill Vin and set her free.

It never occurred to her that Vin, too, harbored a secret life. His days seemed openly laid out on the table for anybody to read. He worked, he went to "the club," he visited his papa and his uncle, he screwed her now and then; when he was home he watched the TV news religiously and an occasional special program; he ate his meals and he slept soundly.

She was used to quiet men. Her father was a quiet man, but she had always felt the agitation under her father's silences. There wasn't *any* animation in Vin, except when he sat in front of the TV news. TV news brought out a stream of agitated comment.

"Looka that. Right in our country. Would ya believe it? Bunch of horses' asses."

He was demanding her participating outrage.

She didn't understand what she saw. Disconnected, too fast, the images that aroused him were only movies to her: crazy milling crowds, police, bodies dragged around, hosed, clubbed; war scenes in unpronounceable places against an enemy too different-looking to be believed in, close-ups of serious faces making statements she couldn't comprehend. The war news was either too disgusting to watch or too boring to listen to.

"Ya feel so strong about it, ya oughta join them nuts downtown," she said.

He threw her a contemptuous glance.

She referred to what the marchers called a "peace vigil," pacing around the Capitol Building on State Street. Mostly women, gotten up in long old-fashioned dresses or sloppy blue jeans, or some outlandish mess of costumes, their hairdos a disgrace, slow-walking with their faces lifted in an expression of belligerent saintliness. Nothing but rich phony lazy hypocrites, was what she thought of them. If they wanted to do good, there was plenty needed to be fixed right in town.

The kids at the college made a half-assed attempt to seize an administration building, copying the big actions in the big cities, but the revolt was put down in a day. She drove over to the edge of the campus after her shopping, curious to see what was going on. Rebellion at hand intrigued her, especially by people her own age. She was surprised. While she hadn't been paying any attention to the outside world, college kids had changed from uniformly dressed, quiet, clean-haired kids to loud slobs, worse than her sister Dorothy's boys.

"Ya c'n see right through the slobbiness to how rich they really are," she commented to Vin. "That's the weird part."

Vin had no use for local protests.

"Damn-fool bastard kids. Tearin down things. Not interested in buildin anythin. Only interested in tearin things down. And those old fools approvin every bit of their foolishness. Sittin in front of the TV night after night givin their stamp of approval to every bit of foolishness."

He meant his papa and Uncle Arturo.

She hardly saw Papa Ciomei now. She was made shy by her feeling for him, and afraid—afraid he'd prove disappointing. She used any excuse to avoid family gatherings. Said she was sick, said Laura had an upset stomach, said anything that came into her head, said she had a doctor's appointment, said she was waiting for an important phone call about school. She murmured to Vin from time to time that she was planning to go back to school, though she never made a solid gesture to get going.

Vin glanced at her with contempt. "B'lieve that when it happens," he'd say.

If he loved her, he'd encourage her. But she didn't love Vin the way a wife should either. It galled her that her father had been right after all. She shouldn't have married him just because she was fifteen and pregnant. Now she was condemned for life?

And then their life was totally shaken up—out of the blue.

Vin returned fom a Sunday visit to Papa Ciomei's, pale and deeply still. Heart attack? She daydreamed herself independent, sole owner of the house (worth maybe $30,000) and two beat-up cars (not worth much) and the beneficiary of his insurance. Widow's benefits (she didn't know how much). She'd have the world's sympathy. She could be free—and a good woman too, if he was having a heart attack.

But he wasn't sick, only upset. He wouldn't talk about what was upsetting him. He didn't want to eat anything, not even a sandwich snack. He went to bed early in the evening right after Laura did, muttering mysterious grumbling hints.

"It ain't all my fault, by Jesus. Somebody else had somethin to do with it. Workin my balls off in conditions worsen hell froze over, cold enough down there to freeze the balls off a brass monkey, but nothin's enough for some people, can't do enough for some people, neva satisfied, neva satisfied with what I done. Gotta have this, gotta have that. More gadgets and more gadgets and more goddam gadgets. Nother hair dryer. Can't eat hair dryers. Comes time to eat, can't eat a hair dryer."

She didn't rise to the bait.

She wrote a poem that night about a woman giving birth to a dead baby.

> *Claimed by death*
> *She drew in her breath*
> *Went on with life*
> *The steady wife.*

She studied the poem. She tried again.

> *Claimed by death*
> *Sucked in her breath*
> *Continued that life*
> *Of good, steady wife.*

She studied the new poem. She changed "that life" to "the life." She was happy working on the poem. She changed the second line to "She sucked in her breath." She studied the poem again. She wrote, changing the first line:

> *Marked by death*
> *She sucked in her breath*
> *Continued the life*
> *Of good, steady wife.*

She reread. Her good feeling dwindled. The poem looked rotten now. She stopped studying it. She went to bed, placing the poem in the drawer under her nightgowns and panties along with the others she had written.

Their life erupted that weekend in a big powwow at Papa Ciomei's. Vin had been gambling at cards, losing steadily, at "the club," a back room at Ginny's Place, an Italian restaurant in a little wooden building almost sliding into the river at the foot of the street that ran up the hill to the Capitol Building. Her father was right again. The ranch-style she had fastened herself upon as on another body to feed her didn't belong to them, just as he had said, and though it was mortgaged to the Branden Falls branch of the New England Banking & Trust, the house really belonged to a trust governed by Vin's brothers and sisters. The family was selling the house out from under them. They had had their meetings in Italian without her and made their decisions. She was supposed to follow without question. She and Vin and Laurie were to move in with the two older men, help take care of them. The family was punishing Vin in a kindly, family-style, caretaking way.

She didn't know she was capable of the anger she tried to control.

"Ya not goin to let them do it, are ya?" she said. "How come it's not our house? How come ya never demanded ya name on the deed? Wasn't it us that was payin the bills?"

"Us? Where'd ya get 'us'? Ya can bet ya ass I was payin ya goddam bills. Neva enough. Always pushin, pushin, pushin. Ya'd push a man clear over a cliff if it was a choice tween him and a new hair dryer. Never pleased with what I done or what I brought home, always lookin for more, more, lookin for more and more, like a regular Jew."

He said, "I'm sick a talkin about it. Okay? Okay?" He could barely get the words out through the tears choking him.

"What are we, some kinda goddam babies? Takin orders from ya goddam family like some kinda goddam babies?"

Vin turned his palest, sickliest green. His hands trembled, his lips tinged blue, his flat black eyes bulged and reddened. Heart attack. Did she really want to kill him?

It was intolerable. If Vin's family wanted to push Vin around, let them, but she and Laura didn't belong to the goddam family. They belonged to themselves. They had a right to their own nest. She clung like an animal to wood chunks of security—her modern matching bedroom set, Laura's child-scaled dresser and youth bed, a living-room wall unit she had been especially proud of. Everything else was sold.

She knotted the tangled threads of her disrupted life into an obsession with the old Ciomei house to which she had been exiled, entering into a madness of renovation—replacing peeling wallpaper, painting ceilings, refinishing floors; she even tore down a wall and waded in plaster for days. She reupholstered a few pieces of furniture, sewed slipcovers and drapes, insisted on fitting her modern pieces into uneasy spaces by tossing out what had been there—standing gaudy vases filled with paper flowers, leather recliners, huge radio-phonograph consoles, heavy mahogany headboards, chests, dining-room pieces. There were things she couldn't do anything about, like the linoleum cemented on the floor of one room or the sad, dark pictures in heavy frames she was forbidden to touch—the family pictures and religious pictures. There were walls and walls of family pictures, dark, posed, still figures, framed and hung —reproaches to her innovations.

Some nights she couldn't sleep, planning her next line of attack. The two old men retreated from her onslaught of vengeance. Vin faded into a submission that allied him with his papa and his uncle against her. The worst betrayal was Laura's. Laura had never been happier.

The child had been loosed into a garden of delights. Real gardens, chicken-wire fenced, and entered by makeshift latched gates, odd-lot areas secured against deer and smaller marauding animals, the kitchen garden, the herb garden, the strawberry patch, the blueberry, raspberry and blackberry patches, the squash, cucumber and corn areas, the potato field, the asparagus rectangle, at this time of year a spread of magical, delicate fern. There were miniature fenced pastures for the horse, the two lambs, the goat. The pigs were penned in their own clean housing. The geese, turkeys and chickens had the run of the place. Loving the animals indiscriminately, the child watched calmly the slaughtering of the pigs and lambs when the time came, prepared by Papa Ciomei for that inevitable moment. It was Sally who hid in the house when they shot the pigs. Blithely, Laura shifted her love to the horse. She rode the ungainly pale horse with ease. The dog loped behind, the three cats scurried to cover. She rode her bike safely on the long, curving driveway set in the woods, and out on the quiet town road beyond. In the fruit orchard, as in a fairy tale, three groups of ornately carved stone benches and little stone tables were set among the trees; stone animals hid in the trunks—rabbits and skunks, frogs, even a lizard and a snake. Posted at the entrance to the orchard, two long-nosed dogs carved of a rough gray stone stood guard.

Sally thought it a queer way to live, okay for the old men, maybe, but not for her. She resisted it, bought eggs at the supermarket, chickens, regular milk. The others drank goat's milk, ate fresh-laid eggs, fresh-killed chickens, turkeys; they ate one of the geese one Sunday. There was an immense freezer stuffed with food raised by the two old men. She ignored it, as she did their pickling and their preparation of relishes, their processing the immense crop of ripe tomatoes and corn, freezing the vegetables and preserving the fruits. The old men even made their own brandy and wine. She jangled the pots, slammed cupboard doors, growled to herself as she prepared meals for herself and Laura and Vin. Let the old men eat whatever they liked. She had turned against Papa Ciomei now that she was forced to live with him.

The old men set up a private kitchen in the heated shed in which they worked. Uncle Arturo avoided her as if she were bad weather. Papa Ciomei smiled and nodded, nodded and smiled, courteous, diplomatic, all conciliation and warmth. Yet he was stubborn in his insistence on maintaining the core of the life she was bent on destroying. He had declared certain areas inviolable: the two old men's separate bedrooms, the back porch, the warren of cold areaways connecting the main house to the main barn, and all the outbuildings. These were their domain. The rest was hers.

She kept the household in a limbo of remodeling where present comfort was daily torn up as a sacrifice for what was to be. The three men slunk from her vision of their world, as if they were guilty of having shaped it to her disgust. "Nice, nice," Papa Ciomei said, as she tore out the chair-rail moldings, tore off wallpaper, painted the walls light colors, sealed the fireplaces. "Nice, nice," when she covered the ceramic tile bathroom floor with vinyl tile.

Spookily, the discards of her redecorating surfaced in their bedrooms, and the large back porch, now enclosed, was reborn as a miniature of the former house: worn rugs, more family portraits, paper flowers, vivid flowered pottery, crocheted doilies and woolen throws, recliners and a big old radio-phonograph. A little wood-burning stove kept the men toasty warm. A new color TV was for amusement. A mahogany card table that folded double for narrow placement against a wall remained open before the wood stove, ready for play at any time. A wrought-iron stand held the small round birch logs.

The outsider, she stood in the doorway calling Laurie out from among them at the child's bedtime, and felt herself indefinably yet definitely wrong and foolish. The three men sat at the table, playing cards, and except for this brilliantly lit spot, the ornate table lamps she had dumped in the barn had been reinstated to suffuse the room with a softness that dimmed the glare of the TV and seemed even to quiet its blare. The dog, Biff, slept with his head on Laurie's thigh. One of the cats slept on the child's chest. Half asleep, stretched out on the floor, Laura was hazily watching the TV screen. Sleepily she objected to being interrupted. In Italian

Papa Ciomei suggested through Vin that Laurie would fall asleep watching and Vin could carry her up to her bed.

"None a that," Sally said. "When it's bedtime, it's bedtime."

Assured of sympathy, Laurie whined and cried, but, obdurately angry, Sally insisted. And also insisted on banning the child's pets from her bed.

"I hear ya wheezin lately. Ya wanna become sickly like ya cousins? Wheezin all over the place? Kids get allergic, ya know."

In the candy-striped bedroom she had finished for Laurie almost to her own satisfaction, alone with her child, she became herself, kissed Laurie on her rich, thick hair, sang her to sleep with two choruses of "Lullaby and Goodnight," the song her father had sung her to sleep with as a child.

"What's 'bedite,' Mommie?" Laurie said, and drifted off before Sally could think of a concocted answer. Sally didn't like to say she didn't know.

She couldn't find the word in the big library dictionary, couldn't figure how to spell it and was ashamed to ask.

"With roses bedight" ran circles in her head for a couple of days, tormenting her with its mystery, and when she had decided *the hell with it, forget it,* she found the word by accident in big letters at the top of the page among the b's, and tracing downward read, "arrayed, adorned." She was proud to be able to explain it to Laurie the next time she sang her to sleep.

"It means roses are all round ya, honey, for ya to look at in dreamland."

That was one for her side in this contest against foreign influences.

She made a point of visiting her father more often. One morning she drove over to Hartshead to treat him to lunch. What the hell. Vin's people weren't going to have everything their way. Economizing off her hide. She put aside five dollars one week and five dollars the next out of the food money and treated her father to the Lobster Pot. Fried clams with all the fixings. Her dad took an extra hour for lunch. It was good to be with him, and it was bad. Very hard to find enough to say to keep conversation moving along. She thought of the murmured limpid foreign secret speech of the three men in the back room, its constant music sometimes rising to laughter, to shouts, to passionate dispute, to tones so tender it sounded like endearments, like lovemaking. They always had something to say to one another, the brothers and the son and nephew, her husband who was so silent with her except for his new sudden bursts of rage, the same man who acted so hard and boastful with his friends, a man in disguise from himself, from his background, from his daily reality, a man so strange to her it frightened her to remember that he was indeed her husband, and her child's father.

Impossible to explain in response to her father's repeated question: "Well, now, how ya doin up there in the woods? Stuck out there with the family—with his family?"

She had said, "Doin good, Dad," each time.

Dissastisfied, he asked again, while they were drinking coffee, eating apple pie.

"Well, now, Sally, how is it, how ya doin back there in the woods?"

She said, "Real good, Dad. Ain't complainin."

He said, "Dunno. I ain't so pleased thinkin of ya alone back there in the woods. They ain't like us, ya know."

"Who?" she said.

"Them people," he said.

"They're okay," she said. "Nothin bad about em."

"Ya know what they say about the two ole fellers? Anarchists," he said.

"Who?" she said.

"People."

"People talk about em?" She was surprised.

"That's what they say. Anarchists. The two ole men and that barber feller alongside that Eyty restaurant, Ginny's, or somethin like Ginny's, ya know the place I mean?"

She shook her head, No.

"Well, I'm glad to hear ya ain't hangin out in them places."

"What ya said about the two old men. What is it? That word ya used."

"Anarchist," he said. "Ya know, bombs n overthrowin the government."

"Oh," she said. "Yeah. I knew bout that in school."

"Bout them?" he said.

"No," she said. "History and stuff." She said, "They ain't doin nothin like that, Dad."

"Now how would ya know, not understandin the lingo and all?"

"I know they ain't," she said. "Just two old men gettin along. One's over eighty years old. The other's right after him."

"Yer father-in-law's over eighty?"

"Uncle Arturo."

"What kinda name is that?"

"Papa Ciomei's seventy-eight or maybe eighty-eight, I think."

"That what ya call him?"

"That's his name," she said defensively.

"The two ole men and that ole barber feller were supposed to be the leaders of it."

"Of what?"

"Some kinda newspaper in that lingo of theirs. Meetins and stuff. Rousin up the Eytys."

It was unimaginable.

"Some time back, some bunch who didn't appreciate what he was doin doused the barbershop in red paint. That feller didn't mind a bit. Went and painted the whole shebang red, right up to the roof, went right on barberin like nothing happened."

She said, "That so?"

"Ya know im? He come round visitin?"

"Never seen im," she said. "Dunno im."

"Well, it's somethin at least that ya ain't forced to hang out with them kind."

His spoon, scraping the last pearly spots of apple pie, screamed against the plate. Finished, he constructed a pile-up of his dishes, then moved them from in front of him. He pulled a napkin from the dispenser, roughly wiped his mouth and the table, squeezed the napkin into a ball and jammed it into the coffee cup. Only then, he met her eyes with a direct message of blue burned-out anguish.

"Keep worryin bout ya up there alone, worryin bout where ya life's headin."

He dropped his gaze, shy and bitter.

"Nowheres," she said, reassuring him, "like everybody," and smiled her bright, bright smile.

10

SHE HAD BEEN STRUGGLING like a madwoman to cover with new vinyl tile what seemed like miles of old tile on the kitchen floor and countertops, repeated on the back wall of the cookstove and around the fireplace behind the wood stove. The mantel was a deep reddish solid marble, as was a section of the countertop. She figured the old tiles couldn't be good design, as they said in the magazines she read, because nothing matched, though there was a blending of colors, deep red and a deep yellow with little dots of blue as blue as the sky on a clear, clear day, and the deep red, more like a deep pink, repeated in the solid marble. The tiles were different sizes too—little around the borders, and larger solid ones on the floor, with another kind of border. She couldn't find anything like them in the do-it-yourself magazines she was buying. She used as her excuse to destroy them the fact that some of the tiles were cracked. Besides, if she accidentally dropped a dish or a cup or a glass on them, it always broke. She spent a whole day friggin with the vinyl tiles, trying to get them to stick evenly. It was hell. She had bought so much material at the local housewares store that the owner offered to come out to advise her on his way home from work when she called to complain that the product wasn't satisfactory.

"Ya sure ya wanta cover it?"

He tapped the file floor with the toe of his boot.

"Nothin much wrong with it. Coupla cracked tiles. Maybe we c'n order some for ya from the importers. Maybe not. This stuff coulda come from Italy, Portugal, Spain. Don't look like the Mexican stuff to me. That marble slab there is for the bakin ya know, for rollin out the dough."

She didn't know.

"Lotsa the new expensive houses are puttin in ceramic tile. Costs, boy oh boy, it costs!" He rolled his eyes heavenward. "Costs going way up, way up. Not like in the old days when they put this here in. Ya gotta have a pile to put in ceramic tile today. I see ya got a ceramic roof on the place too. Never wear out. That stuff'll never wear out."

She felt a fool.

He gave her credit on the vinyl tiles, said he'd look into matching and replacing what needed repairing.

"If not," he said, "if that don't work, it'll look good anyway. Ya get the cupboards and ceiling refreshed with a little paint and it'll look real pretty, them tiles will really shine out then. It won't matter at all, those coupla cracks."

It put her in a temper that she had been so ignorant, and she worked even harder the next day emptying the cupboards, repairing and repainting the insides. She removed the cupboard doors, drove as far as Newton to deliver them to a fellow with a stripping vat, spent an hour choosing the right new brass hinges. On the way home she bought a hanging planter and a plant whose name she didn't know, with deep-green leaves and a tiny starlike blue flower to pick up the blue in the tiles. She had an idea now how the kitchen should look, but at the fabric place on Route 60 she almost went into a fit trying to choose cloth for the kitchen windows from among the hundreds and hundreds of patterns. Nothing seemed right. What was on the windows now was too far gone in grayness and snags from the cats to be saved by laundering, but she recognized they had been perfect—filmy white, delicately embroidered, filtering in daylight with a soft brightness. She spent twenty-two dollars, wasn't sure of the yardage, and when she got home and held the new cloth up against the old stuff, the new material seemed hard as a board compared to the old.

After supper and the washing up, trying to figure how to sew up the new curtains to somehow duplicate the old, she burst into tears.

Vin stood in the kitchen doorway. He hung there, a limp, sorry, sad figure, fear of her tears in his aspect.

She threw the fabric across the room.

"Hey, Sally, what's a matter? Gettin ya period?" he said.

"I ain't had a period in half a year, ya idiot," she yelled, and having started, couldn't stop. The hollering speech she made was one she didn't know she had been harboring. "Ya turned me inta some kinda fuckin slave. Don't even own myself. The lot a us is owned by ya goddam family. Don't own a thing. Everthin we got belongs to ya goddam family."

"Ya stop that cussin," he said.

"Well, it's true, ain't it? We got nothin, ain't that right? We got *nothin*. I neva counted on livin like this."

"Ya neva counted!" His voice shook. "Ya ain't the only one what neva counted. How bout me doin some countin on ya. Stead ya stuck me with a baby and no choice but to marry ya."

She heard herself screaming at a pitch she couldn't imagine reaching.

"Ya goddam complainin son of a bitch. Ya nothin but a ole woman. Ya don't give a shit for me or for Laura. I'm sick a ya. I'm gettin outta here so fast ya won't see me goin. I'm gettin out right now. Takin Laura and goin."

"Goin where, boss? Goin where?"

He was putting on a good act, but she knew, even in her uncontrollable rage, that his bravado might instantly fall in on itself.

Papa Ciomei appeared at the kitchen doorway then, sweeping into the room with broad, calming, operatic gestures of his long arms. His deep, liquid voice made a song of the broken English speech. "Nice, nice. Kids, whatsamatter, nice, nice, kids, kids, no fight, no fight. Cenzo, whatsamatter, Vincenzo, whatsamatter, you go crazy? Nice, nice, no fight, shame, shame. Sally, whatsamatter? No fight, please, please."

He looked imploringly at Sally; Vin he grabbed by the shoulders and collapsed him under a torrent of Italian. She lost the father and the son to their passionate private language. The liberating rage that had entered the fight was seized from her. She stood apart, crying, half laughing at the spectacle of their dispute, intensely jealous of the heat they were generating—her heat, stolen from her, just as this family had stolen her house out from under her and were stealing her self, swallowing her whole to feed their own fires.

She wasn't prepared for an apology from Vin, even if there was ice in his delivery, and an irritation so intense she could feel it in her teeth.

"Let's forget it," he said. "Didn't mean nothin, all that hollerin and yowlin, forget it."

"Don't tell me ya sorry just cause ya papa says ya hafta," she said. "Ya some little kid who hasta do what ya told to do?"

"Ya neva heard me say I was sorry," he said. "I said to forget it."

He turned back to his father in another burst of Italian, pointing to his wife, saying something about her, his dead-black eyes streaking Sally with a buried hatred that strangled her.

"Goddam it, don't talk about me like I ain't even here," she yelled. "Like I don't exist. I ain't deaf an dumb, ya know. Just cause I can't talk ya goddam lingo."

"Seems to me," he said, "I dunno nothin anymore. Dunno what I am or I ain't anymore. Everybody tellin me what to do like I was born the day before yesterday."

"Well, that's how ya been actin, ain't it?" she said. "Blamin everybody but ya self. Nothin's ever ya doin. Ya neva the one responsible, neva."

She recoiled from the sheer misery of what she was doing to him. Right in front of his father too. This was the man she had planned her life around; he would save her life, make it all come out right. If it was a mess now, did she have the right to blame him any more than he had to blame her?

She couldn't look directly at his misery. Anyway, he'd never allow it. Carefully he kept his gaze averted, his dark head down, his lids lowered over the blank, dead-black eyes.

"C'mon, forget it," she said.

There wasn't any use fighting.

"Ya wanna forget it? Forget it. Whyn't ya go to bed? Ya look beat. Ya look dead. Got a hard day's work ahead a ya."

He kept his head down. Was he crying? She heard the dull thud of her own heart in the long space of silence. A weight heavy enough to kill blocked her chest. What kept anybody going on living? What was this struggle all about anyway?

"Ya want some of that meat loaf I made for ya lunchbox? I c'n put it between a English muffin, if ya like."

He nodded. He was crying. He couldn't speak. Now she could see that Papa Ciomei's grasp on his son's shoulders had become supportive. He half led Vin to the stairs, pulled him to him, kissed his son on his head, gave him an encouraging shove forward, and a series of strong pats on his back. The old man towered over his son. Papa Ciomei turned back to the refrigerator. She knew he had decided on a beer as an excuse to be with her. Can in hand, he smiled at her with piercing sweetness. It was astonishing how powerfully he conveyed sympathy while doing nothing at all. Both elbows on the kitchen table, her head between her hands, she studied him through teary eyes. He was a handsome man. Tall and broad, his head and upper body matched the huge sloping shoulders and full, rounded chest, but below his sex his legs oddly dwindled and his toes turned inward like a shy little boy's. That weakness was appealing. The great black spots on the skin of his face were too. His imperfections made him handsomer.

She said, holding her voice steady, "Ya know, Papa Ciomei, that stuff on ya cheek looks like it's spreadin.'"

She could see the effort it took him to understand her English.

"Ya should see a doctor. Ya never know with that kinda thing." He waved his hand in dismissal.

"No important," he said and, widening and then narrowing his liquid, dramatic eyes, managed, "No look, Sally," smiling, reassuring. "No look," he said, "no nice," dismissing his ugliness from her vision.

"It ain't the way it looks," she said. "It's, it's . . ."

She couldn't say outright, "It'll kill ya, Papa Ciomei, if it's cancer." He divined what she hadn't said. In a burst of Italian he assured her that dying was nothing. He was eighty-one years old. It was nothing to die at eighty-one. What difference did it make what one died of at his age? She couldn't account for the ease with which she understood the deep music of his speech. He showed her his teeth, opening his mouth wide. He had an enormous bright-pink active tongue. All his own teeth. He grabbed his abundant iron-gray hair in his huge fist, tore it at the roots to show her it was all his own. She smiled and nodded. Triumphant at having stopped her tears, he leaned back against the refrigerator, sipping his beer.

Suddenly he was seized by an idea that he couldn't convey to her, though he tried in a mix of Italian and some English. Deeply excited, he ran off to get Vin to translate. Vin, in pajamas, came in, quarreling with the old man, gesturing in her direction.

"What ya tellin him?" she yelled. "Ya doin it again, actin like I'm not here. What ya tellin him?"

"I'm tellin him ya don't have no interest in cemeteries and anyways you've been there hundreds of times."

"I ain't neva," she said. "What cemetery ya talkin bout?"

"Mount Peace Cemetery, on the Hartshead-Palermo road. The big one ova to the quarries. Course ya been there."

"I ain't neva," she said.

"I told him ya don't have no interest in any a that."

"In what? I don't get it. Is ya mama buried there? Does he want me to drive him? Tell him I'll be glad to drive him. Tell him. No problem."

Sullenly Vin relayed the details of an outing with Papa Ciomei.

"Four thirty tomorra. He's gonna drive. In his old Plymouth. That's how he wants it."

"Well, if he don't need me to drive, why does he want me to go?"

"Beats me," Vin said. "I can't enlighten ya. If it embarrasses ya to go out with the ole man, tell him no."

"Listen," she said. "He wants me to go, I'll be glad to go. No problem."

She didn't want to tell Papa Ciomei No. On the contrary, she washed her hair first thing in the morning to look her best, and carefully chose her good black pants suit. Restless, she drove into town at noon, bought a silky-looking apricot turtleneck to replace her stretched-out, washed-out tan cotton one, and then, wandering in desultory boredom along the main street after a burger and Coke at the luncheonette, she noticed a display of travel books and foreign dictionaries in the window of the gift-and-book shop. The problem, of course, would be language. It took an effort to enter the shop; but once in she went straight to the paperback section, as if she knew exactly what she needed to buy, plucking the first Italian-English, English-Italian dictionary she spotted on the shelves, and, paying her dollar twenty-five, she headed home in the car as if on a special mission. She took the book to Laura's room. If she was discovered, she planned to say she had bought it for the child—to help her learn her granddaddy's language. She closed the door and began her studies with the cover.

MONDADORI's
POCKET
Italian-English
English-Italian
DICTIONARY
An Indispensable Aid For Students,
Travelers, Home and Office Libraries
    by Alberto Tedeschi and Carlo Rossi Fantonetti
    with the assistance of Seymour A. Copstein
OVER 25,000 VOCABULARY ENTRIES
TWO VOLUMES IN ONE
    Over 600 Pages

Seymour A. Copstein was a definite encouragement among those names.

The lower half of the book's cover was in Italian.

DIZIONARIO
Tascabile MONDADORI
ITALIANO-INGLESE
INGLESE-ITALIANO

No problem about the first word. She identified it in a surge of pleasure. She tried saying it aloud, aiming to reproduce the open, limpid, rich music the three men made on the porch, but like a tune heard perfectly in the head and voiced hopelessly off key, her tentative whisper was nothing like the sound made by Uncle Arturo or Papa Ciomei—or even Vin. Anyway, she knew what the word meant; that was something.

Mondadori was a name, she knew that from the top part of the cover, and the rest was clear enough, but whatever could *tascabile* mean? She said it over and over in her head, tried it aloud to see if it had a familiar ring, was appalled again by the result, glanced about self-consciously, listened to the silence of the empty house in

which her flat attempt to voice an Italian sound floated like a dese-
cration.

Okay, so this book had her beat? Too soon to give up. She could
look up the word. Of course, that's what the book was for. However, that meant opening the book, really diving in and testing herself. Well, sooner or later she would have to open the damn book,
wouldn't she?

The first page hit her like an insult. It was entirely in Italian.

*Il più accurato ed economico dizionario tascabile Italiano-
Inglese, Inglese-Italiano finora pubblicato . . .*

As if a reader had only to open the book to understand Italian, it
went blithely on:

*è un' opera concepita espressamente come strumento pratico per
tutte le categorie di pubblico: dagli studenti agli insegnanti, dai
turisti . . .* The strange accent marks, the hints of meanings mas-
querading in thin disguises, first encouraged, then baffled her further. What did an opera have to do with students, tourists, dictionaries? And there was *tascabile* again, whatever it was. Along
the bottom of the page, she discovered real help. Seymour at work,
no doubt. "The above text appears in English on the back cover."
She could read and understand the back cover okay, but it didn't
serve as proper enlightenment. There wasn't a word about an
opera, for one thing, and *tascabile* remained a closed mystery.
Okay, she would move on ahead. She would break the back of this
problem, no matter what it took.

It would take more than she was ready to give, she decided, after
an hour of intense concentration on intimidating introductory items
—the table of contents and the list of abbreviations alone were
overpowering to her sense of what she was capable of absorbing.
She read all about Italian pronunciation, instructions in vowels,
consonants, stress, accent, apostrophe and syllabic division. Of no
use in making her sound more like the real thing, she was immensely pleased to learn that "the Italian alphabet consists of 21
letters: a, b, c, d, e, f, g, h, i, l, m, n, o, p, q, r, s, t, u, v, z . . ." and
that j, k, w, x and y were "found only in words of foreign origin."

She experienced a kind of beginner's luck, euphoria—she had
made a successful attack on a landmass of knowledge that she had
not expected to yield to her grasp—at least not in this solid, satisfy-

ing, generalizing way. Progressing was another matter. She bent under the weight of THE NOUN with its genders and plurals. It didn't help that she wasn't sure what a noun was in English, and if she had begun with a comfortable sense of the superiority of her own language (English, the best, the only), she became lost in the complications of suffixes, articles, prepositions, adjectives and adverbs—followed by pages and pages of irregular verbs. How did anybody ever learn Italian? Did Vin know the rules of this book? She could imagine Papa Ciomei mastering them—but dumb Uncle Arturo? The whole subject of language opened before her eyes as an impenetrable mystery.

She was resolved to come out of her foray with something tangible, no matter what. At least *tascabile* would give up its secret. Sure enough, it was listed, though slightly fractured into *tascábile*, adj. pocket. And turning back to the cover, she found *tascabile* under *dizionario*, working the puzzle through as if she were on the trail of a major discovery—solving it—*pocket dictionary*—there it was—hey, how about that!

She had also looked into "Phrases for Travelers, Prepared by Robert T. Giuffrida, M.A., Ph.D., Department of Foreign Languages, the University of Rochester," and among the statements irrelevant to her purposes, "Do you speak English? Where is the police station, the train station, the airport, the center of the city, a church, a travel agency? Help, I've been robbed!" and "I'm seasick," she had located *Ciao* for "So long," *Mi scusi* and *Desidero* for "Excuse me" and "I want," and *Grazie,* of course, for "Thank you." She tried those out on the empty air. Only *Ciao* rang out sounding faintly similar to Papa Ciomei's speech. More to the purpose, she practiced eradicating "Syomy" from her lips, aiming for the softness and openness with which the Ciomeis themselves pronounced their name, ending her first attempt at self-teaching only when it was time to meet Papa Ciomei downstairs.

Sitting beside Papa Ciomei in his unbelievably well-preserved 1950 Plymouth four-door sedan with its high little windows and comfortably high seats, she was too terrified that the old man would kill them both in the heavy traffic on the Eatonville-Hartshead road to even think about the problem of language. Her involuntary warnings to watch the car ahead, go a little faster than twenty-five miles an hour, use his turn signal when he changed lanes, and the series of other directions were given him in rapid English, but he went right on using the old hand signals that nobody understood anymore, driving as if there were nothing else on the road, nobody in the world but himself in his 1950 Plymouth and his passenger beside him. He was so sweet to her, so courtly, and his concern for her nervous chatter had him concentrating so hard on her comfort and peace of mind, further endangering them, that just out of town on what seemed like the longest ride in existence, she gave up and resigned herself to death on the highway with her eighty-one-year-old father-in-law. There were worse ways to die, surely. *His* reassurances were all in Italian, and by the time they reached the gates of Mount Peace Cemetery, she accepted as a natural state of things that they were communicating in separate languages without much difficulty, though with a lot of shouting.

He had told her, for one thing, that he had kept Vin from accompanying them. She was sure of that information, though she couldn't explain how, and she was glad he had insisted on this meeting being private. He had dressed up for the occasion, just as she had. He was in a black suit, white shirt and black tie. He had obviously just showered and shaved. Sweet smells hovered about him—smells of soap, talcum and something he had rubbed on his unruly head of white hair. Physically he was as endearing as a baby. Only the black patches of diseased skin put her off from embracing and kissing him; and once again she urged him to see a doctor, sketching with her finger in the air around the disfigured sections an imperative need for care, which, in a long, passionate and apparently humorous speech, he again rejected. They were parked just inside the high, imposing iron gate, pulled over to the side during this part of their conversation. She could watch the full display of his liquid eyes under the constant motion of his expressive, heavy eyebrows. His deep voice, a voice of remarkable range and brilliant timbre, rumbled its vibrations through the seat they shared, and reverberated in the car as if they were indeed characters in an opera. That's what she had expected of life among Italians, though it hadn't been that way with Vin at all. Forget Vin. This moment was between her and Papa Ciomei, and so far so good

—it had already come through for her in warmth and excitement, in feeling alive and happy.

If he had been a younger man, she would have said she was falling in love. Before their outing had hardly begun, she lamented the afternoon's coming to an end. She mourned the loss of attention, of admiration—yes, of love—in his responses. He had complimented her at once, before they got into the car—"Nice, nice"—for her clothes and her hair and face; and the sense of rich, good feeling that rushed in with his greeting was keener than anything she had ever experienced. She really didn't care *what* he wanted to show her. She would have gone anywhere with the old man.

Now he was demonstrating that she must close her eyes and seal them with her palms until he signaled to uncover. Laughing together at their foolishness, she complied, aware of his seriousness underneath. The car lurched ahead. She had never been to Mount Peace Cemetery; it wasn't where her mother was buried, and that would have been her only reason to visit, on the insistence of her father. But those grave-site journeys with her father and sisters to the town cemetery had been unspeakably dreary—no connection with this adventure—and the stillborn baby hadn't been buried. He had been done away with quickly—as if he had never happened. No markings.

She had no idea where they were going, and it was lovely to be wholly in the old man's charge, her eyes shut tight, the car perilously making its way first up, then down, on what seemed to be an endless, narrow, rutted road. The air up here blew clearer than in town, and she could smell lilacs and something even sweeter, honeysuckle, probably. When the car stopped he still kept her from uncovering her eyes until he had come around to her side of the car and led her out, steering her by her elbow until she was positioned just as he wanted her to be.

Looking about, it seemed to her that they were at the farthest end of the cemetery on a roadway that circled a bluff overlooking the river, which here widened abruptly on a curve of swift-flowing white water, totally cut away from the presence of the paper mill a mile or so below. They might have been deep in isolated country; looking down the lush spring growth of the gorge falling to the wild river below, it was hard to believe that immediately behind the entrance to this spot were highways, shopping centers, traffic lights, the huge installations of the quarry, the power plant and the paper mill.

The two were alone at this end, and for a split second it occurred to her that the old man meant to harm her.

But instead of pushing her over the edge, he grasped her shoulder with a big hand and indicated that she should follow him. He moved quickly on his long, little-boy legs, led by his powerful shoulders; he was on his own territory and knew exactly which path among the crisscrossing confusion of grave sites he wanted. He's terrific, she thought, I bet he can still get it up, and was ashamed of herself.

It was hard to figure Papa Ciomei's love life. Mama Ciomei had died the year before she and Vin had married, but Sally had had more mother-in-law trouble with that dead woman than most wives had with live ones. Up over her ears in blessed memories of Mama, Mama, Mama. And letting it get to her, too, trying to meet those standards of perfectionist slave labor. Wasn't she doing that right now—breaking her ass redecorating that stupid old house? And there was no way to measure up. Mama Ciomei was perfect. She never complained—not even about dying. She never went out. She never did anything but have babies and work, work, work. How Papa Ciomei had managed to lay that sainted woman seven times, once for each kid, was unimaginable, not to mention a couple of lays they must have had for the hell of it in between.

Who was the best cook in the world? Mama Ciomei. Mama Ciomei washed and waxed and polished; she sewed all the children's clothes; she raised the girls like dolls, the boys like little gentlemen; she set a table that made every day a holiday; she ironed a shirt so perfect you'd swear it had just come brand new from the store; she was infinitely wise, good, loving, patient, always available, and what's more she sang as she worked in a voice so beautiful she could have been the leading singer in any opera house she wanted. Quote, unquote. And the worst of it was there didn't seem to be a single note of false reverence in their praises.

The hell with Mama Ciomei.

Papa Ciomei had stopped. In his most courtly manner, he welcomed her to a grave site, ushering her to the entrance from the path. His eyes glowed with the promise of exciting wonder to come. In his resonant voice he made his announcement: "Mama Ciomei."

Her heart sank. She had expected more than a forced visit to her mother-in-law's grave, a place she had managed all these years to avoid, while Vin paid his regular respects. For Papa Ciomei's sake, she assumed a properly sober face and moved in the direction he indicated. The plot was small, dominated by a large imposing stone beautifully lettered with the family name. She murmured approval and giggled nervously. Now Papa Ciomei was explaining something too complicated for her to follow, involving the names of all his children accompanied by vigorous shakings of the head, "No, no, Theresa, California, no, no, Giovanni, Detroit, no, no," covering the list, "Vincenzo e Sally, si, si," with appropriate head signals and a brilliant smile. When she didn't catch on, he repeated, "Theresa, no, no, California, Giovanni, no, no," the use of formal family names further confusing her, "Vincenzo e Sally, si, si," until in desperation she pretended to understand. Only she and Vin were to be buried here? Right away? Did Vin have a fatal disease?

Satisfied, now Papa Ciomei was indicating another headstone a space forward and below the larger one, where a contented middle-aged couple sat up in bed, seen from the waist up in neatly pressed pajamas with the piped edge of the lapels wonderfully reproduced in stone, faint smiles upon their modeled lips, their deep-set eyes gazing pleasantly upon the prospect of their buried bodies which became a natural extension of the stone figures lightly covered by a satin-edged blanket. They were holding hands. Behind their dignified heads, the stone out of which their faces were carved formed the headboard of the double bed they shared so easily in death, a bed shaped exactly like the matched bedroom suite that still furnished Papa Ciomei's bedroom.

"Mama Ciomei," he said again.

So there she was. She had worn her hair long, parted in the middle. It was thick hair, thick as Laura's, pulled back to cover the tops of her ears, the lobes exposed and adorned with little pierced earrings; and though the stone image was flat, Sally coud tell that Mama Ciomei had twisted her thick plaits of hair into a firm, fat bun sitting squarely on the back of her head.

Should she fall in line and revere this woman too? Easy enough to love this quiet, undemanding image. But did she want to become it? And iron shirts to look as if they had just been bought in a store? What kind of deal was Papa Ciomei offering?

"*Sono io.*" He was so deeply excited, it seemed more like agitation. His deep voice was weightier than she had ever heard it. "*Sono io,*" he repeated over and over, until, in desperation again, she nodded, and nodding *before* she understood, suddenly she did understand. The man sharing the bed, waiting for his body to join his wife's, was Papa Ciomei.

Not that the image was a true likeness of Papa Ciomei, except in a generalized resemblance to his handsome features. Too quiet, too composed, *too* handsome. That was a revelation that served to quiet her envy of Mama Ciomei. Mama probably hadn't looked exactly like that classic beauty against the headboard either.

But it seemed that Sally hadn't fully understood, because Papa Ciomei kept repeating "*Sono io,*" bending his powerful upper body toward her and then swerving to embrace the figures with extended arms, demanding her comprehension, while his lower body seemed about to have a child's foot-stamping tantrum if she failed him.

She would not pretend that she understood. If her comprehension was so important to him, how could she fake it? Smiling, shaking her head, she tried to emanate enough sympathy to console him. Because she really did care for him, this flesh-and-blood passionately vivid old man with the black claim of death staining his cheeks and his state of excitement threatening to put him in his assigned place under the double-bed headstone.

He led her now from headstone to headstone. Was he giving her a tour of dead Ciomeis? That didn't seem likely. Some of the names weren't even Italian: "Henderson" in ornate lettering, surrounded by a border of carved roses; "MacKenzie," over a centerpiece of marble hands clasped in prayer. He moved so rapidly from one to the other she hardly had time to admire the beauty and variety of the pieces. There was an open Bible resting on a stand, the book so real she swore she could turn a page. It wasn't these he particularly wanted her to see, but came to a stop before a full-length figure.

It was a marble statue of a young woman with close-cropped curly hair, sitting at a little table, one slim-fingered hand pressed to her forehead, her downward gaze pained, yet held in a stilled dignity. Every fold of her 1950s full skirt was marvelously reproduced, as was the silk shirt she wore, with all its tiny buttons down the front and on the cuffs of the full sleeves. On her slender throat in the open-collared shirt, she wore a double-strand choker of graduated pearls, pearl after pearl carved to perfect size. She sat on a chair Sally knew was called a Windsor chair, at a little side table trimmed by a delicate, fine railing. Her feet, in pumps with narrow, medium-height heels no longer fashionable, were crossed at her slim ankles and tucked under the chair. The folds of her skirt draped her knees gently. How could stone yield such softness?

She saw that the dead girl's name was Angelina Conti, that she had died in 1957 at the age of twenty-two, and that her family's thoughts would ever be with her. The girl meant nothing to Sally, apart from being close to her own age, so why this wrenching pain at the well-shaped head with its modern haircut and the downcast, stoic eyes, and at the row of tiny, silk-covered buttons down the soft shirtfront, and the narrow-heeled pumps on the crossed feet? What was more surprising, why this joy that the girl was there to be seen, that she was glad to see her, and glad *for* her, for the girl herself, glad that she existed in the cemetery in a stone image that Sally loved, whoever she was.

Papa Ciomei had taken a big blue bandanna handkerchief from his pocket and was vigorously wiping the statue's face. Then he bent down and rubbed away at her feet, almost as if he were shining her shoes. Bits of leaves had gathered in the crevices.

He stood up and back, calmer now, looking into Sally's face for her reaction. Angelina was a favorite cousin or niece? She had no notion of what Papa Ciomei wanted from her here, but she smiled and nodded agreeably.

"Beautiful," she said. "Sad," she said.

That she was glad, too, was harder to convey to him, but he seemed satisfied with her response, and moved on at his rapid pace, no longer holding her hand but expecting her to understand what they were about.

They tramped to another section where he stopped before a group work of two children, a boy seated on the floor, a girl, higher than the boy, on a child's rocker, an open book on her lap, her eyes down, reading to the younger child, who listened intently, his head tilted upward in devoted admiration. The girl's hair was long, the boy's cut boy-fashion, and both were dressed in Doctor Denton sleepers. The girl was shown full face in her serious concentration; one slim finger of the delicate hand emerging from the too-big Doctor Dentons pointed out the words as she read. The boy was in profile, his little features perfectly worked and the little neck heartbreakingly frail. His legs were spread under him and on the underside of the feet of the Doctor Dentons, Sally could see the ridges of the plastic sole reproduced.

Papa Ciomei's grandchildren, wiped out in an epidemic? The date was August 12, 1961, but the name was Atwater. Amy and Forrest Atwater, ages five and three. Dead to the world, the smart little girl who could read at five, with her silky hair and serious face, her delicate pointing finger, and her knees clamped together to hold the big book securely on her narrow lap. The too-large Doctor Dentons extended beyond her fine little feet in folds of extra cloth deeply carved into the pinkish stone. Marveling again at how touching and pleasing these children she had never known were, Papa Ciomei's actions came perfectly clear to Sally. It was Papa Ciomei who had made these statues. This was his work. He had brought her here to show her his work.

How could he have done so many? There were moments when she thought she must be wrong—he couldn't have carved all these statues and headstones, it wasn't possible for one man to have produced all these. Her exclamations and appreciation were now so genuine that he rushed her from one to the other, hurrying her on too quickly for her to enjoy them.

She wouldn't let him pull her away from a life-size figure of a small, elegant, fiery man, the kind of marble statue she knew only from book illustrations or historical movies, an old-fashioned figure with a trim moustache and pointed beard and wavy hair curling above the beard. He was dressed in an elegantly cut formal suit, a long, broad tie flowing across the jacket lapels, the crease in the narrow trousers carefully pressed. His trousers were a little short and showed his high-button shoes. His head was lifted as if he were speaking, his lips slightly parted, his open eyes under the narrow, lowered brows seemed alive, and one gesturing hand was flung out as if he were addressing a crowd, while the other was drawn into a tense fist at his side.

Papa Ciomei became so excited at her pleasure in this figure that he let out a long stream of talk in which she caught some English words. "Good man, man for the people," and "Prince, anarchist, Malatesta," repeated again and again dotted with urgent pleas of "You know? You know?"

But she did not know and the name on the statue's base wasn't Malatesta. It was more like something to eat—Cacciatore, Antonio Cacciatore.

She said, "That's terrific, Pop, terrific, but please take it easy, Pop, calm down."

He would not calm down. He was so pleased with her pleasure, he led her back to the car to drive to another area, a more recently enlarged section of the cemetery where she was not so taken with the more usual pieces he was showing her (elaborate crosses, Bibles, praying hands) until he arrived at what he had been looking for. He laughed out loud as he displayed it. It was a rocker carved out of granite, on a pedestal. There was nobody in it; it sat there at rest with its formal marker underneath, "Catherine Whiteside," and her dates.

When Papa Ciomei laughed, his whole body shook, and that made her laugh too.

She said, "What's the idea of it?"

"America," he said, "Crazy. That's what they want. Crazy people." And he led her to another memorial he found even more hilarious, a TV set, complete with rabbit ears, its dials and controls minutely detailed in granite, resting on a carved table. On the TV screen, beautifully lettered, appeared the name and dates of the dead man.

He laughed so hard she became afraid for him again.

There was less traffic on the drive home, but the ride was equally dangerous because Papa Ciomei was very talkative, pouring out an impenetrable mess of language, lifting his hands clear of the wheel in his expansive gestures, turning his ardent eyes fully toward her, letting the road and the car take care of themselves. Miraculously they did. She felt protected, in a charmed circle of Papa Ciomei's world, deeply satisfied. She was sorry she had prepared a meat loaf for supper following a *Family Circle* recipe, resisting Uncle Arturo's method that used a hard-boiled egg in the center and grated cheese and garlic and parsley fresh from the early-growing herbs in his garden. So what if Uncle Arturo's recipe gave them all heartburn? It was better-tasting than the dumb *Family Circle* meat loaf, and Papa Ciomei would have enjoyed it better. She wanted to please Papa Ciomei, to return pleasure for pleasure. She was glad she had bought fresh strawberries at the roadside stand; and there was vanilla ice cream in the freezer. He would like that.

Greedy, happy old man, proud as a rooster, eager as a boy, self-loving and mischievous as a child, glowing with the natural surge of his great ego, had he brought her to Mount Peace Cemetery just because he was a show-off? She was too weary by now to penetrate his hopelessly distorted language mix. She smiled and nodded, nodded and smiled at the outpouring of speech yielding no coherent meanings, no longer listening to words but only to the beat of what he was. Beautiful, joyous, good man, a man who had carved out a whole world where work was love and love was work, and one man and his one woman, smiling serenely, held hands in an eternal harmony, sitting up in a double bed.

Are you telling me that Vin and I can be good too, Papa Ciomei? She did not ask him, and heavy with regret, did not tell him that she knew they couldn't be, but that for his sake she'd give it a real try with his son.

It wasn't easy, though she gained something from the effort to be good in Papa Ciomei's sense. She was happier in a way. She learned to cook the best lasagna in New England, for one thing, and picked up a little Italian just by breathing in the family's sounds and smells, the wild gestures and the distorted facial expressions at their noisy gatherings. She was getting to be more of an Italian than Vin was. When Duane didn't have her car ready that he was supposed absolutely to have fixed by Tuesday morning, and she saw it sitting there untouched, with nothing even started on it although it was already five in the afternoon when she arrived to pick it up, she enjoyed letting herself go. She yelled at Duane in a passionate outburst that it really hurt her to be so disappointed in a person's promises.

Took him by surprise.

"I never meant to hurt ya, Sally," Duane said. "Been busy as I dunno what. Busy as hell, that's all."

"Well, ya hurt me, Duane, ya really hurt me," she yelled. "Ya messin up my whole week, besides the hurt of it, too." She felt good, felt the way Cousin Clementina must have when she started smashing the wineglasses a while back during a big family fight, and the way Papa Turo must have when he zipped and unzipped his pants, inviting his bossy niece to become the man of the family if that's what she wanted. What's more, her fit got Duane going on her brakes right away, and he even fixed the dimmer light he'd been breaking his promise about for weeks.

At home, suppertime was almost pleasant now with her new attitude. Not that any changes in her got the slightest rise out of Vin. She was invisible to him. Or he was to her. Or he was invisible to himself. Or there was no more to him than a dim little man carving out as little space for himself in the world as he dared to without disturbing anybody. That was the most frightening thought of all.

Her best times were the mid-afternoon treats she fixed for Papa Ciomei and Laura when Laura got off the school bus. Uncle Arturo napped, Vin was at the quarry. The three gathered around the card table on the enclosed back porch and ate ice cream topped with one of Uncle Turo's preserved fruit sauces. Sometimes Sally made whipped cream to go with it, not that Cool Whip stuff, the real thing, since they had the good cream right in the refrigerator anyway. They'd joke and laugh like three kids, she and Laura and Papa Ciomei. Cold days the little wood stove warmed them, and Sally made hot chocolate, dressing it with whipped cream or marshmallows. And she'd bake cookies or brownies or muffins some days.

Vin came home in the middle of one of their afternoon treats. He said his head ached so bad he couldn't go on working. Said it was because of the intense cold. "Cold enough to freeze the balls off a brass monkey. With the wind chill factor makin it a hundred percent worse." He looked feverish, both sallow and flushed, his eyes dark-ringed and sunk in his head. He was slumped in the big leather armchair, watching them, a glance that was filmed over and terribly sad, maybe because of his not feeling well, maybe because it was just his nature to turn a party into a funeral. She gave him two aspirins and some hot broth and turned her back on him. She was sick of him, of the heaviness of him.

The two old men had initiated an ambitious project—a miniature replica of their old village, carved out of a red granite boulder planted there by God, Uncle Arturo believed, just for that purpose. The work advanced slowly. Not enough days of good weather for steady progress; not enough times when the two old men could reach agreement on how to proceed. If Papa Ciomei was volatile and good-natured, Uncle Arturo was volatile and argumentative. He'd go off like a madman in a disagreement.

Watching them chip away, she was inspired at last to do something, to look into some schooling for herself. The family agreed it was a good idea and that she could have the money. She began part-time classes at a secretarial school downtown.

She had always been a good student. She cut through the course work with ease. When the school director called her in to encourage her to enroll in some special courses that could take her further, he told her they wouldn't have a bit of trouble placing her in a job as soon as she was ready.

He was a local fellow. Arthur Powers. She knew his whole family. She had gone to school with his kid sister, Ernestine Powers, subject to boils on her face, otherwise pretty, but stupid. Arthur was six years older than Ernestine, seven years older than Sally. She knew his mother and father, plain working people like her folks. Like a lobster shedding, he had sloughed off the clumsiness he had been born to and had become quick and sharp, fast-talking and easy-smiling. He had slid into the new skin of his narrow-striped Dacron suits, color-matched with his tie and shirt, and the handkerchief just tipping out of his breast pocket. He had erased his local speech, except for a Kennedy touch, proudly hanging out the flag of his New England origins, the flat A even educated New Englanders clung to.

She could learn a thing or two from a man like Arthur Powers. She listened carefully, studying, tutoring herself, aping, copying not only Arthur Powers but TV news announcers, actors and actresses, out-of-staters. She was going into the world of work where nobody would be laughing at her if she could help it.

Arthur Powers called her out of a class where she was being

taught how to use the copying machine. He never mentioned the word "interview" and she was so casually introduced to a plain-looking older woman, and so occupied by trying to locate this woman within the limited categories known to her, that Sally never knew she was being interviewed to temporarily replace the woman until she was hired. Sighing as if the decision was painful, the woman said that she guessed Miss Syomy might be able to handle her job for three weeks. She had been hired as a temporary fill-in. Executive Secretary to the President of an architectural firm. How about that?

The nondescript, sighing, fussing woman who permanently held that impressive title showed Sally around what would be her temporary place of work. The offices looked dazzlingly handsome to Sally. A partitioned entryway, the desk she would be using set in a window niche overlooking Main Street, bright with light and hanging plants. Red leather desk chair, a red phone, an IBM electric typewriter. In the large open space beyond, the feeling of a living room. Oriental rugs, a heavy carved desk and an ornate upholstered desk chair. The surface of the desk was startlingly tidy—even the pencils and pens were lined up in parade rows of matching colors. There were other work areas, also rigidly neat: drawing boards, high worktables, a couple of stools. In the corner near the windows another grouping: leather-and-chrome lounge chairs with matching footstools, magazines neatly piled on a glass-and-chrome coffee table, a glass bowl of fresh flowers, another sort of rug in bright-colored stripes. One wall of exposed brick was hung with old tools. The other, a smooth white wall, held architectural drawings and color blow-ups of details of houses, and at the farthest end a group of framed diplomas from Harvard and the Rhode Island School of Design. She recognized tones and shapes familiar to her from the magazines she had studied while fixing up the old Ciomei house and the one before it. She straightened her back, tossed back her hair. She'd better become a fit companion for this luxurious background.

The architect was a curlyheaded, round-faced, youngish man. His eyes held a fixed stare, then suddenly, unexpectedly, they would dart out of reach. Joseph Santelli. He might have been born in the area like Vin, but he didn't talk like Vin.

"Good to meet you, Miss Syomy. I'll leave you with Mrs. Preston now, leave you in expert hands."

Staring and darting away.

To Mrs. Preston he said, "Luncheon engagement, Mrs. Preston. Back soon."

And again, staring and darting, to her he said, "See you Monday morning, Miss Syomy."

"Ciomei," Sally said. If he was Italian, let him pronounce her name as he should. But she smiled her best smile. "Or call me Sally."

He stared. "Ciomei," he said. "Right. Glad to have you on board, Miss Ciomei. Sally."

Mrs. Preston sighed, and sighed again, fussily showing Sally around. At the far wall another partition hid a bar sink, liquor, glasses, an electric coffee-maker, cups and saucers, a refrigerator. Mrs. Preston showed Sally how to make coffee.

"I've made a lot of coffee in my day," Sally said.

Mrs. Preston sighed. She was sending out a lot of "don't touch" signals, making everything seem wildly complicated and mysterious.

"Don't open this drawer," she told Sally. "You won't want to disturb this center drawer either," she told Sally. "Don't bother with anything in this tray. Just let the filing pile up till I return. Don't annoy Mr. Santelli with questions. He doesn't know a thing about the office routine. Here's a number to reach me. Keep it posted right here for any emergencies."

Mrs. Preston was traveling to Naples, Florida, on some grave family matter. She said, "Naples, Florida," as if the place were God's heaven and anybody, even Sally, had to know where it was.

Throughout the weekend the elegant assignment she faced worried her. She hardly spoke of it at home, downgrading the entire event. Not exactly lying, she managed to create the impression that she would be reporting to an office for the next three weeks, an unpaid part of her training. In fact, once she had installed herself at the desk in the window niche under the hanging plants, on the red chair, answering the red phone, there wasn't much to do, and the job was easy as pie.

Joe Santelli usually arrived late. When he came in he said,

"Good morning, Sally." Then he drank two cups of the coffee she had prepared in the electric coffeepot and politely declined the homemade doughnuts she had brought as an offering. He read the morning paper while he sipped. In the late morning he dictated one or two letters sometimes, rarely as many as four. His dictation was dotted with interminably long pauses during which he worked out the exact phrasing to follow. She had no difficulty transcribing her notes. Waiting, poised for the next phrase, she marveled at how different the real thing was from the classroom speed exercises. Then he left for lunch.

In the late afternoon Joe Santelli returned sloshed and harried, spending the remainder of the day in prolonged telephone conversations. A half hour before she left the office she placed before him the perfectly typed letters he had dictated earlier. He smiled and said, "Goodnight, Sally. I'll sign these and leave them on the desk." At first, she couldn't understand how any work was done, but after a day or two she learned that all the real work was performed at night apparently, because in the morning, neatly laid out on his desk alongside the signed letters, appeared the completed solutions of the problems he had discussed on the phone the day before, the plans drawn, the design finished, the architectural drawing signed and carefully covered with its protective skin of onion paper.

Joseph Santelli, who wasn't supposed to know a thing about the office routine, kept his own books and records and signed all the checks. The complicated and mysterious instructions left her by Mrs. Preston boiled down to dictation, typing, answering the telephone, recording messages, acting as a receptionist and keeping fresh coffee at the ready. Her salary was one hundred and fifty dollars a week. After deductions and Arthur Powers' placement fee, her take-home was less. Even so. Wow.

The money remained her secret. Her heart pounding, she opened a savings account. That was after spending freely, buying herself good lunches, a new outfit to match her new position in life, a deep-blue dress with a touch of red at the neckline and wrists. She bought Laura an expensive velour top, and in an outpouring of generosity or guilt bought Vin a handmade fisherman's-knit sweater. Passing the bookshop on Water Street on the last Friday of the three weeks, she bought a picture book displayed in the window. *Great Cities of Italy.* It had originally cost thirty-two dollars, but it was marked down to six ninety-five. She bought it for Papa Ciomei, whose joy in it was the sweetest part of the venture, next to her one-hundred-dollar bank account. Papa Ciomei spent hours looking through the color pictures, pulling out and studying the folded maps of Rome, Florence, Venice, puzzling over captions in the Engish he had never mastered.

Papa Ciomei wasn't feeling well. It had begun with toothaches. The dentist wanted all his teeth out. It was the dentist who brought the doctors into the picture. Papa Ciomei hadn't been checked in more than ten years. His heart wasn't right, the blotches on his cheek were skin cancer and he had cancer of the prostate too. Papa Ciomei wasn't a man to enjoy being ill. Doctors buzzing around him were an indignity and an irritation. Grumbling, he took his medications, let them pull the first batch of teeth from his rotting gums, stared ahead angrily as Dr. Bradley listened to his chest. Dr. Bradley wanted him in the hospital, but Papa Ciomei wouldn't go.

And so he died one morning resting on the living-room couch right after finishing the breakfast Sally had served him of stewed prunes, oatmeal, coffee and the lunch biscuits he preferred to toast. Uncle Arturo was out on the back porch tending the wood stove. Laura had left for school, Vin for the quarry. Sally was tidying up the kitchen. She had heard an odd noise from Papa Ciomei's throat and looking into his alert, terrified eyes, she ran for the bottle of little white tablets and put one under his tongue.

He held one hand clenched at his chest. The other hung limply over the side of the couch.

He whispered, "Cold. Very cold." In English.

She pulled a crocheted throw from the back of the couch. She heard herself saying, "Oh, God. Oh, God. Oh, God."

She covered him, tucking him in carefully, lifting the drooping hand, kissing it, rubbing it, placing it under the covers.

She called the hospital from the hall phone, where she could watch Papa Ciomei. He lay still. She asked for Dr. Bradley. The secretary said he would call back.

She whispered, "It's an emergency. I think he's having a heart attack."

The nurse said, "Do you want an ambulance?"

"Yes," she said. "Yes. And Dr. Bradley."

"Dr. Bradley will call you back," the secretary said. "Your location?" the secretary said. "And directions?"

When she returned to Papa Ciomei he was dead. The hand she had kissed and placed under the covers had slid out and hung limply over the side again. His eyelids were partly open, showing a glimmer of expressionless pupils. On his large, slack cheeks, the black splotches triumphed. Except for his strange dead color, he seemed asleep.

She went back to the phone to call the quarry.

"Tell Vin Ciomei to get right home," she said. "This is his wife. His father's been stricken."

Stricken. It was a word she didn't know she knew.

The proper thing to do was to cover Papa Ciomei's face. She pulled the openwork throw up over his face. His big features stuck through the openings as if he were kidding around, playing dead, and now his little boy's legs, lying slightly twisted and pigeon-toed, had been exposed. She pulled the cover back down over his legs.

She knelt at his side and took his limp hand in hers. It felt natural and warm, Papa Ciomei's dear, good hand. She placed it flat on the couch and, on her knees at his side, pressed her cheek against the back of his hand until she heard the ambulance sirens and the medics pushing in and then Uncle Arturo calling out in a panic.

She had had her moment alone with Papa Ciomei. She was grateful for that. The family took over and shoved her aside. Engulfed by their extravagant grieving displays, she held herself dry-eyed and silent. At the wake, the irrelevant notion struck her that she was the only "white" in the room, even counting her own daughter. Not that there weren't plenty of dyed blondes, looking even more Italian-exotic than if they had kept their hair black. Well, anything wrong with that?

If not with that, then with something. She had made up her mind to leave Vin. As soon as she had a steady job and found a place to live, she'd take Laura and go. It wouldn't matter a bit to Vin Ciomei whether she went or stayed. It had only mattered to Papa Ciomei.

PART THREE

11

THE FIRST TIME Sally saw Morgan Beauchamp Sweetsir she almost killed him.

She was pulling into the Hilltop parking lot, going like a streak, thinking of something else. Of what? Something dumb about one of the girls she played volleyball with one night a week. The "girls." Three were married and mothers, one was a grandmother, two were lesbians, one was divorced (herself). Only two qualified as anything resembling a "girl," and of these only nineteen-year-old Debbie might be a virgin, though there wasn't any reason to suppose she was. Sally had worked with them all at her next-to-her-last job at the district high school, in administration, and had gotten caught up in a weekly volleyball game. They usually met for a burger and beer and a round of gossip before leaving for the district high school gym, tossing the ball around for an hour and a half, and then stopping back at the Hilltop for a nightcap. Not Sally's idea of a particularly great way to spend an evening. That was what she was thinking as she zipped around the back of a big trailer truck, skidded slightly, and came as near as *that* to plowing into a man getting out of the cab of his truck.

He jumped clear at the exact second she hit the brakes, stopping short of where he would have been if he had stayed put. She hadn't touched him. He came after her in a rage.

He was a very handsome man.

"Would ya like to give it another try, lady? Ya didn't quite succeed the first time around, maybe ya'd like to try again?"

Heavy sarcasm. She got out of her car, calling out, "Sorry. I'm sorry."

It was a penetratingly cold night with a light, wet snow that turned to slush as it settled on the hardtop surface of the parking lot. He was a large man, made larger by swathes of clothing—a down vest over a bulky wool sweater. He wore a crazy-looking wool hat on his head. He was huge enough and handsome enough to dominate his clothing. He was astonishingly handsome, like a movie actor, glowing with a dark, hungry beauty of a kind that made others turn and stare, thinking, I know him, I've seen him in the movies or on TV. He was that kind of handsome.

She revved herself up to deliver a charming performance—fluttery, apologetic hands, pleading eyes, dazzling smile. She wanted this man to like her.

She said, "God, I'm sorry. Honest, I'm a nut in a car. I get lost in my thoughts and start speeding up, I just forget where I'm at and start driving automatically. I can't tell you how sorry I am. I bet I'm more shook up than you are. Look." She held out her gloveless hands, making them tremble for his benefit.

He stood planted, immobile and unimpressed.

"I'm really sorry. I'm really, really sorry," she said. "I really am shook up."

"Maybe ya the one shook up, but it weren't me did the damage. It'd be me smeared all ova the parkin lot," he said, "if it weren't for a little bit a luck."

"Listen," she said. "Were you heading for the Hilltop?"

He looked at her with no expression. The wet snow drifted on their faces, melting into instant wet discomfort.

"Don't see any other place attached to this particular parkin lot," he said.

Sarcasm seemed to be his thing.

"Don't seem to know what I'm doing or saying tonight," she said and again flashed her dazzling smile.

"Ya bet ya don't know what ya doin or sayin," he said.

She plunged in. "Let me buy you a drink, show you I'm really sorry. How about it? C'mon."

He studied her.

"Ya buy guys drinks?" he said. "Ya one a them liberated females?"

She knew he was interested now, even if he wasn't enchanted.

"Figures," he said. "Sure. That the reason ya can't drive worth a damn?"

She laughed. Cute shake of her head.

"Just want to show you how sorry I am."

She'd slow down, back off a little, give him room to make the next move. She couldn't read the tone of his messages. It occurred to her that some of his resentment was directed at the way she talked. Maybe she should revert to local speech, make him more comfortable with her. Maybe he wasn't attracted to her at all. She was so heavily bundled against the cold, there wasn't any way for him to know what she looked like. She pulled off her wool hat, shook her hair free.

"Ya goin in there alone?" he said, nodding at the Hilltop entrance.

"I'm meeting a bunch of girls for a snack. Ladies' volleyball night at the Eatonville gym. Usually we come back later for another beer—about nine or so."

He nodded. "Now wouldn't ya say I'd be runnin a big risk, drinkin with a lady who tried to kill me?"

She laughed and held out her hand. "Safe. Safe as can be. I'm as gentle as a lamb, ask anybody in town, wouldn't hurt a fly."

He looked at her hard for what seemed like a long time before he took his right hand from the side-slit pocket of his down vest and gathered her icy fingers into his warm grasp. She had been through too many tries since leaving Vin to believe in love at first sight, but she believed in the power of touch, and knew in her body that power was working between them. And something else. Beneath the command of his large, warm palm, a trembling ambiguity pulled away from contact, a vulnerable fear of such delicacy that it shocked her, coming from the sarcastic, swaggering giant of a man she had assumed he was. It was as if a wolf had been turned into a fluttering bird. It was as if the hand that had set out to grasp hers had wavered into a shy, rare catch that her strength had secured against its will. If she had been pulled toward him before, the moment their hands made their strange contact she had become so deeply intrigued that everything else paled.

"What the hell," he said, releasing her hand. He stuck his hand back in his pocket. "Lemme buy ya a beer at nine o'clock. Meet ya back here at nine o'clock. But *I'm* buyin," he said. "Ain't reduced to bein paid for by wimmin yet. Ain't sunk that low yet."

"Sure," she said. "Delighted. Long as ya forgive me. See ya later." And ran off before he regretted it.

She was going to give him the best time of his life. Take all the tremble out of his fingers, put him at ease, be herself with him, talk the talk she had been born to talk. It was going to be terrific between them.

She soon quit playing volleyball with the girls. Sweets occupied all the space around her, all the space within her. It was as if they had been starving for each other until the moment they met, and now falling upon the feast couldn't get their fill. Not very communicative with others, they had endless messages to convey to each other, flooding their time together with love and talk, calling each other the moment they separated, calling each other during the day at work, two and three times a day. They went right on doing that, calling each other two and three times a day from work every day, even after they decided to live together and Sweets moved in with her and Laura. Now there were three of them bunched up in the little two-bedroom apartment in town on Water Street over Pheasant's Drug Store, a perfect place for her and Laura alone, fixed up sort of nice with secondhand furniture, and its pretty view out over the river. Two weeks of Sweets in the apartment and the whole shebang was coming apart. Even the floorboards loosened up under his heavy tread, and the plumbing gave out. No matter. They were too wound up in each other to care much about houses or furniture, anyway, and she put aside her overriding concern about Laura growing up too fast for her own good. Was the girl suffering? Could she hear them through the rickety walls?

The important thing was to keep love from spoiling.

If she was too busy at the office to call him by noontime, he'd call her.

"Checkin on ya. Somethin the matter? How come ya ain't checked in with me yet?"

No matter how often they spoke during the day, each time his voice on the telephone was like a first time, pulsing for her with a romantic resonance she responded to as if she were a teenager successfully negotiating her first date. She hadn't loved Vin except like a brother or an uncle, feeling sorry for him mostly, not wanting to hurt him; but her blood had really pounded for a couple of men since. If suffering could be counted as strong feeling, she supposed she had been in love, and had even had some joyous times until the men proved out frauds, and the connection died in a rotten, depressing nothingness that negated the bits of pleasure along the way.

With Sweets it was so different, it was as if a new language needed to be invented to describe it. She didn't want to talk about Sweets to anybody. She hugged this love to herself, the only treasure in her life so tenderly valuable she couldn't bear it to receive another's touch.

Out of the blue, Bill Grandstone asked her to lunch. He said he had something of personal importance to discuss with her. She assumed it was of personal importance to him, but no, it was supposed to be of personal importance to her. He was warning her against getting involved with Sweets. He knew that she and Laura and Sweets were living together in the little rented apartment over the drug store on Water Street. Everybody knew it. That's how it was in town. Everybody knew everybody else's business. Gossiping behind one's back. She had to credit Bill Grandstone for being open with her, at least.

But what she felt at the moment was irritation. During the period she had worked for Bill they had done it together a couple of times. It hadn't been any good. He couldn't even get it up. Sally always felt it was her fault when she couldn't get a rise out of a man, and cut her losses and quit; but maybe Bill Grandstone was one of those men who felt they owned you if they laid a finger on you. He murmured something about "taking the liberty because of their past intimacy" and because he "had such a high regard" for her.

It didn't seem to occur to him that he could be plain envious of another man making it with her with no trouble.

"You're a first-class lady, you're a great lady, Sally."

Bill came from California. He had an odd way of talking.

"You deserve the best. The best of the best. Others can take punishment. They've earned it. You've earned good in the world. You're a good lady, Sally, and that fellow is bad medicine."

She had taken a couple of sips of her Bloody Mary. Liquor got to her so fast the drink somewhat dulled the edge of what he was saying; even so a thumping anxiety started in her gut. The barbecued spareribs didn't look delicious anymore. This fancy lunch was going to be ruined for her.

She said, "I know all about Morgan Sweetsir, Bill."

She knew about the short jail term when he was really only a kid. His army stint would have made anybody crazy. She knew about his four marriages. Was he supposed to hang because he was looking for love, real love, and hadn't found it until he met her? She knew about his kids scattered around among the wives, and she knew he was battling for custody of his kid from his last creepy wife, Kay. What's more, Sally was going to help him get his kid when she and Sweets married, which it looked as if they would soon now. She knew about his heavy drinking. She knew he had a lot of debts. Anything else?

The drink had loosened her tongue. She was ashamed and angry with herself for sitting over lunch talking to Bill Grandstone about Sweets.

He nodded, very grave over his roast beef and mashed potatoes, then glanced at her with his prominent blue eyes. His whole face flushed a bright, bright pink.

"Not talking about that kind of thing," he said.

"Well, what?"

"He's bad medicine," he said.

The color receded slightly from his full, mottled cheeks. He couldn't have been more than thirty, but he looked middle-aged with his thin, fair, receding hair and pudgy face. He's jealous, she consoled herself.

"You don't even know Sweets," she said.

"I'm concerned about *you*, Sally. You're too good to get trampled."

She gave up on the sparerib she was nibbling. She wiped her hands and her mouth carefully. Her hands were shaking.

"What does that mean? If you don't know Sweets, what are you talking about? What's the big mystery? If there's one thing I hate, it's hinting around, creating a mystery."

He said, "I'm not at liberty to divulge my sources. You understand, Sally."

What she understood was her urge to sock him in the face. Bill Grandstone was in criminal law. She had worked for him as a temporary legal secretary right after her divorce from Vin. She knew how successful he was, how many clients he had. He was in a position to know everything about everybody in the county. He knew something about Sweets that she didn't know? His innuendos lit up a swampy, scary dark patch of her love for Sweets that she didn't want to look into now. Angry panic destroyed her speech control.

"Are ya at liberty ta tell me what the hell ya talkin about, Bill? Or are ya havin fun scarin the hell outta me about nothin? That ya idea a fun?"

"Sally," he said, his babyish blush deepening. "Don't be angry with the messenger of bad tidings. It's not the messenger who's at fault."

She wouldn't bother to answer that.

He said, "You know I have the highest regard for you, Sally."

"Well, thanks for nothin," she said. "I ain't aimin to become a saint, ya know."

The waitress brought their coffee. Embarrassed with each other, they busied themselves opening the packaged containers of coffee cream and sugar, pouring and stirring. She seized those moments to pull herself back to her earlier control.

"Listen, Bill," she said, smooth and smiling, "I really appreciate your concern, but I just don't know what you're leading up to. I mean, what am I supposed to do? Call the cops and tell them to get Morgan Sweetsir out of my house because Bill Grandstone heard something about him he's not telling?"

He dropped his eyes, his blush a full-blown red, red rose now.

"You understand I can't supply details, Sally, you just have to take my word for it. The man isn't safe to live with. He's violent. He sent at least one woman to the hospital. You know I can't say who, but it's documented. There were certainly other incidents. It's your welfare I'm concerned with, Sally. I care for you too much to see you . . ."

She stood up, interrupting.

"Gotta get back to work, Bill," she said. "Thanks for the lunch. And thanks for the warning. But you might be interested to know I've had nothing but the best times of my life with Morgan Sweetsir and if he *ever* did put some woman in a hospital with a black eye or something, all I can say is she sure must have brought it on herself—because Morgan Sweetsir is a total gentleman and a first-rate man if you know what I mean."

She meant to crush him with that last phrase. Instead, his face hardened and saddened into a coldly dismissive mask.

"It's your life, Sally," he said, and picked up the check.

12

SHE DIDN'T TELL Sweets about her lunch. It was Friday of a long
holiday weekend. Laura would be spending the time away at a
girlfriend's house. Why spoil the possibility of perfection—she and
Sweets alone with hours and hours of happiness for themselves.
They would talk about what was ahead. No need to go back, to
force Sweets to face disagreeable past events. She knew he had had
a hard time in life; why shove his face in early failures, remind him
of former wives and ugly reports to lawyers? The precious point of
their love was that it was powerful enough to rescue them from
their histories. And not only rescue for Sweets—she too was being
opened up by love, and her body and yes, her soul, her mind and
heart, her whole self opening, growing, shooting out into colors and
shapes she didn't know existed in her—changing all over. She was a
different person since loving Sweets. And he, so beautiful and vi-
brant and yearning. She wasn't going to harp on his unlucky past
when she knew she could move him forward to the man he really
was, the best man in the world. She didn't care what he had been
with other women, if with her he was different. She knew Sweets,
knew him better than anybody, knew his true inner nature, his
sweetness and his physical beauty and his weaknesses and moods,
knew him inside and out, as well as she knew the shape of his cleft
chin and the colors of the tattoos on his chest and arms. Nobody
needed to tell her anything about Morgan Beauchamp Sweetsir. He
was her lover, her best friend, better than a father, the brother and
the son she had never had; he was perfect for her and she was perfect for him. Bad medicine? Their love was magic. It ran through

their veins igniting hope. They were going to have a great life, she and Sweets.

She wasn't going to say a word to Sweets about jealous Bill Grandstone and his creepy hints.

She thought she knew what Bill Grandstone had gotten wind of. Sweets liked sex games—liked playing around with boots and straps and whips and costumes. Strapping her to a chair. The other way around. Switching master-slave roles. Nothing dangerous to it. One of Sweets's wives must have accidentally gotten hurt, decided to turn it into a federal case, brought her lurid stories to goofy, repressed, innocent, incompetent William Grandstone, Esquire.

The thought made her laugh.

You had to be a total stranger to fantasy to be bothered by Sweets's games. They weren't even all that different from Vin's flights of fancy at the motel, limited though Vin's were to changes of sexy nightgowns and a little bit of help from the wine. Her private fantasies had been wilder than anything Sweets came up with.

But it was a lot more fun for two to play, especially if the partner was Sweets. And it wasn't as if he was a nut. When she got the giggles, overcome by a ludicrous mirror view of herself in a black bikini and bra, white vinyl hip boots and long white leather gloves that were so large she was having a lot of trouble manipulating the whip on Sweets's bare hairy ass, Sweets didn't get mad, he waited patiently for her to get over the giggles. He was straddled on a rocking chair positioned upside down. The rocking chair was their most important inert prop, but he came up with others. Sometimes Sweets himself became a horse and she the rider, the master, as later she would become the horse stripped of her weapons, her gloves and her lace bikini. It was Sweets who put together the scenarios with the help of a sex manual and some magazines he owned. Ridiculous to take seriously this tame, silly playacting he invented.

Unless the games got out of hand. He hurt her, strapped to the rocker, entering her from behind. It hurt like hell, she hated it, and he let her holler and cry and didn't stop until he finished.

He had had a lot of beer that night. The few times when the games turned weird and scary, it was usually because of too much beer. The scariest part of one particular time was that it matched one of her recurrent childish fantasies, except in her fantasy she was in control of what happened. Here with Sweets, she was afraid of what might happen.

She was strapped across the middle on the overturned rocker, on her back, her legs and arms spread wide, anchored to the chair at the ankles and wrists too. Sweets stood over her, his penis not so much erect as grotesquely engorged.

"I'm gonna piss on ya goddam face. I'm gonna piss on ya goddam bleached-blond hair. Take the curl outta ya, by Jesus. And ya gonna love it. Ya gonna beg for more. I'm gonna piss in ya mouth, ya gonna lap it up. I'm gonna piss in ya twat, in ya asshole, ya gonna be nothing but piss inside and out. Ya gonna love it, ya gonna beg for more."

Astounded at her fear, she heard herself, a miserable baby girl, sobbing, pleading, "Daddy, Daddy, don't, don't, don't, I'll be good. I'll be good, don't do that to me, please, please, I'll do whatever ya say, swear I will, Daddy, please, please."

His face was alight with pleasure.

He smacked her across the side of her head with his open palm. Again—astonishment—not so much at the pain as at the rushing noise the blow created in her ears, the instant, powerful, humiliating depression, tinged by a terrible elation at the depths they were daring. She heard herself scream, "I'll kill myself."

"Do it for ya," he said, and smacked her again. "Save ya the trouble"—and readied the enormous trembling palm to strike again.

The blow seemed to loosen her connection to herself. As if she were following a script arranged by a power beyond her, she sobbed and writhed, calling, "Mama, Mama," in an infant's long-drawn-out wail, "Mama, Mama, I want my mama, I want my mama," dying away into a whimpering "Please, please, I want my mama, I want my mama," almost luxuriating in letting herself down into the grieving depths of a monstrous humiliation.

He didn't hit her again. He stood over her laughing, and with a couple of wide-arching gestures of his arm, emptied what was left of his can of beer in her face, then threw the can at her. It hit her stomach. That didn't hurt, and the splash of cold beer could be considered oddly pleasant and refreshing. What was terrifying was the union between them. He was no longer the Sweets she knew; she was no longer the person she knew herself to be. The man standing before her was a huge, violently blue-black creature, covered with hair and menacing tattoos, a naked animal, awesome in his strangeness, his brilliant eyes shining with an intensity of angry joy. She loved him. Was she prepared to go along with him to whatever depths he invented? A little click went off in her muffled head, switching her to the self that was securely inviolable at the core of her being. Enough.

She forced herself to smile as naturally as possible. She made her voice flat and matter of fact, steady above the ecstatic panic of fear and pleasure, of pain and joy.

"Hey, Sweets, I'm gettin kinda tired. Ain't ya gettin tired? We both put in a day's work today, y'know. How's about we get inter bed now and do it straight?"

She thought she had enraged him, but if she had, his anger passed rapidly. He stared vaguely, laughed loosely, said, "Yeah," then turned his back and walked away. She heard the full rushing sound of his urine hitting the toilet bowl and smelled its strong odor. Soured supper backed up into her throat. She swallowed with difficulty. Her throat was swollen and raw. She heard the rough intake of her own breathing.

It was taking a chance, but counting on his "Yeah" as consent, she wriggled her hands free of the loose ties binding them, and by the time he returned, she was mostly out of the straps holding her down. He padded by her on his naked feet as if he had forgotten not only their game but her very existence. He flopped on the bed and was instantly asleep. That was okay. He was never any good when he was full of beer, anyhow.

That was the only time Sweets hit her before they married. She didn't think of the scene as a beating. One of their games had gone out of whack, that was all. Still, she had learned to respect a certain click that went off in her head when their games threatened to enter dangerous terrain—and even at other times. Caution had been imposed on the perfect freedom of their union. She blamed it on the drinking. She tried to discourage beer drinking during games, and tried to keep their scenarios lighthearted and silly, but the little warning click still went off in her head from time to time, went off during their best times, when love took a natural, easy shape without the need for stimulants. The great stimulant was talk. Their talk was a miracle to her. They had endless stories for each other: there wasn't enough time, counting the day and night, to tell each other everything there was to tell, everything that had happened before they met, and everything that was going to happen now that they had met.

A lot of the talk was nonsense—some little nothing event, a new supper plan for the evening or some errand to be done in the next few hours. They were on the phone to each other three or four times a day about such details, or about a trivial occurrence that must immediately be communicated, or some minute change of plan that necessitated instant touch, instant contact. But it was the long, confessional talks accompanying their lovemaking that was the real glue holding them together. They had never trusted themselves to such talk before.

It wasn't consecutive narration. Their stories came out in bits and pieces. She told him about her mama dying when she was too young to know what was going on. He described the death of his father—a vivid drama of a heart attack that arched his daddy's body into a clutching hoop of pain that killed him in two minutes. Sweets was ten when that happened. She told him about her daddy and how there wasn't any warm feeling between them. She told him about meeting Vin at the fairgrounds and getting pregnant and marrying into an Italian family. She told him how Vin was a good man but she never had had any real love feeling for him. She tried to tell him about Laura but couldn't. She couldn't reach down that far into what she felt for Laura. Oddly, she cried. He held her in his arms.

"I know how ya feel," he said. "I know how ya feel about ya kid. I got my kids scattered all ova, but I know how ya feel. I know how I feel."

Talking about her sisters, one moved out of her life to Lincoln, Nebraska, and the other disappeared into fat and drudgery, she conveyed a picture of loneliness and a drought of love. She didn't speak of Papa Ciomei. Again, as with Laura, she didn't know how.

Their deprivations bound them further. They had both lost their mamas when they were little, and he had lost his father too. He had been raised by a sister seventeen years older than he. She was dead now.

"I thought I loved her. I thought I loved her bettern anybody in the world."

He became highly agitated. Tears reflected blue lights in his black eyes, brilliantly different from Vin's dead-black pupils that no light ever seemed to penetrate. Sally knew that his fears were for himself, not for his dead sister—but that was all right. The perfect gratification of their talking love was that it included the luxurious shared embraces of self-love and self-pity.

"She died when I was twenty-one," he said. "Only thirty-eight herself. Died of leukemia. Went inta the hospital for tests so they could figure out what was wrong with her and six weeks later— dead. Just like that. So fast I couldn't hardly believe it. Jennie. I neva even had a chance to mourn her. My aunt comes up to me at the funeral and throws me a bombshell. 'Ya sister Jennie was ya mama,' she tells me. 'It's time now for ya to know.'"

A click went off in her head. He was dramatizing—making up stories?

She said, "Y'mean she was tellin ya that ya sister did it with ya father, with her own father? . . ."

They were lying on the bed in her bedroom. They were alone in the apartment. Friday night was payday night, good-feeling night. They had met right after work, shopped for food together, dumped the week's supplies at the apartment, bothering only to put perishables in the freezer and refrigerator, leaving the rest in the big brown grocery bags on the kitchen table, and then had driven right on out to the Hilltop for a couple of drinks, entering like royalty, she and Sweets, greeting people, "Hi ya? How ya doin?" laughing together at the big-screen TV commercials and news, sitting by themselves, feeling themselves wonderfully endowed, good-looking, happy, going to make it, going to do good, no matter what anybody said. They came home to a dinner quickly prepared by her while Sweets eyed the TV. They had steak and french-fried potatoes, salad, apple pie and coffee, and all the while they were talking, talking, talking, laughing and talking, bathing in talking, smiling love, the messy room obscured in the haze of cigarette smoke and the soft focus of a continuous flow of beer, the crummy apartment and their crummy jobs fading away in the soft, dreamy vista of the great shared life to come for them.

But now she had said the wrong thing.

She had ripped apart this magic fabric with her dumb remark. She felt his anger rising not only against her but against the fragile structure of love itself, striking at the illusion that veiled the messed bed, the ashtrays filled with butts, the empty beer cans, the clean laundry in a basket on the dresser, the dirty clothes in a heap on the chair, seeing her, his Sally, his love, not as the glamorous girl coming in with him to the Hilltop, everybody eager to call out, "Hi, Sally, hi ya, how ya doin, Sally?" Seeing instead a fading thirty-year-old woman who'd been around plenty, saddled with a kid, leeching onto Morgan Sweetsir to suck him dry, to do him in.

Click.

He said, "I ain't neva yet come up with a woman who knows how to listen. Goddam bitches think they're some kinda private investigators. Okay, Rockford, ya wanna check me out?"

She left him. Said she had to put the kitchen in order. He didn't follow, as he liked to when things were going good between them, helping with the cleanup, rattling on about anything at all, or urging her to tell him more about her boss and his creepy kid, and about the boss's clients, people from away, each with an exotic cast, something remarkable for her to report to him. He stayed in the bedroom. His mood pervaded the air of the apartment, its power to disturb following her to the kitchen, spreading a dark mist of raging despair.

He was asleep when she returned to the bedroom, the TV on.

Click.

But the next night he was sweet again, wonderfully, wonderfully sweet.

He told her that night about bursting into his older brother's room to show him a new transistor he had just bought to find his brother with his head at work at a fellow's crotch.

"Y'know what that felt like—right after the other shock? I was through. Beginning right then and there, I was finished. I lost my faith in human nature. If I could find my brother in that kinda situation, I give up on human nature."

Another elaborate lie?

She was afraid to respond except with a serious nod. If her words were wrongly chosen, it would set him against her. She silently nodded at his accusing eyes, covering an inner twinge of contempt for his carefully treasured grievance list and for the way he tilted his head with a childishly defiant lift of his cleft chin and pursed his full lips. Like a woman looking for sympathy.

Click.

One night he cried like a baby. He was telling her of a long car trip he had taken with his daddy into Maine and Canada during a snowstorm. The heater wasn't working right. His daddy had a woman with him up front. They stopped from time to time when they hit a town with a bar, to warm up with a drink. The boy wasn't admitted. Under age. Once they brought him a cold dry ham-and-cheese sandwich. For the rest, he went hungry, thirsty, cramped to his bones, frozen with loneliness and a sense of desperate neglect.

"They left me to rot in the back of the car like I was some kinda dog, worsen a dog. They woulda treated a dog bettern me. Then the two comin back to the car together, laughin and warm from their food and drink, tellin themselves, 'He's okay, he's asleep, he's havin a good time, he's dead to the world'—well, I wasn't, I wasn't dead to the world, I was up, pretendin to be asleep, wishin they were dead, wishin they would die."

He had rolled on his stomach to bury his sobs. She wormed her way under him, cradling him with her body, rocking him with her whole body until the sobs ceased, and had the triumph of knowing him aroused. She undid his clothing and hers, fitted him again into her cradling body, locked her legs and arms around him.

That had been a right response. In the morning, over coffee and a cigarette, and right in front of Laurie, who kept her head down and acted as if she hadn't heard him, he told Sally, okay, since she really wanted to get married so much, maybe they oughta get married.

"It don't make no sense goin on keepin my own place when I'm practically neva there," he said.

They were married at City Hall with borrowed rings. Sweets's best friends acted as witnesses, Tyrone and Helen Parsons, the only people he wanted present. No kids. If he couldn't have all his kids there, they wouldn't have any. Then the two of them drove all the way to Boston to buy matching rings and have lunch, and then drove all the way back, just for the hell of it, singing along with the radio on the turnpike, having fun, feeling great. They had found exactly the rings they wanted in an elegant department store that Sweets wasn't too pleased to be entering in his down jacket, but he looked splendid, looked like an actor or a rich man knocking around in sport clothes. It wasn't possible to be as handsome as Sweets was and not look right.

They really splurged on the rings. Sally laid out the money. Sweets was a little short of cash because it was the end of the month and he got paid once a month. She banished the click in her head. Sweets earned a lot more money than she did. If he was planning to live off a woman, he'd do better with some one richer than she was—and he could get a rich woman, he could get anybody he wanted, any woman in the world. He spent the money he made a little too freely, that was all. Had a backlog of debts to work off.

On the sidewalk, under the store's canopy, right there on an elegant street in Boston, she kissed the full, cushioned, warm lips of this terrific man who now belonged to her. He was embarrassed at first, then pleased.

"Show these big-city assholes how a real man and a real woman act," he said, pulling her to his side. He lifted his chin to dare anyone to challenge them. None of the passersby streaming in both directions paid any attention.

His bravado fizzled out at the ordeal of entering a restaurant she chose. She wanted snails on her wedding day. She had learned about snails and garlic-butter sauce from Papa Ciomei, and had had them at a restaurant she was taken to by Bill Grandstone. Snails in garlic-butter sauce and French bread was what she wanted to eat on her true wedding day. Marrying the man she loved. She wanted red wine, soft lights, a white tablecloth and cloth napkins, real flowers, the authentic smells and sounds of rich people—perfume and shaving lotion, hearty bass laughter, the high shrieks of women as the liquor settled in.

She had made a mistake. The restaurant she had thought so glamorous from its outside windows was almost entirely filled with women alone. There were no snails or garlic bread on the menu.

Homemade muffins, dieter's salads, a special luncheon plate of filet of sole, mashed or french-fried potatoes, broiled tomato . . . They might as well be back home in Eatonville. She wanted to leave, try another place, but Sweets wouldn't, it was too embarrassing for him to walk out after being seated. They ordered the luncheon special and toasted their marriage in beer.

She found a big house on the hill near the State College that rented for more money than they could afford, and took it for a year. "We'll show them," they said. They used that phrase to cover a lot of ground. "We'll show them." They both knew what they meant.

As soon as they moved in, Johnny and his dog Blackie joined them, and Sweets started a suit for custody of his kid, Judy, as well. She agreed to everything, agreed almost before he asked. She entered wholeheartedly into his obsession to gain custody of Judy; it became her obsession too. Because she had worked for Bill Grandstone, she knew a thing or two about courts and the law. It would count in Sweets's favor if they had a decent home to bring the child to, and she devoted herself to furnishing and decorating as if the result was to be a feature story in *House Beautiful*. It wasn't like the other time, redoing the Ciomei house. This was the happiness and hope of their marriage made solid. It was the child they had promised one another they wouldn't have. She traded in her beat-up mess of a Dodge that ran perfectly for a neat-looking used VW squareback that was giving her nothing but trouble, but the VW was the right kind of car to be pulling into the curved driveway of their house. She bought a London Fog coat with a fake-fur lining and a collar for too much money, to go with the car, with the house, with her new shorter hairdo fluffed around her face in a backward turning wave.

Laura was a worry to her. She hadn't developed into a real terrorizing teenager; she wasn't out to kill her parents—or her stepparent either—but Sally was aware of depths she had no method of sounding in this beautiful dark girl who was her daughter. She worried about Sweets not liking Laura, and more about his liking Laura too much. She worried in the same way about Johnny and Laura, alone in the house during those hours when she and Sweets worked, or dropped into the Hilltop for a drink, or took off for a long drive to talk and sit in the car looking at the sunset over Serpent Hill, or went out for a bite and took in a movie once in a great while. She worried about Laura baby-sitting for faculty families at the Academy. The professor who brought her home was a creepy-looking guy.

The floating, dreamy softness of her daughter worried her. It was unbearable to imagine Laura headed for disaster at the same age she had.

She told herself the right thing to do was to spend time alone with Laura and she aimed for one evening a week—a movie, shopping at Jerrie's, a Big Mac and a shake at McDonald's, something like that, but however good her intentions, in practice there seemed never to be more time available for Laura than once a month, and after a couple of months even that faded out to nothing.

A phrase ran around in her head, materialized out of the air Sweets created. *If he ever so much as touches Laura, that'll be it.*

It was only Johnny he beat up on. She interfered the first time he went after Johnny. He turned on her, taking a swipe that glanced off her shoulder but knocked her to the ground. She told herself he hadn't meant it, that he didn't realize how strong he was, that the blow had caught her off balance. She had fallen against the table. In the next few days a hideous discoloration flowed down her side, under her right breast. She displayed herself to Sweets.

"Ya tryin to decorate me?" Smiling, forgiving.

He kissed the bruises. She kissed the birds, the snakes, the hearts and twined leaves of his tattoos.

Sweets would change, he had to, he'd become the man she knew he really was inside. She knew he loved Johnny. Hadn't he always taken care of him? He hit him because he loved him. She understood. She only had to do more, to keep working at regeneration of his gentle, loving side, relieve the causes of tension, take over the bills, give Sweets hope and the freedom to do as he pleased, make him happy. He was terribly tense. He needed so much. Right now, he needed his baby, Judy. She'd do anything to help him get Judy. Then he'd be happy. Everything was coming under control. She was putting everything in order. She had taken out a loan to pay off Sweets's debts and the lawyer's fees for handling the custody suit.

She had drawn up a budget. If they stuck to the budget, they'd manage.

Sweets agreed to whatever she proposed.

"Anything ya say, Sally. Ya take care of it, okay?"

On his first monthly payday he bought a color TV, a neat little set that cost a lot, and that used up almost all the part of his pay due to go into the joint budget. He plunked the set down on a living-room side table. He was flushed with good intentions and a couple of beers.

She was dismayed. She let her anger show.

"If we got an agreement, we got an agreement," she said.

"I gotta be able to count on ya, Sweets," she said. "We gotta be countin on each other, stickin to our plans, or we won't get nowhere."

He seized the TV with both hands and held it over her head, as if ready to drop it. There was a terrifying loss of control in his manner. As always when he was mad at her, instead of the hollering she expected, his voice was lower than usual.

"That's the thanks I get. Tryin to do somethin nice for ya. Tryin to give ya a surprise, give the kids a treat. That's the thanks a man gets."

Laura and Johnny were naturally on his side of the argument. He was the best daddy in the world. It was the best surprise in the world. A color TV was what they wanted more than anything in the world. Under cover of their compensating praise she backtracked as fast as she could. Said she was only kidding, made a prominent place for the TV to sit in the living room, hugged him, kissed him. He suffered her thanks coldly.

To even out that month's budget, she arranged to do some babysitting. Her boss was divorced and needed help with his seven-year-old boy's regular visitation weekends. And if they all cut down on lunch expenses, that would help. She packed lunches for everybody and planned cheap dinners—lots of spaghetti-and-ground-meat variations. They'd squeeze through. None of that was important anyway. What was important was that Sweets feel good.

He felt wonderful when they won custody of Judy. He wanted their whole world to know. He headed with her directly to the Hilltop to celebrate. To the "Hiya, how ya doin" greetings from all sides, he responded not with the usual "Doin good," but with a tri-umphant "Got custody a my kid, y'know." "Y'hear bout me gettin custody a my kid?" "Got custody a my Judy." "Court give me cus-tody a my kid." And as he got cockier on beer, "Goddam court give me the right to my own kid, ain't that somethin, they damn well better had, or they'd a seen somethin, legal or illegal," his arm loosely hung about Sally's shoulder in absolute ownership of his good woman who had stood by him.

She had stood by him. She had splattered the walls with the blood of his former wife.

She dismissed that image. It wasn't *her* doing. Miserable woman had done it to herself, coming into court looking like something the cat dragged in, a safety pin holding her eyeglasses together, be-draggled and crying, admitting she was on relief, admitting she couldn't afford to keep Johnny and his dog, that's why she had turned them over to Sweets, getting the judge so mixed up about Johnny and impatient with her talk that it was plain he believed Johnny to be her illegitimate child and was figuring that Sweets had more compassion for the boy than his own mother did. In a cold official manner, he questioned Kay. Didn't she know she was Sweets's fourth wife? Mr. Sweetsir hadn't hidden his three former marriages, had he? Wasn't it *her* third marriage, anyway?

Kay seemed to become lost in the judge's questions.

He called her back impatiently. "Mrs. Sweetsir? Mrs. Sweetsir?"

Vaguely staring about the room, she accidentally met Sally's eyes directly.

"It ain't just me. He can't live with nobody. He gets too mad, is why."

"Mrs. Sweetsir, we're discussing the custody of your child. Do you understand the nature of these proceedings?"

Vague stare, then a blubbering collapse. "It ain't right. It ain't right to separate a mother and daughter."

Impatient, cold pause for her to recover. "How do you plan to take care of your daughter, Mrs. Sweetsir?"

"Ain't he gotta help? Ain't he gotta support her? He makes good money on them road crews."

Along the outer leg of Kay's green stretch pants, a split in the seam revealed a gleam of pink underpants. Unpleasant, that glimpse of grayish-pink. Sally had heard that this former wife of Sweets's was supposed to be young and pretty. The woman on the stand was a cracked vessel. She seemed middle-aged. A purple wool turban was wrapped around her head, obviously because her hair was a mess underneath. She had to be color-blind to come to court in a purple hat, a green pants suit, a yellow turtleneck and her pink-gray underpants showing. Some of her clothes hung on her like hand-me-downs, too large, and some were too tight, like the stretch pants bursting at the seams. Yet she was skinny, wasted, with an unhappy pastiness in her fair skin. And the pin, holding her eyeglasses together.

Sally could have burst into tears over her—or kicked her senseless into a corner of the courtroom where she couldn't be seen. She would have liked to wipe her out like an infection. Unbearable that she and this smashed wreck were both called Mrs. Sweetsir.

Sally Sweetsir knew how to dress to appear before a judge. She knew it never hurt a woman to look good. She wore high heels to show off her legs. She had spent half a day locating a pair of panty hose that wouldn't wrinkle at the ankle. She had washed her hair, tinted it, blow-dried it into shape, made her face up carefully, the eyes shadowed meticulously, easy on the mascara. She knew she looked terrific. That gave a woman confidence.

She had advised Sweets on his outfit too—flannel shirt and contrasting tie, houndstooth sports jacket over solid gray pants, low Hush Puppy boots, high dark socks. None of those falling-down ankle socks showing hairy legs for her husband, Morgan Beauchamp Sweetsir. She bought him executive socks. She kept Bill Grandstone firmly in mind as she helped Sweets choose at the best men's store in town. On Sweets, Bill Grandstone's kind of clothing looked like a million; Bill Grandstone couldn't look that stunning no matter how much money he spent.

Sweets's lawyer had rehearsed him carefully. Still, her heart pounded when Sweets took the stand. If he blew it, if he failed, what then, how would they survive his disappointment and anger, he and she? It took awhile before she could control her nervousness enough to sound out the way the hearing was going. The judge was listening without that tinge of impatience he had brought to Kay Sweetsir's bumbling behavior. Energetic, straightforward and charming, Sweets talked about his work, told how much he made, how long he had been married to Sally and where he lived, proudly ringing out their impressive address. When he got to Judy he produced just a touch of emotion, not too much, pleading for the right to raise his daughter in a decent home where the child would be given what was needed—a peaceful, happy atmosphere with a good woman who knew how to manage a household. Lowering his eyes, as if it hurt him to expose intimate troubles to public view, he said, "I ain't sure my ex-wife is strong enough to carry the burden, ya honor, raisin a child all alone."

He could have been an actor, the way he repeated what the lawyer had told him to say, just as if he meant the words from the bottom of his heart.

"And it was her idea, separatin and divorcin. It was her idea," Sweets said, quietly, as if it pained him too much to say anymore.

Kay blubbered and wept.

Then it was Sally's turn. No problems. Wipe the floor with Kay Sweetsir by being a bright contrast to that hunk of misery.

Happy ending?

She told herself that there was always a letdown after the high of a victory. Natural for Sweets to be depressed following the court decision in their favor. She awoke every morning to a speculative terror. Was Sweets in a bad mood? His head was under the covers and he lay curled like a forlorn puppy. The first one up in the household, she tuned herself to the spirit of his mood. When Sweets felt good, he'd get up with her, stay at her side, kidding around, joshing the kids into action; he liked to run out with Johnny's dog. Not the help so much as the noisy, happy confusion he created buoyed her afloat through the rest of the day. These days mostly she got up alone, drank a cup of instant coffee before she started the pot of real coffee. She roused the kids, a bad scene one way or another. Then she got dressed. Finish her makeup later. Back into the kitchen to dish up breakfast. In and out of the bedroom, she checked out the mood weather. Sweets's head stayed under the covers, though she knew by the stillness and tightness that he was awake. His wrapped mummy sent out waves of violent, disturbing despair.

Fighting anger, resisting depression, she prepared the lunches, fed the dog, urged the kids along, took something out of the freezer for supper, made a note to herself to pick up a couple of items on the way home from work, dumped a laundry in the machine—she'd run it when she made dinner, fold and put the clothes away before she went to bed. Now the dog again. Damn leash law had her crazy. Johnny was supposed to walk his dog but he never did without a fight and she had this thing about being especially nice to Johnny and Judy, so as not to bug Sweets. She yelled at Laura to walk the goddam dog, and Laura pulled on her sweater, grabbed the leash and went without a word of protest. That would show Johnny how a human being should act. Then Judy appeared in a sleazy thin, sleeveless dress her idiot of a mother had bought her for her birthday and Sally had to holler Judy back into her room to get into proper clothes goddam it, hollering softly so Sweets wouldn't think she was being mean to his kids. That would be all she needed, the mood he was in.

Mornings like that, lucky to get out in one piece looking nice, it was a relief to leave the house to concentrate on her work, to deal coolly with people in and out of the office, in a world not connected with the dark tensions of the household.

Was she inventing her troubles?

At eleven o'clock Sweets's first call usually came in. She was no longer astonished by the buoyancy of his greeting, however blackly silent she had left him earlier. Now he was all friendly good humor. He called her honey. They talked about the weather, the traffic on Route 60; they talked about the kids, supper plans, and TV watching that evening. It was lovers' chatter. Made her whole day right, that first call. She called him at the hut during his lunch break. Told him she had the boss's kid in the office driving her up the wall. He called her again at his next coffee break. Told her a guy had mentioned a good buy in a truck. She called him at five, just before she left work. See if he needed anything she could pick up on the way home. She hurried toward home as to a source of renewed joy and strength. Everything was great; everything was going to be all right.

She stopped to see her daddy once in a while. They had a cup of coffee at the Wadeway Luncheonette. Mrs. Wade liked her daddy so much, she always served him herself, coming out from behind the cashier's spot to carry his cup of coffee to him. A nice-looking red-haired woman of his age. Dyed, of course. Give more of his attention to flirting with Honey Wade than he give his own daughter. Then the put-down she had come to expect.

"Still livin with that new man a yours?"

"What ya mean by that, Daddy? We're married."

"Well, ya don't expect it to last, do ya?"

"Sure I expect it to last."

Shake of the head. Dart of the vivid blue eyes. "There's no changin ya. Ya fall in a pile of shit, it's pearls to ya. There's some that's like that. They hafta believe that whatever they got is special, even if it's shit, to them it's gotta be gold."

"You saying I'm a fool?"

"I worry about ya, is all."

"Well, stop worrying. Might do me more good if you felt glad about me once in a while."

Bill Grandstone called her at the office. "I owe you a lunch. Jerry Greenspan told me your husband's a terrific guy. Always the first to admit I can be wrong."

Okay. He was inviting her to lunch because he had shot off his mouth without knowing what he was talking about? Good. She'd savor every nuance of his apology. She asked Jerry for extra time. She dressed specially for the occasion. She meant to luxuriate at the Lobster Pot.

"Take all the time you want, Sally," Jerry Greenspan said, "as long as you get those letters out by the end of the day. And better make sure the phone's covered. Don't leave it to those birdbrains in the outer office."

That was more or less Jerry Greenspan's way, collecting a little more than he was donating.

He and Bill Grandstone were tennis friends. They played twice a week at the Holiday Inn courts. She had a vision of them gossiping about her in the locker room. Screw them both. So she had, in the days before Sweets. No more of that now. It didn't add up, not for her anyway, never had really except as part of a search, and now it had absolutely no attraction for her. The possibility of becoming tired of Sweets, getting bored with him, made her laugh aloud, it was such an absurdity.

"Jerry told me your husband's a very impressive man," Bill said at lunch.

"How come?"

She meant to give him a hard time.

"Appearance. Manner. He said he was very impressed by him when he came to pick you up at the office. He's an engineer, I understand?"

He was foreman of a road crew was what he was, making good money working on the northern extension of the throughway, but she just smiled vaguely.

She ordered snails in garlic butter, French bread and a salad, a glass of white wine. She'd have a couple of cups of coffee later—no dessert.

"That's pretty gourmet of you," Bill Grandstone said.

She hated his smug, pink face, his pudgy hands. Flatlanders loved to think of others as ignoramuses, especially about the good things in life. Well, she knew about food, that was one thing she knew about. She hadn't lived with the Ciomeis for nothing. She thought of saying something cutting, then decided against spoiling a good lunch just to score points. Better to sink into the warmth and soft lights and the Lobster Pot's romantic piped background music. She sipped her wine, sang along with "It Was Just One of Those Things."

"Soothes the savage breast," Sally said.

He looked up, surprised.

"Most people get that wrong," he said.

She thought he was referring to the words of the song.

"Most people say, 'Music hath charms to soothe the savage beast,'" as if he were awarding her a prize for coming up with the right answer on a game show.

"Wow," she said, "that is one major error for most people to be making," smiling mockingly.

It pleased her to confuse him, to see his deep blush rise to engulf the flat lids of his washed-out blue eyes. The edge of her pleasure was crumbling under a dull wave of depression. A little too much wine in the middle of the day? But why did she feel so mean about Bill Grandstone? Why wait so expectantly for his apology?

Why did men count for so much with her? And most depressing of all, what if Bill Grandstone was right about Morgan Sweetsir?

Try it out for size on Bill Grandstone. *You know, Bill, there really is something wrong with my husband. I love him a lot and he loves me a lot, but I think there's something wrong with the way he is. It's hard to explain. I don't know what to do about it.*

Over coffee, Bill Grandstone said he was truly glad to see her so happy. That was as far as he went in apologizing. She forced a bright smile. She would rise to the occasion, as Jerry Greenspan liked to say.

"I'm the happiest woman in the world," she said. "I'm the luckiest woman I know."

Again he flushed pink and then laughed oddly, a short bark that irritated her.

"Sally, you're incorrigible."

She knew the word, knew how to spell it and type it, but didn't really understand what he meant by it. She looked brightly and steadily at him. Take it as a compliment.

"You know how I'd describe you?" he said.

If he wanted to tell her, he'd tell her, she wasn't going to beg.

"You're an incurable romantic."

"Is that good?" she said. "Or should I be taking medication for it?"

He shrugged. "It's preposterous. That's what worries me. You have no idea how preposterous."

"Jesus," she said, "if I had a buck for everybody worrying about me I'd be doing a lot better collecting than listening. For all the good your worrying is doing me. But thanks for the lunch, anyhow."

13

FROM HAVING STOPPED menstruating at all, she now bled so often and so long, there were hardly more than ten or twelve days during the month when she wasn't flowing. Sweets turned a squeamish back on her, lying curled into himself, falling asleep without a word or a fingertip touch.

She heard herself nagging, grumbling. Sick of everybody being so goddam sloppy, dumping their soiled clothes for her to pick up, dropping their wet towels on the bathroom floor. She kept her complaints general, but he knew she meant him along with the kids.

He hit her, whamming her hip against the edge of the washbasin. This time she didn't laughingly display the rainbow bruise. It shamed her to show him her nakedness now that he didn't touch her, now that her bleeding was obviously disgusting to him. His disgust translated into her self-disgust with this bitch she was becoming, as if on demand, to meet an essential male need she couldn't fend off.

Terrified at the risk involved, she opened a discussion of money, since it had become plain that they couldn't make out on what they were earning, couldn't pay the rent on the house and meet the various car payments and clear up the outstanding loans and debts and have enough left for food and clothes and gas and oil with the heating bills mounting sky-high. It was then the damn dumb dog got his hip broken, not having enough sense to stay clear of the automatic garage door. The accident cost a couple of hundred bucks to the vet right there, but first thing Sally knew, Sweets had subverted the conversation into a fit about hair dryers.

"Ya might start out by savin some money on those fuckin hair dryers ya always buyin. If ya cut out buyin a fuckin hair dryer every other day we might be managin a lot better."

She laughed at first. What was it that drove men mad on the subject of their wives' hair dryers? But when he didn't stop, going on and on in his low menacing voice, she was driven a little mad herself.

"Those fuckin hair dryers are built to blow out the second the guarantee is used up. Is that supposed to be my fault? Ya think I'm spendin my time misusing the fuckin hair dryer? Got nothin better to do than misuse a fuckin hair dryer? Those companies set ya up—build em to blow the minute the guarantee is ova. What am I supposed to do, go around town lookin like a pig, lookin like something the cat dragged in? Ya want me lookin like Kay Sweetsir, lookin like ya ex?"

He hit her, a hard whack across the side of her head, using the full swing of his upper arm. It rocked her. He immediately hit her again in a deliberate yet abandoned rage, accompanying the blows with his low-voiced command: "Shut up. Shut up, ya goddam bitch, or I'll shut ya up," hitting her again and again.

He was hurting her. He was meaning to hurt her. Oddly, she had no consciousness of physical pain—only a paralyzing absorption of extravagant emotional shock. This incident was different. Easy to excuse his other rages as not really directed at her. Sweets would just as soon kick the TV or Johnny's ass or knock over a chair as hit her, exploding in general rage at a vague maddening circumstance floating out there in the air. This was different. He *hated* her. He meant to hurt *her*. He wanted to terrorize her, to squash her, to shut her up forever if he could.

She ran from him to Laura's bedroom and locked the door. The kids were not yet home from an early movie. She listened to the silent house, alert to further movements from Sweets, but she heard nothing. She kept the lights off in Laura's room. It was a cold, brilliant night and beyond the window a blue-white light reflected the luminous moon on the snow, and the long, silent shadows of the pines surrounding the house issued a message of calm beauty and understanding. The contrast between her inner agitation and the outer peace of the scene created an unbearable tension. Still, there were no tears in her, not for the blows, and not even for the inexpressible pain of what was happening to their love, that living entity they had created between them by loving one another, a growth existing of them and apart from them, as real as the moon's glow, and as fragile. He was blasting that beauty out of their world, with her help. They were committing a crime together.

It was as much her fault as his. She had pushed him too hard. He was a good man but he'd had a hard life, he'd had his bad times. Couldn't wipe that all out overnight. And he worked too hard. He tried to do too much. Taking responsibility for Johnny and Judy. He didn't have to do that. Everything would be fine between them if it was just Sweets and Sally. They were so good together. All this other stuff weighing them down, responsibilities and bills, prices of everything going up, people's attitudes. And she was no angel, that was for sure. She shouldn't have said that about Kay, shouldn't have rubbed his nose in his ex. Any man would explode at that. She was beginning to learn what got him mad—why couldn't she just shut up when he started on her? He'd get over it. Their love was more important than all that other shit.

She was going to go out of the room, find him and apologize. She'd tell Sweets she knew she had earned those whacks. Maybe then he'd never hit her again.

When she attempted to reason coolly, it astounded her that making up could appear so sweet or that she could believe again, and again and again, that he would never again flare up at her, that he did indeed love her as she wanted to be loved, that he was truly penitent, that he needed her as much as she needed him. And she did need him. Loving him gave her her only sense of being useful in the world, apart from Laura. But Laura would grow up and grow away from her. Only Sweets was truly her other self when he was his best self, that glorious whole man she knew hidden behind his most shattering rages.

She shut her ears more and more to his comments. Clicked off the warning system that alerted her to his view of what was wrong between them. Her fault. It was women, by Jesus, with their fuckin crazy ideas that brought marriages to disaster. And he oughta know, as he said.

"I been married enough to be a expert. If ya'd only straighten

out, Sally, ya'd see, there wouldn't be a spot a trouble between us."
He used her father's harsh "Huh? Huh?"—a sound that cut her into
jagged pieces of anger she couldn't pull into place. "Ain't that
right? Ain't it? Ya gotta get ya head together, then we'll be perfect.
Huh? Huh?"

She nodded, avoiding his pleading, stupidly domineering expression. She refused that final submission she knew he demanded of
her, but it gave her no pleasurable victory to do so. She knew it was
her stubborn insistence on simply being herself that defeated him
more than anything else about their life.

Okay, she'd let him run things. She'd let the reins hang loose, let
him govern the driving. A dizzying chaos threatened. Who
shopped? Who cooked, who forced the kids to take their baths and
straighten their rooms, who changed the linens, did the laundry
and the ironing, prepared the meals and the bag lunches, paid the
bills, planned the budget? And what about the dog? Who worried
about that dumb hulk if she didn't?

The trick was to do what had to be done and act as if she wasn't
doing anything. The trick was to make Sweets feel that it was he
who was doing everything.

It was exhausting.

She managed her new technique for two weeks. On Friday her
car broke down again. Sweets picked her up at her office after he'd
finished work. His entrance brought an animal power and beauty
into the soft routinized emptiness of the office atmosphere as if the
clanging of a bell were waking them to the consciousness of what
real life was about.

Jerry Greenspan's wacky kid was hanging around the office waiting for his daddy to finish signing the letters she had typed. Sweets
played around, boxing with him, and even that impossible kid followed Sweets with adoring, shining eyes and was tamed.

Jerry Greenspan emerged from his office, a batch of signed letters
in his hand. Standing alongside Sweets, the little man was shrunken
to a dried-out husk. He tried to greet Sweets man to man, slapping
Sweets on the shoulder, but he seemed a little boy lifting himself to
be hugged by a big daddy.

She took Sweets's arm and walked out of the office like a queen
leaving with her king.

"They ain't a woman in that office wouldn't give her right arm to get ya," she said.

They had stopped at the post office, so she could tend to the office mail. It pleased her that Sweets was standing by while she completed her work. It restored some of her natural self-esteem. She heightened her compliment by suppressing the cultivated speech she had taken such pains to learn. She knew he didn't like her to talk like an out-of-stater. She exaggeratedly broadened the flat vowels, dropped her endings, raised her voice.

"Ain't a woman in my office wouldn't give her right arm gettin her hands on a man like my husband."

Let everybody in the post office hear her pride in him.

He kissed her when they were settled in the cab of the truck out in the parking lot, kissed her not with the routine attention of a husband but as if they were lovers on a date, insistent, hot, yet slow-savoring. It was a good evening. They hung out at the Hilltop for a while, handsome King and Queen of the Hilltop, greeting the people, then home to eat a little, and drink more. With the house to themselves, Sweets toyed with the notion of playing one of their old games on an overturned chair, costumes and all, but they were uncomfortably worried that the kids might return soon. On so good an evening, it seemed they didn't need any games, didn't need more than their bodies and their hungry love and the new delicate tenderness their quarrels had taught them about their fragilities. They hadn't done it in so long it was almost like a whole new thing. And she was okay, too, no bleeding.

She ignored his hiding under the covers the next morning. How could he be depressed—after the beautiful night they had had? It was early in the afternoon when she decided to rouse him; almost one o'clock. She had let Sweets sleep late while she did the weekly grocery shopping and took the dog for his last checkup at the vet's, using the truck for the errands. When she got back, she washed her hair, did the weekly cleaning, kept the kids as quiet as possible during breakfast, shooed them out. She drove Judy to Kay's for her regular visit. Back again, she ran a laundry through the machine, folded and put the clean clothes away, tiptoeing in and out of their bedroom without disturbing Sweets. She saved scrubbing the bathroom until after Sweets used it. She watered the plants. She cleaned the dog dishes. Her orderly house, clean and polished—all its gadgets intact—was working perfectly. A good sign. Only now it was time to rouse Sweets. He was interested in a sale on down jackets at Benny's Bargains. That would be their first stop after he finished the good breakfast she prepared. No, first stop was the dump. She had bagged and tied the garbage. All Sweets had to do was swing it into the truck, handle it at the dump. They'd take their time at Benny's, looking at a jacket for him. Or anything else Sweets wanted to do. Then home. She had taken pork chops out of the freezer, no big deal to cook dinner. Then maybe take in the Walt Disney movie over to Hartshead; do something as a family with all the kids, for a change.

She freshened her makeup before she woke Sweets. She looked great; her hair looked great. All would be well, she insisted, even while he still lay curled in an inward S with the covers over his head. She turned off the click in her head. Harder to control the anxious banging of her heart. She forced her voice into gaiety. She was happy. Love was safe as she playfully stripped the covers from him and announced the day's plans.

She knew before he hit her that she had done it all wrong. No way to start a man's day off. Preplan his whole schedule. Throw the garbage in his lap, along with chops for supper and a family outing to the movies. Stupidest piece of managing she had ever done in her life. *Mis*managing. Forget happiness, forget safety—think *manipulation*, she told herself.

He hit her again. Quite suddenly, from her reasonable stance, she had never hated anybody so thoroughly as she hated Sweets—crazy, naked, raging beast, murder in his blue-black eyes, and limp death strangling his penis. When she hit the floor, he pulled back, his scarlet face a stranger's mask of answering hatred. No longer pretty, the birds and snakes of his tattoos were now part of the alien menace of his anger.

He said, "Shut up. Shut up, ya goddam bitch, orderin me around like a goddam sergeant, shut up, shut up," in the low voice that terrified her more than if he shouted.

Was he going to kill her? Some part of her welcomed death at his hands. If love could swing so easily to cold hatred, then whether they ended in a blaze of bliss or a blaze of rage made no difference.

She heard the thump of his bare feet on the floor and the slam of the bathroom door. She heard Laura whispering, "Mom? Mom?"

If he ever touches Laura, that will be it ran in her head.

"Ya glasses broke, Mom," Laura said. "Did ya hurt ya eye? Ya got a little cut over ya eye."

She had no sense of being hurt at all. She felt nothing, no pain. She couldn't remember any blows, or how or where she had been hit or even that she had been hit at all and was lying on the floor. She allowed Laura to help her up. One lens was intact in the broken glasses Laura handed her. She stood irresolutely, then carefully picked out the remaining shards in the shattered lens.

"Mom?" Laura said. "Ya okay?"

Laura stood too close to her. She could see the clear, innocent liquid in Laura's round, black eyes.

"Ya watch is broke, too," Laura said.

She gathered the watch into the same hand. The crystal on the tiny face was smashed and the metal clasp broken. When had that happened? She slipped the glasses and the watch into the pocket of her jeans.

In a few minutes, when she'd begin to feel more normal, she'd attend to the problem of fixing what had been smashed.

If she were somebody else looking at herself, she would have despised herself, turned her back on herself. As it was, she tried not to encounter herself but simply to move from task to task, from moment to moment without acute consciousness. Aware, from the sounds of his movements, that he would be coming back to the bedroom, she shooed Laura out and pretended to be entirely preoccupied with making the bed. He gathered his clothes and dressed, ignoring her presence. She kept her back turned when he left the room. She heard him slam out of the house after yelling some directive at Johnny. She heard the truck's motor starting up, then cough out, then start again. She was consumed by a rage so sudden there was no way to ward it off. She raced to the stairs. She'd stop him leaving in the truck if she had to throw herself in front of it. Out in the yard of the house she saw only the green tail end of the truck taking the corner.

"Ya bastard," she heard herself yelling. "Ya goddam fuckin bastard, come back."

They had no near neighbors, but she was ashamed, in that split second, of the possibility of anyone's hearing these sounds she was making. Then a secondary rage, fiercer than the first, carried her up the stairs to the bathroom she found in the mess she had envisioned while still in the front yard, and full of energy, as if on a job, she pulled down anything in sight not already on the bathroom floor, wet and dry towels, soiled underwear and socks, bathrobes and nightgowns, and then stamped, her breath whistling in her throat in a not-quite-uttered sobbing laugh, and then, as if on a more important mission, tore off into the bedroom to yank all Sweets's clothes from the hangers where she had so carefully arranged them. His clothing made a high pile in the corner of the bedroom. She stamped on them, grinding out of his slacks and jackets his smell and his presence, the sexual smell of him rising as she jumped and danced, mingling with her own smell, the smell of rage, like the smell of love, rising from their union even now while she cursed him, she cursed him, she cursed him and wished him dead.

Exhausted, she stopped.

Laurie was in the doorway watching with round worried soft eyes.

"Mom?" she said timidly. "Mom? Mom?"

"Get the fuck outta my sight," she heard herself yell.

Between exhaustion and the terrible hurt on Laurie's face, her rage evaporated. She had to lie down at once. She ached badly along one entire side. Flat on her back, weakness ruled, and she sobbed uncontrollably. She was a newborn infant howling its animal misery.

Then this release evaporated, too. Behind the howls, a concept was forming that stopped her tears. There was an emptiness beyond and within her so jammed with nothingness it left no space for anything else. There was nothing out there and nothing within— no love, no tears, no longings, no, not even the connection of hatred. There was nothing. Nothing out there but nothing.

She didn't know how long it was before she got up to place all the clothing neatly back into the closet. She walked across the landing and tidied the bathroom. She washed the cut below her eyebrow, applied makeup to cover. A bruise was forming. She wore her dark glasses in case her eye blackened entirely. She brushed out her hair. On one side, her body was stiffening into a long, massive ache. She took a couple of aspirins, then went into Laurie's room, and in the disguise of her grooming and the smile she used on strangers, she kissed her daughter.

"Forget it, baby," she said. "Go out and enjoy your Saturday. Call one of your friends. Don't pay attention to us fucked-up so-called grownups."

She grabbed her shoulder bag from the hall table, called out "So long" to Johnny, "Have a good day, Johnny," gathering her storm coat and scarf from the coat rack, checking again for the broken glasses and the broken watch in the pocket of her jeans. She'd get that started first. Get her glasses and watch fixed. Pick up the car. Then she'd come back and haul the trash off to the dump. Then she'd see. Maybe Sweets would come back to the house by then.

Returned to the house after a trip downtown and two trips to the dump (she couldn't fit all the trash in her little car in one go) her numbness threatened to be invaded by—what? She shoved aside whatever emotion struggled to express itself. No more. Nothing from now on. Remember that.

Her side was ablaze with pain. She searched among Sweets's dozens of pill bottles for a pain killer, then decided against taking anything stronger than more aspirin. Make her too sleepy to drive, and she had to keep moving, had to get out of the silent, empty house. She rechecked her appearance. The eye was definitely bruising noticeably, and there was a cushiony distortion forming on her lower lip. More lipstick. Make her mouth look as if she had smeared the lipstick in applying it.

She was so thirsty, it was like an illness. For an instant she entertained the idea of a swig of hard liquor. If there was some in the house Sweets hadn't gotten to. Fat chance. That's it, she thought, that's where he's at, that bastard's enjoying himself over to the Hilltop, fuckin dog, enjoying himself getting wacked, well he won't get the satisfaction of seeing me follow him in there like some kind of bitch hound, tracking the fuckin bastard down over to the Hilltop, apologizing like I always do, giving in to him, giving in like I always do, that bastard can sit and wait at the Hilltop till hell freezes over. . . .

She poured herself some white wine from a bottle in the refrig-

erator. She added mostly soda. She sipped at the mixture. Very
hard to swallow. She left the almost-filled glass on the kitchen
counter. Impatience drove her out to the car again. She had no idea
where she was going when she started out the driveway, but it was
clear when she entered the highway that she was headed for the
cemetery. Almost there, she swung back, detouring past the Hilltop. Sweets's truck was in the parking lot.

Big news. Ya knew it. So now ya know it for sure. Ya knew ya
knew it all along. So now ya know ya knew it. Big news. So what
else is new?

She drove on past and parked at the entrance to the cemetery. It
would be just her luck to have her dumb car break down on one of
the cemetery's icy roads. She walked through the deserted paths to
the end plots where Mama and Papa Ciomei sat up in the bed he
had carved in imperishable stone, side by side, holding hands in a
calm and loving companionship—forever and ever. Or till shattered
stone shall them part. A thin film of ice did not mar the perfection
of their communion.

"Crap," she said aloud. Vapor formed as she spoke. "Fuckin, lyin
crap. A load of shit."

She looked directly into the serene stillness of Papa Ciomei's self-
sculptured eyes. "Crap, Papa Ciomei," she said. "It's all nothing
but a crock of shit, and I bet you knew it too. Deep down."

She walked to the very end, to the high spot over the river, now a
blocked mass of grayish, milky ice. Fling herself over the edge and
it was done with, the whole messy try at living and loving. Yet
when a branch broke and fell below her, she drew back in instinc-
tive self-protection. After a while she turned and walked to her car.

Sweets was standing beside his truck, his down jacket flung open,
his arms spread wide to embrace her, his handsome face glowing
with excitement, his wonderful voice warming the air.

"Pretty smart detective work, huh? Huh? We got ESP, us two. I
just knew where ya'd be, when I didn't find ya to home, I just knew
where to find ya. It just come to me."

Underneath the glow of his energy and exultation, she recognized that he was afraid of her and that his fear carried an attendant threat. She could turn him down. She might not be ready to forgive and forget. He'd smash her then. If she wasn't ready to come

round, he was ready to smash her. He wasn't a man to take No from his woman.

She walked into his inviting arms, put her pounding head against his hard, broad chest. She was flooded with relief, with love, and with dumb hope again.

Yet the very next time he acted up on a Saturday night, arriving at the supper table looking for a fight, pushing away the food she had piled on his plate, muttering his surly "Ya really expect me to eat this shit?" she reacted before she had given her action a thought. She did it, she grabbed his plate of food in one hand and hers in the other and flung them at him—no, not exactly flung, but sort of ground the plates of food into the sides of his head, one slightly after the other, using both hands in a syncopated beat, first mashing in the left plate and then the right. She performed this unthinkable procedure in front of the kids, who sat frozen around the table in expectation of what awaited Sally in retaliation.

Sweets sat totally silent, his eyes closed. Spaghetti and chicken cacciatore ran down the wall, drapped itself about Sweets's hair, decorating his ears and lodged in his eyelashes, streaming down his undershirt and jeans, piled in a final mess on the kitchen floor.

Judy bolted from the table. She ran to her room, slamming the door behind her. Muffled screaming laughter filtered back to the soundless tableau around the table. Johnny and Laura were mesmerized into idiot statues. She wanted to laugh herself. She didn't care what Sweets did to her; it was worth the exultation of having hit first.

After what seemed like a long time, she saw that behind the closed eyes and forced stillness, Sweets was crying. She was struck by a panic Sweets's blows had never inflicted. She had done the unthinkable. She had humiliated him to the point of tears, and in front of the kids too. She waved Johnny and Laura away from the table. Released, they sprang free, accessories to a crime, getting off easy.

Her only defense would be to make it appear to him that she had gone crazy. She put on a hysterical tone, babbling apologies, desperately cleaning up with a roll of paper toweling, licking the food from his face, becoming hysterical in fact, crying and laughing, kissing him, calling herself crazy, an idiot, begging for forgiveness.

He opened his eyes. She was astonished to find a cowering fear behind the black hatred of his glance. His voice was almost too low to be heard.

"Listen, ya damn crazy loon. Ya better get ya head together, ya wanna make it with me. Cause ya ain't gonna make it with me, ya keep on the way ya doin. And somethin else." He shook a trembling fist at her. "Ya gonna clean up this shit, ya gonna clean up every last drop a this shit all by yaself, ya hear?"

He kicked a glop of the mess that had accumulated on his boot in her direction, and gathered a fistful of the guck from his T-shirt, smearing it on her face. She caught his hand in hers, kissing it, begging forgiveness. He struck her, and though she acknowledged the blow, she breathed easier. He was okay. She hadn't harmed him beyond repair. He still retained the courage to be mean and to hit to hurt.

14

To CELEBRATE their first anniversary, they went to Florida. Her idea. Two weeks' vacation. Judy was sent to her mother, Kay; Laura to Vin; Johnny stayed at the house, caretaking and dog-sitting. A leisurely trip south, three nights and four days on the road each way, stopping at Howard Johnson Motor Lodges all the way—Sweets's choice. Felt homey coming into the same room with two oversized beds, big enough so his feet didn't hang over the edge, color TV, terrific bathrooms, and the same dining rooms and menus wherever you went—Connecticut, Delaware, Georgia. Felt like coming home night after night after the long interesting day of shared driving, two hours off, two hours at the wheel, down Route 95, easy as pie following the Florida route, passing the same vacationers in their cars along the way, getting to know the typical occupants, old retired couples, neatly dressed, their clothes hanging on a rack across the back seat of their well-kept cars; messy family groups, two parents, two kids, one dog and a carful of junk to keep the kids amused; jazzy young fellows in their jazzy new cars, cutting in and out of lanes; college kids poured into sloppy vans, running from something, running to something.

On the road she learned that Sweets was shy of strangers and of new situations. Once they shot past Harmon Junction and the places where he was a big man, he shrank a bit, quieted down. He kept his tattoos under wraps, was how she described it in her mind.

Alone in the car with her, he behaved more like his usual self. He sang along with the radio, off key. He made a lot of noise, said anything that came into his head, told her all his old stories—service stories, sex stories, fight stories, sad family stories, out-with-the-guys funny stories, laughing his rippling laughter at her joking responses, roaring at his own jokes. He kept touching her while he drove; kept an arm around her, a hand on her thigh while she drove. They went to dinner in the Howard Johnson dining rooms, having spruced up first, like on a date. They made love every night in the big Howard Johnson beds. They were happy. It was the best time she ever had. Ever.

They spent the week in a queer structure on the beach at Clearwater, a hotel built in the round, their room facing a sea as smooth as glass, multicolored with wide stripes of water as warm as a bath, exotically different from the white water of the rushing rivers of their own state, the fierce cold depths of their open bays or the hermetic quiet of their secluded ponds, reeds swaying at the edge, a blue heron on the far opposite shore. Here the beach invited human action. A long pier was constantly filled with vacationing families fishing. The miles-long stretches of snowy sand beaches were peopled by bathers sunning on blankets, running and playing in bathing suits that exposed a lot more than was exposed in New England. There were always bathers in the sea. It was so tepid and calm, she and Sweets lolled for as much as an hour at a time on a float they had bought that was as big as a bed, riding the sea together like a couple of kids.

Even on the beach and on into the salt sea, Sweets kept his tattoos covered. He said he couldn't take the sun; she knew he was ashamed of his snakes and birds. He wore a long-sleeved V-neck thermal undershirt over his bathing trunks. His body was beautifully proportioned, but his eccentric outfit made him look a bit odd, like an older man pretending to be young. First thing in the morning, awakened by the excitement of day after day of hot, gloriously sunny weather, they took a walk before breakfast on the luminescent hard wet sand releasing the receding, passionately tinted waters. Little sandpipers ran before them. She stopped every two or three steps for another uniquely wonderfully convoluted shell, a perfect starfish, a stone as smooth as a pearl. They ate breakfast at the hotel. Sweet Florida orange juice, fresh-squeezed. Bitter-edged taste of chicory in the coffee. Virginia ham and fried eggs, grits on the side.

Sweets put on a show of being hushed and polite, made a point of nodding pleasantly to the help, to the other guests. He wanted everybody in the world to like him. He lied, put himself out, put her out on a limb in the name of making himself more pleasant, more likable to absolute strangers. Didn't matter whether they were waiters, little kids, ice-cream vendors, salesgirls, big spenders at the hotel, bars, restaurants, fancy shops in town—high or low, he needed to have humanity's approval. She hardly listened to his lies. He told a chance acquaintance on the beach that he was "in construction," letting the man assume Sweets owned his own company. Told another couple his wife didn't work, she was too busy raising their three kids. Told the couple they had been married for seventeen years. She smiled and nodded. What did she care what he said, as long as he stayed pleased and happy? She rubbed more lotion on her now stunningly tanned legs, rolled over on her stomach, sifted the fine white sand through her fingers and smiled to hear him telling the wife of one couple who had mentioned a college reunion that his wife was a college graduate.

She broke up later in their room, remembering the honorary degree he had conferred on her. "Ya forgot to mention the name of the college. After all, I don't wanta be the last to know. Yale? Harvard?"

"Don't ya know nothin?" he said. "They don't allow women in those schools."

But he avoided any follow-through. They spent their time alone, together. He used her as his excuse to get out of invitations he had encouraged from strangers, couples bored with one another, looking for diversion. They didn't want that kind of company. They only wanted each other.

"Thanks, we'd love to, but the wife ain't up to it. Not feelin perfect, little tired, ya know what I mean."

She didn't mind if strangers concluded she was a drag on this handsome, outgoing, social man she deserved to lose immediately to some livelier mate.

At night they cruised the strips, ate hot dogs, pizzas, wheatcakes, waffles, tacos, fried shrimps, deviled crabs, crayfish; they ventured over the long causeway toward Tampa, tasted Spanish food, black bean soup, paella, Cuban sandwiches. An incredible sunset put on a special show every night, night after night.

Nothing in her native New England had prepared her for this flat green terrain, these immense low-lying skies flushed with heat and extraordinary color, this soft night air, the lushness, the ease, the fun. Her own landscape, so admired by the thousands of winter and summer tourists, squeezed her heart; this landscape opened her veins to joy.

Alone, she boarded a tour one morning when Sweets preferred to sleep off the previous day of strenuous sun and sea bathing and a heavy night of beer drinking. At a stop called Sea Wonders, she fell in love with Peri, a killer whale.

Sweets thought she was kidding about how beautiful and smart and friendly she thought the whale was.

"I wished I owned a salt-water lake and could buy one," she said.

They were on their way home by then, driving north on the same highway they had traveled south a week earlier, stopping at the same Howard Johnson Motor Lodges with the same oversized beds and the same bathrooms (extra washbasin in the dressing room area); same dining rooms and menus (chopped beefsteak platter with french fries, tomato and lettuce and a slice of spiced apple); same roadside signs of SOUTH OF THE BORDER good for their laughs miles before hitting and passing beyond the actual complex; same turnpikes, gas stations, rest stops, same kinds of carloads passing and being passed along the way, same couple of drinks before going to bed, same close, loving nights.

Sally was driving, talking over the din of the radio announcer.

"Ya know that killer whales have a capacity for more intelligence than human beings?"

"Big deal," Sweets said. "Ya gone crazy on this subject? Or ya puttin me on?"

"Honest, Sweets, ya shoulda seen that whale. Ya know that it's been scientifically proven that the killer whale has a real sweet nature? They're very willing to help man, only the marine biologists can't figure out how to communicate with them. Ya know it's believed that the killer whale is the most intelligent creature on earth, on the whole earth? Including human beings?"

"Where'd ya get all this information?"

"Right there at Sea Wonders. I bought a whole book on it. Paperback."

"Ya musta read it wrong," Sweets said. "That can't be right. It ain't them that are smart, it's dolphins. Ya got it all wrong."

"I'm tellin ya, Sweets, it's the killer whale."

"How come it's a killer if it's so goddam smart and sweet?"

"That's just prejudice," she said. "The book explains it all. Whales been very misunderstood. And very mistreated. The pamphlet I read—"

"Don't care what ya read in that pamphlet," Sweets said. "From what I seen on the TV they are the ugliest creatures on God's earth, so I dunno where ya come up with beautiful. Maybe smart, I'll grant ya smart, but not beautiful."

"I'm tellin ya, Sweets, that creature was so huge and powerful and graceful and cute. And smart! Ya know when a killer whale is about two hundred yards from an object in the water, whatever that object is, whether it's on the surface of the water or under the water, without even trying hard the killer whale can tell the size and shape of the object, y'know, like a fish or a man or a boat or some other object, and it can tell if it's alive and if it's alive whether it's healthy or sick and what its state of mind is."

"Oughta hang out a license," Sweets said. "That's bettern an M.D."

She laughed.

"Okay," he said. "But has that Peri fellow any tattoos? And is he any good in bed?"

"Ya jealous of Peri," she yelled, delighted. "Ya jealous of me fallin in love with Peri. Well, she's a girl, nothin to be jealous of."

"Wouldn't ya know?" he said. "If it's a killer, it gotta be a female."

They had passed Harmon Junction by then and were less than two hours from home.

15

CLOSE TO THE TIME of their second anniversary, their finances got so bad they had to give up the house and move into an apartment, one of a group of run-down buildings owned by an old lady, a Beauchamp relative. Sweets was allowed to live in it rent free for some kind of half-assed caretaking of the place. For Sally, giving up her own house again was like suffering a death, but since she'd been through that loss before with Vin, a hard, coarse membrane of memory pulled her through. To hell with trying to live nicely. Some of the furniture had been repossessed. No matter. There was no way to make that dump look good. Or feel good, with Helen and Ty Parsons across the porch listening in on their private lives. Only good thing about the Beauchamp apartment was that they were living rent free.

She was on edge all the time these days. Screaming at the kids. Long periods of bleeding running eight, ten, twelve days, then a couple of clean days, and on to the bleeding again. Headaches, backaches, nervous as a cat. Dr. Graham's diagnosis was early menopause. At thirty-two years of age? Finishing her off before her life had hardly begun. She went to him regularly. Spread out on the table, knees bent, thighs opened, her gynecologist was into her more often than Sweets was.

Sweets's moods were worse than hers. He was drinking too much, smoking too much.

They were going to quit smoking together. She had made an appointment to visit a nonsmoking clinic, less hopeful about the value of the treatment than she was of the value of a trip bringing them closer. He had a layoff vacation coming up. She could tell he was depressed about spending two weeks doing nothing special. All the kids were at home. School hadn't yet started. They savaged the house with their constant bickering and snacking, their bedroom and bathroom messes, the empty Coke bottles and cans and crumbs all over the living room, the incessant music of the player, the blare of the TV. He beat up on Johnny at the drop of a hat. Surly as a beast to Laura. Avoiding Sally like the plague. Only Judy was getting fair treatment—not good, but fair.

Again, unbidden, the final warning in Sally's head: *If he ever lays a hand on Laura, that'll be it.*

She'd leave Sweets?

She worried about Laura, and not only because of Sweets. There was Johnny too. He and Laura were often thrown together alone in the house. They scrapped as if they hated each other, but what did that mean? And there was that pale, limp professor whose baby Laura minded. He drove Laura home, his tongue practically hanging out yearning after her young flesh.

And sixteen-year-old dumb baby Laura pleased that she was getting a rise out of a wornout asshole of a professor with a wife and three kids.

"Keep your mind on your work, baby, you go on to college and make something of yourself. You can do anything you want to, become anything you want to. I'll back you all the way. Don't make all the mistakes your mother did, okay?"

She never had the solid sense of having gotten through the dreamy vague heat of her daughter's black eyes.

She was working hard, creating overtime work, baby-sitting for Jerry Greenspan's kid, trying to earn enough to straighten out their finances. Sweets had bought way beyond the limit on his credit cards. She had gone to the bank and made a deal to pay off the debts, a heavy amount a week. She had given up trying to talk money with Sweets. It was too dangerous. She knew it would end in a fight. Yet she remained determined to get out of the mess they were in, out of the hole they were living in alongside Helen and Ty Parsons, where Sweets couldn't resist getting wacked with Ty at least two three times a week—almost every night these days.

What was unbearable for Sally was how easily Sweets was reconciling himself to the death of the life they had planned for themselves. Had it all been bullshit for him? Love was workable for him only before marriage? Natural as peeing for love to wither with marriage? Was that his real philosophy? And the good times were meaningless, the rare, fragile, nourishing love didn't exist except in her stupid dreams?

It didn't help her state of mind that it was a very hot summer. Muggy. Raining a lot. Downtown was so crowded with tourists it was exasperating to get around. Long lines at the supermarket, the main street jammed with gawkers gawking at nothing, heavy traffic on all the highways. There was no way to cool off that damn apartment. When she could drag Sweets away from Ty, it was to hang out at the Hilltop keeping cool in the air conditioning, drinking beer, watching the new big TV screen Gil had had installed.

Nothing dissipated the tension between them.

She planned the nonsmoking clinic as a diversion, but he emerged in a strange state. For her the whole experience had been a joke, but she had allowed the doctor, or whatever he was, to believe he had successfully hypnotized her.

"Do you love your child? Do you love your husband?"

Pretending to be asleep. "Yes. Yes."

"Would you poison your child? Would you poison your husband?"

"No. No."

"Cigarettes are poison. You detest cigarettes. You would not give poison to anyone you love. You love yourself, don't you?"

"Yes. Yes."

"You refuse to poison yourself. You refuse. Repeat, I will not poison myself."

She did a takeoff on the hypnotism routine, but Sweets didn't find it the least bit funny.

"Wasn't *my* idea, goin to a hypnotist," he said. "But if ya let yaself in for somethin ya might as well believe it. Might as well believe it's gonna do some good. Not as if it didn't cost plenty to take the treatment, ya know."

She drove in silence. She thought he had fallen asleep. But he spoke again. "Ya mean ya ain't gonna follow through? Ya gonna start smokin again—right away? Throwin out good money?"

She knew he was fixing for a fight.

"Listen, I'm havin enough trouble with bleedin as it is. I ain't aimin to start bleedin from the lungs too."

She couldn't have chosen a more distasteful comment. He turned aside and went to sleep. She tuned in the car radio, low, to keep her company as she drove. He hardly woke when they arrived, woke just enough to get himself into bed and soundly asleep by the time she was ready for bed. She had locked up, settled the dog down for the night, yelled the kids into their rooms.

When the alarm woke her, it was to the sight of Sweets turned from her, the sheet pulled over his head. It was suffocatingly hot, and Sweets had his head covered. He had to be in one of his shit moods. She reached for her cigarettes, then remembered and put them aside. One of these mornings she'd surprise him good. She'd pull the covers over *her* head. Blot it all out—breakfast, the kids, the dog, work and worry, Sweets and so-called love. See how Morgan Beauchamp Sweetsir liked that kind of behavior when it was indulged in by others. Do unto others. If she ever did unto others as others did unto her, the whole damn world would go to pieces.

She got up, showered and dressed. She was bleeding again, probably dying of cancer. That's the way it happened, no pain, just some little symptom, check into the hospital for tests and never come out again until dead. That's exactly the way it happened.

Let everybody shift for themselves that morning. It was too hot to worry about anybody but herself. Bad day ahead. She had promised to take care of her boss's kid. She had an appointment with her gynecologist at five thirty. She should be thinking of something nice to do with Sweets this evening. It was a vacation for him, even if he didn't really want one right now. She should take something out of the freezer for supper and let the dog loose and feed him. She did nothing. She didn't even look in Sweets's direction when she left the bedroom. She knew he was awake. He wasn't fooling her with that sheet-over-the-head routine.

Yet by noon, having had a relaxed light breakfast at the luncheonette and a calming morning at the air-conditioned office, she was ready to face any mood Sweets was in, ready to meet, handle, deflect, manipulate, tame—she was ready to make it all better between them.

She called the house. Johnny answered. "The bedroom door's closed."

"Can't you go see if he's up?"

"Not me," Johnny said.

She called again at twelve thirty.

"Still shut up tight," Johnny said.

"Well, when he wakes will you remind him to register Judy for school? And you and Laura have to register too, don't forget, it's the last day."

"Not me," Johnny said. "I'm not tellin him nothin. Ya better call again."

"Well get yourself registered and tell Laura. Can you do that at least?"

"Okay, okay," Johnny said. "Don't get hysterical."

She had chewed a lot of gum and eaten a lot of Life Savers to help with the nonsmoking. She was feeling jumpy and sick to her stomach, so she hardly had any lunch—cottage cheese and fruit and a cup of coffee. Then she called the house again.

Laura answered. She could hear Laura shouting, "Phone, Sweets, it's Mom."

"Yeah?" he said.

"How ya doin, Sweets?"

He grunted in reply. She had meant to be loving and pleasant but his tone turned her off.

"I just wanted to remind you that you have to register Judy at school. The big kids can register themselves. Just be sure they get over to the high school."

"Okay, boss," he said. "Anythin else, boss?"

She hung up.

He called her right back, yelled, "Don't ya hang up on me, ya hear? Might be ya think ya a big shot downtown but . . ." and hung up without finishing.

She phoned a half hour later. To apologize? Johnny said Sweets was out. She didn't believe that.

Dr. Graham's office called right after Jerry Greenspan had dumped his little boy on her and left her in charge of the kid and the office. It was the secretary telling her that the test results were in and that Dr. Graham would like to move up her appointment. "Three thirty okay for you?"

"Why?" she said.

The voice said, "Doctor would like to see you at three thirty instead of five thirty, Mrs. Sweetsir. Can you make it then?"

"Well, do you know why? Something about the test?" Sally said.

"Dr. Graham will explain when he sees you," the nurse or secretary or whatever she was said in that tone they reserved for patients who used more than two and a half minutes of their time.

"Okay," Sally said, "but I'll have to bring a kid I'm baby-sitting for."

The voice ignored her. "I'll put you down for three thirty," it said.

She locked her office at two o'clock and left the girl in the outer office in charge of the telephone. There was a limit to what she could do.

Her boss's kid was in one of his worst states. She could not figure what Jerry Greenspan and his ex had done to that kid. Hyperactive, they called it now. Plain spoiled rotten they used to call it when she was a kid. She bought the boy a Matchbox car before she took him into the supermarket. He busied himself driving it across the shelves and the stacked cans and boxes while she dragged him up and down the aisles. It was hard to think about supper. Spaghetti. Little hot for it, but everybody always liked spaghetti. She gathered all the fixings for a spaghetti-and-meat-sauce dinner and a big salad. She bought a lot of cold drinks and grabbed a handful of gum and fruit drops for the nonsmoking.

It was a shock to hit the heat of the parking lot. She was pushing the filled shopping cart with one hand, the other firmly hanging on to Ricky, but she had to let go of the child to load the bundles into the truck, and he took off, naturally, tearing across the parking lot in a weaving pattern, transforming himself into a siren-wailing vehicle. She dumped the grocery bags, raced after him, and gave him a good whack on his poor skinny behind. That slowed him down a bit, though he started whimpering and kept droning out his troubles until they pulled into the space in front of the house.

Sweets was lounging in a beat-up upholstered chair in the garage. The doors were wide open. She could see Ty Parsons and a couple of other guys in there with him—Eddie Duchamp and Billy Handy—laughing and jawing and drinking out of cans. Soda, she hoped, but it could have been beer. Sweets was sucking a lollipop too.

She knew he hated her barging in on him when he was hanging out with the guys. Loaded with bundles, clutching Ricky, she found herself breathless and nauseated. She made a great effort to keep her voice friendly. "Can I talk to ya a minute, Sweets?" Remembering to talk regular, none of that flatlander speech. That's what had gotten him so mad before, probably.

He took his time rising out of his chair, very deliberately replacing a tool he had been holding, rolling his eyes at the guys as if he was the most pussy-whipped man in the whole state. They kept their heads down as if she wasn't there.

She said, "Hi, Sweets. How's it goin?"

He rolled the lollipop around in his bulging cheek. She leaned her face toward him for a kiss, but he pulled away.

"Too fuckin hot," he said through the lollipop, "for that stuff."

She said, "I need to talk to ya a minute, Sweets. Could ya please come inside?"

He rolled his eyes back toward the guys, looking for their understanding sympathy. He shrugged his shoulders elaborately. But he followed her in. He didn't help with the bags until she almost dropped one trying to maneuver the screen door. Then he held the door for her. He acted nice to Ricky, rumpled his hair, patted his head, admired his Matchbox car. Nothing told her more clearly than that hypocritical pat that he was mad at *her*.

"Ya okay, Sweets?" she said, unloading the food. "Ya feelin okay?"

"Can't ya quit naggin for a minute? Jesus." He drew the stick of the lollipop out of his mouth, threw it past her into the garbage. The sound of his strong teeth crunching the hard candy affected her like an act of brutality. He took another lolly from his pocket, unwrapped it and stuck it in his mouth.

"Not smoking gettin to ya?" she said.

"Nothin's gettin to me," he said. "Ya wanna ask me somethin?"

Not only love created a living presence. Hatred also could be touched, breathed. It burned like heat in the room.

She said, "Ya mad about somethin, Sweets?"

He said, "Ya got somethin to ask me or ain't ya?"

Laura came to the kitchen door, tested the atmosphere, found it untenable, murmured, "Hi, Mom, ya home early," and quickly melted away, but not before Sally yelled out a reprimand.

"I'm sure nobody thought to get something out of the freezer for supper, did they?"

"Ya talkin to *me?*" Sweets said. His voice had gone very low.

"Talkin to myself," she said, "like always."

"Ya got things so bad in ya life, ya know what to do about it," he said.

"What's that supposed to mean?" she said.

"Figure it out," he said. "Ya so smart."

They studied one another.

"Ya wanna tell me somethin, what the fuck ya got to say?" he said. "I got better things to do, ya know, than listenin to ya asshole whinin and complainin."

"Please," she said, prodding for the good Sweets, for the loving Sweets who needed her, the Sweets she needed. "I'm nervous about this doctor's appointment. And I got the kid with me. I thought maybe ya could help me out with the kid."

He said nothing.

She said, "Come on, Sweets, let's not fight."

"Ain't me that's fightin," he said. "Ya wanna see fightin I'll show ya fightin."

She laughed. "No thanks," she said.

He rolled the lollipop on his tongue.

She said, "I'm afraid to bring Ricky to the doctor's with me. He's gonna humiliate me there."

"I ain't no fuckin baby-sitter," he said. "Ya should be askin ya daughter, not me. She some kinda privileged character around here? Huh? Huh? Not by my lights, she ain't. Ya could stand some straightening out on the subject of ya daughter, couldn't ya, huh? Huh?"

She detested that huh? huh? Did he think he was her goddam father? He turned away abruptly and went out, letting the screen door slap shut.

Laura was in the doorway to the living room.

"I'll take care of Ricky, Mom. He's a real pain in the ass, but what the hell."

"Don't do me any favors," she said. She was so consumed with bitterness it had to be dumped somewhere. Easier to unload on Laura than on Sweets. "I'll take Ricky with me. Just get the spaghetti sauce started, will ya?"

Big sigh from Laura. "Ya got the directions somewhere? So I can follow a recipe?"

"Oh, forget it," she said. "I'll be back in time. For all the cooperation I get around here, nobody would take the time to bury me if I dropped dead."

"Oh, Mom," Laura said.

Johnny walked in, imitating Sweets's swagger. He headed for the refrigerator.

"Ole martyr routine comin up again?" He smiled, cruelly. "Ya boss's kid is wreckin the livin room for us civilized people, Sally," he said.

"Be my guest," she said.

She mounted the stairs to her bedroom, less to check her appearance than to be alone for a second, but there was too much disorder in the room to find any peace there. In the full-length mirror behind the door she looked okay. It was the room that needed attention. She pulled the double bed together, covered it with the cotton spread Sweets had thrown on the floor. She hung up the good pants Sweets had worn to the clinic, flung on the back of a chair. Trying to determine whether the sport shirt he had worn could be used again without laundering, she found herself in a rage against the unoffending shirt, stuffing it into the hamper violently, as if, at last, she had located the true villain in her situation.

She splashed her bare arms and throat with after-bath cologne, changed into flat heels, brushed her hair and was ready to go.

The living room was a scatter of newspapers, comic books, empty cans and bottles, overlaid by a smell of adolescent sweat and stale cigarettes. Ricky had moved the smaller pieces of furniture to the center of the room and tied them together with a length of clothes line.

"What the hell?" she said.

"I dunno what it is with this kid," Laura said.

"Well, you could have stopped him," Sally said. "You kids been smoking against our orders?"

Laura shook her head in a wide-eyed transparent lie.

Johnny said, "Hey, Sally, ya know where the *TV Guide* is? We had it around here somewhere before that kid began his search and destroy mission."

"Just about all I have to concern myself with," Sally said, and sensed more than actually saw Johnny tossing his head and mimicking her. What she clearly saw was Laura smirking in appreciation of the stupid act he was putting on.

Screw them.

She yelled, "Get that stuff in the living room untied and put it all back where it belongs before Sweets sees it, if ya know what's good for ya. Make yourselves useful for a change."

Behind the wheel of her car, pulling out of that decrepit spot they called "the front yard" though it was nothing but a back alley, she ripped out making as much noise as she could, for Sweets to notice, but when he didn't, she backed the car around and ripped in again, screeching to a stop in front of the garage. That brought everybody to attention.

She called out to Sweets to please come over. She didn't clearly know what she had in mind. He approached her very slowly and stood off some distance so she had to speak up. He had a lollipop sticking out of his mouth.

She said, "Sweets, honey, please tell me what's botherin you. I hate to leave this way. . . ."

He interrupted. "I been listenin to ya shit all day. Ya keep askin me and askin me what's the matter with *me*. There is *nothin* the matter with me. There's somethin the matter, baby, but it ain't with me. Ya better get ya self straightened out. That's where the straightenin-out crew needs to be reportin for duty."

Helen Parsons was with his buddies now, and Eddie Duchamp's girl was also there, Corine Duchamp, Eddie's ex. They had taken up with each other again after their divorce. With Eddie and Ty and Bill Handy, that made quite a crowd. The hell with all of them, listening in, adding everything up all wrong.

Only she and Sweets knew what they meant to one another.

She said, "Please kiss me, Sweets." She tried to keep her voice low enough for intimacy but she had to speak up to be heard. "I hate to leave for the doctor when we're in this kinda mood. It's like I'm bringin bad luck along."

His face softened. Brightness glowed in his eyes as if tears were forming. He took the damn lolly out of his cheek, grunting, half-complaining, but some part of him was clearly pleased by her plea. He put his head down and leaning in kissed her on the lips. She clung to his mouth. Touch would melt away the meanness between them. His lips quivered with the familiar ambiguity she recognized from their first meeting in the Hilltop parking lot. He had always been cut right down the middle—his need to cling on one side and his need to flee, to get loose, on the other.

16

THE DOCTOR told her that the Pap smear, the second Pap smear, had also come back positive and that he wanted her to go into the hospital for a D and C and something she heard as "a colon biopsy." She had asked him what a colon biopsy was.

". . . cells on the cervix which are probably cancerous," she heard. He couldn't be sure, only the biopsy would tell for certain. And if they were cancerous then they'd do what had to be done.

She said, "I don't want to be waking up in the hospital with my insides gone and my breast cut off."

He looked disgusted with her. "Mrs. Sweetsir, we are doing tests at this point."

She couldn't remember any more of the doctor visit. Ricky had taken his clothes off and was jumping up and down on the office furniture, and she was preoccupied with calming him down, collecting his clothes, and apologizing to the nurse and the receptionist and to the other patients in the waiting room, explaining that he was her boss's kid and a hyperactive child, as if all she had to worry about in the whole world was that people understand Ricky wasn't her own child or her responsibility.

She was so confused that she had to turn around and drive back to check on what she was supposed to do next. Nothing, apparently. The receptionist said arrangements would be made for her to go into the State Medical Center as soon as possible. Question of an available bed. They'd let her know the next day. She'd be entering the hospital within a few days.

Automatically she drove into town to pick up Jerry Greenspan's

laundry and his boots at the repair shop. It was then she was sure
she saw Sweets and Ty Parsons going by in Ty's truck. She still had
Ricky with her, so it must have been then.

Where could Ty and Sweets be going? Heading out to the Hilltop probably. Helen and Corine already there with Eddie and Bill
Handy, waiting for Sweets and Ty, all of them feeling good in the
cool dim Hilltop catching a buzz. She'd never be able to talk to
Sweets about the hospital once he was wacked.

She made a U turn right in the middle of the Main Street bridge,
tearing through town like a nut until she picked up the truck ahead
on Capitol Hill. She honked so they'd stop. She could see Ty and
Sweets identifying her in the big side mirrors of the truck but they
kept on until they got to their stop, which wasn't the Hilltop after
all but the Trading Center. She pulled in and stayed in the car
waiting for Sweets to approach her. He took his time. When he
finally did, he was mad.

He said, "Ya better have a damn good excuse to be follerin me
all the way through town."

She said, "There's something important we need to discuss."

He said, "It better be important. Anyway it's gonna hafta wait
till me and Ty finish buyin this frigerator."

"What for?" she said.

"Because I'm busy," he said.

"What are you and Ty buying a frigerator for?"

"We figgered it'd be handy to keep out in the . . ." and stopped.
"Ya mind if I wiggle my ass without checkin it out with ya first?
What the fuck's come ova ya? Practicin to become a private eye?"

She said, "Ya know how tight our money is. Still payin off what
ya *already* bought," and at the fierce anger that hardened his face,
she quickly added, "I mean we bought."

He turned away in a rage. She hung around, suffering Ricky's
earsplitting noises while he drove his Matchbox along the back seat
and the roof of the car, waiting for Sweets to return and ask what
was so important for them to discuss.

Was it then she went back to the house? Yes, after she gave up
on Sweets, and it was too hot to sit in the car waiting.

She still had Ricky with her. She fixed the spaghetti sauce. Even
the kids were in an awful state. The tension in the household had

been injected into their bones, and they were all hyper, as bad as Ricky. There was the heat too. Laura had started the spaghetti sauce, but of course she had done it a little wrong. Sally fixed it, browning the meat separately and then the sausages. She drank some chilled wine as she prepared supper. It calmed her a little, but only a little. She was so alert to her body that she had the illusion her blood was running erratically in her veins, taking little nervous jumps and detours. She made a salad, heated a loaf of Italian bread she had stashed away in the freezer.

Sweets didn't appear. Had he really gone off to the Hilltop?

About five thirty she served the four kids their supper and left them on their own with their squabbles and their teasing of Ricky. She couldn't stand the noise.

No, that wasn't the way it had gone.

She had called New England Projects, where she knew Jerry Greenspan was supposed to be. She did that before supper, hoping to get rid of Ricky, but they told her that Jerry wouldn't be in until after seven, so she decided to feed the kids before she took Ricky to his daddy.

No, Sweets came back before she fed them. She remembered him slogging up the steps. That was before everything was ready, while dinner was cooking. It was still very hot, but there was a promise of coolness in the low, hazy sunlight. Backed by that romantic light, he looked beautiful in the doorway, relaxation and ease in the stance of his hips. The wine helped her open her arms to him.

He brushed past her. "Ya can smell the wine on ya all the way ova from here," he said. "No trick to stop smokin and start drinkin."

"Just havin a glass of wine," she said. "We'll be eatin pretty quick now, Sweets."

"Neva mind the food," he said. "I dunno when I'll eat. Don't feel much like eatin." He was chewing gum.

She said, "Honey, you've got to eat, you haven't had anything to eat all day."

He said, "How the hell would ya know? Ya don't give a shit about me."

She said, "Honey, what's the matter with ya today? Please tell me what's botherin ya. We haven't had a chance to talk all day. I still need to tell ya . . ."

That drove him right out of the house. But he must have come back in because wasn't that when the matter of the chain saw came up? He said he had to pick up a chain saw he was having fixed, it was supposed to be ready at six o'clock.

She said, "Aren't you comin right back? I'll wait supper for you."

She thought he said Yes. She must have had two glasses of wine by then. Maybe not. She drank liquor so slowly it took her a long time to drink two glasses of wine. Impossible to remember any of it clearly. She remembered asking Laura to look after Ricky.

"Like lookin after a hundred-mile gale," Laura said. Sally took that for consent.

She called out, "Wait up, Sweets. I'm comin with ya."

He said, "Ya ain't comin with me, wherever ya goin it ain't with me."

She said, "Honey, we always go places together."

He said, "Get the hell away from here," and opened the door of his truck.

She said, "How come suddenly I can't go someplace with ya?"

He said, "Ya gettin to be a real pain in the ass, ya know that?"

Ty Parsons came out of the other end of the house. Maybe it was because of Ty that she couldn't go along. Something between the two men that Sweets didn't want her in on. She knew how important it was to him to present a certain front to the world. Everybody's great guy.

It must have been then she fed the kids. She didn't eat herself. She was sure of that, because she waited to eat supper with Sweets. She called New England Projects again and glory be to God, Jerry Greenspan was finally there. She got Ricky's clothes together from where he'd dropped them around and she cleaned him up a bit though it was as exhausting as a wrestling match to manage him. Jerry was outside the building waiting for Ricky, so she just opened the door, let the kid out, waved at Jerry and took off again, but at the corner she remembered Jerry's clothes and boots in the trunk of the car. She made a U turn. She wasn't functioning right, that was for sure.

The air was definitely cooling off by then. Sweets wasn't home when she arrived, but the kids had cleaned up the kitchen in a manner of speaking and settled down, in the same manner of speaking, in front of the TV set.

She made an attempt to reason out her position. Sweets definitely had to be pissed at her. He was probably at the Hilltop working off his anger. The thing to do was to fix her face and hair again and join him at the Hilltop. They'd have a drink and talk it over and everything would be peachy keen again. Then they'd come home and have supper. She told the kids she was leaving. The Hilltop was almost empty. Too early in the evening, and a Thursday at that. Nobody had money left for the Hilltop by Thursday. Sweets wasn't there. She felt odd coming in alone, so she sat at the bar and jawed a bit with Gil. She ordered a Bloody Mary. Talked about the heat and prices going up. Fern Bowdoin came in and sat one stool away from her, but after he ordered his drink and it came and he sipped it and they were talking all the while, he picked up his drink and hers and suggested they go sit at a table. It wasn't the right thing to do but she did it anyway. She didn't care if Sweets came in and found her with Fern Bowdoin sitting at a table drinking and talking. She had a right to some human company, didn't she? She had known Fern since grade school. She could talk a little to an old friend.

No, she was getting things out of their proper order again. Before that, the doctor's office had called and the secretary gave her a date and a time to enter State Medical Center. That got her very nervous. That's why she talked so loosely to Fern Bowdoin, telling him she had to go in for a cancer checkup and how worried she was about Sweets. If she had to go into the hospital for a major operation and give up her job, how would Sweets manage? Just when she was trying to get them straightened out financially and all his debts cleared up? Fern was good to talk to, sympathetic and quiet, not pulling against her talk the way Sweets always did, as if Sally's having an opinion was damaging to Sweets, was an attack on him in some way. All Fern Bowdoin had to say to her was, "How ya doin, Sally, good to see ya pretty face again, how ya doin now?" and all that stuff troubling her poured right out of her.

She spent more than an hour with Fern Bowdoin. The sun was setting by the time she got home. Sweets was really pissed now.

The house was ominously quiet. Sweets must have put the fear of God in the kids.

She said, "Hi, ya ready to eat now?"

"Ain't hungry," he said, moving toward the screen door.

She tried to catch him and embrace him but he backed off.

She said, "For God's sake, Sweets, ain't ya even interested in what the doctor told me?"

He paused at the doorway, one hand ready to open the screen door, holding his breath in an elaborate show of pretended curiosity.

"Can't wait," he said, "I'm that interested."

"Well, it ain't as if we're discussin an ingrown toenail," she said.

He half opened the door. "Ya got somethin to say, ya betta say it fast."

She said, "I don't believe this."

He started to move out further.

She said, "Dr. Graham said it could be cancer."

He brushed aside the air in front of his face as if she were some kind of pestering bug.

"I hafta go inta the hospital next week. State Medical Center. For special tests. Then if it's, y'know, what he thinks it is I hafta have an operation, I guess."

He looked at her then, coldly and angrily.

"Oh, great," he said. "Great."

She said, "I'm scared, Sweets."

"Great," he said. He opened the screendoor wide. "Just what I needed. More problems."

She said, "Sweets, where the hell ya goin? We hafta talk about this. I could be in the hospital for a long stay. I could be havin to leave my job. What's the matter with ya, honey? We hafta talk about it."

He said, "What the fuck is there to talk about?"

"Jesus," she said, "is that all ya got to give when I need ya? Don't ya even care?"

"Shut up," he said. "Ya fulla shit. All ya lookin for is pity. Ya lyin about the whole business, I know ya and ya fuckin dramatics. Ya lyin. I'm gonna call ya doctor and prove it. Sick a ya lyin. Sick a ya self-pity. Ya'd do anythin to get attention. Everybody knows that about ya."

An unmanageable rage seized her. She was clearing the dish drain of the washed dishes and found herself smashing the colander against the faucet, cursing and yelling.

"Ya cut out that commotion or I'll smash ya," he said, very low. "Ya drunken bitch, went out and got yaself wacked, didn't ya?"

"If it comes to that," she said, "I c'n smell the beer on *you* from way ova here."

He turned back. His face was so bright that she thought he had relented, and she went toward him expectantly.

He said, "Got more important things to talk about. I sold ya car. I sold ya car for two hundred dollars. Ya better be glad that's what ya got for it because it ain't worth a cent. Did ya a favor."

She said, "Ya gone crazy on me? Ya must be crazy thinkin ya can sell my car."

He said, "Well, it's sold. To Helen Parsons. And I already got the money, so forget it."

Laura was in the kitchen, searching for a Pepsi. She headed right back out to the living room.

"That what ya bought the frigerator with?" Sally said. "My two hundred dollars?"

"Get off my back," he said. "Ya gonna be one sorry cunt, ya don't quit actin up. Ya turnin into one fuckin asshole, ya know it?"

"I'm sorry enough," she said. "Right now. Sorry I was ever fool enough to count on you."

"Ya don't know what sorry is," he said and shoved her.

She was caught off balance and fell against a kitchen chair. It tipped, rocked, crashed with her, and came apart as if it were made of paper.

Then he was gone. With Ty, no doubt, laughing at her. She got up off the floor, disentangled herself from the kitchen chair, kicking it. She heard herself yelling, swearing, crying, raging. She'd smash her car to bits before Helen Parsons got it. She ran out into the yard, slid behind the wheel of her car, accelerated so abruptly and drove out so fast she almost hit the old couple who lived in the first building down the alley. They were standing at the open trunk of their beat-up Buick, their arms full of grocery bags, glaring at her with sick, gray terror and fierce judgment. She swerved sharply and luckily didn't hit them.

Where was she going? There was nowhere to go. She drove to Denby Hill, pulled into the overlook, watched the last of the setting sun light up the farthest mountain tops while the great valley mysteriously darkened. Supposed to be beautiful. Cold, uncaring landscape attending to its own business of existence, spiteful and ignorant of a humanity that craved comfort. She would trade this melancholy blue-tinged sunset any day for a lush crimson Florida sky opening its hot arms to her.

All those out-of-staters loved this harsh landscape, and even plenty of locals pretended to love it, bending their stiff necks to its authority, submitting to its hard-luck demands. Sweets loved to fight it, to force it to yield some satisfaction, to subdue it to ribbons of roads out of hard rock, wiping out the swamps with hard dirt and packing a road on the earth's soft sinking surface. Up above Hartshead, where he and his work gang were putting in the new spur and cloverleaf, it was like being dropped into World War Three. Only a bare crew worked, but the area was blocked with enough equipment for an army, even choppers, and huge hunks of machinery drained the lower portions of the ground, sending out great gushes of whitened, pulverized sand and water. Hell must look something like this ravaged spot, with the last light of the sun falling on it like God's finger, pointing out a warning.

A couple of other cars pulled into the overlook. Youngsters in pairs or threes. She paid no attention to the first ones, but other cars were coming and going in such numbers she began to wonder. There was a van full of youngsters at the far end, and from the bustle it didn't take much study to understand there was some kind of drug transaction going on.

She pulled out. She went home. There was nowhere to go but home.

She parked out in the yard for a while, sitting behind the wheel, her tongue in her mouth dry and rough as sand. She could hear the kids fussing about a program, Judy's high-pitched voice screaming and Johnny's high-handed attempt at authority. Laura silent, of course. *Brought her up to be silent and to smile, like her asshole stupid mother.* Brought her up to think, *Be good and life will be good to you.*

She could hear the unsteady loud tones of the TV coming from Helen and Ty's living room, and from somewhere else the deep sound of men's laughter. It was Sweets in there with Helen and Ty. Laughing at her. But Sweets materialized in the yard alone, sucking a lollipop, strolling across from the garage to their porch with his free-swinging, conquering-hero walk. He saw her in the car, and he smiled, actually smiled, as if nothing had happened between them.

"Ya get any beer?" he said. "We're outta beer."

He hitched the belt of his blue jeans, moving the lolly from one cheek to the other.

"I ain't *been* anywhere," she said.

He looked baffled. "Thought I heard ya take off."

She got out of the car. "Ya oughta have somethin to eat, steada more beer." Her concern was automatic. "Bet ya ain't et anythin all day cept lollies."

"Ain't hungry," he said and started up the porch steps. He seemed to be losing all interest in her. "Ty might have some extra beer."

"I bet," she said. "Ya can count on Ty havin beer."

"If it comes to a choice," he said, "ya'd rather be sarcastic than breathe and eat."

She began to cry. She grabbed his forearm to keep him from walking away from her up the stairs. His skin was amazingly cool and silky to touch. Touch would heal all rifts between them. She tried to hold him by his arms as she teetered on the edge of the stairs, pleading for reconciliation. She recognized that what she said was incoherent.

"Honey, please, I'm so scared, what the hell's goin on, please hold me, will ya, let's calm down, I promise. Let's talk. I promise to be reasonable and calm. I need ya, honey."

He pushed her away. She fell awkwardly, sprawling down the broken steps, the uneven stair edges cutting into her flesh.

She yelled, "You bastard, you don't give a fuck about me. Well, if that's how it is, I don't give a fuck about you either."

There wasn't anything left to build on, nothing left to lose, so she wasn't going to pretend she was his pal talking the way he and his ignorant cronies did. She was going to talk right from now on, the way she had taught herself.

He said, "Shut ya mouth, shut up. Shut up."

She picked herself up off the ground at the base of the steps, brushing dirt and leaves from her bare feet. The debris clung stubbornly to her jeans.

"Oh, fuck it," she said.

He took her words for himself.

"Get off my back, Sally, I mean it, ya gonna get it good ya keep this up. Ya been a pain in the ass all day."

He walked into the house. She followed him, crying now.

"You don't care, you don't care. Mr. Nice Guy. Mr. Nice Guy to the whole world. But not when I need you. You don't care—I could die of cancer tomorrow and the day after you'd be drinking and laughing and having fun at the Hilltop."

He said, "Shut up. Shut up," in his low, low voice.

It was then she pulled her wedding ring off. They were in the kitchen. In a frenzy, she attached herself to his arms, hanging on with all her strength, clawing up his shoulders, pushing the ring at his chest, telling him to take it, it didn't mean anything to him, he didn't care anymore, he didn't care, he might as well throw it away.

He fought to get free but she fought as hard to stay close. One way or another she'd keep them close, if not in love, then in hate. This was one fight he wasn't going to walk away from and then return scot-free, smiling and acting as if nothing had happened.

He yanked himself loose and slapped her hard twice, once on each side of the head.

"Shut up, shut up, ya fuckin asshole. Get off my back."

He snatched her ring and pulled his matching wedding band from his hand, throwing both straight at her face. They missed, hit the wall behind her, rolled away.

He no longer looked like himself. He looked like a kid, trying not to cry.

"Gettin the hell out," he said. "I've had it with ya asshole complainin. That's how ya want it, that's what ya gettin."

She clung again. He hit her on one side and then the other, pushing and pulling her wildly. She felt no pain, only an exultant, airy fury.

"You can't do this to me, Sweets. You can't. You hit me again and I'll get you. I'll get you, Sweets."

He did hit her again. She landed up against the kitchen cabinets facing the open drawer. As if blossoming through some natural evolutionary process, the long knife became an extension of her clawing hand and of her liberating anger. She was glad to see fear on his face when she turned on him. He grasped her wrist, hitting her hard with his other hand, then grabbed both wrists, pushing and pulling her. They were locked into a hot spinning void where she no longer knew where she or Sweets began or ended.

What she knew for sure was that this was one fight she was going to win.

PART FOUR

17

THE LAWYERS were driving her crazy. They were looking for something from her she couldn't deliver—a definitive explanation, of herself and of Sweets and of their life together right down to its inconceivable end, that they could grasp in one hand and hold up to the light, a transparent glass ball, concrete and simple. Here it is, judge and jury. See how it was? So possible and inevitable and understandable?

Their aim was to have her walk away from the trial scot-free.

But they had an alternate approach. They showed her a paper they were filing.

OFFER OF PROOF FOR CONSIDERATION AT HEARING HELD PURSUANT TO RULE 11, etc. etc. etc.

INTRODUCTION

Sally Sweetsir is a 32-year-old woman who resides in Eatonville with her 16-year-old daughter, Laura Ciomei. She is charged with the crime of first-degree murder as a result of the stabbing of her husband, Morgan Beauchamp Sweetsir, which took place at their home on the evening of . . . etc. etc. etc. This presentation of background is made in support of the defendant's request for a sentence of probation in the event that a plea of guilty or nolo contendere is entered by her to this charge, etc. etc. etc.

She didn't read all the papers she was given to consider, not every word, that is. She was suffocating under a mountain of papers she couldn't connect with Sweets's death. There was the mourning emptiness of Sweets gone; and there was Sally Sweetsir charged with first-degree murder. The two didn't come together for her.

She was having coffee at the luncheonette with Ellen Mahoney, one of her lawyers. Of the three lawyers working on her case, she liked Ellen Mahoney the best. She usually preferred men to women, and when she first met the Public Defender team her attention gravitated to the male members, a thin nervous New York Jew who headed the team, Michael Bronenfeld, called Mike, and Kris Kerkorian, supposedly another New York Jew according to local gossip, actually a second-generation Armenian born and raised in Providence, Rhode Island, and, in fact, a practicing Catholic.

It amazed Sally how hard these three were working to get her off. She went through the motions of expressing gratitude, though she wasn't sure that she actually felt any.

"It's our job," Ellen Mahoney said, brushing aside Sally's thanks.

Ellen was an enormous woman, broad-boned, solid-fleshed, monumentally solid, so that Sally never thought "fat" looking at Ellen, but responded to her bulk with a sense of coming to rest, of harboring against anchored rock. Her hazel eyes in her open Irish face looked straight into Sally's—a gaze as clear and direct as a child's. *No bullshit.* There was absolutely no bullshit about Ellen Mahoney. She was Boston Irish. She hadn't been poor, but she understood poor—she understood what it meant to be considered one step above shit underfoot. Sally knew that in her bones about Ellen Mahoney, just as she knew about the no bullshit.

She had heard about Ellen before she met her, the usual town mixture of truth and misinformation. She was forty-one years old. She was something of a feminist heroine, written up in those magazines, *Ms.* and *Working Woman,* one of the first women to graduate (with honors) from Yale Law School, entering in her thirties, with three kids and a Ph.D. in something or other already behind her, plus marriage to a leading American artist. Sally arrived at their first meeting coated with reservations about this brilliant, privileged woman who was supposed to defend her. "New York smart Jewish rich," Sally had been told. She was expecting a knockout—

tall, willowy, swishy-skirted, big tinted glasses, masses of curly hair, loop earrings.

Instead, Ellen. She wore a loose cotton jumper (she was always too hot; all that flesh, probably) and an open-neck, long-sleeved shirt. No jewelry. Her legs, thick as furniture, ended in surprisingly small, pretty feet in black suede pumps. Her hair was short, straight, parted in the middle, hanging free in two clean, brown, gleaming sweeps on either side of her broad, flushed cheeks. She shook Sally's hand, smiled, looked directly into Sally's eyes with her clean, warm gaze.

Her artist husband had a long unpronounceable name, Roberto del Castillo. Everybody called him Castle. Ellen used her maiden name. From town gossip, Sally imagined Ellen's husband as an exotic foreigner, Fernando Lamas and Ricardo Montalban combined, speaking with a heavy accent, full-bearded, with burning eyes and a red mouth, sensual and ardent. Castle walked into the Mainway Luncheonette, where she and Ellen were having a cup of coffee, to give Ellen some message about picking up their littlest kid. Sally was introduced to a short, frail, clean-shaven fair man. Afterward, once she recognized the name Roberto del Castillo as one of America's leading artists, she began to come across all sorts of articles and little bits about him in magazines and papers. It seemed his family had arrived in Massachusetts practically on the Mayflower.

There *was* something wildly intense struggling in the depths of his strangely narrowed eyes, as if he were constantly squinting to sharpen his view of a scene, but there was nothing exotic about his speech—just the usual broad A—and he was so shy he hardly spoke at all and couldn't get away from the two women fast enough.

"Could I get the death penalty?" Sally said as soon as she and Ellen were alone. It seemed a foolishly dramatic question. Yet wasn't murder in the first degree punishable by death? "I mean isn't it the same as Murder One, like in the TV shows?"

"Sally, don't even think about the death penalty. It's on the books for very special cases, murder of officers of the law, and so on, but there's no way they're going to convict you of murder in the first degree. They have to prove premeditation."

"But if they prove it, if they do, what can they do to me?"

"Life imprisonment."

Ellen put both her hands on the tabletop, leaned across, close to Sally.

"We're going to get you off, Sally."

"Tell me more about the law," Sally said. "If you don't mind, that is."

"I'll tell you anything you want to know."

"I don't know anything, that's the trouble. What else can they do?"

Ellen looked at her directly. "You mean how can you be charged and what are the penalties?"

She nodded.

"It's complicated, but here it is—in a highly simplified form. In this state the next charge is murder in the second degree. That's without premeditation." She paused, flushed a little. "You understand what premeditation is?"

"Yes," Sally said.

"Okay," Ellen said. "So murder in the second degree is without premeditation but with malice. We're not concerned about that either. We're looking toward . . ."

"Wait," Sally said. "What could I get if they prove malice?"

"Life—or whatever sentence the court orders. But we're not planning to defend you on those charges. . . ."

"Well, what about that probation of sentence document," Sally said.

"You play every angle," Ellen said. "We're just at the talking stage. It's your case. You make the final decisions. We're talking about manslaughter at the worst, justifiable homicide at the best."

"What do they mean?"

"Justifiable homicide is a killing occurring during a just and necessary defense. Manslaughter is either a recklessly negligent killing or an intentional killing that has been sufficiently provoked into commitment through the heat of passion."

"But what do they mean in terms of penalties?"

"Justifiable homicide—you're home free. There's a wide variation of sentencing for manslaughter—the law calls for one to fifteen years."

There was a short silence between them.

"Any other question?" Ellen said.

"Do they call it manslaughter if a woman's killed?" Sally said.

Ellen smiled. She had begun to shuffle through the mass of papers in search of a particular one. It seemed there was some question about Sweets's last words that could be very helpful to Sally's case. Sally picked up a couple of documents Ellen had pushed aside.

"Can I look?"

"Of course," Ellen said. "Just stop reading if you hit something that upsets you, love. There are quite enough taxing things you'll be required to do."

"Love." "Taxing." Ellen used affected expressions that irritated Sally. "How are you coping?" The only thing she didn't like about Ellen Mahoney.

She picked up a document, read:

COMES NOW THE STATE, by and through Lyman Bannister, Hartshead County's State Attorney, and respectfully submits the following Memorandum of Law:

1. WHETHER EVIDENCE INADMISSIBLE AS A PART OF THE STATE'S CASE IN CHIEF IS AN APPROPRIATE SUBJECT FOR CROSS-EXAMINATION WHEN THE DEFENDANT TAKES THE STAND AND TESTIFIES AS TO THE FORBIDDEN SUBJECT AREA.

She put that down, picked up another, read:

COMES NOW SALLY SWEETSIR, by and through Michael Bronenfeld . . .

It was a very long document. She put it aside. COMES NOW THE STATE AND COMES NOW SALLY SWEETSIR. IN A FIGHT TO THE FINISH. COMES NOW SALLY SWEETSIR ON A WHITE HORSE. COMES NOW THE STATE ON A BLACK HORSE. TOURNAMENT OF THE WEEK. BEST SHOW IN TOWN.

She leaned her head back against the high wooden back of the booth.

"You okay?" Ellen said, looking up from her search.

She nodded, lit a cigarette, ordered another cup of coffee, tried to create an isolated zone between herself and her situation.

Kris Kerkorian joined them, sliding into the booth with difficulty in his heavy down jacket. He too had a briefcase filled with documents that he put down on the table. He said hello, then stood up again, hung up his jacket, excused himself to make a phone call, and when he finished at the phone, she saw him go around the corner to the men's room.

It seemed they had all these different sworn statements as to Sweets's last words. It took her awhile to understand that they were shopping for the best one, the one that had him forgiving her. And of all people, Ty Parsons had supplied the useful statement.

Judy Sweetsir had sworn that her daddy's last words were addressed to her:

"Goodbye, baby Judy, be good to ya mama and never forget ya daddy loved ya, honey."

Sally laughed. "Nobody believes that, do they?"

Kris Kerkorian explained that Judy's statement didn't weigh on either side. She was only eight and she wasn't clear whether "mama" referred to her stepmother (Sally) or her real mother (Kay).

"He never said it," Sally said. "She's a baby, keep her out of this, can't we?"

It was hard to follow what they were hoping to achieve. She had stabbed Sweets. She was guilty. She was prepared to pay for what she had done. She expected to pay. What were they dragging baby Judy into it for?

Johnny's version was quite different. Kris Kerkorian was clearly worried about Johnny's version. It began with a long rambling account of his name being Matthews, not Sweetsir, though Sweets was the only goddam human being in the whole world who gave a goddam about him. Sweets had taken him in just like his own son since the time he was nine years old. Sweets was the best goddam guy in the whole world. He wanted that clearly understood. Then he explained that he had been in the living room with his sisters Judy and Laura, who weren't really his sisters of course, Judy was Sweets's kid with Kay, and Laura was Sally's kid with her first husband, and like he said before he didn't belong to either one, flesh and blood, or to Judy or to Laura either, even if he was living with them all together like one family since Sweets and Sally married more than a year ago he guessed it was, and it hadn't been bad, he'd say it had been pretty good, better than his daddy's other marriage even if Sweets and Sally did go in for a lot of scrapping. Sally's fault. She kept after him and after him. She was always on top of him, there was no other way for Sweets to go. Sweets had to clobber her like any fellow had to now and then, a woman like her.

Anyways he hadn't been paying that much attention to them fighting and yelling cause it had been going on for days, at least it seemed like days. Since the night before, he thought it was, and getting hotter and hotter by the hour and the minute. All he was interested in was watching a special TV show about the FBI and the KKK coming on just about the time slot that Sally and Sweets were beginning the clobbering part of the fight. But he went into the kitchen at the first station break for something to snack on and that's when he heard Sally yelling, "I'll get you, Sweets." He heard his daddy pleading with Sally, "Now, honey, stop, honey, please stop, I love you, honey, what are you doing, you just calm down and stop." Then he saw her stab Sweets, he saw Sally stab his daddy. He heard Sweets say, "Honey, what have you done? Stop, stop, please stop." Then Sally yelled to get help, to call an ambulance, and Johnny ran across the porch to get Ty Parsons.

Kris Kerkorian assured her that Johnny's highly damaging version was easy to attack. Johnny was young, upset and very impressionable, but most important he had rushed to the neighbors hollering that Sally had shot Sweets.

"All the first reports to the police and the ambulance were of a shooting," Kris said. "Question of reliability."

With all the down off him, Kris Kerkorian was small, short and fair to the point of being colorless. To Sally, his way of bringing his lips together in smug satisfaction when he finished a sentence made him seem silly.

Sally said, "Why don't we leave Johnny out of this? He's got enough to put up with. He's just a kid. I don't want to attack his reliability. He was frantic."

"It's not entirely up to us, Sally. The prosecution is definitely going to use him. They'd be idiots if they didn't." And Kris rested his lips smugly on the thought.

Helen Parsons' version. She was sitting in her living room with her feet up on a chair watching the TV special about the FBI and the KKK, not paying attention to the fight going on next door. Fighting in there wasn't that unusual. She had heard enough screaming from Sally Sweetsir to last her the rest of her natural life. Sally was always screaming at her kids and screaming at Sweets and screaming at the dog, she just didn't pay that much attention to it anymore, though she had it in mind that they were banging one another around in there, so when Johnny came tearing over saying Sally shot Sweets it didn't even surprise her that much and she got up and followed her husband Ty on over there and Sally Sweetsir was crying and sitting on the floor in her bare feet, carrying on begging her husband's forgiveness and saying she was sorry, she was sorry, and Morgan Beauchamp Sweetsir was laying on the floor dying. Sweets was laying there bleeding to death and he opened his eyes.

He said, "Ya shoulda thought a that sooner, honey, ya shoulda thought a that before ya killed me, honey."

Then Sweets closed his eyes and died, one of the sweetest guys in the world. Ya couldn't locate a sweeter guy than Morgan Beauchamp Sweetsir, and she had known him all her life practically and so had her husband, Ty.

"It's interesting how they make up all those honeys," Sally said. "They've got me honeyed outta sight in those stories they're making up."

"Nothing like that was said?" Kris said. "Your husband said nothing like that to your best knowledge?"

"Come to think," Sally said, "I think something like that was said, but I'm sure it was Helen Parsons who said it. I seem to remember her saying something like that."

"Try to remember everything you can," Kris said. "Try to sit down and write it out, if you can, just as you remember it, but don't show it to anybody but us. Okay? Can you try to do that?"

She said, "I'll try," but the thought of doing so was sickening.

There was still another version, sworn to by Ty Parsons.

"On the night of the event, after Johnny Matthews came to get me and my wife Helen and while Morgan Sweetsir was lying on the floor and I was tending to him, and while we were waiting for the ambulance to arrive, I heard Morgan Sweetsir say to his wife, Sally Sweetsir, 'Honey, I love you and I forgive you. And I know that you love me and that you didn't mean to do it.'"

They presented the statement as if it were a piece of cake, Ellen and Kris expectantly half-smiling at her across the table. A bullshit affidavit from Ty Parsons was some sort of triumph?

"Bullshit," she said. "Forget the idea of Sweets saying anything like that. He couldn't have if he wanted to. He didn't have the breath for it."

She saw the eager look fade from Ellen's eyes. It must have been Ellen who turned Ty around and got that statement out of him.

"He never said it," Sally said. "I heard everything Sweets said." She spoke in a light, quiet tone that labored to rise from the weight of the depression lodged underneath and the sadness that lurked behind the smiling surface of her eyes. It was an effect that baffled Ellen Mahoney—that combination in Sally of massive depths of grief and a surface of almost merry toughness.

"Besides," Sally said, smiling and shrugging in apology for undermining Ellen's accomplishment, "that's not the way Morgan talked."

She caught a veiled exchange of glances between her two lawyers that enraged her. Kris said he had another appointment, he'd have to leave her with Ellen but he'd see her at the office the following day when they all would meet together.

"Okay?" he said.

She smiled brightly. She knew what they were doing—throwing the two women together alone, for Ellen to work on her woman to woman so that she'd come around to agreeing to whatever they said.

Nothing wrong with that, was there?

Bill Grandstone had told her that Ellen Mahoney had done so well at Yale and gotten so much public notice she could have had her pick of the best openings in the big-city law firms. He said he had to admire her decision to go into Public Defender work in a New England town instead. Sally was supposed to be grateful to Ellen Mahoney for becoming a public defender instead of heading

for a big-city law firm and making a pile of dough? Kris Kerkorian
and Michael Bronenfeld were her saviors also? If they were, let
them work for it. She wasn't going to hand them her life on a silver
platter. She wasn't going to sit around saying Yes yes yes to all the
nonsense they dreamed up. They knew damn well Sweets hadn't
handed her a pardon before he died.

"Why are you smiling?" Ellen said.

"Am I smiling?" Sally said.

"Sometimes I think you're smiling when you aren't," Ellen said.
"It's your eyes. They always look as if they're smiling."

Sally said, "People have told me that."

"She's lovely. She's immensely appealing," Ellen Mahoney had
reported to the team after her first sight of Sally at the arraignment.
"It's not going to hurt our case one bit that she's as lovely as she is."
She could see Sally's appeal even though Sally had been a mess
after the night spent at the hospital and in jail. She was exhausted,
pale, dirty, her hair stringy and flattened. It was possible to understand one of the cops' description of her as "a plain-looking fair-
haired woman in her forties."

"It's a strange effect how your eyes smile," Ellen said, "because I
know how hard it must be for you, and how terribly sad you are."

Sally said, "I think I'd like another cup of coffee."

Ellen half rose from her seat, gesturing to the counterman to
refill Sally's cup, and caught Sally's mocking glance at her deferen-
tial act. *She thinks we're manipulating her,* Ellen told herself. *Are
we?*

"I want to win this case, Sally. We all do. I mean to win it. I always want to win any case I handle, but this is special. I want to
get you off. I mean to get you off."

The waitress came to refill Sally's cup. It was Brenda Poole, making a little extra money waiting on tables.

"You're in luck, Sally," she said. "Just made a fresh pot."

"You got to get lucky sometime," Sally said. "Right, Brenda?"

"Right," Brenda said and half patted, half hugged Sally.

"Some people have stayed real nice," Sally said to Ellen,
"through this whole thing."

She took a long sip of the coffee she drank black, then lit another
cigarette.

"Not Helen and Ty Parsons. It's been hell living alongside them."

"That's an important statement," Ellen said. "He's a hostile witness. That statement is a tremendous help to the case."

If she knew how, Sally would have liked to explain to Ellen how she, Sally, and her case, The State vs. Sally Sweetsir, were two different entities, but she couldn't catch hold of that concept solidly enough to pass it on.

"Don't you understand? It gives us a handle. We need a handle on this case."

She didn't understand. She saw Sweets, his head fallen to the side, his eyes fixed on her.

"He was dying so fast he couldn't have made a long speech like that. He didn't have the breath for it," she said.

"There were other people in the room," Sally said. "No two people heard the same thing. Y'know what I mean? Did anybody else hear Sweets forgive me?"

Ellen Mahoney was sure she was being mocked now. "We're trying to keep you out of jail, love," she said.

"Good luck," Sally said. "Isn't that where I should be? In jail?"

The ambiguously sad smiling elements in Sally Sweetsir's eyes moisturized into a mist clouding the prettiness of blue eye shadow and black mascara. After a long draw on the cigarette, she replaced the one she was smoking. She pressed a manicured finger against the straight bridge of her small nose.

"That's a funny habit you have," Ellen said, "pressing your nose when you inhale."

"I know," Sally said. "It drove Sweets nuts. At first he thought it was cute. I don't even know I do it."

"What kind of man was Sweets?" Ellen said. "Tell me about him."

Her life on a silver platter, delivered on order to her lawyers.

"I hate the world for what it did to him," Sally said.

"What did it do to him?"

"Ruined a beautiful man."

"How did it do that?"

"By being the way it is."

"I don't understand that," Ellen said.

"That's because you don't live in our world," Sally said.

"We all live in the same world," Ellen said. "You lived in his world, didn't you, love? And look at you, it's terrific the way you're sticking things out, living in the same place, staying on the same job, seeing it through."

The moisture was gone from Sally's pretty blue eyes. The smile persisted in them.

"That's a funny expression you use a lot," Sally said. "'Love.' Where'd you get it?"

"It's a family expression. My mother and my sisters and I all use it. If it bothers you, I won't . . ."

"Doesn't bother *me*," Sally said. "Just wondered."

"People here say 'dear' a lot," Sally said. "Even when they hate you. Dear. Honey."

She finished her coffee, put the cup away from her.

"I did it," Sally said. "You know I did it. And I said I did it. I said it a hundred times. I said it and I said it. And I signed those papers."

"We know," Ellen said. "The law's a little more complicated than that. That's our job. But we have to have your cooperation."

"I'd give my right arm for Sweets's forgiveness. He never said it, Ellen."

Ellen brushed her hair back from her broad cheeks. She took both hands and rubbed her eyes hard for a while, then she leaned forward across the table.

"Listen, Sally, in an event like this you get very confused reporting from the participants and witnesses. The lawyers play with that. You have to use everything. We're not asking you to lie. You're not the one saying he forgave you. Ty Parsons is. Just let it be. Forget it. It's not important. It will be introduced as evidence, Tyrone Parsons' statement about the event . . ."

Sally couldn't bear the use of the word "event." It was impossible to endure her lawyers' coolness, their documents, their terminology. Kill someone you love and hear it called an "event."

She interrupted, "You know what Sweets's last words were? The last words he spoke to anybody before he died? He said them to me. He said, 'ya stupid shit,' those were his last words. 'Ya stupid shit.' Anybody hear that?"

Ellen rested her head on her hand. "We have all those contradictory reports."

"Like what?"

Ellen straightened her broad back, began shuffling through the mass of papers again. "Well, we have Johnny and Helen Parsons and Judy and the ambulance crew. Ty Parsons, of course. Your daughter Laura. The arresting officer and the other cops."

"And what do they say?"

"Mostly their reports are on what you were saying."

"Why didn't I shut up?"

"Don't blame yourself," Ellen said. "You weren't in a state to govern yourself."

"What about Laura? Where's her statement?"

"I have it here somewhere," Ellen said. She glanced at her watch. "Damn," she said, "I have to pick up my boy."

"Okay," Sally said. "Forget it."

"They'll keep him till I get there," Ellen said.

"Here it is," Ellen said. She began reading rapidly, turning the pages. "Laura Ciomei, age sixteen . . ."

She stopped, startled. "Sixteen? How can she be? You're so young."

"It's easy," Sally said. "All you do is become pregnant at fifteen."

Ellen returned to her reading in a rushing whisper.

". . . fighting in the kitchen . . . watching that TV special but I could hear Sweets calling Mom a fuckin asshole, that kind of stuff . . . heard Mom say, 'You can't do this to me, I'll get you.' Then Johnny was yelling Mom shot Sweets and we all run into the kitchen and he was laying on the floor looking terrible, his eyes rolling up showing the whites, and Mom was like I don't know what, not understanding where she was or what was going on, and she kept saying 'Oh, did I hit you?' And Morgan said 'Yeah ya stupid shit, ya hit me all right,' and he closed his eyes. Then Mom yelled for Johnny to get help and she was pleading with Sweets to 'breathe, breathe, honey, please breathe,' and 'I love you' and 'I didn't mean to do this . . .'"

"Okay," Sally said. "Don't read anymore. Unless there's something more about what Sweets said."

She watched Ellen reading rapidly, her lips moving, the words shaping in a whisper under her breath.

"Mom was begging us to help her take Sweets to the hospital cause the ambulance wasn't coming fast enough but we couldn't lift him up and Ty and Helen wouldn't let us touch him and maybe we shouldn't, his eyes were all glassed over . . ."

"Okay," Sally said, her head down. "Okay."

"He didn't say anything more, according to Laura's statement," Ellen said.

Her chest was tight with the pain of forcing Sally back into the event. She thought Sally was crying, and it was a shock as Sally lifted her eyes to see them mysteriously and mockingly smiling. If they were smiling.

"You have to admire my kid Laurie," Sally said. "She was the only one there with an accurate memory."

Did Ellen imagine it or were Sally's eyes even more mocking when she spoke again?

"Sounds more like the real thing, wouldn't you agree, love?"

18

THEY WANTED her to write about what had happened. Mike had called it "recalling your exact, as far as possible, *exact* remembrance of the event." Alone with Ellen later, she said she couldn't do it.

"I can't. Don't you understand? I can't."

"Yes." Ellen understood. She came up with a compromise solution. She would prepare a batch of documents for Sally to read and comment on.

"Don't read anything that's upsetting. When you hit something that's too upsetting, go on to another affidavit. Just put down on paper your reaction to the statement. That's all. Don't worry about how you express yourself. Just get it down. Or anything else you feel like getting out of your system."

"Will you be the only one to read it?"

"I can't promise that, Sally," Ellen said. "I'll do my best by just passing on the general nature of your information."

And added, after a pause, "We all want to win your case, Sally. You know that. That's the only reason we're pushing you so hard."

"I know," Sally said. "Don't think I'm not grateful."

"Don't say things like that," Ellen said. "No need. Come by the office after work tomorrow and I'll give you material to start on."

There were two stuffed briefcases of documents for her to take home. She began her work after supper following Laura's nightly ritual of cheerleader optimism about the outcome of the trial.

"We're gonna win, Mom. We gotta win, Mom, nobody could blame ya for what ya done. Nobody will. Not when they hear it like it really happened."

She'd settle for fifteen years in jail and count herself lucky not to be given life imprisonment—if it weren't for Laura. She didn't want Laura with a mother in jail.

She steeled herself against large, dangerous possibilities by concentrating on small, hard tasks. She forced herself up and out every morning, properly put together. She had been bitten by those descriptions of herself in various affidavits as "plain," "about forty years old," "broad-hipped woman wearing blue jeans," "stringy-haired," "dirty feet, bare." She kept her hair washed and color-rinsed, her eyes made up, her clothes in good shape. She defiantly stayed put in the same house where everything had happened. Nobody was going to get her to run until she was ready to move on. If she went to jail, she'd go to jail. If by some miracle she was let off the whole thing, she'd—she didn't know what. Laura talked of "just the two of us, Mom, just the two of us from now on." That didn't appeal to her much. A slimy, cowardly solution—holing up with a sixteen-year-old daughter.

Nobody was going to transform her into a scared mole, no, not even now while waiting for the trial, an assignment as difficult as running through water. She kept on working, at the same job, with her same boss. She even baby-sat for Ricky once in a while. There was nothing else to do unless she and Laura went on relief. Johnny had taken off. Okay. She could understand that. Whatever she and Sweets had owned jointly was in escrow along with whatever he had owned alone—truck, life insurance, pension. There were even death benefits waiting on the verdict. Not to mention all his debts. Benefits and penalties. If she would be found guilty she'd pay the penalty. Innocent, she was a bona fide widow, walking away free—Morgan Beauchamp Sweetsir's legitimate heir.

Innocent, she'd pay off Sweets's debts and blow whatever was left of the insurance money on a new Toyota. Take off for Florida with Laura. Get rid of everything they had here; it was nothing but junk. Pack their few clothes, shove everything in the trunk of the new car and go, go, go. In a Toyota Celica GT Liftback—"lean, clean, and a little bit mean." AM/FM stereo all the way. A daydream of blurred detail. Florida's soft, seductive heat, the flat landscape endlessly extending in its thin washed colors, bursting into gaudy party sunsets. Leave this confining valley shut in by hills and the dark depressing pines and never come back. On the white, white sand of the playfully inviting beach a man waited for her, so vaguely defined he was inexpressibly and perfectly beautiful.

She disgusted herself, daydreaming of a new man.

It was essential to keep her feet firmly on the ground. Get up every icy morning and get out looking nice. Brave the porch, take the chance of running head on into Helen and Ty Parsons. "Good morning." Shove it down their throats. I'm alive. I'm managing. Get into her beat-up car, struggling with starting up the cold motor. Move it down the snowy driveway. Run head on into the neighbors who hated her. "Good morning." Up yours. Bright smile for old Mr. and Mrs. Hedges in spite of their sworn affidavits made of their own free wills with no threats or pressures used against them.

"Sometime in the late afternoon of the day that Mr. Sweetsir was killed my husband and myself were returning from shopping after work. We were unloading the groceries. Our house is the first of the Beauchamp houses at the end of the driveway from where the Sweetsirs live. A car came racing out of there. I saw Mrs. Sweetsir at the wheel. She was driving in a hurry, coming out so fast that she didn't have control of her car. She almost hit my husband as she passed us. She was driving much faster than she should have. There was another person in the car with her at this time in the front seat. I yelled at her to slow down because our road wasn't a raceway. She just kept right on going without stopping and not a word of apology."

That was Geneva Hedges' contribution. There was Taylor Hedges':

"On the day that Mr. Sweetsir was killed I heard a car racing its engine in the direction of the Sweetsir residence. When it came roaring up, I recognized Sally Sweetsir as the driver. The car was going so fast its wheels were spinning and digging ruts. At one point it was aimed right at my wife and I. When it went past us, it seemed like it was less than a foot on top of us. We yelled at her to slow down but Mrs. Sweetsir just drove out toward the road without even stopping to check if she had done any damage."

Those were the first documents she read. She put a sheet in the typewriter. At the top she wrote:

COMMENTS ON THE AFFIDAVITS BY SALLY SWEETSIR
GENEVA AND TAYLOR HEDGES' STATEMENTS

I did come out of the driveway fast, but I didn't hit anybody. They make me sound like a natural born killer.

She studied what she had written, and added:

Oh yes, Geneva Hedges says there was someone in the car with me. There wasn't. I was alone.

That hadn't been too bad. Encouraged, she reached for another document. She typed.

STATEMENT OF OFFICER BRYANT: COMMENT

Officer Bryant gave a long, rambling account of coming to the house, then to the hospital. He was the one who reported that her feet were bare and dirty. He affirmed that she repeated over and over that she had stabbed her husband.
What was she supposed to say about Officer Bryant? She typed.

I don't remember this guy at all. Who is he? I can't even remember talking to him. He says I said, "He hit me so I stabbed him." I don't remember saying that but I never stopped talking. I was just blabbing my head off. For all I know I said I was the Son of Sam and the Boston Strangler. Everybody knows I admitted it.

She picked up another long statement by a man named Carson, skimming it carelessly once she saw it was a recapitulation of her admission of guilt. Reading these was becoming upsetting and making her angry. She typed.

CARSON STATEMENT: COMMENT

Don't know him either. Can't remember him. Someone at the
hospital? On page 3 he says I said "I stabbed him." I did say
this. I said it many times. That's what happened. I stabbed
him. I said I stabbed him. I did it and I said I did it. So what
else is new?

The next document was a statement by Jeanine Southby, the
mental-health worker supposedly helping her in the emergency
room. She read it in a mounting fury, then typed:

STATEMENT OF JEANINE SOUTHBY: COMMENT

This woman has everything absolutely wrong. Maybe her
heart's in the right place, but she sure misplaced her ears and
brain, if she has one. Everything she says about the knife is
wrong. Everything she says about the rings—wrong. Everything about my feelings—wrong. Everything about the nonsmoking clinic—wrong.

She was going to leave it at that, but went on.

Incidentally this mental-health creep drove me nuts with her
false sympathy. She hung on to me like a leech. All I cared
about was Sweets. All I wanted to know was what was happening to Sweets in the operating room. Maybe she thought
she was helping but she sure wasn't. That cop bugging me
with his questions. Even after I said everything and signed everything, she kept hanging around me, even after I knew
Sweets was dead and all I wanted was to be left alone. They
ought to give them some better training than that if they're
calling them mental-health workers.

She was shaking. She lit a cigarette, smoked it slowly, leaning
back in her chair, her eyes closed against the mound of paper evidence. When she opened her eyes, the mass of sheets remained.
She ran through them idly, without reading. They were documents

in mourning. The Xerox had added to each page a thick black border and turned the holes for the loose-leaf binders into solid black holes of grieving.

She had dreamed of Sweets that morning, having fallen asleep only after hours of wakefulness. It was a mess of a dream. They were fighting. She was trying to explain to Sweets how she had come to kill him. He wouldn't look at her, wouldn't listen. In a low, sad mutter, he repeated, "Shut up, shut up, shut up." His color was blue-white. The tattoos on his naked body were violently livid.

Or were those marks his wounds?
Was she supposed to tell her dreams too?
She put a clean paper in the typewriter.

STATEMENT OF HELEN PARSONS: COMMENT

She forced herself to read Helen's and then Ty Parsons' statements. It took an effort that ground into her gut. She sat for a long time before she began to type.

Said she heard me and Sweets fighting all the time, heard me screaming at the kids. No argument. We fought a lot, I scream a lot. But I'd trade me and my love for my kid and for Sweets's kid and I'd trade me and Sweets for a whole carload of Helen and Ty Parsons. Married people fight. Mothers yell. She wasn't born yesterday, was she? Helen Parsons hates me, that's all there is to it.

TY PARSONS' STATEMENT: COMMENT

Said I was grouchy about not wanting to sell my car to Helen—this is all messed up—he says that's why I kept calling Sweets all day, that we were quarreling about selling my car to Helen Parsons. But I didn't know a thing about the car during the day. I called Sweets a few times that day to talk with him because I wanted to, that's how we were, we were always on the phone to one another during the day—we missed each other when we weren't together, but he was acting weird that day.

He wouldn't talk to me. He came right out and said he just plain didn't feel like talking to me. I was calling about supper, I wanted somebody to take something out of the freezer and I was calling about Ricky because I had to go to the doctor. I was just calling. Because that's what we always did, that's how we stayed in touch. We liked to talk to each other a couple of times a day.

She stopped.

If she could write a poem, maybe then everything could be explained.

She flipped through interviews with Judy, with Johnny, with Laura, and put them aside. Some other time when she felt better. Idly examining what else was in the briefcase, she found a group of documents clipped together. On a file card Ellen had scrawled, "Don't bother with these, Sally. No problem with this material."

They were all medical documents, beginning with the court-ordered internal examination the morning after she had been arrested. Her lawyers had advised her to go along with that. She had blotted out that ultimate humiliation, but it was on the record, forever and ever.

You are hereby ordered to appear at Central Hartshead Hospital in the town of Hartshead, at 1:30 P.M. on September 5, for the purpose of permitting the within-described nontestimonial identification procedures in order to aid in the investigation of the offense of homicide in violation of 13 V.S.A. Chapter 53, committed upon the premises of the Sweetsirs' residence in the Town of Eatonville, on the evening of September 4. Probable cause exists to believe that you have committed the offense of homicide in the Affidavit of Officer Harding LeVeen sworn to before me on this date, relating that you admitted having fatally stabbed your husband Morgan Beauchamp Sweetsir and that this stabbing was witnessed by your stepson John Matthews; and, an Information charging you with said offense, and supporting affidavits, filed with the clerk of the Hartshead Superior Court.

The nontestimonial identification procedures to be conducted at the time and place above stated are the following:
(1) Procedure: A physical examination
   Methods: By accepted medical practices
   Approximate time required: One Hour
(2) Procedure: A Pap smear
   Methods: By accepted medical practices
   Approximate time required: Fifteen Minutes
IF YOU FAIL TO APPEAR AT THE TIME AND PLACE ORDERED, YOU MAY BE HELD IN CONTEMPT OF COURT.

She held off the invading remembrance of the examination. She'd lose herself if she forced herself to face that day again—the arraignment, Bill Grandstone's putting up bail ("I warned you, I warned you, Sally"), the hospital examination, going home to the same bed, the kitchen where it happened, the mess, his clothes, Laura's round, innocent eyes, Johnny's hatred, the dog whining and howling. Yet, unable to keep herself aloof, she looked further. There was an affidavit from Dr. James Graham, the gynecologist who told her she probably had cancer. She skimmed, reading rapidly, her heart beginning a slow, pounding beat.

. . . when I examined Mrs. Sweetsir my nurse, Catherine Robertson, was present. The nurse and I found Sally to be very upset, very emotional. She was crying and looked ten years older than her age. She reported abnormal bleeding since adolescence. I administered a Pap test which resulted in a class 2 finding, indicating an abnormality and the necessity of retesting. Mrs. Sweetsir reported marital problems, and that her husband would not make love with her because of the bleeding. Mrs. Sweetsir was on birth control pills. She was anemic. On examination she appeared gynecologically normal. However, Sally was very upset and practically asking for a hysterectomy immediately. She said, "Why don't you do something? This has been going on all my life." I informed Sally that the hysterectomy procedure was inappropriate at this point in time.

She was registering an anger so intense it came in visions of physical violence, of kicking, smacking, clubbing that bastard of a doctor. Goddam nerve he had, calling her Sally.

A class 2 Pap test result indicates abnormal cells, not necessarily malignancy. It is usually treated as an infection, and watched, and retested. Pap tests are not 100% accurate and must be evaluated with other methods.

Covering his ass now. He hadn't given her any of that information.

I instructed Sally to stop taking birth control pills. I prescribed iron for anemia, and I told her to come back into my office in four to six weeks. The interview was quite long, lasting about an hour. Sally exhibited an abnormal amount of fear of the prospect of cancer, though the possibility of cancer had not been emphasized, simply the need to do further tests.

At her second visit I asked Sally if she and her husband were having sexual intercourse, and she said no, not much. The Pap test result was again a class 2. I felt that her condition indicated a D & C (Dilation and Curettage) and a Cone biopsy, to positively determine whether or not she had cancer.

A D & C is a routine surgical procedure in which the cervix is dilated and the inner wall of the uterus is scraped. The scraped material is sent to a laboratory for a biopsy.

In the Cone biopsy, a more complicated procedure, a piece of the cervix is removed for testing, entailing risk of bleeding and the possibility of transfusions, plus possible post-surgery problems.

I explained the test procedures to Sally and that they were necessary because of the possibility of cancer being present. I made an effort to quiet her fears. I believed that I had made it clear to her that the chance of a malignancy was very slight, but that is difficult to convey when the patient is irrationally fearful.

Mrs. Sweetsir left the office with the understanding that she would be hearing from us the following day as to the date of surgery.

She shoved the document aside and lit a cigarette. The Mrs. Sweetsir of these papers—what did that woman have to do with her, now or then? She remembered the visit to the doctor as a monstrous distraction in her already monstrously distracted days. What stuck in her memory of that day was Ricky. When she had come out of the inner office she had found the kid undressed in the waiting room, climbing up the bookcases like a goddam monkey, the other patients and the receptionist gawking at the child and, accusingly at her. *Bad mother.* Did she have to wear a sign? Not his mother, damn it, I'm just taking care of him. He's my boss's kid.

What she remembered was driving home to Sweets as to a haven. In spite of everything, Sweets would come through for her, hold her safe against fear and aloneness.

Instead, he wouldn't listen to her. Then when she insisted, he turned away. *Oh, yeah, great, just what I need—more problems.* That was his response. *Ya lyin. Ya just tryin to drum up sympathy. I'm sick a ya self-pityin lyin and carryin on. I'm gonna call ya doctor and show ya up. I know damn well there's nothin the matter with ya.* That's what Sweets had said.

She stubbed out her cigarette. She forced herself to pick up the next document, another medical report. Sally Ciomei, age 17, husband, Vincent Ciomei. She read a record of a minor procedure she had almost totally forgotten. It was after Laurie was born and before the baby that died. What was this document doing here? Were her lawyers laying her out cut open for the whole world to look in?

DIAGNOSIS: Dysfunctional uterine bleeding; chronic cervicitis with erosion
OPERATION: EUA; D & C; biopsy and cauterization of cervix
PROCEDURE: Tissue obtained: Uterine curettings: 4q biopsy of cervix
Blood loss: Approximately 10cc.

The patient was taken to the OR and give a general anesthetic and placed in the lithotomy position. The perineum was prepared, the bladder was catheterized and the patient draped in the usual manner. Bimanual examination was then carried out which revealed a parous introitus, Skenes and Bartholins negative. There was erosion around the entire circumference of the internal os with small lacerations at 3 and 9 oclock. The uterus was anterior, normal in size and configuration, both adnexa within normal limits. 2 single tooth tenacula grasped the anterior lip of the cervix. Uterine sound was inserted and the uterine cavity measured 2½". The cervix was then dilated with Hogar dilators. Ovum forceps explored the uterine cavity and no evidence of polyps was found. Sharp curettement was then carried out and a moderate amount of tissue was obtained. 4q biopsy of the cervix was then done. The cervical erosion was then cauterized. No vaginal gauze was inserted. Immediate post-op condition of the patient was good.

She called Ellen at home, her heart pounding.

"If you have any questions, call me. Any time. At the office or at home. You have my house number?" Ellen had said.

She reached a baby-sitter.

"Ellen and Castle won't be home until real late. I'm sleeping over tonight because they had to go all the way to Woodstock. Any message?"

"That's okay," she said, "I'll call her in the morning."

"Ya sure there's no message?"

"No, it's okay," she said.

Underneath the medical report of seventeen-year-old Sally Ciomei there was a hospital summary on Morgan Beauchamp Sweetsir, age 26, male, dated eight years ago.

She called Ellen's number again.

"Sorry to bother you," she said to the baby-sitter, "but just in case Ellen Mahoney gets in while you're still up, even if it's midnight or one o'clock, will you ask her to please call me? It's very important."

"I could leave her a note," the girl said. "Is that okay?"

"Terrific," Sally said. "Tell her Sally Sweetsir would like her to call whenever she gets in—no matter what time it is."

"Okay," the girl said.

"Thank you," Sally said.

"Oh that's okay," the girl said. "She has your number?"

"Yes," Sally said, "she has it, but maybe you better put it next to the phone, just in case, right along with the note." She gave the girl her number.

She read the documentation of Sweets's long-ago medical problems.

DIAGNOSIS:

1. Chronic anxiety
2. Gastrointestinal discomfort in upper abdomen accompanied by intractable headache.

This was the first admission of this 26-year-old garage mechanic. Physical examination revealed a tense, slim, immaculate young man of normal physical development. Long-standing complaints of nervousness with knotlike pain in the epigastrium followed by nausea and vomiting provoked by environmental stress. Upper GI series done. Revealed a sliding esophageal hiatus hernia. There was no relation of pain to position or bending and no response to antacids. Severe headache originating over right eye radiating to the right occiput constantly present for the past four years. Urinalysis, CBC, BUN, FBS, A/G ration, Alkaline phosphatase, phosphorus, calcium, retic count, skull films and chest X-ray and perimetry work-up by an ophthalmologist were all within normal limits.

Personal history revealed a traumatic childhood, two unsuccessful teenage marriages, a questionable unsuccessful third marriage and three hospitalizations for psychiatric problems while in the services. He is presently married, allegedly happily. His wife underwent a hysterectomy about a year ago. She is now 22 years old. There is one female infant. An attempt at adopting an older male child was frustrated by the social investigator's opinion that the couple's home was too compulsively well kept.

At the bottom of the page, the admission and discharge dates were recorded. Sweets had been in the VA hospital for more than a month. Half of January—more than halfway through February. Upstate in Black River Forks. Cold as hell. Kay visiting once a week, riding a smelly bus that took the long way round, stretching a three-and-a-quarter-hour car ride on the interstate into a six-hour ordeal. Leaving baby Judy and Johnny in whose charge? In their compulsively neat house.

Somebody was conning somebody. Sweets doing one of his numbers on the doctor. Here I am, Doc, greatest guy in the world—even compulsively neat.

She skipped a page, then began again:

Mr. Sweetsir was seen daily by the Chief of Psychiatry in Consultation during which treatment the patient gained much insight into his problems and enjoyed considerable relief of symptoms except for the constant headache. It was recommended that he be discharged CBOC for followup to be arranged by the patient. The patient reported being out of work and that his first priority was to seek new employment.

Discharged on Fiorinal one tablet q.i.d. prn for headache and Maalox one tablespoon q.i.d. with meals and at bedtime and prn for burning discomfort.

She reached toward the typewriter, her fingers poised on the keys. To put down on paper the sentences that had blossomed in her head? *I have stilled forever your burning discomfort, Sweets. My love that promised you everything delivered you from this.*

She was crying. She turned from the typewriter, reached for a ballpoint pen, and in an automatic secretarial response began to look for misspellings and typos in the medical summaries, until, unsure of the technical terminology, she stopped.

She wiped the tears from her cheeks. No crying. She had sworn herself to no more crying after all the blabbing and crying she had allowed herself when Sweets died.

There was another medical document with its Xeroxed black holes and mourning bands. At the top was a case number and autopsy number. Parts of the document were printed, the rest typed.

CIRCUMSTANCES OF DEATH: This 34-year-old white male, Morgan Beauchamp Sweetsir, was allegedly stabbed by his wife in the left arm and chest at approximately . . .

She slapped her open palm over the page to cover it, to stop reading it. But began again, further down.

. . . A chest tube was inserted in the 8th left intercostal space from which air and blood returned. Pericardio-centesis was done four times with no blood noted. The left chest was opened but the patient remained nonresponsive. Following opening of the chest, the thoracic cavity appeared relatively empty.

She saw Sweets on a table, his chest opened wide. Inside Sweets nothing but a bone-white, sweet-smelling cleanliness.
Now she saw that certain passages were underlined.

No wounds were entered or touched according to the Emergency Room physicians.

Further down she read:

. . . superficial abrasion of the lower left lip—in opposition to the left upper medial incisor.

The neck below the angle of the jaw shows dried, red, superficial abrasions 6¼″ from the top of the head, 3½″ to the left of midline; and on the right 8½″ from the top of the head and 4½″ to the right of midline. There is an oozing ¼″ incised wound of the pinna of the left ear and a ½″ abrasion behind the pinna of the right ear. There is a blackheaded comedo on the anterior surface of the right shoulder. There are multiple tattoos: birds on the anterior chest bilaterally, snake forms symmetrically on the lower . . .

She must stop reading. But read on:

There are three stab wounds: #1 is disposed vertically and is in the left lateral upper arm . . .

A black-banded printed box on the right side of the form carried the heading

ORGAN WEIGHTS (GRAMS)

Heart	400
Lung—R	850
—L	750
Liver	1875
Spleen	175
Kidney—R	125
—L	125
Brain	1575
Other (Adrenals)	5 ea.

She studied the figures as if a mystery were to be solved through the resolution of a mysterious formula.

The liver weighed the most. Brains weighed a lot; the heart, not so much; the spleen was light. One lung was heavier than the other. The kidneys and the adrenals were even.

Why was the word "Adrenals" typed in beside the printed word "Other"? Didn't everybody have adrenals?

She clipped together the group of papers, fixed Ellen's file card under the clip, and shoved the batch back into the briefcase. She lit a cigarette. She poured herself a glass of white wine. If she knew a decent doctor she'd go ask for something for her nerves. The doctor who had checked her out at the hospital on the day of her arraignment seemed like a nice man. There was that new girl in the outside office who swore she'd never get through the day without Librium. And Jerry Greenspan popping Valiums.

It was only ten past nine. Could she stand reading more documents?

She picked one out at random. It was taken from a technician at the hospital, the night of Sweets's death. This was a question and answer interview—just like on a Perry Mason show. The fellow's name, Walter Brown, was entered at the top of the page, and the whole page was circled as if somebody had decided it was important.

Q. Was he conscious?
A. No, sir.
Q. He was unconscious?
A. Yes, he was.
Q. Did you hear him say he was knifed?
A. To my knowledge, he never spoke.
Q. You were with him constantly?
A. Well, there was a lot of stuff going on. I went out once to get more equipment.
Q. Could you describe your actions in detail?
A. I was getting material as the doctor requested it—you know and doing whatever the doctor requested. I put the monitoring daisies on the gentleman's chest—and the heart compressions—we monitored with paddles—and I catheterized and that kind of thing.
Q. Did you at any point talk with the victim's wife?
A. Well, I was after an IV pole and I had to go into the X-ray department and I was hustling and went past her. She grabbed at me and said, "What's the matter? What's the matter?" I just told her I needed more equipment. That was all she said, as I remember. I think maybe she also said, "Is he going to be all right?" She was sitting on the floor outside the emergency room door, on the floor.
Q. Did you hear her say that she was responsible for the knifing?
A. No, no. I didn't hear anything like that. But I rushed right back into the emergency room.
Q. Did you have any impression of the woman's attitude?
A. Well, I don't know exactly what you're getting at, but I had the impression of a woman whose husband had been badly hurt and she was very concerned, that was my impression.

Attached to the Xeroxed sheet was a typed note: "Walter Brown. Possibility. Reluctant to get involved, but obviously sympathetic." Underneath, the name Fern Bowdoin was scrawled, followed by a question mark.

She turned back to her typewriter. She typed:

WALTER BROWN: COMMENT

Don't remember him.

She read rapidly now, picking up statements in no particular order, skimming and keeping her comments very short, until she came across still another interview with Ty Parsons. What a man for shooting off his mouth. She read pages of inaccurate, self-important posturing distortions of her life by Ty Parsons.

She let out a long sighing breath, took another sip of wine, lit another cigarette. Then she began to type.

TYRONE PARSONS' STATEMENT TO OFFICER LEVEEN: COMMENT

Ty Parsons reports that I'm grouchy and not very social. This is complicated. Sweets probably gave this impression to Ty because this is one way he manipulated people. Quite often when Sweets just didn't want to go someplace or do something with someone who had asked us to join them in some outing or to come over to their house or something like that, he'd use me as an excuse so he wouldn't have to tell them he didn't want to do it. We both acknowledged this fact. I didn't care. Sometimes he'd use me as his excuse without telling me about it. It didn't bother me usually because I knew it mattered a whole lot to him what people thought of him and he needed people to think he was a great guy. I didn't care about it one way or another. I could take the blame easier than he could. I'm not saying this situation was right or wrong, it was just the way it was.

In fact, she had always resented his manipulation of social situations in which the end result would be that he looked good and she came on as the nagging witch of the world. He had done that to her a lot. Twisted her nature so he could sport a carefree generous profile. Shouldn't her feelings have mattered more to him than the opinions of relative strangers? He'd sell her out any time for the good will of the crew he worked with, or any Hilltop regular, he'd even try it on her own kid, and on his, and of course on his good friends like Ty and Helen Parsons; but he'd extend his need for approval to gas-station attendants, waitresses, checkout women, bag boys, bartenders, everybody who crossed Sweets's path had to be impressed with what a great guy he was. And if he shone at her expense, so what? Sweets was the center, Sally his satellite. That's the way it was.

She didn't write down her reaction. She sat immobilized, her heart banging in a raging beat.

To quiet herself she read a report by a state policeman. She couldn't remember him. It was a jolt to find following the heading MOTIVE—"Personal Satisfaction."

She looked through the group of reports by officers to locate Officer Harding LeVeen's. He had been the arresting officer, his words would carry more weight, wouldn't they? She read through the entire long report, though it was somewhere in the middle that he supplied under MOTIVE—"Anger, resulting from a family quarrel."

In a rush of confused self-blame and self-exoneration, she typed rapidly without pause.

GENERAL COMMENT

If I were a stranger to myself reading these documents, I wouldn't know what to think. I might think, she's guilty as hell. From the things said by others it would be apparent that I did stab Sweets and that I did take the knife out of the drawer and threaten him and normally if a person threatens another person and that person gets killed you would assume that there was the carrying through of a threat. Only that wasn't the way it happened. Ty Parsons said that I said "I only meant to stab him a little." I couldn't have said that because I never meant to stab him at all. Maybe I said I meant to scare or frighten him into backing off, meant to scare him with the knife, but I'm dead sure I never said I wanted to stab him, because I didn't want to. I want him alive this minute. I don't remember anything I said to Ty Parsons. I remember that I wanted him to help me get Sweets to the car and he said he wouldn't, then I remember he told me something about "You've done enough already." Or maybe that was Helen Parsons.

Everybody says I said all those things they say I said. Maybe I did. I don't remember what I said. I would have talked to anyone about anything just to get them the hell away from me that night.

All the cops and the hospital people say I kept saying, "I did not know it would do what it did." That sounds awful, that sounds like I meant to cut him, but that wasn't what I meant. They are presenting a picture which indicates I meant to stab Sweets but that I was too dumb to know it would hurt him so much or something. Do they think I haven't any common sense? Nobody in their right mind would go waving around a 10" blade and think it couldn't do any harm. I had no intention of using that knife. When I realized he had been hit, I thought his arm had been accidentally cut, and I couldn't figure out what was happening to him from an arm wound and when they cut his shirt away I saw that the wound had gone through his arm and into his chest—

She stopped. There didn't seem to be any use to what she was doing. She had done it. She'd go to jail for it. Still, she continued reading and commenting.

In the gospel according to St. Harding Leveen, he says my motive was anger. That other cop says it was personal satisfaction. If what I'm getting out of this horror is personal satisfaction then I don't know the meaning of those words, and if what I was feeling was simply anger, then I don't know anything about my own feelings and my love for Sweets.

Johnny's statements are the most damaging. I understand that now. I don't blame him for what he says, he hates me for what I did, but what he says is all wrong, it's all confused. Johnny really loved Sweets and I understand his feelings. I don't want to make hash of Johnny Matthews in court. He's got enough to contend with. I took him into my house as our son,

Sweets's son and my son. I saw some writing that indicated
you were playing with the notion that Johnny is Kay Sweetsir's
illegitimate son by Sweets before he married her and that's
why he tried to adopt him. What difference does any of that
make? Why dig up all that old dirt that will only harm Johnny?
I don't want to do Johnny harm to save my own neck.

There was nothing to do but give up. She tried to imagine being
jailed for life, but instead of images of herself, it was Laura's fate
that chilled her.

Unless a miracle occurs, they're going to get me, no matter
how hard you lawyers are working for me. It's easy for them to
prove their case against me, I see that now. But what they're
all saying isn't the way it was. In the end what matters is what
really happened. I know what happened and Sweets knows
what happened. It was between me and Sweets. If he were
here . . .

She was X-ing out the beginnings of that last ridiculous sentence
when the phone rang. It was Ellen.
"I just got your message, Sally, I'm calling from a booth. Do you
have a pencil? I want to give you this number in case we're cut off.
It's 348-2100."
"Where are you?"
"At the hospital in Woodstock. I called home to see if everything
was okay and Terry gave me your message. My baby-sitter. I'm
sorry I didn't get it sooner. Did I wake you?"
"No, no. Listen, forget about me. Why didn't she tell me where
you were? You've got your own problems. What's the matter?"
"It's Adam. Croup. I can't believe it. I thought it was a nine-
teenth-century disease. They put him in a steam room, and it
relieves the condition very quickly. And they let the parents stay, so
that's good."
"Go back to him," Sally said.
"No, it's all right," Ellen said. "Castle and I are spelling each
other. Castle's with him now. It's a relief to get out of that mist."

She laughed. "Maybe it'll melt away some of my weight, knock off two problems at once, mine and little Adam's."

"Ellen, I'm sorry I bothered you, this can wait," she said.

"No, tell me," Ellen said.

"I'm sorry but your time is up," a recording announced. "Please deposit—"

"Call me back," Ellen said and hung up.

Ellen picked up on the first ring.

"I feel awful bothering you now," Sally said. "Let's leave it for next time we meet."

"Okay, but just give me an idea. Was it too dismaying going over the papers? I know it must be very hard. We waited as long as we could. But with the trial date set, we really have to pull our case together now."

She became calmer listening to Ellen's reasonable voice discussing "the case," using an affected word like "dismaying." It helped to remove the situation to an antiseptically unreal distance, retreating into a news event or a town project, impersonally engrossing.

"Well, that's what I was wondering about," Sally said. "Like all that medical material . . ."

"There has to be forensic medical testimony in a murder trial. There's no need for you to cope with that kind of material. Put it aside, Sally."

"No, I mean all that ancient history about Sweets's hospitalizations and all those gynecological reports on me. Is that stuff going to have to come out?"

"Sally, what in the world are you reading those for? They weren't even supposed to be in the briefcase. This booth is so hellishly hot," she said without a break, letting out her breath in a long sigh.

Sally envisioned Ellen's bulk shifting to accommodate itself to the little seat in the narrow, glass closet. Then Ellen's voice recovered—very brisk, very reassuring.

"There was a question of your credibility involved. The court-ordered internal examination put you totally in the clear. You don't need an operation, you haven't got cancer, all you needed was some very simple treatment, but Dr. Graham was clearly recommending surgery and scaring you with the possibility of cancer. You weren't lying to your husband. You weren't self-pitying, or creating a fake situation to get sympathy. You weren't making a big deal out of nothing. You were following your doctor's orders, and if you were upset and worried, you had a right to be. Also, the court-ordered physical upholds your account of having been hit and knocked down. They found bruises consistent with your story. We have other witnesses to testify to Morgan Sweetsir's brutality toward women."

"What?" Sally said.

"I think we've got Kay Sweetsir ready to talk. I'm working on it."

"She's got nothing to do with this," Sally said. "What are you dragging her into this for? It'll turn on us. I helped Sweets win custody of her kid. She'll start yakking about that. She hates me."

She heard herself yelling, pictured Ellen's hazel eyes with their calm, direct gaze—listening. *I like her, I like her so much, why do I give her such a hard time? She's only trying to help me.*

She said, "I don't get the drift of the defense. What are you after?"

"Whatever we can get," Ellen said.

"How about the plain truth?"

"Have you told it to us, Sally?"

"What does that mean?"

"Have you told us what it was like living with Sweets? Every day, day by day?"

"Listen, Ellen, I'm no Kay Sweetsir. Don't get any ideas like that."

"I would never confuse you with Kay Sweetsir in a million years," Ellen said. "But if Morgan Sweetsir was a brutal man to live with, that would make our case. Do you understand that?"

She didn't respond.

Ellen said, "We'll talk some more tomorrow. I have to get back now. I'll call you tomorrow. Trust us, Sally. Try to write down whatever can be of help. We needed a handle, and I think we have it, especially if you help."

"What about the plain simple truth that I took a knife and stabbed him?"

"The law isn't ever that simple," Ellen said. "Only trouble is that that tricky maxim works both ways."

"What do you mean?" Sally said.

"Works as well for the prosecution as for the defense. I've got to get back," she said.

"Ellen," Sally said, "I'm sorry I bothered you. I'm sorry about Adam. I hope he's better real soon."

"He's better already," she said brightly. "They've put him on antibiotics and his breathing is normal. I'm sure he'll be fine now. It's just that he's so little. I couldn't stand it. Okay, love, we'll talk tomorrow."

"Thanks for calling," Sally said, but Ellen had hung up.

Apprehension immobilized her. They were going to turn her inside out, her whole life, her life with Sweets. And they were going to turn Sweets's life inside out, his own life, the life he led before he even met her.

In a rush, she added a final paragraph to her general comment.

One last thing. Suppose Morgan Beauchamp Sweetsir was the worst person ever born. That wouldn't make my killing him any better. It doesn't make it a right thing to do, it isn't any better to kill a bad person than a good person. Thou shalt not kill doesn't say anything about good or bad. I feel this pressure on me to help dig up a lot of bad things about Sweets, all the things we tried so hard to put to rest, the things we were both working so hard to change. Anybody can be made to look bad. They can make me look like the worst slut in town if they want to. So I don't want any of that stuff brought into the case. Our life was between me and Sweets, and that's the way I want it left. So what I'm saying is please don't go around digging up any more of that stuff. I'd rather take my punishment than ruin Morgan's reputation.

She felt better then. Yield to the inevitable. She'd go to jail, there was no other way. Then she heard Laura, dropped off by friends with a car, mounting the porch stairs. She had forgotten her daughter for the moment.

19

THE NEXT DAY, a Friday, a woman called her at the office. June Easton. She was someone Sally knew well enough to say "Hi" to. Librarian at the district high school. Pulled herself up in life, got herself educated, married a man who had made his way up too, now running a small construction outfit. Both had wormed their way into the company of out-of-staters. At least that was the local gossip. "Those flatlanders are laughing at them behind their backs." June Easton invited Sally to the house of one of her friends to meet with a women's group that evening. Sally was so surprised by the call she said, "Sure, June, thanks." June would pick Sally up and take her in her car.

Ellen called a few minutes later. Little Adam was being discharged from the hospital in the late afternoon. They made a date to meet Saturday morning at ten o'clock in the Public Defender's office.

"That building better be heated," Sally said.

"That's the least we can do for you," Ellen said.

"What about this women's group I'm supposed to be meeting tonight. Did you set that up for June Easton to call me?"

"She already called? She was supposed to wait till I spoke to you. Did you say No?"

"I said Yes like an idiot."

"Maybe you'll find it interesting," Ellen said. Her voice was acutely doubtful. "Most of them are great—my best friends are in that group. There are a couple of very annoying phonies. A couple of arrogant fools. And a couple of really crazy ladies. What have you got to lose?"

"God knows," Sally said. "They're women's libbers?"

"They're feminists," Ellen said. "Whatever that means these days. Each feminist to her private theory. But that's okay. They want to help. There's nothing to lose."

"Maybe there is, maybe there isn't," Sally said. "Most people around here aren't exactly hot supporters of women's lib. Suppose the jury decides to hold it against me that I'm rubbing shoulders with women's libbers?"

"Your decision," Ellen said. "There's something to what you say about local attitudes. That's a minus. But there are possible pluses. The case might get national coverage through the women's movement."

"No," Sally said. "No, please, I don't want any of that."

"Do what you think best," Ellen said.

June Easton arrived in a brand-new Buick Regal that took the rough, climbing, badly snow-plowed back road they entered from the Branden highway as if it were a carpet path. Big impressive modern house, all peaks and angles with lots of glass. Inside, an assembly of about thirty women awaited her.

"They acted like I was some kind of heroine," she told Ellen the next day.

Sally Sweetsir, husband murderer, feminist heroine. She didn't say the last part to Ellen.

Huge leather couches, glass-and-chrome tables, recessed lights controlled by dimmers, thick exposed beams so low around the staircases she slammed her forehead on her way to the bathroom, itself more of a tiled cathedral than a toilet. On the living-room walls, huge paintings with nothing on them but solid stripes of dark paint—blue, black, brown, dirt-red. On the glass coffee table there was a glass bowl of purple grapes, each grape as big as a plum, a green dish filled with mixed dried fruits, bottles of white wine, green cloth napkins, green china plates, thin, green wineglasses. Wood-burning open fire in an immense stone fireplace.

She smiled and smiled, her subdued "I am gentle" smile, shook hands with each woman in turn, not catching or holding on to the names she was given. She estimated there was enough money tied up in their leather boots and bags alone to solve all her money problems for a year.

The sympathy she saw in their faces was real or fake? Either way, she preferred not to accept it. It was her first public appearance as the Sally Sweetsir who had killed her husband, her first self-assigned acting up to the image of the exotic specimen she was supposed to be. It was exhausting.

They called themselves "a support group," and indeed it seemed a rule that the word "supportive" be employed frequently. She began by thinking contemptuously how quickly she could ape their lingo and almost choked on her wine because of a private joke: Gee, I should have worn my supphose.

Draped, curled and bunched on the soft big couches and chairs, they did a once-around-the-room where each woman again told her name and added her profession. Sally announced herself "Sally Sweetsir, executive secretary," but what she felt was that she'd never have made it to that room, among those women, if she hadn't killed Sweets. It was "husband killer" that had bought her entry to their club.

They were all professional women. Nobody said "housewife." Some were students, June Easton said "librarian," there was a lawyer, two psychologists, a gynecologist, a group were teachers at the high school, and a larger group were professors of sociology, English, history, women's studies—teaching at the University. One woman was a weaver, one was a potter. The older woman, in whose house they were meeting, owned a gallery. The rest were journalists, poets, writers, painters.

In a way, it was like being back among the Ciomei clan. Though everybody spoke English, she floundered in an alien language. After the introductions, a youngish woman gave a sort of formal talk. Sally understood the drift okay. Things were bad for women in general. What she had trouble with was the terminology: "matriarchal and patriarchal society" and "the parameters of oppression are not to be measured merely in single sectors—such as the economic, the personal, etc., but within the broader spectrum . . ." She would lose herself, returning to "the idolatry of womanhood and motherhood so celebrated by the society we live in is in fact the obverse side of the coin of . . ." She understood "battered, abused." Then was lost again. The young woman ended in a flurry of words: ". . . in every sphere of existence—the social, the political, the psychic, the physical, the verbal, the sexual, in interpersonal relationships and most particularly within the nuclear family where the great majority of violent acts occur."

But that talk hadn't prepared her for what followed.

A woman with creamy smooth skin and masses of black curly hair moved to the center of the room, and raising her arms to the high, beamed cathedral ceiling, knelt on the rug behind the coffee table. The loose sleeves of her gown fell back from her silky, fleshy arms. Her soft, full breasts were emphasized by a linked gold belt gathering the folds of material under the sweet, inviting swelling. Another heavier gold chain ending in a huge medallion weighed a path between the hills. Kneeling, arms raised, her eyes brimming with power, she held her position until a total expectant silence took command of the group. She had cast a spell.

Watching the woman as if she were at a performance, Sally was astounded to be singled out by the liquid black, thickly fringed eyes. The woman lowered her arms until they were outstretched directly toward Sally.

"Sister," she said. She modulated and rang out her tones like an actress. "Sister."

Her arms still outstretched, she circled slowly on her knees, moving on from Sally to the other women, saying "Sister, sister," to each woman in turn, in an extraordinary tonal variety of caress and embrace until she completed the circle. Then she rose, swiftly crossed to Sally and seated herself next to her on the couch. She took Sally's hand. The woman on the other side of Sally grasped Sally's left hand and so a circle formed of joined women, intoning "Sister, sister," and Sally heard herself in unison with this roomful of strange women, responding, "Sister, sister." It was a lovely performance. She liked it, whatever it was. She was warmed by white wine, surrounded by the soft perfume of women and the embraces of strangers. Someone was very softly humming a lullaby-like song.

The woman who had led the ritual said, "Who will be the first to speak bitterness? Tonight we will speak bitterness against male oppression."

There was a short silence. Then a woman began to speak.

"I lived in Brooklyn when I was a little girl, and I had to ride the subway for my piano lessons. It was only a couple of stations. I would go for my lesson directly after school when the subways were almost empty and would be home before the rush hour. From the very first week, I noticed the same man in the train every day. I think it was about the third or fourth week that I became afraid of how strange he was. He would sit near me, looking at me and moving his hand in his lap, under his coat. It was winter and he had a heavy overcoat on. I was twelve or maybe just thirteen. I'm an only child and my parents were very prudish. I had never seen male genitals except on my little boy cousin—never seen mature male genitals, and though I had been given a bare, biological account of sexual intercourse, animal and human, I didn't understand sexuality in any real sense. I told my mother that there was a queer man in the subway, but she thought I was dramatizing. She gave me one of those mother looks and told me to ride a car with a conductor. If you know the BMT system, those of you who know New York, well, you understand what it's like in the middle of the day, empty and eerie. That trip became a weekly nightmare. Then one time the man sat down right next to me. I was a very good, polite child. I didn't feel free to get up and move away, to dare insult a grownup. He seemed to me to be a very old man, but he was probably in his forties or fifties. He never spoke to me. He gestured with his eyes. I was being ordered to look down at his lap and he kept insisting with his head movements so strongly that I did. I thought I was supposed to do what grownups demanded, especially males. I was always being warned by my mother that my father would have to hear about some wrongdoing on my part. I can't imagine what I ever did wrong, except get less than an A on a test."

She was a tall, slim, middle-aged woman with big, tinted glasses. She spoke with a certain formality, but in an easy flow. Now her voice halted and thickened and it was clear that behind the tinted glasses she was crying.

"I looked down at his lap. He had exposed his genitals. At first I didn't know what they were. Because of all his clothes bunched around them and because his penis was limp, I thought it was a nest of some little animals in his lap, a nest of pink newborn mice. That's what I thought at first."

The tears were streaming down her face now.

"He grabbed my hand and pressed it against that horrible, horrible mass of living tissue and his penis began to stiffen. I can't describe my feelings—the terror and disgust, the unspeakable aloneness and fear. There was nobody else in the car. I fought with him to tear my hand out of his grip and ran to the farthest end of the car, praying, praying that a conductor would come through, or that we would come into a station, and other riders would enter. He sat where he was, working on his penis, watching me intently and I watched him intently. I watched, I watched until he came." She broke down and sobbed. The woman next to her held her in her arms. In a few minutes, she sat up and spoke again. "I don't remember any more about the man. I lost my music, I remember that, and I had a hysterical fit about losing my music books. I begged to be allowed to stop taking piano lessons. I said I hated the piano. But the truth was I loved the piano. There just wasn't anyone to talk to about it. There wasn't anyone who would believe me."

"I would like to kill that man," one of the other women said.

"We will kill that man," the woman in the red gown said.

There was a memo pad and a slim gold pen on a side table holding a telephone. Printed in blue at the top of the pad was a lion's head resting on a crown; at the bottom was the printed name THE RITZ-CARLTON. The woman wrote in a bold hand, more like printing than writing, letters looking as if they were copied from an ancient manuscript. Sally watched her put down: "The nameless man who brutalized and terrified Jane Brenner on the BMT train."

She tore the sheet from the pad, folded it in half, and put it aside on the coffee table.

Another woman began to speak. She was shy, her voice so low Sally had difficulty hearing her.

"I've never told this to anybody. I wasn't allowed to watch television at home as a child. We didn't even own one. My mother and father were professors and they had very high intellectual standards. My brother and I, of course, were always sneaking off to friends' houses to watch TV. My mother and father's closest friends lived in the very next house. People just like us, except they had no children, I never knew why. He was a professor of comparative literature and she was a librarian. He would talk to me as if I were a grownup. I remember him explaining to me what comparative literature meant just as if I could understand, and of course I could when he explained it. They had a room called Philip's TV den, because he was crazy about TV. His wife hated TV, but she didn't mind if he watched. She would read or listen to music in the living room, or talk to her friends on the telephone. My parents permitted me to watch TV there every evening after supper and homework, and before bedtime, because Philip Devit was their friend. There was only one big comfortable chair in the den. We'd watch TV together, Philip Devit and I. I was about ten or eleven. Really, it was more like a closet, that room, but the chair was a big leather Eames chair and he was a very slim man, and though I was a large, almost fat child, we snuggled into the chair easily. It was wonderful to watch in his arms. He held me and stroked me under my clothes and we kissed, and I stroked him. I loved him. It went on for a long time, many months. I was very happy. I don't know the details, nobody ever told me how we were discovered, but suddenly there was a terrible uproar about me and Philip Devit, an uproar kept quiet between the two families. I was forbidden to go anywhere near the Devit home. My mother and father made me feel like a dirty stranger and my brother eyed me as if I were a lewd freak. I heard nothing from this man who meant my whole life. I loved him, heart, body and soul. I used to tell him everything, about school, about my friends and my dreams for myself. He'd tell me everything about his day, about a bird he had seen that morning, he'd explain parts of the programs to me. He was the dearest person in the world to me and suddenly he was gone. The Devits moved, nobody said where. He had resigned his teaching post at the University and his wife resigned from the library. I knew that from other people. A For Sale sign went up on the lawn of their house. Soon it was sold to a family with a lot of children. I never heard from him again. He broke my heart," she said, very softly. "I know that's not the way it's supposed to be, but that's the way it was. It's called child abuse but for me it was true love. He had no right to go away and leave me without a word."

"That's the essence of child abuse," a woman said. "Don't you see the significance of . . . ?"

The woman in the red gown interrupted. "Sister, tonight we listen to our sisters' bitterness without comment. Isn't that what we agreed?"

"Sorry." The woman who had commented turned her head aside, picked up a magazine from a table, leafed through it angrily.

"Shall we write down his name?" the woman in red asked.

"He's probably dead. After all, my father is, and he was a couple of years older than my father." She laughed. "Never mind, let's do away with the Philip Devit who used to be, the Philip Devit who broke my child's heart."

Sally watched the woman write "Philip Devit" in the same strange script. Again she tore off the sheet, folded it and put it aside.

The older gray-haired woman who owned the big house jumped into a diatribe and jumped out as abruptly as she had begun.

"It was always I, I, I, my, my, my, *my* gallery, *I* bought, *I* found, *my* collection, a man who never heard of *we*. I'm there with him working my brains out, working my guts out all my life. Not even about the children, we. The man doesn't have the generosity to say *we*. No, *my* son, *my* son, *my* daughter, *my* daughter, the word *our*, *ours* didn't exist for him. *His* success, *his* money, *his* house, *his* architect, *I*, *I*, *I*, *my*, *my*. 'Last year when *I* was in Italy,' exactly as if I never existed, exactly as if there was nobody there, Hannah Wasserman didn't exist with him in Italy morning, noon and night. The only one who counted in the world was Harold Wasserman, the collector, the gallery owner, the big cheese. *I*, *I*, *I*, that was all that counted with him. Women lose their husbands, they complain of loneliness. They're crazy. I've never been so happy in my life. People say 'The Harold Wasserman Collection' I correct them. 'The Wasserman Collection,' I say. 'The Hannah and Harold Wasserman Collection.' He picked up Larry Rivers cheap, I found Al Held when he was starving. He put his money in Jews, in Kline, Shahn, Baskin, Levine. Abstract, figurative. I bought Calders, he laughed at me. 'Toys you're buying?' Castle, he wouldn't hear from Castle. I had to buy Castle on the sly from my own pocket—the best investment I ever made. Okay, Harold made the original money. True is true. He made it on the stock market. But the gallery, the collection? That he dared to call the Harold Wasserman Collection? I changed everything when he died, brass nameplates, stationery, the telephone book. The Hannah and Harold Wasserman Collection. I hope to live to be a hundred so I can say it a hundred times a day for the next thirty-five years. And still I'm fair, I leave *his* name in. Him with his, I, I, I."

She stopped.

"Put him down, put him down," she said. "Write down his precious name, I, I, I, Harold Wasserman. He's so important, let him die twice."

The woman in red wrote "I I I Harold Wasserman."

A young woman said, "I'm sick of talking about men. Put down men, M–E–N. Then we'll stop talking about them, stop being obsessed with them."

On the Ritz-Carlton memo pad, the woman wrote "Men" in her elaborate script.

A beautiful girl said, "I called my father last night to tell him that Roger and I were separating, that I wanted to try living alone with the children before we divorced. He said to me, 'For Christ's sake, Julie, do you know what the hell you're doing? Who's going to support those two kids of yours? You know your mother and I aren't getting any younger.'"

"Shall we put down your father's name?"

"No, no," the girl said, and cried.

A short, very dark young woman left her seat, and paced the oval center around which they were gathered as she spoke.

"My father went crazy. He had spent his whole life in the regular army. We moved from place to place, wherever he was assigned. When he retired, sort of young, he went crazy, maybe from nothing to occupy his time. He slept with a gun under his pillow. One night he shot my mother. She had gotten up to adjust the air conditioning—we were living in Florida then—and he started yelling about an intruder in the house and he shot her. I was seventeen. The yelling woke me. I rushed into the room just as he shot her. He had shot her in the leg and then he held the gun to her head to kill her. My brother woke too and I told him, very low, to call the police."

She was pacing, pacing.

"When the police came, even before they came in, just the sound of the sirens and the revolving lights drove my father even crazier and he started after my brother, shouting he was going to shoot him. My brother was fifteen. I hated my father. He was the most authoritarian man ever born. But he gave *himself* every license. Drink, other women. I would hear him, like an animal, after my mother night after night. I could hear his animal yells right through the walls. I hated him. I hate him. But I knew I was his favorite. I took a terrible chance. I closed the door. I told my brother, 'Keep the police out until I say.' I put my arms around my father and told him I loved him and that I'd keep him from harm. I kissed him and cajoled him until he gave me the gun. I could have killed him then, I could have said it happened accidentally in the scuffle. I would have gotten away with it. Instead I let the police take him to an asylum. I had my enemy before me at the point of a loaded gun and I didn't kill him. I'll never forgive myself for that. Never. Never. My mother always walked with a limp afterward." She paced more rapidly. "She took him back when the hospital let him out. And she calls me and complains and complains that she can't live with such a madman. I could have liberated her, I held the gun and never shot. I never shot my enemy. I'll never forgive myself."

"Tell his name," the woman in red said.

"Anthony Lopez," the girl said, and stopping her pacing, threw herself face down on the carpet.

The back of the girl's jeans had a French name sewn on the pocket. Sally had never seen that particular label. The woman in red added "Anthony Lopez" to the pile of names, then half turned toward Sally, expectancy in her brimming eyes.

They were inviting her to speak? Sally lowered her head, pretending unawareness that the attention of the room was centering on her.

"Sally?" the woman said, and gestured toward her in encouragement.

She shrank back.

"We understand that it's hard to speak the first time," the woman said in her wonderfully artificial voice. "But try. Share your terrible experience with us."

She could barely respond, she was so embarrassed. "Thank you," she said. "I hope you understand, but I can't. I'm sorry."

The woman who had gotten so angry that she had stayed hidden behind the magazine said, "Of course, this is the result of no content, no ideology. Dramatics, self-indulgence, under the guise of consciousness-raising. Time to move beyond. Time to consider class, the element you refuse to face. . . ."

"We have a ritual to finish," the woman in red said.

"Sorry," the other said bitterly. "Back to our games."

The woman in red ignored her.

"Sally, will you give us a name to add to these? You don't have to speak about it. Just give us the name that harmed you the most."

She wanted to give them Helen Parsons but she understood that only males were acceptable. They were expecting the name of Morgan Beauchamp Sweetsir to be written on the memo pad in that fancy script.

Inspired, she said, "Yes. The arresting officer, Harding LeVeen."

"A Jew arrested you?" Hannah Wasserman exploded. "A man named Levine is a cop in Hartshead County?"

Some of the women broke into laughter. The woman in red hesitated.

Sally spelled, "H–A–R–D–I–N–G, capital L–E, capital V–E–E–N. Some people say he's French Canadian, but that's from way back."

"Oh, thank God," Hannah Wasserman said. "Anybody want coffee?"

Everybody wanted coffee. An electric china coffeepot sat on a long table at the far wall. There were cups and saucers, puffy cookies piled on a raised dish, small dessert dishes, silverware, more cloth napkins. Everything on this table was in matching white.

Again the woman in red raised her arms and again the room came to a charmed silence. She stood and moved gracefully toward the fireplace, the folded Ritz-Carlton memo pages cradled in her outstretched palms. She chanted as she walked.

"For you, Sally, and for all women, we cleanse ourselves and the world of our enemies, man when he acts the oppressor, man when he is the liar, the distorter of love and friendship, man when he is the enemy. For you, Sally, for the good outcome of your trial, in our love and in our sisterhood, in our support and our mutual suffering, with all our inner-directed help and outer willingness to serve in sisterhood, we consign your enemies and ours to the fire."

She had to poke the logs a bit to get the papers properly burning.

The women sat in silence while the notes were reduced to ashes, and then they broke into applause, laughter and talkative groups mostly bunched around the far table where the coffee was ready to be served.

June Easton stayed close to Sally, helping her with names. The discontented woman was arguing loudly near the coffeepot. Another group, on the largest couch, measured the relative merits of their senior high school children applying to Dartmouth, Princeton, Harvard, Grinnell, Bryn Mawr or Goddard.

Sally liked these women. She had thoroughly enjoyed herself in an exotic fashion, she wasn't recording any underground laughter at her or at June, she was convinced they really did mean to be helpful to her. Yet along with the good warmth she had collected internally, resentment and anger burned too, generating a cool, calculating heat that was busy figuring their incomes, telling herself, If I wanted to put on a smooth act I could take this bunch of do-gooders for plenty.

"I just had the weirdest experience of my life," she said to Laura, too exhausted to give any details. She went to bed but not to fall asleep, too overexcited to settle down, startled to her depths by the realization that the strangest part of the evening had been how closely its reality had engulfed her. Why, she could have told those women the most shameful secret truths of her life and it would have been no more or less revealing than their own. Yet something about the group wildly angered her. As if there were an element involved of their fooling her, misusing her. Just before she left, one of the journalists asked if Sally had considered having a book written about her case.

Sally almost ran from her. "No, no," she said. "I don't like any kind of publicity. I wouldn't want my name plastered all over." And she urged June to leave then, please, because it was so late.

What was the good of that kind of talk, what good would it do her, practically speaking, in this tournament of The State vs. Sally Sweetsir? None, she decided, finally. She'd call June in the morning, thank her, tell her she'd rather the women's movement didn't step into the case. Do it politely, act very grateful and a little dumb, sort of scared. No sense turning them against her. Maybe one of them would show up on the jury, for all she knew.

The sound of a car pulling into the yard must have awakened her. Whoever was at the wheel kept the headlights on for some minutes, sitting still and waiting. For what? It was totally dark, and she saw by her illuminated clock that it was four thirty. Then the car door opened, and she recognized the sound of Johnny's dog barking its delirious joy at being home again. Then Johnny thumped up the stairs into his regular room, the dog trailing him as it always used to do.

She couldn't go back to sleep when the house quieted. Johnny had taken off right after the grand jury proceedings ended. He had the state's permission to go, although he had been told to stay in touch and to understand he must return for the trial. The state's most important witness. Poor Johnny Matthews.

It occurred to her to be frightened. Of Johnny? The righteous son returning to execute his own form of justice? Ludicrous. Those women's dramatic stories had gotten to her.

She got out of bed at six when the heat started up again. To hell with the energy crunch. No frigging with wood stoves for her, her furnace burned oil. As long as she could pay the bills she and Laura were going to stay warm the easy way. Let the rich solve the energy crisis—she hadn't created it, she wasn't going to make it better. Not now anyway, when she had enough to contend with. She'd do her bit later. She'd be a patriot, go to Florida, let the sun warm her. If the state treated her right.

A dead field mouse lay on the linoleum just inside the kitchen entrance. The cat's work, but Johnny's dog had forced the cat into hiding. She unrolled some paper toweling, picked up the weightless animal. How elegantly God had fashioned this little creature— smooth gray touched with white. She wrapped it in its paper shroud, dumped it in the garbage bin, carefully closing the swinging top.

"Sweets was afraid of mice," Johnny said.

She hadn't heard him come down the stairs. Had he tiptoed to scare her? She entertained again the notion of Johnny threatening danger, and again dismissed it as preposterous. He had removed his heavy boots, that's why she hadn't heard him. On his huge feet, double pairs of woolen socks showed their clashing colors through holes in the heels and toes. He looked older, messier. His beautiful golden hair hung limp and darkened with dirt. He had let it grow longer than Sweets ever would have allowed.

"Sweets neva woulda laid a finger on that mouse," he said. "Not him. Scared a them."

"More squeamish than scared," she said.

She was glad to see Johnny. She smiled at him, walked toward him to kiss him and cut her caress to a brush of her cheek when she realized that her touch disturbed him. He blushed deeply and pulled away. He smelled dirty.

She said, "Hey, I'm really glad to see you. I been worrying about you, wondering how you were getting on."

He spoke so low she had trouble hearing him. "Ain't ya mad at me? I expected to find ya good and mad at me." Then, louder, "Laura's been explainin to me how I ain't exactly helpin ya case none. I was almost afraid to come down to stay with ya."

"You been talking to Laura?"

He blushed again. "Call Laura two, three times a week." Deeper blush. "Sometimes more." Shy, proud grin. "We been connectin on a regular basis more or less since I took off for Portsmouth."

It was a disorienting piece of news. She couldn't trust Laura?

"That so?" she said. "I didn't know it."

"I made her promise not to tell ya," he said. "Laura don't go around breakin promises. That's not Laura's way."

She didn't know what to make of him and his news. He was different from the boy who had lived with her under Sweets's intimidation.

He said, "I been down a coupla times since, y'know, since everythin happened and I took off. I been down twice a month, maybe more."

"Where'd you stay? You don't ever have to worry about a place to stay while I have a place, Johnny. Don't you know that?" she said.

"Yeah, well," he said and held a long pause.

"Laura was keepin me up to date, y'know, on the trial n all. She kept tellin me ya wasn't mad at me, that ya understood how I felt n all, but it was hard to believe. Now I see ya with my own eyes . . .

"Ya lookin good, Sally," he said. "I like ya hair fixed y'know. . . ." He made a complicated attempt to simulate with his hand motions the backward curling wave across her forehead. His extraordinarily blue eyes were gazing down at her in a look in which defiance overcame fear. He talked in a rush.

"I'm goin upstairs and rouse up Laura now. She wasn't expectin me till later in the day. Decided to leave on the spur a the moment, split Portsmouth and drove straight through. Drivin at night on the highway, I dunno, it does somethin to ya, bores ya to hell and sets ya dreamin about all kinds of crazy things. Like bein all alone in outta space or somethin. Good thing they keep those rest stops open all night, stop for a cupa coffee, pass some conversation back n forth, come back to normal."

He waved vaguely, then turned his back and took off, mounting the stairs two and three at a time, bounding into Laura's bedroom and closing the door behind him.

What was she supposed to do? Not stand there listening for sounds, that was for sure.

What she was going to do was prepare a big breakfast, just as if nothing special was happening except a family visit from Johnny. She started a big pot of coffee dripping, prepared two small cans of frozen orange juice, dug into the freezer for a package of bacon she'd been saving for a big occasion, and while she was at it she hunted out the blueberry muffins she had made at the height of the berry season. Have a party, kids. They certainly were.

Keep her mind pinned to her own business. She had a lot to do before she met Ellen Mahoney at the Public Defender's office. Tidy up, run a laundry, give the living room a proper cleaning, make a stab at scrubbing the kitchen floor, defrost the refrigerator, clean up the stove a little. She had been letting everything go for weeks now. The bathroom was disgusting. They were living like pigs, she and Laura.

She had stockpiled a mess of trash in the garage. Raccoons had torn into the plastic bags twice now. She could move the whole mess in two or three trips with her little car. Empty the waste-baskets and the kitchen trash first. Prepare the elegant, weightless gray mouse for his cremation. There you go, sweetheart.

She drank a cup of coffee, alone at the kitchen table, studiously not listening for noises from above. The knife drawer was partly open. If the drawer hadn't been open that night? Sweets would be here, beating the shit out of Johnny Matthews.

Her love was supposed to change her man. Their love was going to make them the great couple of the world—their love, that temple of gossamer, was going to be more solid than Papa Ciomei's marble, more nutritious than a thousand meals, more gripping than a million TV shows, more romantic than all the love songs. Sally and Sweets in love carving out their chunk of sweet immortality.

Upstairs, there was Laura, in her sixteen-year-old hope and ignorance, taking her first step on that desperate woman's journey the child would insist was *love*.

"We love each other, Mom, can't ya try to understand?"

They were whispering in Sally's room where Sally was making up her face before going out to meet Ellen Mahoney, hushing their talk against Johnny's hearing them, though he was making so much noise in the shower, Sally doubted he could hear anything above the sound of the water and his own singing.

"Why the fuck are we whispering?" Sally said.

She knew why they were whispering. Women were *supposed* to whisper—to fear men overhearing their true talk, even when the man was a little kid.

"Laura," she said, "simmer down. You and Johnny are a couple of kids—"

"Johnny's eighteen now," Laura said. "No kid, Mom. He's got this job lobsterin. We c'n be down here visitin with ya any time. Only takes six hours straight down the innerstate. Or ya c'n come up there with us when we get married."

Was it fair of her to simulate utter desperation? Yes, any device to save Laura was fair. She grasped Laura by the elbows.

"Laurie, please, baby, don't you realize there's a limit to what I can take? I can't take any more than I have to contend with right now. I'm trying to save my ass. I should be on my way right this minute to my lawyers'."

"Mom!" Laura matched desperation for desperation. "We love each other. Don't ya understand?"

"I do, I do, baby. I do, I swear it. But I can't face any more problems right now. After the trial, after the trial, okay? Then we'll talk about it."

"There's nothin to talk about. Me and Johnny ain't neva gonna be parted soon as everything's settled with ya case. Cause we know ya gonna win it. Ya don't ever give me a chance to talk right. I ain't told ya the most important thing a the whole lot. Johnny's gonna talk to ya lawyers. He's goin ova to the Public Defender's office this afternoon to meet with those two guys, y'know, ya lawyers."

"What?" Sally said. "What for?"

"To talk to them."

"What for?"

"To tell it more like he remembers it now, y'know, the night everythin happened. He remembers it more like the lawyers say it happened, y'know, more like it really happened, like an accident."

She said nothing. If there was a connection between Laura in love and Johnny's changed story, it deeply chilled her. Laura had manipulated Johnny to save her?

"Johnny doesn't have to see my lawyers. He doesn't have to do that for me. I don't hold what he said against him. He was upset. I blabbed my head off too. All he has to do is tell the truth as he remembers it, that's all the defense wants from him. How come he changed his mind about what happened?"

"He just did, Mom, he just did. He just remembers better now he ain't so upset." She put her arms around Sally, hugging her hard.

"Don't ya understand? He's gonna tell the truth, just like they want him to. Ain't it terrific? Cause he was the worst the state had against ya, wasn't he? Now it'll be okay, they'll neva get ya now."

It was astounding how much solid woman there was to Laura suddenly—or was it that they hadn't been embracing very much lately? She pulled back from her daughter's body with an unaccustomed delicate distaste. She didn't want leftovers from a sexual feast that had nothing to do with her. And if it did, if there was a cause-and-effect relationship between their sex and Johnny's new "truth," then that was even worse.

"How come?" she said. "I don't get it. He isn't coming over to my side because of you, is he?"

Laura said, "Y'know, Mom, there are times when ya make me so mad . . . What are ya sayin to me? Just think about what ya sayin," and stepped back, her body taut with sexual defiance.

"Don't be mad at me, baby," Sally said. "I just don't want you to jump like I did. Want you to finish school. Want you to know more about yourself before you jump."

"God, ya talkin as if I'm goin off the edge of Harmon Junction bridge," Laura said, tears starting up. "I can't do nothin right for ya. Nothin I do is right. I thought we'd be makin ya glad and here ya are lecturin."

It flashed into Sally's mind that Laura was pregnant. She didn't dare ask, but exactly as if she had, Laura spoke.

"And don't go thinkin I'm pregnant. I'm *not* pregnant. We're not dumb, y'know. Know how to take care a ourselves."

Sally said, "You're smart and I love you and I know you're working your ass off to help me and I'd be a pig if I didn't appreciate it. Now you know I'm not a pig, right?"

"Sure," Laura said, "but ya ain't givin him any credit."

"Give me a chance," Sally said. "I have to get used to the idea first."

20

AT THE PUBLIC DEFENDER'S OFFICE, her three lawyers, inundated by documents and paper containers of coffee, weren't concerning themselves with the question of support of the women's movement, to her surprise, but were arguing the relative merits of a plea bargain. Sally would plead guilty or nolo contendere, to a charge of manslaughter and be sentenced to five years in prison.

Ellen said, "We have very persuasive arguments for probation of sentence . . ."

She picked up a stapled, Xeroxed document of many pages, waved it about.

"What's that?" Sally said. "Nolo—whatever you called it."

"Literally," Ellen explained, "'I do not wish to contend.' What it means is that there's no admitting or denying the charge. It means you don't wish to contest the charge. For practical purposes, the court will treat it as a guilty plea. You understand?"

"Yeah, I guess, sort of." Sally reached for the document. "May I see that? Does it mean that you're asking for the whole sentence to be suspended? That I don't go to jail at all?"

Ellen nodded, handing over the document. Kris and Mike were arguing some matter Sally couldn't follow.

She read, skimming and skipping.

Sally Sweetsir has no criminal record . . . born and lived in this area all of her life. This was her second marriage, her first was of ten years' duration. She has one child, a daughter. Sally Sweetsir is now employed as an executive secretary with the responsibility of office management and has been regularly employed in this capacity for the last six years. Prior to that period, during a time of acquiring and polishing her skills she was employed on a series of temporary assignments. Two of her former temporary employers are prepared to testify in her behalf. One, William Grandstone, is an established and esteemed attorney. Gerald Greenspan, her present employer, will attest to her personal character and to her loyalty, competence and reliability. We would add that if this matter were to go to trial there would be six or seven additional people who would testify as to the responsible, gentle character of Sally Sweetsir as wife, mother, daughter and friend. . . .

She moved ahead to a long section on Morgan Beauchamp Sweetsir.

Severe emotional difficulties . . . married five times . . . drinking . . . abusive behavior toward women characterized by verbal and physical abuse. . . . During his directly previous marriage he subjected his wife, Kay Sweetsir, to frequent severe physical abuse including documented injuries such as loss of teeth, black eyes, dislocation of the shoulder . . . his abusive conduct was not limited to periods of intoxication . . . Morgan's similar conduct toward his wife Sally Sweetsir was soon apparent after their marriage . . . usually careful to leave no visible bruises . . . nevertheless, black eyes caused by blows evident on several occasions . . . Sally's response was always to protect her husband's image. . . . Morgan Sweetsir's history of mental disorder . . .

She skipped. The final part of the document was titled THE EVENT. She pushed beyond the details to the last paragraph.

. . . she was obviously shocked by the seriousness of her husband's wounds, clearly she had had no intention to inflict a fatal wound. She was hysterical . . . remorseful . . . her only concern was for her husband's welfare. Sally Sweetsir loved her husband and never intended to do him harm. Tyrone Parsons heard Morgan Sweetsir say to his wife while waiting for the ambulance to arrive, "Honey, I love you and forgive you. And I know that you love me and that you didn't mean to do it."

Three signatures appeared above their typed names and titles: *Attorney for Respondent,* Michael Bronenfeld, Kris Kerkorian, Ellen Mahoney.

Sally Sweetsir, portrait of a saint surrounded by a halo. Sweets, portrait of a man with horns and a tail. On the state's side, the story would all be turned the other way, by another, different team of lawyers, prosecutors for the state. All this weight brought to bear on one woman, her. It was absurd.

Ellen was speaking.

". . . argue and prove our contention that at the very least the killing was not intentional and at best was an accident. We have it now with the cooperation of Johnny Matthews. And Kris's last memo . . ."

Ellen searched out another long document, flipped the pages, read aloud rapidly. ". . . the assault with the knife in and of itself is a lawful response to the battery upon her."

Her eyes moved down the page, then she continued. ". . . but if the stabbing was an accident precipitated by a struggle for control of the weapon, it may be homicide by misadventure, not criminally negligent and . . ."

Kris Kerkorian was sitting back, his lips pressed together smugly, as she read. Mike Bronenfeld paced, his face darkened by irritation.

"We've all read those memos back and forth between us a dozen times, Ellen. The question is, Do we have it, or don't we have it? The theories are fine, it's all fine, but I'm the one who's going to have to stand up and perform, convince the court."

Ellen said, "We've got Johnny now. We stand a very good chance. Anyway, that's my vote on the subject." She sounded tired.

"It's not Johnny's show, it's Sally's. It's Sally who's the key to the decision," Mike said in his quick, excitable manner.

"That's true," Kris Kerkorian said. "It's Sally's handling of herself on the stand. That's the key. That is the crux of the matter."

"What?" Sally said as if a straight, simple question might have the power to stop all the bewildering talk. Nobody answered her.

"We've still got a very tricky complication if we don't use self-defense. On the admissibility of evidence. And we've got all this hesitation on Sally's part. We can't do it without Sally following a very tight script. There's no way."

Mike seized the document Ellen had been reading from, turned the pages.

"Here it is," he said and read.

. . . admissibility of evidence as to the victim's character or reputation for turbulence arises, counsel for the accused must claim self-defense . . . since if the defendant denies the killing or asserts that it was not intentional, evidence of the bad character of the deceased for peace and quietness or that he was a violent or dangerous man is not admissible. . . .

He ended muttering numbers and initials—"1 ALR 3d 576"—and then burst out again, "and on top of that, Sally's holding back, don't use that, don't say that, I want him protected, we're blocked any way we go with her attitude."

"Don't talk about me as if I'm not in the room," Sally said. "It makes me feel like I'm nothing."

"Listen, Sally, I'm breaking my ass for you. I want to get you off, we all do," Mike yelled. "I want to win this case."

"Well, it's simple, isn't it? I killed him, but I didn't want to kill him. It was an accident. I only wanted to scare him to make him back off. I didn't want to kill him. You all know that. Now you're talking about pleading guilty or that nolo business. I won't, I won't."

"It's your decision, Sally," Ellen said. "We'll only do what you want us to do."

"I'm sorry," Mike Bronenfeld said. "I didn't mean . . . I don't think any of us are going for that plea, are we?"

Kris Kerkorian shrugged, stared ahead.

"Listen," Mike Bronenfeld said, "I have to break now. I have to meet a guy. We'll get together again at one thirty. Okay?"

"Me too. I have to get home and check on my little fellow," Ellen said. "The antibiotic ruined him. His guts are pouring out of both ends."

"Want to have a couple of sandwiches brought in?" Kris Kerkorian asked Sally in a pleasant conciliatory manner.

She wanted to get away, to be alone.

"Thanks, Kris," she said, "but I've a bunch of dumb things to do in town, this and that, may as well do it now."

Once outside, she cringed from the possibility of further contact and headed for the strip on the other side of town, but because it was Saturday the fast-food joints were spotted with people who knew her. Avoiding the inevitable stares and greetings, she erratically pulled in and out of Mary's Heroes, Kentucky Fried Chicken, the Pizza Hut, Chuck Wagon, McDonald's, Burger King. Her stomach was both queasy and empty. She hadn't eaten any of that big breakfast she had prepared for Laura and Johnny. And the talk at the office hadn't helped to settle her insides.

She was already so far out on the strip, it would only take another ten minutes to go on to Mrs. White's Luncheonette on Main Street in West Eatonville, across from the paper mill. Nobody she knew would be there, and in this bitter cold a bowl of Mrs. White's homemade fish chowder and biscuits would be perfect.

As if in entering the luncheonette she had stepped into the middle of a nightmare, she was face to face with Helen and Ty Parsons, seated in the corner window table right behind the door. Sally automatically adjusted her expression to bright, fake heartiness.

"Hi," she said.

Ty half greeted, half dismissed her in a single embarrassed gesture. Helen Parsons displayed such open disgust that Sally's act backed up on her in a wash of uncontrollable nausea. *Vomit up the whole fuckin town, the whole fuckin problem, give it all up, go to jail, go to hell and never come back.* That'd satisfy the damn dumb crew of coarse, mean, ugly bastards: watching her crumble. Expecting it. Enjoying it. She turned to leave, saw Fern Bowdoin outside, dismounting his motorbike. Was she going to skulk around the rest of her life? In a rage, she swung back to Helen Parsons, stood directly in front of her.

"You hate me, don't you, Helen?"

How loud, almost gay, her voice rang out in the little luncheonette.

"That's right," Helen Parsons said, through a mouthful of biscuit.
Her voice was muffled.

"Mind telling me why?"

Helen Parsons looked away, swallowed, then spoke out louder
than Sally had.

"Ya killed a good man, a thousand times bettern ya could eva
hope to be. Don't mind tellin ya at all."

She was astounded at the coolness of Helen's attack. Had she expected Helen Parsons to wither silently before her clear blast as if
she had only to smile and explain for the world to condone and accept her? What was she hoping for from Helen Parsons? Beyond
her ability to control her response, Sally spoke again.

"You hate me so much you'd be happy to see me jailed, wouldn't
you?"

"I'd be happy to see ya hung," Helen said. "Or whatever they do
these days."

"You don't even realize what you're saying," Sally said.

"Don't ya lecture me, not ya kind ain't lecturin me. Ya want applause for what ya done like some are givin ya? Ya go get it from
them kind, and leave us decent people alone."

"What does that mean?" Sally said.

"Ya know damn well what it means," Helen said.

Fern Bowdoin had come in, nodded at Sally, interest and wonder
on his face as he hung up his down jacket. A crazy-looking wool hat
was on his head. She felt disoriented. Helen Parsons' voice bounded
off the walls of the little luncheonette in a booming loop of continuous sound. The hollowness of Sally's insides responded to the
smell of the fresh fish stew, then an odor of french fries in stale oil
turned her stomach. She really might vomit right there in front of
everybody. At each crowded little table familiar faces stared and
listened, as if to a play on a stage. She had started Helen Parsons
going and now there wasn't any stopping her. Ty held Helen's arm,
tugging at her.

"Lemme alone, Ty," she yelled. "She asked for it, she's gonna get
it. It weren't me started it. But so long as ya asked, Sally Sweetsir,
ya may as well know it right here and now that I pray to God ya

get what ya deserve. Since the day ya killed Sweets I been askin God to do me that favor, do the world a favor and put ya away where ya belong wherever He thinks best."

Since she was onstage with Helen Parsons, fighting to defend herself, then she'd have to put on a performance better than Helen's. She raised her head, pulled off her white knitted hat, tossed her hair, managed a big, fake, carefree smile.

"Not very Christian of ya, Helen, prayin ya heart out to see me hurt. Prayin to have me hung, prayin to have me put away for good."

She heard herself reverting to local speech. The hell with a pretense of having moved on and up. She was nowhere. She had gone down as far as anybody could.

Helen Parsons rose from her seat, waving one of her hamlike arms toward Sally as if she meant to whack her one.

"The chair'd be too good for ya," she was yelling. "Putting ya away for life'd be too good for ya. Ya didn't think of *his* life, did ya? Him losin *his* life didn't bother ya none. If ya had any sense ya'd get the hell outta here. Ya shouldn't be walkin aroun free as a bluejay spoilin life for the rest a us. Ya shoulda been locked up from the minute ya done it."

Sally's throat was so tight, her voice came out in a quaver. "Ya mind if they gimme a trial first? Ya mind if Sally Sweetsir gets a fair trial before she gets melted down."

Righteousness kept Helen's voice steady and loud. "Last thing I'm gonna say to ya, so ya betta listen. I neva asked ya to talk to us, and me and Ty'll be pleased if ya neva do again. Just stay the hell outta our way. Get the hell outta here. The sight a ya is spoilin our dinner."

She ran from the little steamy, homey place turned rancid, pulling her wool hat on her head, pushing past Fern Bowdoin. He followed, catching up with her at her car door.

"Hey, Sally," he said, "ya ain't lettin it bother ya none—what went on back there now, are ya?"

He had no outer jacket on, but he was still wearing the silly woolen hat. She hadn't seen him since the afternoon of the day Sweets died, when she had dumped her troubles on him at the Hilltop bar. He wrapped his long arms around his lean, hard body. The wind brought tears to his eyes. She stared down at the messy ground, knocking dirty snow from her boot against the edge of the car. She couldn't speak.

"Not everybody thinks like Helen Parsons," he said. "There's some around town wouldn't agree with Helen Parsons, not by a long shot. There's plenty wouldn't.

"All ya need is a jury with a little common sense," he said. "Plenty a people with common sense around. Plenty."

She didn't respond.

"How's ya health now, how ya feelin?" he said. "Cause ya remember, ya was worryin about that cancer thing."

"Oh," she said. "I told you all about that, didn't I?"

She was coming back to herself, in better control of her shaken speech.

"That all checked out okay, Fern. Thanks for asking, just needed some simple treatment. Wasn't cancer at all."

He nodded and nodded, sagely, but the funny hat ruined the effect. Around the two chatting on the plowed road muddied by salt and gravel, Saturday afternoon traffic moved slowly. In each car, as it passed, faces turned to check them out.

"You better get back," she said, "you'll freeze."

"As long as ya keep ya head covered it traps the heat in ya body," he said. "That's the way the heat gets out, through the top a ya head."

She said, "I thought you lived down my direction. How come you're out this way?"

"Work here," he said, and jabbed his thumb back over his shoulder at the immense sprawling structures of the paper mill dominating the wide curve of the river.

Sally said, "I worked at the mill for a month or so in the office—typing."

"Well, then, ya know what it's like, don't ya?" he said, slightly mocking. "Little different out on the floor—depending on which floor, too."

"I was on the floor once when there was a paper break. Never saw anything like that in my life," Sally said. "Thought the world was coming to an end. Sirens going and everybody running like maniacs."

He nodded, grinned.

Someone had told her Fern Bowdoin was an engineer. She'd have to ask him about that sometime. It seemed too nosy at the moment.

"Ya get used to it. All in the day's work. Gotta move fast, fast— fast and careful, that's the trick."

"I didn't like it working at the paper mill," Sally said. "You like it?"

He shrugged. "Makin good money, considerin. Put myself through some very hard years studyin and workin. Now I'm on the collectin end I'd *better* like it."

"Seemed like working in hell to me," Sally said. "Those departments, either it's smell or awful heat or noise, and the size of the machinery. The size of those rollers. They're scary. The office was okay, nothing wrong with the office, but I was glad to get out of there."

"It ain't too bad," he said. "Ya get used to it, learn to respect it. Anyways I put too much inta this job to give up on it now."

"People say working at the mill makes you deaf," she said.

He overacted deafness, cupping his ear, leaning forward, "What's that ya sayin, ma'am?" enjoying her laughter.

"Fact is," he said, "I'm some deaf. Not bad enough for a hearing aid. Own fault. Wasn't careful enough, but I watch it now, keep those ear guards on whenever I'm on the floor.

"There's worse than deaf can happen to a man in there," he said, "and OSHA ain't much help either."

"What's 'osha'?" she said.

"Federal safety agency. Bunch of assholes. I know more about the risks of that machinery than any OSHA asshole."

He shivered violently.

"You're freezing," she said.

He shook his head, grinned, brushed away a huge tear rolling down his hollowed cheek. She liked him. It was a shocking sensation, liking a man again. Behind him loomed the varied structures of the mill, cottony white smoke billowing from the huge stacks, lifted and blended by the wind into solid clouds in the vividly blue sky reflected in the wide, clear river. Seen from this distance there was charm in the scene—the Tinker-Toy bridge, the height of the buildings dwarfing the massive piles of tree logs into tumbled matchsticks, the railroad a toy-train set winding across model tracks surrounded by a miniature parking lot complete with miniature cars and moving figures of mechanical men carrying tiny lunchboxes. Yet the scene didn't please her. It hurt, as if its power had seized her in a fist and squeezed.

"I'm going to get out of this state and never come back, if I'm lucky, if I stay free," she said.

"Where would ya go?"

"Florida. Ever been? It's terrific. It's warm. You can breathe there."

"Funny, ya mentionin the state a Florida. I been lookin inta the state a Florida. Paper mills down there."

"Really? I went to a place called Clearwater. No paper mills there. Pretty place, everything's pretty."

"Yeah, well, that's it. Some was tellin me, Florida's a state ya c'n find work ya trained in and then maybe enjoy life a little too."

"Are you thinking of moving your whole family?"

"Har, har," he said.

He fixed a bitter gaze at a spot beyond her head, then drew in his breath sharply.

"Ya know I'm divorced, don't ya?"

She shook her head No.

"Right around Thanksgiving," he said. "When ya havin trouble ya think everybody's noticin. I guess ya had ya hands fulla ya own troubles without payin attention to other people's."

She said, "I didn't hear a thing about it. You left Deedee?"

"Other way around. Weren't my idea. My idea is ya make the best a things. But everybody seems to be doin it. The part that hurts is the kids. I got a lot invested in those kids. She took em way the hell out to New Mexico, place called Santa Fe. Supposed to be real nice."

She nodded. An intense restlessness hit her. What was she doing, standing around listening to this man jabbering?

"I musta done something wrong," he said. "Deedee's a good woman down deep."

She nodded.

He said, "Ya didn't get to eat in there," and went on quickly, "Wanna drop in at Burger King down the road? Ya c'n go on ahead, I'll pick up my jacket back there and foller ya, meet ya there. Be an honor to have the favor a ya company," he said with mock ceremony.

She looked at her watch. "I only have a half hour now. I have to get back and confer with my lawyers."

"There's so little meat in them burgers ya c'n swaller the whole thing in one intake."

He himself ordered only french fries and a Coke. "Not hungry," he explained. "Helen Parsons shootin her mouth off give me a pain in my gut. Can't stand to hear that holier-than-God bullshit. Who she kiddin? Pretendin she and Ty is havin a peaceful marriage. Amazin grace! I seen them go after one another at a Legion dance. Ty cracked a rib in that one. It's the hypocrisy I can't take. Don't care who they are, how much money they have or education or what. Ya take ya average married couple, they got a war going between them. Not what I eva wanted with my wife, but that's the way it was. I tried my best, mostly for my kids, that's true, but I tried. She's a good woman and she tried her best, but it don't work, it can't work. Two different human beings, they gotta be different, they're *different*, and each forcin the other inta his mold or her mold. Tryin, neva succeedin, frustratin themselves, frustratin the one they supposed to be lovin till they hardly act human. A man's supposed to be such and such, and a woman's supposed to be such and such, well they ain't, they are what they are and no amount a hollerin and yellin's gonna change em. Wonder is they ain't more killins. What the hell's the use to put Sally Sweetsir away cause she and the man she was tryin her best with got inta a fight and she accidentally killed him? That ain't gonna solve nothin. Them holier-than-God folks are hypocrites. A man gets inta one a them moods, lookin for trouble like a hound dog trailin a telephone pole to piss on. Nothin gonna stop him till he finds it. I got four younger brothers livin at home with my ma. Sweet guys most a the time but mean bastards fulla beer. One a them starts actin up, my mother calls me to come ova and stop em. They all love a scrap. Only thing to do is sock em. I done it more than once. Sock em on the jaw, let em sleep it off. But a woman ain't got the strength. Not a regular woman like you, y'know what I mean, ya ain't a bruiser like Helen Parsons. Up against a big man like Morgan Sweetsir, what ya supposed to do? Somethin gotta stop him. I give my youngest brother a sock, he's a slim, light fellow, caught him on the side a his head, didn't mean to. Knocked him unconscious. Thought I killed him. I coulda killed him, I hit him that hard, I was so goddam mad. Then they'd put me away for twenty years—or whatever, life maybe. Tell themselves they're makin the world safer without me."

He stopped, grinned. "There I go, shootin my mouth off."

"Deedee go off with another man?" Sally said.

"Yeah," he said. "A nineteen-year-old boy. Gonna be fatherin my children. My oldest is only four years younger'n her stepfather."

He paused, sucked in his lean cheeks. "Y'know I c'n hardly say that word stepfather without gaggin."

For an instant she considered advising him to sue for custody. Instead she said, "You drink?"

"My entire capacity's limited to one, two beers at most. Can't tolerate a single shot a the hard liquor. Must be allergic or somethin. What I like is bars. Like to spend a coupla hours at a bar, eatin a little somethin, pickin up on some conversation. Ya get lucky ya run into Sally Sweetsir like at the Hilltop that time."

He grinned.

"I like a glass of wine now and then," Sally said, "with a meal."

"What I can't stand," he said, "is one a them real drunks. Liquored up, thinkin they're havin a great time amusin the bystanders and all the time actin like damn fools borin everybody to extinction ramblin on n on."

He made an open, friendly appeal.

"How about us goin to hell with ourselves over a glass a wine and a glass a beer? Y'know that new bar opened up on Main Street downtown? Like to take ya there any time ya say. Serve a good steak. The salad bar ain't bad either. Got one a those squeamish fellers strummin a guitar doin more talkin than singin. Don't care for him too much. Country's my music. But he sort of fades inta the noise, can't hear him too good, so's he's not too annoyin."

She said she was going to be pretty busy in the coming weeks preparing for the trial and getting through it—but thanked him, anyway.

Her three lawyers were waiting for her at the Public Defender's office. She requested a private conference with Ellen Mahoney. Sally noted the alert glances exchanged. As if she were made of explosive material. What now? they signaled one another.

The two women walked down the windowless hall to Ellen's office in silence. Settled in an armchair, Ellen facing her across her desk, Sally lit a cigarette, inhaled, pressing her painted fingertip against the bridge of her nose. Ellen smiled, but her clear, honest eyes waited anxiously.

"I forgot to ask you how your little boy is," Sally said. She needed a momentary truce before commitment.

"Much better. We took him off the antibiotic, and would you believe that the doctor told us to give him Tums? Adam's delighted. He thinks they're mint candy. He'll be fine now. And Castle's back, so I've the rest of the day to feel free."

She didn't look free. She had the limp, disordered appearance of harassment, and her slight tic was showing up—a compulsive widening of the eyelids accompanied by a tiny sniff.

"Is it about the plea? Do you want to talk about that?"

"My plea," Sally said, "is 'Not guilty.' Of anything."

"Good," Ellen said. "That's been my choice all along."

"You tell me what you need me to do. I'll know how to do it," Sally said.

"I know you will," Ellen said.

Ellen's eyes, clearer, happier than before, still measured some anxiety.

"We need a particular concept of Morgan Sweetsir," she said. "Of your life with him."

Sally said, "I understand."

Ellen excused herself, maneuvered her bulk out of the desk chair and hurried out on her surprisingly dainty feet. Sally knew she was going down the hall to tell the others.

21

Now THAT SHE WAS IN IT all the way, going for broke, each day's serious work was the preparation for the trial—rehearsals as for a drama, the good guys and the bad guys, the big game between two teams, playing their hearts out to win. *The truth*, which had obsessed her since the killing, *why, how*, was obscured by the contest. There was *the Law;* its manipulation constituted the rules of the game; the prize was *winning*.

Mike Bronenfeld passed around a Xeroxed clipping from *Time* magazine that he had tucked away in his folder. She skimmed it, uncomfortable to be identified with such women, seeing herself as a special case, having nothing to do with these others.

More than one fourth of U.S. murders are family affairs, and the courst have never been particularly tough on defendants who act in the heat of a domestic quarrel. In recent weeks, an array of women have managed to walk away unpunished after killing their husbands or even former husbands. In Chicago, Juan Maldonado capped a drinking bout by beating his eight-year-old son with a shoe, so wife Gloria, 32, shot him three times. The State's Attorney ruled there was "insufficient evidence" to warrant her prosecution. . . . In Lansing, Michigan, Francine Hughes, 30, claimed that years of physical abuse drove her to pour gasoline around her sleeping ex-husband and light it. A jury acquitted her of murder on grounds that she had been temporarily insane. In Orange County, California, Evelyn Ware, 29, pleaded self-defense after shooting her ex-husband five times. Accepting her evidence of habitual beatings, a jury found her not guilty of murder. . . .

She skipped a few more examples to the final paragraph of the article.

. . . inform the public of a woman's right to protect herself against physical and emotional attack . . . notes New Jersey Lawyer Robert Ansell, "the cumulative effect of beatings on a woman's consciousness is often considered. A woman may well be allowed quicker resort to a weapon than a man." That worries some lawmen. Says Sheriff Lawrence Schmies of Waupaca: "I wonder if these people know what they're doing. If they get their way, there's going to be a lot of killings."

She laughed out loud.
Ellen looked up. "What's funny?"
"Oh, God knows," Sally said, but couldn't stop laughing.
It was Ellen who had broken down the defense line into parts, leaving Sally a subtle, difficult but absolutely starring role.
"You loved him. You were trying. You thought Morgan's abuses unintentional, a part of his emotional upset, a part of his drinking problem. Lots of time he was wonderful to be with. He acted like a man who loved you. Tell that too. Just tell your story exactly as we've gone over it, exactly as you've told it to me, about the fight and him hitting you and your deciding to scare him with the knife. You didn't know consciously the knife had penetrated. Use your own words. Tell how you felt when you saw he was badly hurt."
"What if I start to cry?" It was her way of asking for a directive. Shall I cry?
"You damn well better cry," Mike called out from across the room. "Just tears, no breakdown."
Mike took over from Ellen the weekend before the trial. They had a run-through rehearsal, Mike directing her and Johnny and Laura. Kris Kerkorian was still up to his neck in case law, precedents. Ellen was grooming all the other defense witnesses.
Sally noticed that Ellen arrived at the office depressed and agi-

tated that morning. Later a telephone call came in for her. Right in front of everybody, Ellen was having a fight with her husband.

"You're talking as if I like the situation, as if I created it. I don't control the court calendar, Castle. I didn't purposely set up a conflict of dates."

A pause while she listened.

"I cannot walk out on this case in the middle."

Pause.

"I've never missed one of your openings and you know it."

Pause.

"If you insist on an either/or approach, you force me into an either/or response. It is *not* an either/or situation. It's just bad luck. I'm not asking *you* to postpone your opening, am I?"

Pause.

"Castle, I don't want to talk about it now. We'll discuss it later."

Pause.

"There's no way that I'll leave this case until the verdict is in. If you insist on your interpretation, then logically, yes, you're right, I'd rather stick with what you call my fucking case than be with you at the most important opening of your career. Is that what you want to hear?"

Pause.

"Yes, damn it, I know what it means to be shown at the Whitney. Do you know what it means for a woman like Sally Sweetsir to be faced with jail?" Pause. "If everything's going along according to plan I can fly down for the weekend. The trial can't run longer than two weeks. With luck, it might only run one week, and there won't be *any* problem. But I will not leave until . . ."

Castle had obviously hung up. Ellen placed the phone in its cradle. She sat at her desk, her heavy shoulders hunched forward, a large, serious, vulnerable child.

Sally stood up, put her arm around Ellen's broad shoulders, her head against Ellen's clean-smelling brown hair.

"I'd never make it without you, Ellen," she said. "Y'know?"

She had never done anything like that before, displayed an open plea for help to another woman, and by extension an open declaration of her thanks.

Now it was easier to approach Laura again.

"I'm only asking one thing, baby. Finish school. Please finish school. Stay with me till you finish school. Then, out on your own with my blessing. Make your decisions, marry, don't marry, your decision."

"I can't stay here, Mom, don't ya understand? Ya know what it's like stayin on in the same school with the trial about to begin? Ya know what I'm goin through?"

"We won't stay here, baby, we'll take off. Go to Florida. You'll love Florida."

"That's if we *win*, Mom, what if we lose?"

It was the first time Laura had said "lose" to her.

Lying awake at night, obsessed with thoughts too loose to control, circling her chances, daydreaming a perfect performance on the stand by Sally Sweetsir, Mike Bronenfeld knocking the jury dead with his summation, she found herself debating Fern Bowdoin.

How about real love between a man and a wife? Forget man and wife. A man and a woman in love. There was no such reality? Only husbands and wives, natural antagonists, their reasons for being to raise kids, and the best to hope for, an armed truce for the sake of the kids. Till death do us part and one kills the other. Everyone circling in space, separate and alone, daydreaming a nonexistent connection. Love. Love between a man and a woman. Not love for Laura or Papa Ciomei or Ellen Mahoney, or her father and her sisters. Love, love for a man, a particular kind of man, a man like Sweets, yes, like Fern Bowdoin, yes. Love between a man and a woman, forever and ever. Encourage Fern Bowdoin, fall in love again, immerse herself in hope and trust, hold out a promise of peace, a haven of love for him, disappoint him, anger him, make him hate her, hate him back. Love. War and its casualties. Did she need love—or whatever it was? Not for the sex. She could do it to herself, she could do it with a stray man whenever she got the urge. Not for support, financial or any other kind; not for companionship. She could support herself, support her daughter, take care of herself, enjoy her own company. She could swat bugs, get rid of dead mice, burglars didn't worry her, lightning didn't scare her. She didn't need a big strong man to lean on. *What*, then? She had no theories defensible in a court of law.

"Do you love Castle?" she asked Ellen. They were alone in Ellen's office.

"Oh, yes," Ellen said, and flushed slightly.

"Does he love you?"

Ellen laughed. "Well, *look* at me. There's no inherited wealth on my side in my family either, so what else can it be but love?"

She did not say to Ellen, Castle demands of you just what Sweets demanded of me—submission. I come first, saith the male, there shall be no others before me. Even a little runty man like Castle. Not Sally's idea of a man at all. Real men were big, dark; they hid a dangerous and exotic element behind their outer swagger; they worked at jobs that demanded strength, skill, respect for enormous, tricky machinery. Their hips grew down toward the earth on a firm base, not the mincing, shuffling, ungrounded stance of a guy like Castle.

"Are you afraid of him?" Sally said.

She had astonished Ellen. "Yes," Ellen said, "I guess I am. Does it show?"

She was a big woman. She could easily knock Castle down if he made her angry enough.

"No, I was just wondering if we all are—afraid of men."

"Yes," Ellen said, "and they, just as afraid of us."

"You believe they are?"

"Don't you?"

She thought of Sweets's ambiguously trembling hands. Of his contradictory need to be simultaneously in and out of her sphere, tied up tight, and free as a bird.

"Do you believe in happy marriages?" Sally said.

"Oh," Ellen said, "*believe, happy*. Who knows? I want to be married to Castle. I'd be miserable if he left me, and I'd never leave him."

"Don't you think Castle loves his work first?"

"Oh, sure he loves his work first," Ellen said lightly.

"Do you?"

"Love my work first?"

Sally nodded.

"I don't know," Ellen said. "Sometimes I think I love my children first."

"Don't you think that really what men love first isn't their women or their children or their work but themselves, their picture in their own minds they make up of who they think they are. Isn't that what's first with them?"

"Yes. Exactly. Maybe that's the right way to conceive of oneself, and women should emulate men in that."

"I always thought men were better than women, I liked them better. Women can be so silly. A real smart woman can be scared to death of lightning, for example. That's dumb."

"It's not dumb. Lightning can kill you," Ellen said. "And men are scared too. They just pretend."

"Y'know, it's funny," Sally said, "men have always been very important to me. Men are important to me right now. I'm worried about what Mike thinks of me. I never worry about what you think. And I like you so much more than I do Mike. There's no comparison, how I feel about you and him. I don't understand myself, I don't understand about love and men and women, do you?"

"No," Ellen said. "I don't, at least not much."

Laura's testimony was near perfect. Mike's only concern was that she "keep it clean, hold the asshole, fuckin bits, okay? We'll bring out verbal abuse through other witnesses and in cross. We want you to come on as a sweet young lady. Got it?" Laura got his meaning perfectly.

Johnny, too, was quick to pick up on what was expected of him, a certain tone, with its measure of confusion since the prosecution would surely attempt to undermine his credibility, just as the defense would have if he had gone the other way.

When they rehearsed with the duplicate knife bought for the purpose, Sally left the room, until Ellen came to tell her it was over. She had heard the scene rehearsed orally. Mike pulled a step-by-step description of what he wanted out of Johnny and Sally. Laura was out of it; she hadn't witnessed that part of the fight. A paralegal assistant was called in to act as Sally, same height and build, more or less. Kris Kerkorian, not tall or broad enough, nevertheless was Sweets. The young woman acting Sally picked up the knife. Kris, acting Sweets, grabbed her wrists, pulling and shaking her violently. The cutting edges of the knife were sheathed during the act.

Because of the shaking and pulling, the knife accidentally and fatally stabbed the man through the fleshy part of the inner arm, entering between the ribs and severing the heart. Johnny described Sally's shock, disbelief, horror. Obviously no intent. They rehearsed over and over and over again. Each time they played out the knife scene, Sally left the room.

Over and over and over again, Mike rehearsed Sally's testimony. She even had to practice rising and walking to the stand, being sworn in. Mike put her through her speech so many times, she was certain she could have delivered it word for word awakened in the middle of the night, half asleep.

She had had a bad day. She was on edge because of the threat of cancer, because it was her first day of not smoking, and because her husband was in a bad mood. (True.) He, too, was on edge because of not smoking, and because of a temporary layoff. He was in a rotten mood, foul-mouthed and uncooperative. He had often been so in the past, but she lived in hope for their future. She would help him to steadily become the man he sometimes was—a good and loving companion. Yes, he could be charming, supportive, at times. He earned good money, but he spent freely and had many debts; there was a history of failed marriages, emotional and psychological problems. He had an irrational temper. He drank heavily, was verbally and physically abusive to his wife and children. She hoped that these traits would be worked out with her help. (True.) When she turned to him for sympathy that day, he struck her, tore her wedding ring from her finger and his wedding ring from his finger and threw them at her. (False. It was she who started the ring incident, she extended the fight, if she had gone away and shut up it would have blown over. She had insisted on a degree of care he simply couldn't come up with. It enraged him. It enraged her. They wanted to kill each other and she had done it first. *Strike all that.*) She grabbed the knife to scare him. (She had no idea whether this was true or false. She could barely remember grabbing the knife, only her anger and a rush of exultation with her determination to win, never to be beaten again. *Forget it.*) They struggled. He grabbed her wrists and shook her violently, pulling her and knocking her about. She didn't feel the knife go in. She was shocked by his collapse, thought it was only an arm wound and only later when his shirt was torn open saw the chest wound. (True.) It was at this point in the telling where she cried, always at exactly the same point, when she described her shock at his collapse.

"I'll never forget my husband lying on the floor and all his bright, dark color going out of his skin. So fast, so fast. I'll have to live with that memory for the rest of my life."

Mike drilled her so thoroughly, the trial version became *the truth*. She had no difficulty assuming the soft, subdued character Mike wanted. Still he wanted more, more of a battered-wife, submissive-animal touch. She wouldn't oblige. She couldn't. She knew he was pulling out the whole bag of tricks to save her, but she wasn't going to become Kay Sweetsir to win her case. He kept up the pressure even after the trial began.

"Cut back on the eye makeup. I want you to look nice, attractive, but you don't want to give the impression of a woman on the make," Mike said, the morning of the first day.

Ellen said, "Mike, I'll stab you myself if you say another word. Sally looks lovely. She's perfect. Let her alone."

She had bought a new suit and three tops, two blouses and one overblouse, turning one new outfit into three. She had bought a long fake-gold chain—no other jewelry. She had her hair carefully cut the week before so it would settle in by trial time. She washed and tinted it every morning, shaped it with her blower, she prepared herself for last-minute runs in her panty hose by purchasing a dozen pair. She wore plain pumps with high heels, avoided the skirt slit all the way up the front, took instead the one with two little slits on either side. She looked right. She knew she looked right.

She convinced Laura to hold herself down to a new navy-blue double knit and quiet her exotic beauty. Mike fussed. Laura had to do something to her loose, long hair. They drew it severely back and secured it with a big barrette. It was startling how the smoothly parted flat look turned Laura into a classic madonna. One of Papa Ciomei's statues. Johnny wore cords, a flannel shirt, new shoes; his hair was freshly washed. The big surprise was Sally's older sister, neat as a pin in a black pants suit—and slim.

"Weight Watchers," she told Sally, hugging and kissing her, the tears welling on both sides. They hadn't seen each other in almost a year.

Slim, Dotty looked strikingly like Sally now, and both sisters looked very like their daddy, Robert E. Stark, manager of the Hartshead supermarket, his blond hair a little duller and thinner, blue eyes defiantly bluer. His loose, muscular body was uncomfortably boxed into a polyester suit, too cool for winter weather but the only suit he owned. He wore long johns underneath.

"It'll lay down eight foot a snow before the night ends, betcha," he said before he went to bed.

Sally was reminded of the Ciomei family gatherings that always turned into a party—one of those meetings to settle a dismal family problem or mourn a death. Dotty had driven in from her farm with a cooked roast chicken, a fresh ham, a meat loaf and a bunch of baked goods, unloading the lot with sidelong glances at Sally, eliciting approval. Lots of kidding around, coffeepot kept full, beer and soda in the refrigerator, snacking junk brought in by Johnny and Laura.

It was Ellen Mahoney who had searched her family out, rallied them to her cause. Other witnesses showed up in the room across from the courtroom where they waited their turn on the stand: Vincent Ciomei, former husband; William Grandstone, former boss; Jerry Greenspan, current boss; Fern Bowdoin, longtime friend; Kay Sweetsir, Morgan Beauchamp Sweetsir's former wife; June Easton, longtime friend; Iris Benton Beauchamp, married to the last living Beauchamp, now dead, a perfect stranger to Sally, eager to testify to the irresponsible and emotionally disturbed behavior of her great-nephew by marriage, Morgan Beauchamp Sweetsir.

They left for the courthouse very early because of the snow, but the roads had been cleared sufficiently for slow-moving traffic. Johnny took the wheel of Daddy's car, but her father was so on edge that once out of the alley he made Johnny stop. Daddy took over the driving. Johnny sat in the back with Laura and Dotty, beating his leg up and down, jerking his knee and shaking his foot in a constant, machinelike motion. It was Sally and Laura who were entirely calm. They had taken a Valium each—Ellen had said they should.

"You're not going to be called on to do or say anything, and it'll help you cope with the shock of the first day."

Sally had been vaguely fearing reporters, photographers, a courtroom so impressive it would overwhelm her, crowds of onlookers jeering harshly. But there was no one around. The outside of the old courthouse building retained its ornate façade, but surprisingly the inside had been renovated into a smoothly modern neutral space. Ellen was waiting for them, showing them where to hang their heavy outer clothing and to change their boots for their new shoes, offering containers of lukewarm coffee, going with Sally to the ladies' room to brush her hair after Mike arrived and upset Sally with his criticism of too much eye makeup.

Nothing about the place was frightening. There was tension, yes —the men, especially, spread tension like an infection—Johnny, Kris, Mike, her father. Maybe it was the Valium soft-pedaling and trivializing Sally's responses, but the courtroom itself was as familiar-feeling as the new high school auditorium. She was disappointed— let down. She hadn't expected a scene as ordinary as the local Holiday Inn banquet room. The witnesses' waiting room reminded her of the jail, or was it the hospital? An element of high drama had been subtracted from the situation because of this everyday familiarity.

Kris dug his elbow into her side.

"Sit up, Sally, you're falling asleep. Stay awake."

"I'm sorry. It's the Valium," she whispered. "And I hardly slept last night."

"Don't take any more Valiums," he said. "I'll give you some of my Dalmanes to take at night." STAY AWAKE, he printed in big caps on his pad and placed the warning in front of her.

But as soon as the jury selection began, her sense of being a distanced, disinterested observer vanished. The bizarre scene came into focus—however much she seemed to be watching a TV show, her future hung on the ending.

The questions asked of the prospective jurors had to do with the privacy of marriage.

"How do you feel about relationships between a man and wife, family arguments and physical violence?"

"It's their private affair. I don't hold with gettin inta family arguments one way or the other."

"Well, don't like to see a man abusin smaller weaker ones, like a wife or kids."

There were questions about excessive drinking too.

One side or the other used their challenges. She became fascinated by her attempt to penetrate to the quality of the members of the jury panel, not so much through their actual responses as from a missing element of inner precision that frightened her. Many of the responses were almost word-for-word copies of earlier ones. Were they just trying to get turned away so as not to have to serve? She was asked each time by Kris or Mike or Ellen, "Know anything about him?" "Know anything about her?" Sometimes she did, a wild irrelevancy, such as that Nancy Parker made the best biscuits in the county. She knew a lot of the men were heavy drinkers. In that town it might be impossible to put together a jury of nondrinkers. A few times a lawyer requested to question a juror in the judge's chambers. It went on and on.

The courtroom had gradually filled with people. Hit show. Sneaking a backward check of the house, she was amazed to see among the crowded benches the entire group of women she had met at Hannah Wasserman's house, clustered in two rows of seats. They smiled, nodded; one tiny young girl she couldn't remember from that night, now sitting alongside Hannah, made a little raised fist in salute.

It was just then the judge said, "Step down," in a terrible voice to a prospective juror. She hadn't heard how the man had earned his rebuke. There was a disturbance of buzzing, hissing, some laughter, and the judge reprimanded the spectactors. Later she learned what the man had said on the stand.

Mike had been questioning him.

"How do you feel about working wives? Working mothers? Would you say you are prejudiced in that respect or not? Would you say about a wife and mother making a career for herself, well I approve of that, or not?"

"I ain't what I consider a prejudiced man, but women are out ta wear the pants these days and gettin a little too big fer their britches. Don't hurt none ta cut em down ta size now n then."

The judge was clearly a sophisticated man, from away, she could tell by the way he spoke. She decided then that he was on her side. Mike dismissed her notion at the lunch break.

"Sally, he's one of the toughest on the bench. He's not on anybody's side. He's on the side of the law."

THE LAW. Invariably she saw those words in capital letters.

But she saw Mike's point later, when the judge ordered a woman to "step down" in that same voice of authority.

The woman had answered the question of prejudice by saying, "If I do have any prejudice it'd go in favor of the woman. I'm a woman myself, after all. I know what it is being knocked around and hollered at, scared a—"

"Step down." The judge interrupted her.

Again there was a buzz of excited response from the audience, and again the judge's reprimand. Jury selection continued for the whole long day. The length of the day was like the length of the night everything had happened, endless, bewitched time. Yet, finally, both sides settled for a jury neither was satisfied with and the judge adjourned the proceedings until the following morning. THE JUDGE, too, was now seen in capital letters—priest of his religion, THE LAW.

She had never been so tired. She thought she'd need nothing to help her sleep. She and Dotty and her daddy went to bed early. Supper was delicious but a jumpy affair accompanied by nervous, excited comments and dumb laughs. They read the short notices of the trial in the local papers. Dotty was disappointed that the story wasn't being given a big splash. Sally was relieved that it was being buried. They all helped clean the kitchen, then watched the first half of an awards special on TV to calm themselves down, but it wasn't especially quieting. Only the kids, Johnny and Laura, stayed up to the end. No rehearsals that night.

Sally set her alarm for six o'clock, leaving enough time in the morning to wash her hair, make up right, all that. She wasn't used to sleeping with Dotty, wasn't used to sleeping with anybody anymore. Dotty went off into dreamland like a baby. Through the badly joined closed doors, Sally could hear her father snoring in Johnny's room. On her way out of the bathroom earlier, she had caught sight of him in the darkened bedroom standing in his long johns and high socks, carefully folding his pants along the crease and arranging the jacket over the back of a chair. Her heart thudded; it would have howled if it knew how. She imagined she heard

Helen and Ty Parsons through the wall, laughing and getting laid. More likely, Johnny and Laura, in the living room. It was then she got up and took the Dalmane Kris had given her.

It was like going to work, the most important work of her life. She wore a different blouse the next day. Printed, with an attached scarf that she knotted to fall softly under the gold chain; she kept her dark jacket on. Everybody was more nervous than the day before. The weather was worse, and Daddy drove, gritting his teeth audibly. The windshield wipers weren't working too well.

Again, tension, jokes, comfort, support, containers of coffee, excitement—combining into an exhausting effort to hold herself together. More of a crowd than the day before. There were legal maneuvers she didn't understand, rulings by THE JUDGE, conferences at the bench. Suddenly the show was on the road.

THE STATE presented its charge. THE STATE dwindled as she listened to the State's Attorney—a little man whose voice squeaked when he pushed for power. Back to small letters for the state. He strutted back and forth as he argued. She surreptitiously studied the jury to read their expressions, but from where she sat, it wasn't possible to see clearly.

Sally Sweetsir was angry with her husband because of a complicated, boring story of a sale of a car. Mr. and Mrs. Sweetsir were quarreling and had been extremely quarrelsome for some time now. He was tired of her, and of quarreling. He threatened to leave her. He threw their marriage rings at her. She fought with him, scratched his face and pulled his hair; he defended himself by shoving her away. She took a knife from the kitchen drawer and stabbed him in the heart. Sally Sweetsir had admitted her undeniable guilt before dozens of witnesses. In a rage, during a family quarrel, Sally Sweetsir had taken a knife from the kitchen drawer with the intent to kill her husband and had killed him.

She scribbled on her pad: "He's got the whole bit about the rings all wrong."

She stopped, crumpling the paper in her hand. A sharp image of herself fallen at the foot of the porch steps shook her. Wasn't it then she had torn the ring from her finger? That wasn't the rehearsed version. In a panic, she turned to Ellen, seated on her right.

Ellen's calm, clear gaze was fixed dispassionately on the little figure haranguing squeakily, pacing.

THE JUDGE interrupted. "I should like to remind the State's Attorney that there are no television cameras present. Unfortunately dramatic pacing is quite lost under the circumstances. It is very difficult to clearly understand your words if you turn your back squarely upon the bench and the jury."

Suppressed laughter, a buzz of noise from the audience. Their turn next.

"May I remind visitors that it is entirely within my prerogative to clear the court if I see fit?"

Sally half turned, caught a glimpse of Kay Sweetsir and Judy in the front row, sitting primly, two little kids in school. Damn fool woman, bringing Judy. To this. Somewhere in the middle were two solid rows of feminists, ending with Fern Bowdoin on the last seat. Made her smile. Nearer front, Vin alongside Laura and Johnny, and right behind her, Bill Grandstone, his flat-lidded pale-blue eyes fixed on the State's Attorney in bulging disdain.

The State's Attorney had wound up. Mike Bronenfeld was rising to do his turn. A whooshing in her ears deafened her. She was sickeningly dizzy.

When she was little, she had been caught in a breaking wave, rolled in its disinterested power until it released her gasping on the beach. Daddy had driven with her and her sisters miles and miles to a cove of the open sea. Special treat. They packed a lunch, chicken sandwiches, a thermos of hot chocolate. It was a brilliantly clear, cool windy late summer's day, following a week of storm. The usually protected shell-shape of sea was wild, rising to enormous waves crashing in a great green wall, rushing toward the sandy beach in a mass of foam. The three girls dashed in, fighting the white swirl, letting it tumble and float them, screaming and laughing. Then something went wrong. She was dragged too far back, ruled by the undertow, swept into the turbulence of the breaking wave, rolled and held under, her chest bursting, colors exploding into pulsing stars and rainbows, flashing lights of exquisite pain. Neither her sisters nor her father had noticed what was happening.

The trial was like being caught in a wave. She missed a lot of what was going on, then a detail would spring at her clearly. Janie

Paulsen, state's witness, little Janie Paulsen who sat in the outer office, doing nothing much, testifying for the state.

"On the day that Morgan Sweetsir was killed, I could see that Sally Sweetsir was very upset and angry with her husband, and when Mrs. Sweetsir left the office early with Ricky Greenspan, our boss's son she was taking care of for Mr. Greenspan, leaving early because she had a doctor's appointment, the doctor's office had called and moved up Mrs. Sweetsir's appointment, Sally was definitely acting angry and upset. She said, Mrs. Sweetsir said, 'This is definitely *not* my day, Janie,' and she was upset and nervous when she said it and mad sort of," Janie Paulsen said.

Mike cross-examined.

"Would you say that Sally Sweetsir is a difficult person to work with? Bad-tempered?"

"No, sir. Very even-tempered."

"And that day she was very different? Noticeably different? She quarreled with you?"

"No, sir. I could just kinda guess she was actin a little peculiar, kinda tense."

"Did Sally say anything about her personal life to you that day? Confide in you in any way?"

"No, sir."

"Say she was angry with her husband or imply it in any way, directly to you?"

"No, sir. Except that statement she made on her way out, 'This is definitely *not* my day.' But she kept callin home a lot and she an her husband were fightin on the phone."

"You and Sally Sweetsir work in different offices, is that right?"

"Yes, sir."

"I wonder how you would hear the content of a telephone conversation between Mr. and Mrs. Sweetsir? Listening in?"

"No, sir, no, sir. I don't have no idea what they were sayin. Just knew they were havin a lotta real short conversations, hangin up quick on one another, y'know."

"Mrs. Paulsen, wasn't it entirely usual for Mrs. Sweetsir to keep in close touch with her husband, to call out and for her husband to call in frequently? Wasn't their behavior in this respect that day much like their usual behavior?"

"Yes, sir, but not as often, I mean it was more often that day, y'know?"

"Mrs. Paulsen, isn't it a fact that the sum total of your knowledge of Mrs. Sweetsir's alleged intense anger at her husband consists of your knowing that there were a number of telephone conversations between a husband and wife who ordinarily called one another frequently during the day . . ."

"Yes, sir," Janie said, "and . . ."

". . . and that Mrs. Sweetsir left the office taking charge of a difficult child on the way to a gynecologist's office to be checked for possible cancer, making the remark, 'This is definitely *not* my day,' and that constitutes your sole knowledge of her alleged state of mind. Is that correct, Mrs. Paulsen?"

"Yes, sir," she said. "I just want to say she's always been good to work unda, neva been ugly to me."

"Thank you," Mike said and excused Janie Paulsen.

During the lunch break, the witness room was a party. Sandwiches and coffee, talk, jokes about the strutting State's Attorney, congratulations on the speech by Mike, which Sally hadn't absorbed. Laura was so hopped up she was acting drunk. "It's gonna be okay, Mom, I know it, I just know it."

In the afternoon, medical testimony went on and on. Endless testimony about hair.

"What we do is take samples of hair from each of the two samples and put them separately on microscopic slides and put material on it called Permount, which renders the hair almost transparent. We look at them under the microscope and look at the particular features which are inside the hair. There are twenty different features that we look at and we compare them in both samples."

The State's Attorney asked, "Could you give us some idea of what particular features you would be looking at in making your comparison?"

"Well, inside the hair, the hair is composed of three sections. Outside part is called the cuticle. Looks like—if you look at it under a microscope, looks like scales on a reptile. Inside of this is what is called cortex, and this is where the pigment is that gives your hair where color is formed. There are also other features in there which are like, either air spaces in there. There are other little bodies which are formed in there which give distinct patterns. Inside of that or very center of it there occurs a material called medulla which is the central portion of the hair and it has different characteristics particular to shape, in color and the way it's formed. These are the type of things we look at."

"Okay. Between the sample from A1 and the same Number Six did you notice any particular similarities in those samples?"

"The two samples, Six and A1, were found to show exactly the same characteristics."

Sally scribbled a note to Ellen. "What's this hair all about? It doesn't make sense."

Ellen whispered, "Trying to prove you started the fight pulling his hair out."

She lost track, but again later they told her Mike had been wonderful in the cross.

Now it was human blood under examination, as if there were proof needed that the blood spilled was actually Sweets's. She picked up on snatches of technical speeches.

". . . in sampling any stained material one must first determine if the specimen is blood. To do this a number of examinations are performed or tests are performed. A screening test using a reduced phenolphthalein, which detects peroxidies, a substance found in blood. Secondly, an examination for the presence of hemoglobin component of blood is done. This is known as toxianmocrystal. This is a Japanese test. Once these two examinations are performed, one can determine if a specimen is indeed blood. It is even a specified group using a pertritant-type test involving combining the stain with known antiserums, and these antiserums are determined specifically to detect human or other species types.

"Antigens we found in dried stains can best be grouped by a system known as absorption agglutination. The antigens substance, as I said, was found on the blood cells and so it is insoluble in water and other things. One takes a blood sample and incubates it with a specific known antiserum. Now, actually one does this three separate times. You take a sample and you incubate it with known antiserum. You take a second sample and incubate it with known antiserum and you take a third sample and incubate it with a substance which is essentially antiserum. It is called Lecton H. If an antigen is present, you will form an antigen and antibody complex. A reaction will occur where the antibody is absorbed or held on to by the antigen. If you then wash all the excess material away you can add some saline solution to each of these test spots and by washing break this bond, this holding ability, and so you can form antibody again in solution. Otherwise, you have initially taken an antibody and attached it to some dry blood stain, and by warming you can disattach and then by reacting it with known blood cells you can observe agglutination, or clumping."

"What would this tend to show, Dr. Warren?"

"This will give you the specific . . ."

These experts presented their impressive credentials. Bachelor of Science Degree from State University of New York at Purchase, Doctorate in Chemistry at Boston University, graduate credits from Harvard University, courses given by the FBI in Quantico, Virginia; Bachelor of Arts Degree from University of Maine at Orono, Master of Science Degree in Chemistry and a Ph.D. in Organic Chemistry from the University of Vermont. The cops held degrees in Enforcement and Criminal Justice; Officer Harding LeVeen had attended the Harvard Associates Homicide School in Baltimore, Maryland.

His testimony was the longest session of the afternoon. Officer LeVeen's power to harm her had been burned to ashes in Hannah Wasserman's fireplace, but not even Mike Bronenfeld could ruffle Officer LeVeen as he hammered away at him in cross-examination. The proceedings faded in and out of her attention. Sally kept her body erect, her face turned toward the man who had questioned and arrested her, pretending to be alert, interested, friendly.

The knife had been introduced in evidence—the actual knife. Her skin crawled.

"I then advised her of her rights but she responded, 'I know all about that rights shit,'" Officer LeVeen was saying.

"Was it at that point, after advising her of her rights, that she refused an attorney?" Mike said.

"Yes, as I told the court earlier, first she said, Okay, then she said, No, don't bother, I don't want to bother anybody, and then she made that remark."

"Was Mrs. Sweetsir looking at you?"

"Sure. I guess off and on."

"Were there tears in her eyes? Was she crying?"

"Not that I noticed."

"You never saw Mrs. Sweetsir crying?"

"Wouldn't say never. She cried in spurts but she wasn't crying that particular minute."

"I see. And then you asked her to tell what happened between her and her husband?"

"I never asked Mrs. Sweetsir a thing. Didn't ask the woman a single question. She just began to talk. Volunteered to give a statement. She said, 'I want to tell you what happened.'"

"I see. Did she include anything in her story about cancer?"

"Yes, she did."

"What did she say?"

"She stated that she had been to see a doctor that day and he suspected cancer, that the argument occurred because her husband didn't believe her and that he threatened to call the doctor the next day to check it out, and that's why they argued."

"In your earlier testimony you didn't mention anything about the cancer incident, did you?"

"I don't recall it coming up, no."

"I see. Officer, while you were taking Sally Sweetsir's statement, the surgeon came out of the operating room and reported to Mrs. Sweetsir that her husband was dead. Did that upset Mrs. Sweetsir?"

"Sure."

"What length of time would you estimate transpired between Sally Sweetsir being informed of her husband's death and your continuing the interview?"

"I can't remember to the minute."

"Well, perhaps the official reports might be of help, since they furnish exact times. It's my understanding that there was a lapse of approximately four or five minutes between the time Mrs. Sweetsir learned that her husband was dead and your continuing the interview. Is that about right?"

"Probably. I'd say more like five or six minutes. The whole thing took about half an hour to forty minutes, including the interruption."

"When you say 'interruption,' you are referring to the doctor giving the information to Mrs. Sweetsir that Morgan Sweetsir, her husband, had died on the operating table?"

"That's correct."

"Officer LeVeen, as a police officer with fine training and a good deal of experience, would you say that interviewing an alleged suspect so close to a point of extreme trauma, that is, immediately after receiving information on a death of a husband, say, as in the case of Mrs. Sweetsir, would you say that was good police practice?"

Flurry of objections, counterarguments, then THE JUDGE allowed the question, rephrased.

"In terms of the accuracy of what Mrs. Sweetsir might be reporting, would you say it was good practice to pursue questioning at a moment of such trauma?"

"Yes, I do."

"In your opinion, would you have characterized Mrs. Sweetsir as emotionally upset at that time?"

"Well, off and on she was a little upset. She was upset when I first saw her. Then she calmed down quite a bit, then she got upset again when the doctor told her about him dying, but she calmed right down. I wouldn't say she was as calm as you and me sitting around conversing here, but yes, I felt it was a proper time for her to complete her story. While it was fresh in her mind."

"Did Mrs. Sweetsir indicate she was sorry?"

"Y'mean did she say she was sorry?"

"Yes. Was she expressing sorrow?"

"I never heard her say she was sorry."

"Did she tell you that she was very surprised that her husband had been so badly hurt?"

"No, I don't believe she was surprised, no."

"Did she state that she loved him? Did you hear her saying anything to the effect that she wished she had died instead of him? Did you hear her say anything of that nature?"

Flurry of objections, then LeVeen answered.

"I don't recall hearing any such statement."

Tossed in the green wall of the wave, she alternately drowned and surfaced, surfaced and drowned. The three ambulance-crew members testified next, portraying a distraught, sobbing hysteric. But Mike got them to admit hearing her say that she loved her husband, that she was sorry, that she was concerned.

A whole big thing was made of the rings, her interfering with the crew because of the rings.

She scribbled, "What's this about?"

Ellen whispered that the state was establishing her motive as anger because Morgan was planning to leave her, had threatened to do so and had thrown away their wedding rings.

The old couple down the alley described her as a madwoman running them down in her car. Other prosecution witnesses were easy on her, good for her. The hospital technician testified that she was "sobbing and hysterical, blaming herself and saying she loved him and only wanted him to recover."

Then another fuss. About display photographs of Sweets's dead body. The defense objected that color blowups of the dead man would be inflammatory and prejudicial. There was an adjournment to the judge's chambers.

In the hallway, Hannah Wasserman put her arms around her and kissed her. In the witness room, coffee, jokes, falsely hearty expressions of confidence. Her father's face was gray; exhaustion had sucked in his cheeks. Dorothy passed around cookies she had brought in a plastic bag. From across the room Sally heard Vin in big-man fake-hearty talk with Fern Bowdoin. They had all hoped to be called to the stand that afternoon—unlikely in any event, but with the fight about the showing of the photographs, they might not now be called even the following day.

She couldn't swallow her coffee thinking about the possibility that the photographs might be shown. Her throat closed in protest. Sweets exposed to a roomful of strangers—naked, dead, gashed, bloody—his birds and snakes and flowers ruined by the wounds. Unbearable. She had been shown the pictures, smaller, in black-and-white, to blunt the shock if the ruling went against them. His limp penis and his innocent, unharmed feet hurt her the most.

The blowups were placed on a stand turned toward the judge and jury. She kept her head rigidly locked to the right to avoid the sight. The medical witnesses testified that Morgan Beauchamp Sweetsir had died of a fatal stab wound. They too had amassed degrees. Bachelor of Science Degree from Middlebury College, Tufts Medical School, three years' schooling in pathology, certification in anatomic and clinical pathology, special training in forensic pathology.

She could avoid looking but there was no way not to listen.

"It entered the left chest, laterally and superior to the left nipple, penetrating the left third intercostal space, passing through the medial aspect of the left upper lung, which caused hemorrhaging. It passed through the anterior pericardial sac or the front of the sac and into the front of the heart and into the anterior left ventricle where it passed through the wall and into the left ventricular cavity, between the capillary muscles that are part of the inside of the musculature of the heart."

If she were to be taking this down by dictation, there'd be a lot she couldn't spell.

She glanced at the doctor, a tall, thin, kindly-looking man wearing thin metal half-glasses that he looked through and over alternately when Mike Bronenfeld cross-examined.

"Would you explain, Doctor, the results of your examination as to the relationship of the left arm stab wounds to the left wound in the chest?"

"Yes, I understand the nature of your concern. Yes, your question is, do these wounds approximate one another? In other words, could this have been a single stab wound or a series of stab wounds? By raising the arm approximately thirty to forty-five degrees in a normal anatomic position, without troubling about the position of the elbow, it is possible to line up the inner arm wound with the chest wound, yes."

She missed the next exchanges, concentrating so hard on keeping her head turned away she ached down to her thighs.

Then heard again, ". . . when you're dealing with a dead body on a table the muscles are all relaxed. At the moment of impact, for example, the biceps may have been flexed and tightened and the exact position of the heart is therefore, you understand, difficult to

. . . oh, because if a man is in a lying-down position the heart may slide upward a fraction, and if the person is standing or the upper body is in the upright position, the heart moves. The differences are usually slight but . . ."

"In your opinion, would you describe these wounds as consistent with a single blow of the weapon in evidence?"

"There is such a possibility, yes, depending on the force of the blow. The wounds could be consistent with the possibility of one blow of perhaps even not very excessive force. As I said earlier, with the arm in the position I described, a measurement taken from the arm wound to the wound in the heart, with the man's body in a supine position on the table, the measurement was approximately the length of the blade of the knife in evidence, that is, approximately nine to ten inches, but as I also commented earlier, it is difficult to determine exactly, since if a man were in an upright position the heart takes a more dependent position. . . ."

She was very tired. As if on a damaged record, the last phrase ran a repeat in her head, drowning out what followed. *The heart takes a dependent position, the heart takes a dependent position, the heart takes a dependent position.* She printed on her pad:

THE HEART TAKES A DEPENDENT POSITION.

Exorcise the words.

Kris Kerkorian leaned over to read what she had written, looked at her questioningly. She held her head stiffly in position, turned to the right, away from the photographs, not responding.

At the end of the second day the prosecution still hadn't finished presenting their witnesses. They brought the rest of the cast on the following morning, Helen and Ty Parsons, guys Sweets had worked with, gone to school with, hung around bars with, two women he had dated between marriages. Sweets was the best guy in the world, fun to be with, generous, knew how to have a good time, very attentive to his wife, good family man, loved his kids, terrific worker, perfect gentleman.

In the cross-examination Mike extracted the precious statement Ellen had wheedled from Ty Parsons.

While we were waiting for the ambulance I heard Morgan Sweetsir say to his wife Sally, 'I love you and I know you love me and that you didn't mean to do it.' "

The last witness was Timmy Beal, one of the men working on Sweets's crew. Knew Morgan Beauchamp Sweetsir since they were babies, started kindergarten together, knew Sweets as well as anybody in the world, he guessed.

"Don't care how hard or how careful ya looked, don't care if ya searched the whole wide world, it'd be hard ta find a man as good as Sweets, that is, Mr. Sweetsir, sir. He was a good man, sir. Work, that man understood work, better worker'n anybody but never askin another ta do the dirty work he wouldn't do hisself. Couldn't find a better friend ta have a good time with. Sure Morgan'd drink a bit on the heavy side, get a little outta control, thumped his squaw now n then, but none a that's unusual. . . ."

Sally heard the muted uproar in the court before the expression used by Timmy Beal registered with her.

Mike shoved it into Timmy Beal's face in the cross-examination, playing dumb.

"Just exactly how would you define *thumped his squaw now and then*, Mr. Beal?" he asked.

"It's fer keepin the women in line. Ya gotta, that's the way it is."

22

It wasn't until very late in the afternoon that the prosecution rested and the defense brought on its first witness, Iris Benton Beauchamp, widow of Robert Cole Beauchamp, great-aunt by marriage to Morgan Beauchamp Sweetsir. She was a white-haired woman in her early eighties, looking younger because of her fine nose and bright smile and the lively amusement in her large, intelligent eyes. Her hair was carefully arranged, and, though her body was unshapely, the loose-cut wine-colored wool suit she wore was elegant. She spoke with deliberation and in detail, drawing out her connecting words to amazing lengths: "a . . . a . . . an . . . and . . . al . . . tho . . . ough . . . bee . . . cau . . . se . . ."

She had demanded that she be the first defense witness, informing Ellen during the lunch break that though she was quite willing to help in this sordid matter of Morgan's unsavory end, out of the highest motives and in the interest of truth, nevertheless, if she could not appear that afternoon, then she would have to decline to appear at all, since the following day, Thursday, was her women's bridge luncheon club, gathering this week at her home, and that Friday was also unfortunately promised because she was president of the Friday Afternoon Club, and, heaven help her housekeeper, this meeting as well was scheduled to be held at her house through some confused mishandling of her appointment calendar. Ellen tried to explain that Fern Bowdoin, Vin Ciomei, and Sally's father, Bob Stark, had to get back to *jobs*, but Ellen was afraid to lose so distinguished a witness, and Mike put her on the stand first.

Sally had never met her. The old lady knew a lot about Sweets.

In her deliberate delivery, savoring the gossip and enjoying her own performance, she told of Sweets's repeated efforts to get his great-uncle Beau to help him out of a series of difficulties beginning in his teens. It sounded worse than a soap opera. They bailed him out once or twice. He never repaid their loans, their kindness, never showed them the slightest consideration "al . . . tho . . . ough . . ." he would always reappear when he needed additional help. She told about the failed marriages, the extraordinary variety of jobs, the emotional breakdowns, the scrapes with the law. She ended, her eyes shining, with a final shot.

"I must confess that I don't believe that young man had a drop of Beauchamp blood in him, al . . . tho . . . ough . . . I can't actually prove it. The Lord alone knows what his grandmother was up to in *her* day, a . . . aa . . . an . . . and . . . everybody knows throughout this region that the Sweetsirs were supposedly of Indian origin, so . . . oo . . . ooo . . ."

Mike let the sustained objection end her direct testimony. The State's Attorney was either too weary or too intimidated by Iris Benton Beauchamp to accomplish anything to speak of in the cross-examination. She swept out of the courtroom with a gracious nod of her head for THE JUDGE alone. She was the kind of woman who knew who rated a nod, Sally figured.

She was more concerned about how her father would perform next on the stand. He was good. He was good. Quiet, authoritative, believable.

Sally was his youngest daughter, dutiful, smart and pretty. Got married too young to a fine man, too bad the marriage didn't last, though they both did their best. Sally raised a fine young girl of a daughter. Sally always conducted herself orderly and decent. A gentle, reasonable, dependable and independent woman.

"A man doesn't like to brag about his own, especially when it weren't her mother who raised her, dying as young as she did when Sally was little, leavin the raisin to me, her daddy, but my daughter is as good a woman as ya could find existin anywhere, don't care where ya looked, by Jesus, and if this awful thing happened to her, I c'n swear to God it weren't her . . ."

He was stopped by objections, of course, but she had had her moment of gratification. She smiled and smiled at him, still on the stand, his hands resting stiffly on his knees, his vivid blue eyes suffering angrily through the cross-examination, smiling her tearful thank you, Daddy, thank you, thank you, a prayer to pull him through an ordeal she had never meant for him to endure.

June Easton, Bill Grandstone, her sister Dorothy were the first witnesses the following day. She began firmly to believe in this character they were inventing among them, Sally Sweetsir, Woman of the Year, practically. Jerry Greenspan's circumspection came as something of a surprise. He pulled against Mike's interjection of Ricky into the proceedings, insisting that Ricky was *not* a hyperactive child. She knew Jerry Greenspan had his personal reasons—he might risk losing visitation rights, or his wife could demand more money. Something. He hedged. During the cross he was more of a prosecution witness than he was a help to the defense.

Fern Bowdoin took the stand next, joking about his credentials when Mike asked his personal history.

"Graduate degree in school of hard knocks," deadpan, after listing his degree in mechanical engineering.

She could see the jury liked him right away.

The state pushed at him hard in the cross-examination, playing on the innuendo that there was intimacy between him and Sally Sweetsir, but Fern didn't budge, didn't get outraged or ruffled.

"I happened on Sally at the Hilltop the evening of the incident n I run inta Sally at the luncheonette once near the mill where I work at, n that's about it so far as I c'n recall, except for seein her here now."

He had known Sally since they had gone to school together and he'd known Sweets separately since they were all youngsters together. "Sweets was a coupla years oldern me, but we hung around some, I'd run inta him at the Hilltop. Liked him a lot, very friendly fella, nothin against him I eva heard."

"Except from Mrs. Sweetsir?"

"Beggin ya pardon? Don't get ya meanin."

"The night you met Mrs. Sweetsir at the bar, a few hours before the event, didn't Mrs. Sweetsir complain to you about her husband's treatment of her?"

"No, sir, not one bit. Sally was worryin about that cancer report and about havin to go to the hospital and leavin all the family responsibilities on Morgan's shoulders. She was expressin her concern that Sweets couldn't manage. . . ."

"Was Morgan Sweetsir incompetent? Would you characterize him . . ."

"No, sir. Morgan was a helluva good worker. But there weren't nobody didn't know, I mean if ya knew Sweets at all intimate ya knew he had a drinkin problem and a spendin problem, everybody who knew Sweets knew that, knew he had a woman problem, takin it out on his women. All I saw that night was a woman worryin. I remember thinkin to myself, she's gotta be plenty upset talkin so much, cause she was generally quiet. She was busy worryin about her husband. It's like she was feelin she was guilty or somethin for gettin cancer and causin the man she loved more problems than he c'd handle, y'know?"

Even the State's Attorney liked him, Sally was convinced, and THE JUDGE liked him.

She was convinced too that THE JUDGE liked her from the way he'd look at her from time to time studying her, though he kept his face impassive and expressionless, like all official people did.

Mike blew up at her when she referred to her sense that THE JUDGE liked her, during a break after a legal dispute in his chambers.

"He doesn't like or dislike anybody, Sally. He's a *judge*."

Vincent Ciomei, correcting the clerk's pronunciation, Syomy, told of ten years of marriage to Sally.

"Maybe we got inta two arguments the whole time. Describing my ex-wife as a violent woman, no way, no way. Violent just ain't a word to go with Sally. She's calm and sensible. She was a good and faithful wife, a good mother to our only child, she kept a beautiful house and though we took some bad blows in our marriage, financial blows and losin another child, and she'd been disappointed in life like everybody is, she neva took it out on no one, she just ain't that kind. She was good to my old papa, my daddy, when he was in his last years, carin about him like she was a daughter, I'll neva forget that, long as I live, how she was with my old papa."

In the cross, the State's Attorney asked why such a perfect marriage as he described had ended in divorce.

"Weren't no wish a mine," he said. "I went to my regula doctor to talk about it, I was so upset, and he told me somethin interestin that made sense. He said, now she was just a child when she married ya and didn't know her own mind, so now she has to try the world on her own. That made sense to me. Like my papa trained me to be a letterer, I couldn't do the real fancy carving nohow, so he taught me the letterin but when I got older and I knew my mind better, I neva woulda gone inta that line a work at all. I wouldn't a had nothin to do with stone at all. Not even workin in the quarry. Ya understand?"

He was asked to please just answer the questions.

"Isn't it true, Mr. ah, ah, isn't it true that you were forced to marry your wife at the age of fifteen?"

"No, sir. I loved Sally, that's why I married her, no other reason. And while it lasted it was as good a marriage as any. I don't care how it ended. Statistics show that a higher percentage of marriages end in . . ."

Vin talked right up, none of his fading-away silences overcame him on the stand.

They were doing good, she felt it in her bones, exhilaration spreading through her system. They were going to win; they had to be winning.

A doctor she couldn't remember was led in by Ellen Mahoney. He listed the usual credentials and degrees, then straightened out the whole cancer false alarm. He went on to describe bruises on her body consistent with her story of having been hit and thrown. She scribbled a note to Kris, because Ellen was gone again, setting up the next witness.

"Who is he?" she wrote. "You said you wouldn't go into all this gynecological stuff, what's going on?"

Kris pushed the pad aside, not responding.

In the cross, the doctor was shown full- and side-view pictures of Sally Sweetsir, taken when she was arrested.

"You saw Sally Sweetsir the morning following her arrest, Doctor?"

"I believe it was early afternoon."

She now remembered him vaguely. She had forcibly thrust out of her memory the humiliation of the court-ordered medical examination.

"Would you say these pictures represent Mrs. Sweetsir's appearance accurately, as you saw her early the following day?"

He studied the pictures, glanced up at Sally, then back to the pictures.

"They are definitely pictures of Mrs. Sweetsir, yes."

"Are there any facial bruises evident in these pictures, Doctor, consistent with a beating?"

"No visible facial bruises, no. However . . ."

"And there were none evident when you examined her?"

"Mrs. Sweetsir showed no indications of having been hit in the face. Blows to the side of the head are not discernible unless made with an instrument sharp enough to draw blood or heavy enough to raise a swelling. Hard slaps to the ears, for example, may cause considerable pain and leave no evidence whatsoever. If I may add to this—"

He paused before he began again.

"Mrs. Sweetsir was crying as I examined her. Not crying aloud, but I noticed tears streaming from the corners of her eyes, when I completed the internal which I described earlier. I settled her into a more comfortable position, her feet out of the stirrups, etc., and apologized to Mrs. Sweetsir for having had to hurt her slightly. She said, 'That's okay,' but she continued her silent crying. I judged her to be in a state of traumatic mild shock and deep grief. I would say she had no voluntary consciousness of her tears. I was struck by her bravery in controlling herself, by her stoicism under her very grave circumstances. In examining the bruises on her body, I asked if she had received any other blows. She said, 'He hit me on the side of my head, he kept hitting me on the side of my head, first one side, then the other.' I asked her if her husband had ever hit her before the incident leading to his death. She obviously didn't want to respond. I judged her to be under the impression that she was legally obliged to do so, because she then said, 'Yes, when he'd get mad or had too much to drink.' I asked her if he generally knocked her down as well as hit her head, and she responded again, reluctantly, 'Yes, shoving or knocking me down. He'd mostly try to hit me where it wouldn't show, but he gave me a black eye a couple of times and a wrenched wrist once.' I asked her if she had reported his abuse to the police. She said, 'I'd never do that, he couldn't help himself.' Then she said, 'I guess I never really believed it was happening to me and to him. How could it be? We loved each other.' I completed my examination and told the nurse to assist Mrs. Sweetsir in getting dressed and to give her a Valium before she was turned back over to the police."

There was another break for some legal squabbling, then a short adjournment.

"Judge probably has to use the john," Mike said. He was jubilant. "Lyman Bannister doesn't know which end is up," he added. "He'll win this case for us yet. Probably giving the judge diarrhea." He was talking of the State's Attorney.

"He's letting us get away with murder," Kris said, and out of nervous hysteria, they all broke up laughing.

When the court reconvened, Kay Sweetsir took the stand. Ellen stayed in the courtroom, sitting alongside Sally, her eyes reminding, shaping, encouraging Kay's testimony. She had warned Mike to lead her gently.

"I can't believe you got her to go through with it," Sally said to Ellen.

"I have a confession to make," Ellen said. "She thought we could force her to testify. There isn't any way we could do that, but I wasn't about to tell her so."

The doctor had been impressive, but it was Kay who firmly established Sweets's wife abuse. Pitiful, powerless Kay set the issue in the middle of the case. In a voice so low that THE JUDGE repeatedly requested that she speak up, she recounted three hospitalizations for broken bones, black eyes, a tooth knocked out, smashed eyeglasses with permanent slight injury to one eye, permanent hearing loss to one ear. She was dressed in her usual horrible combination of colors. Her hair was a greasy mess, there was a run in her panty hose, and she had brought little Judy, sitting up on the front bench of the visitors' section, swinging her legs, sucking on a candy drop, listening to her mother's testimony with no more emotional response than a dog swishing its tail as it rested.

Mike led Kay carefully through the maze of proofs: dates, hospitalizations, medical records of the clinic, calls to the police. Then he turned her over to Lyman Bannister.

The State's Attorney made another mistake. He got tough with

Kay Sweetsir, becoming a swaggering little man again, putting on a show of ironic amusement to share with larger, smarter personages than this confused wreck of a woman, addressing the jury rather than Kay with his questions.

"Why didn't you press charges against this alleged monster you've been describing to us, a monster you managed to live with for almost a decade?"

The question had to be reworded before Kay understood it. She shrank from her own defense, murmuring in tones that grew progressively lower. THE JUDGE repeatedly reminded her to speak up. Sally suffered again a mixed response to Kay. Kay was helping her, she was returning good for evil, kindness for ugliness. They had hurt her badly, she and Sweets, and instead of gratitude she was experiencing only her usual irritation at this cowering woman who shared her name.

"Y'mean when I called the cops? Get Morgan put away?"

"Exactly, Mrs. Sweetsir."

"They always acted the same, the cops, gimme a lecture not ta rile him up when he was drinkin. But it weren't only them times. Sometimes he'd be drunk, not always. When he weren't drunk he'd just walk out when he was tired a knockin me around, n come back drunk later. They'd gimme a lecture, the cops. C'mon, it's only a family fight, he'll calm down, ya put him away, where ya gonna get a weekly paycheck? Ya'll be in worse shape."

THE JUDGE asked her to speak up. She apparently had nothing more to say.

"But you did leave him, Mrs. Sweetsir, you did eventually leave this terrible person you've been describing, and lost custody of your children to him, didn't you? How did all that come about? It took some organization, did it not? Who helped you organize your moves?"

She could barely be heard.

"Didn't organize nothin. Didn't move nowhere. My sister dragged me ova ta the free legal aid. They tole me, this woman there tole me, change the lock on ya door, lock him out, we'll get ya a divorce, cruel and something treatment. It was afta a beatin n it was a Saturday so I had money in my pocket fa the shoppin n my sister dragged me ova ta Bennie Smith's place n he come ova n changed the lock n that's all I remember, the legal aid people did the rest. Only afta, *they* got the kids, the court give em the kids, and I only got a little money ta cova Judy visitin. But I didn't care anymore. I figured I couldn't be worse off ifn I tried. Nobody'd eva wanna marry me afta what I become. I already had a hysterectomy ova ta the State Medical Center coupla years earlier. It weren't no sense hopin fa nothin."

"Are you presently employed, Mrs. Sweetsir?"

"No, sir."

"Are you on unemployment insurance?"

"No, sir, ya can't get it less ya work."

"Are you saying you've never worked, Mrs. Sweetsir?"

"No sir, Sweets neva liked the idea of me workin."

"How do you support yourself and the child the court has now returned to you?"

"Relief. Food stamps."

She was whispering. With a flourish he dismissed her.

Mike returned for one further question.

"How old were you when you married Morgan Sweetsir?"

"Sixteen."

"And your age now?"

"Twenty-nine next time around."

She looked forty, fifty; there was no telling what age, the way she looked. Excused from the stand, she left with a barely discernible genuflection directed toward THE JUDGE, who stared ahead without expression.

At the lunch break Sally attempted to thank her. Kay turned on her.

"Thank me for nothin. Think ya some kinda glamour doll. All ya hafta do is smile and ya gets what ya want. Two-faced and schemin. Lemme tell ya, Kay Sweetsir wouldn't be here if the law didn't make her, lemme tell ya the truth, swearin on the Bible. I hope ya go ta jail fa what ya done."

"Oh, Jesus," Laura begged. "Kay, please, Kay, please, don't say 'jail' just before I hafta go on the stand."

"Not *you*, Laurie, got nothin against *you*, Laurie, it's *her*."

Mike herded Laura and Johnny into a separate room for a final quick rehearsal. Sally drank coffee, sitting alone with Ellen, soothed even by her silences, by her clear eyes.

"You know, if it keeps moving this way without any hitches, we'll wind it all up tomorrow. He really *doesn't* know what he's doing." Ellen was referring to Lyman Bannister.

"Then it will be up to the jury?"

Ellen nodded. "And I think they'll be quick, too."

"One way or the other," Sally said, and added, "that'll be good. You'll be able to make it down to New York to Castle's show then."

"That *would* be good," Ellen said, "but the good I'm looking for is the jury walking in with a verdict of Not Guilty."

Sally thought in terms of acts. One or two acts to go? Three main performances to come on their side: Laura; Johnny and the knife-struggle enactment; Sally Sweetsir on the stand. Then, summations, THE JUDGE's charge to the jury—the finale, the verdict. Ellen laid it out for her in that order.

She grabbed Mike's arm as they were walking back into the court, covering up her panic.

"Will I go on this afternoon?"

Mike was distracted, burning with more immediate inner concerns.

Unnerved, she heard Laura's testimony only intermittently.

Laura was perfect, Ellen said later. She slipped once, started to say "shit," caught herself, switched to "crap," and actually blushed, adding an air of innocence to her new, exquisite simplicity put on for the occasion. The State's Attorney hardly cross-examined, and he made his usual mistake of trying for irony.

"Would you describe your relationship with your mother as angelic?"

"No, sir."

"Well, that's what you've been describing, young lady, a couple of angels. You and your mother never quarrel?"

"Y'mean, like, ain't she eva a pain? Oh sure, y'know, like all mothers are. But the thing is my mom has this special thing, like she *knows* she's bein a pain when she's bein one and that keeps everything very simple, y'know?"

The jury smiled. Laura had put the whole room in smiles, even a faint smile on the face of THE JUDGE.

There was another break. Four attorneys approached the bench, arguing in voices too low to overhear.

Sally passed a note to Ellen. "Will you stay with me while Mike rehearses me later?"

"Of course," Ellen said, and pressed Sally's forearm. "How cold you are." She rubbed Sally's hand between her two palms, distracted too, her eyes fixed anxiously on Kris and Mike and the State's Attorney and his men at the bench, until the conference broke up.

"Okay," Mike said, "it's okay," and Johnny Matthews was called.

A self-protective coating came unbidden to carry her through. She knew what was happening, but heard only snatches. A veil descended between her and the actors standing in for Sally and Morgan Sweetsir recreating the blow that killed Morgan Beauchamp Sweetsir. Mike questioned Johnny, leading Johnny through his directives to the two figures: ". . . Then he like grabbed her wrist n he was pushin and pullin, yeah, like that, and shakin and hittin her all at the same time like that, yeah, and she was strugglin, n all the time they was like movin backwards, yeah, like that, but more like dancin, y'know, he was backward n she was forward n the knife was up more, raised straight up and then down, from the shakin n pullin . . ."

When Lyman Bannister began his cross, she felt faint, at the point of vomiting or, strangely, falling asleep. The tension in the courtroom was so palpable it was sucking all the air out of the room. After being chilled, she was now flushed by a sick heat churning in her stomach. Pity for Johnny? But Johnny was all fired up with the excitement of his moment in the limelight.

"No, sir, I don't know nothin about my parents. I'm what ya call, y'know, illegitimate. I mean my blood parents, natural parents, like they say, I don't know who *they* are."

"You never wondered why Morgan Sweetsir took parental responsibility for you?"

"When ya illegitimate, ya wonda a lot, ya dream a lot, this n that, ya could dream ya a king's son, what's to stop ya, but dreams don't prove nothin, n it's proof what counts."

Fair as an angel with his extraordinarily blue, blue eyes, Johnny Matthews looked nothing like Morgan Sweetsir, or like Kay Sweetsir, either, for that matter, which was the state's next innuendo.

Mike objected, THE JUDGE sustained. Lyman Bannister took another tack, driving at Johnny. Hadn't he reported a shooting? How was it possible that he was now able to recall a knifing in minute detail, having erroneously reported a shooting at the exact time of the event? She lost contact again, the room heaved, her head was oddly empty, as if blood was draining out. If Johnny finished quickly enough, couldn't the court insist she appear directly after him? But court was adjourned to reconvene the following morning. Johnny, Kris, the paralegal and Mike had done wonderfully, everybody said. The defense had successfully presented an entirely plausible account of justifiable homicide.

Mike needed his evening to round off his summation to the court. Could they go over Sally's direct testimony right away? The kids, high on their own brilliant successes, went home ahead. Ellen would drive her out to the house later. Mike ran her through her paces quickly. She performed without errors, but Mike held his head in his hands and groaned at almost every response.

"You're not putting anything into it."

"You're not going to reach them."

"You didn't even *cry.*"

"What the hell's the matter with you? You want to blow this trial on us?"

"You've got to put some emotion into your testimony, Sally," Kris said. "You want to win, don't you?"

By emotion she understood they meant her to come on like a squashed bug, like Kay Sweetsir, asking the court to pity and forgive her.

She said, "I'll be okay on the stand tomorrow."

Ellen said, "Sally knows what she's doing."

"Knows what she's doing? Heading herself straight into a Guilty verdict, that's what she's *doing*," Mike said.

"She was a hundred times better last week," Kris said, as if she weren't there.

"What's the matter with you? Overtired?" Mike yelled, rather than excused.

"It's a rehearsal," Ellen said. "Like singing in half voice. Let her alone. Stop undermining her at the last minute. Of course she's tired. I'm exhausted. Aren't you?"

23

LAURA AND JOHNNY had eaten their supper. They had set the table again for one, had left a leg part of Dotty's roast chicken heating on the stove for her. She ate alone to the sounds of the Muppets coming from the living room where the kids watched and listened, punctuating the TV performances with their own banter. Dotty and Daddy had gone back to their own lives and duties for a day.

She tidied up the remains of her meal. There was a note Scotch-taped to the refrigerator door. "Mom: out of toilet paper. Your afectionate daughter and frend for life, Laura."

That girl would never learn how to spell.

She went up the stairs, waving goodnight to the kids. It was an abomination for her, staying on in this house, this town, her old job. If she was found guilty, maybe her lawyers could plead for her as lawyers had for Nixon. *This woman has suffered enough. Her humiliation has been punishment enough. Case dismissed.*

In her bedroom she picked up an almost-full box of facial tissues for the bathroom. Mondadori's Italian-English, English-Italian dictionary was lying on the top of the toilet tank. She had never read in it again, just moved it from house to house. Someone had taken it from the shelf in the hall outside the bathroom. Odd reading matter for anyone in the house. She ruffled through the pages. Chunks of sheets had been roughly torn out. Her first reaction was rage at the destruction of a harmless book, before she realized that the limp pages had simply been needed and used as a tool. Johnny's dumb work, or her father's. Someone else had hung a handful of paper napkins over the toilet-paper holder. That would be Laura's work—signs of the female mentality.

She was up very early, washing her hair, dressing carefully. She chose the soft blue blouse with its own flowing tie. It was pitch-dark, snowing heavily again. She turned the heat way up. She couldn't get her hair right that morning, and if she wore a wool hat her hair would go absolutely flat on her. Johnny and Laura were up by that time, making breakfast. She wanted only coffee. She asked Johnny to rummage through the closets for an umbrella she remembered Sweets's receiving as a Christmas gift from a Beauchamp. He found a huge black umbrella with a heavy cane handle, still in its plastic sheath. Now she wouldn't need a hat or run the chance of ruining her hair dashing to and from the car.

Before they reached the door, Laura halted them.

"Wait. Wait," she said. "Take hands. Make a circle."

She closed her eyes, her head thrown back, her long neck yearning upward. Was she praying? Johnny bowed his head, embarrassed until she released them. She threw her arms around Sally, hugged her, kissed her hair, her ear and one eyelid, and her hair over and over. Her hair was being flattened by all this emotion.

"Kissing me goodbye?" Sally said.

"Ya gotta win. Ya *goin* ta win," Laura said. "Say it, Mom, say it, Johnny."

"C'mon," Johnny said, "we'll be late, ya fruit."

When Sally was called, she stood up and walked to the stand as she had practiced a dozen times, but with a new element in the actual performance, a metallic self-consciousness, a steel frame upholding intact a core of herself she yielded to nobody sitting in judgment of her. She was enmeshed in a mix of clean fury and muddled love, for herself first, and then for what remained outside her, those she loved and those she hated, stuck with one another in the only world they all shared, God's mysterious world which included THE JUDGE and THE JURY and Sally and Sweets, all of them just as they were, no matter what they were pretending to be. She had uncovered a truth during the process of the trial, essential to impart to the court. Not in words. Words were part of the legal game, she had the words down pat—knew all the right plays and how to follow the rules. The trick was to impart this other essence. I, Sally Sweetsir, alleged murderer, am a woman much like you, loving a man much like you, in a marriage much like yours. Ours went over the edge, but what happened to us could have happened to any of you in a family fight. Admit it.

Not by shoving it in the court's face. She told her story quietly, expressing love, and wonder, and horror at its terrible end. She cried when she was supposed to, dropping her brimming eyes when she spoke.

"I'll never forget how his head fell to the side, and all his bright, dark color was running out of his skin."

Lyman Bannister created another uproar during the cross, driving at her like one of Sweets's bulldozers working the interstate spur.

". . . it's all very well to piously declare you never intended to hurt your husband—*but*, Mrs. Sweetsir, *but* you had every opportunity to choose another weapon, a harmless weapon. From the variety of kitchen implements in the drawer, Mrs. Sweetsir, isn't it true that you seized a lethal weapon, a ten-inch blade, sharp kitchen knife? Isn't that true?"

"Yes," she said, "but . . ."

"But what? Mrs. Sweetsir. But what what? Surely there was a potato masher near at hand, or a rolling pin. Why didn't you choose a potato masher, why . . . ?"

There was a commotion among the audience, talk and laughter. Mike objected but THE JUDGE upheld the question, banging his gavel, bringing the court to order.

"I explained that I only meant to scare him, to stop him hitting me. I knew he was afraid of knives, I don't know why, but he was. He was afraid of bugs and mice and snakes, too. If there had been a snake in there I would have grabbed that.

"I don't know how else to say it. If I could make everything go back to before it happened, I'd give . . . I'd give . . . but that's the trouble, there's no way, I haven't got anything to give and it wouldn't bring back . . ."

It was then she cried, her lovely blue eyes flooding and spilling tears.

She lowered her head and wiped away her tears, sat up straight, faced the State's Attorney's next question.

"Mrs. Sweetsir, isn't it the real fact of the case that you stabbed your husband to keep him from leaving you?"

"No," she said. "I didn't stab him. I never meant to stab him, just scare him so that he'd stop hitting me, but he grabbed my wrist and . . ."

"Isn't it true that you said repeatedly as he was being tended in the emergency operating room, 'I won't bother him anymore, I'll go away, I'll leave him if he's okay'?"

"I guess so," she said. "I don't remember exactly what I said then. All I was concerned with then, in the hospital, was that Sweets be all right. My husband, I mean. I wasn't watching my words. If people said I said that, I guess I did, but what I meant was, I wasn't going to try anymore, try for my idea of what a marriage should be, of what love should be, that if he was okay, I'd give up and go away and let him alone because it was too hard, it hurt too much trying, it was hurting him too much . . . turning him into hating me . . . and hurting me . . ."

She had done it. She was sure she had done it. Ellen shone full approval from her broad face, and she could see Mike and Kris were pleased. In a few minutes, the State's Attorney was beginning his summation. Lyman Bannister, playing the bad guy, vigorously repeating all his errors, earning the kind of glances from THE JUDGE one might see on the face of a man accidentally slipping on cow dung. Especially when Bannister repeated the bit about the potato masher. Then it was Mike's turn and they were back into the soap-opera emotions Mike was playing on.

The jury retired. The party atmosphere in the witness room was unbearable. "You were terrific," she heard from everybody. Even Mike hugged her. She had meant to put on a great show, but she didn't want to have the performance acknowledged. Mike basked in an impresario's glory. He too was told he'd been terrific. She sat in a corner close to Ellen.

Fern Bowdoin approached. "I know ya gonna get off, Sally, so don't be disappearin on me now, will ya? I mean if ya take off for faraway places, lemme know where ya at, okay?"

She shushed him. "Bad luck to say out loud what you're wishing for."

"I ain't exactly wishin for ya to take off," he said. "But I know it'll be easier on ya to get outta here."

"I meant bad luck to say I'll win, say it out loud."

"I know it. I know it in my bones," he said.

"You sound like Laura," she said.

He grinned. "Turnin inta a teenager since I . . ." and didn't finish.

"Listen," she said, "if your bones are so smart, and know so much, maybe you can play your hunches on the stock market and get to be a millionaire."

"Okay," he said. "If ya promise to still like me afta I get to be a rich bastard."

That was smart of him, she thought, because she wouldn't go on liking him if he was a rich bastard. Waiting, she daydreamed herself and Fern Bowdoin together. His name was Fernald Bowdoin. When they called him up to the stand, they called out: Fernald Bowdoin. But revulsion took over. She needed space to recover. She didn't want to be close to a man so soon. And she'd never marry again. Never. That was a promise.

Court was called back into session. Her lawyers tensed visibly at the summons.

"So fast?" she said, walking with Kris and Ellen, Mike striding ahead.

"If it's the verdict this fast, then be prepared for Guilty," Kris said, and she wanted to smack the satisfied smirk of his mouth clean off his face.

The jury wasn't ready with a verdict. They had a list of questions concerning complicated legal points. THE JUDGE, who had clarified THE LAW earlier, drew in his breath and clarified it further, defining once again the subtleties of the burden of proof of murder by premeditation, murder with intent to harm, justifiable homicide and manslaughter, speaking this time more slowly, and with greater weariness. It was late afternoon. The last spurts of heat had overheated the courtroom. Outside, the dark day had turned into black night.

The jury listened, stupefied.

". . . and may find that the death was the natural and probable result of a reckless or culpably negligent act, the equivalent of criminal intent. You may examine the evidence to find that an accidental killing occurred where the slayer was proceeding upon a lawfully protective act unaccompanied by any criminally careless or reckless conduct. The accused would then be entitled to acquittal. If the purpose of the protective act was to frighten as a means of causing another to desist in an unlawful battery upon the . . ."

Still looking mystified when he finished, the jury filed out, returning to their deliberations.

She heard Mike. "Late Friday afternoon, everybody wants to finish and get home—and relax—they'll come in with a verdict fast."

"Yes," Kris said, "but is that good or bad? Hurrying could tip the verdict either way."

Exhausted, the waiting going on forever, she stayed close to Ellen's solid comfort, both silent. It occurred to her that she had paid little attention to this jury—a group of people of such vital importance to her. She knew that the foreman was a man, and that there were women on the jury, one very fat and pretty; she had noted two young, good-looking men. In listening to her, they had presented a collective sympathy. She had a strong sense of their good will.

She didn't put her estimate into words. She had been wrong about so much else, in her willful expectations of plentiful love in the air drifting to latch on to her. As if she specifically deserved love, more than anybody else. Less, now? Or more? *This woman has suffered enough.* Sweets's head fallen to the side, his color drained. From that moment, she knew that she had killed him. Time stopped, all the elation of the fight run out. That's why she cried when she came to that point in telling her story. Because she knew she had wanted to kill him. Anything, anything to win, to stop him. She was sick to death of humiliation and defeat. She wanted to win—if it meant killing him, if he killed her back, she didn't care.

The jury was filing in, but again not with the verdict. They were in search of further clarification. Could his honor please explain once more about "illegal battery"? And had they understood him correctly that it was unlawful for a husband to hit his wife? They had been arguing back and forth.

THE JUDGE stroked his nostrils in a deliberate dreamy gesture of his thumb and index finger, looking down at his desk, questioning its surface to witness this development.

The foreman stumbled on. "Some are sayin what about a man's

home bein his castle and what about love, honor n obey n all that, n some brought up this business a consentin adults . . ."

THE JUDGE held up a restraining hand, still gazing sorrowfully at his desk. He drew in a long breath, expelled it in a long sigh and began what was obviously going to be a long speech.

"A husband," he said, "does not have the permission of the law to beat his wife. Is that clear? Have I said that as simply as possible? Let me repeat, let me repeat that in another form. In this state, to lay hostile, threatening hands on any person is an illegal act, unless specifically armed with the legal authority to do so. A husband does not stand in relation to his wife as an officer of the law. He holds no legal authority over her. He is not licensed, solely by means of his marriage ties to a particular woman, to physically chastise, whip or inflict bodily injury upon her. A wife does not constitute her husband's physical property. A husband who physically attacks his wife acts at the risk of being met with sufficient force and violence to overcome such assault. Such assault is illegal battery. The law does not require a wife, solely because she has taken the marriage vows to love, honor and cherish . . ." He lifted his head. "I believe the word 'obey' is no longer in universal usage—" pausing before he continued. "I repeat, the law does not require anyone, man or woman, to submit meekly to indignities or violence to his or her person. He or she may lawfully repel such violence. The question, therefore, does not address itself to hypothetical rights of a husband over his wife or of a wife over her husband but to the larger issue, or rather the more specific details of . . ." and he was off again, enmeshing the jury in the legal rigmarole of premeditation, murder in the first degree, criminal intent, self-defense, manslaughter and justifiable homicide.

She kept her face turned toward him, interested, polite and grave. But in fact she had blotted him out. This jury would decide whether she was guilty, part guilty, wholly innocent or part innocent in the eyes of the state. If they found her guilty THE JUDGE would sentence her according to the laws of the state, but all the real questions and answers were beyond this group of men and women no better than Sweets, no better than herself. She wanted to win against the state as she had wanted to win against Sweets, but winning had no bearing on the real questions; these were not subject to the jurisdiction of her neighbors and an out-of-state judge sitting in judgment. The real questions were between her and Sweets—and God—or whatever it was that shaped existence. These lay outside—waiting for her.

Sweets was conjured up for her then. She saw him in the winter woods behind their house, the nice house they had been forced to give up to move to the broken-down Beauchamp place. It was a Saturday afternoon. She followed the sound of the chain saw through the woods thickly hung with snow and found Sweets cutting birch for the living-room fireplace and for the little wood stove in the kitchen, trimming and burning the brush and splitting the logs to size. He had been working for hours and had cleared an enchanted space that she entered as if into his secret joys. It was all contrast—the deep rich evergreens, the startling white of the birch bark and the silken exposed grain of the sliced wood, the golden fire and the blue smoke rising into the patches of bluer sky, the flaming streaks of sunshine on the dazzling snow, the whole mysteriously enclosed in dark tones of overarching trees. At the center of the magic was Sweets, brilliantly dark and dreamily happy, drunk on daydreams and sweated work, a crazy woolen hat on his head, his long arms spread wide to let her in. He loved to master what he loved, cutting his splash of roads across soft earth, through granite and woods, subduing, punishing, killing to close in on what he loved.

But it was she who had killed—like a man, like Sweets.

She saw Sweets standing in the center of the field on Allen's Hill, a flat tabletop of Queen Anne's lace bobbing and nodding their lighthearted heads in a clear, fresh, late August wind. He was laughing as he knocked off the flower heads with cutting swings of a slender stick he had picked up for the purpose.

"Stop it," she called out, running to join him from the car parked on the road. "Stop knocking their heads off." But she was laughing too.

"I like to," he said, continuing his swing. "Plenty more. More 'n enough."

No. Not enough. Never more than enough. That was what she had failed to pass on to him.

Once again, the jury was back with a question. The foreman introduced it with a long apology which THE JUDGE attended to with his head in his hands.

"We seem to be kinda slow on this one, sir, but we just can't seem to agree."

"What is the question?"

"Ya see, sir, we understand it's unlawful for a man to kill his wife —or, y'know, the other way around. What we're havin our trouble with is this other question. Now, does the law hold it's illegal for a man to slap his wife around, n then the law turns around n says it's legal for her to protect herself anyways she manages to, bein weaker 'n him and him bein stronger? Is that the gist of it?"

THE JUDGE sighed so deeply, it was a groan. With his head cradled in his hand, he began to speak, slowly. He reminded the foreman and the ladies and gentlemen of the jury that they had been present at a full trial, that they had listened to a great deal of testimony, that they had heard lengthy summations by the prosecuting attorney and the defense attorney.

"I, myself," he said, fixing them finally with a direct glance of admonishment, "I, myself, took careful measure of the legal explanations due you. I deeply appreciate, the court deeply appreciates the seriousness with which you are approaching your verdict. I gather from your question that there is some confusion in your minds as to the legal authority of a husband over his wife." He took a deep breath. "Perhaps I can simplify the concept. It is not lawful for a man to beat his wife, he does not have the permission of the law to assault her. Assault, in and of itself, is illegal, it is an illegal act. Is that clear? The question then is not whether you believe, in retrospect, that the defendant's use of force was necessary. The question is whether the defendant, under the circumstances as they appeared to her at the time of the incident, actually believed she was in danger of bodily harm, and could reasonably hold that belief. It is defensible to ward off an illegal assault, even if the assault is being made by a husband upon his wife. The marriage contract is not a law unto itself. The marriage contract is subsumed within the larger laws of the land, the laws of the state. As I tried to make clear earlier, you may be addressing yourselves to the wrong questions. The questions are: Did the defendant act in such a manner . . . ?" and she heard again the fine verbal lines drawn about the terrible moment that ended Sweets's life.

The jury listened, intent and puzzled.

He said, at the end, "Any further questions?"

They had no further questions. They filed out, and when they filed in again, it was to announce the verdict. She was told to rise. Her blood pounded in her ears so that she heard nothing, but she knew that she had won because of the joyous shouts and the rush of her people to her side hugging and kissing her. Above that, she heard angry shouts, clearly heard Helen Parsons' roar of disgusted disapproval and the noises of the court disbanding.

Well, she had won. Now she had only to face what waited for her beyond her victory.

ABOUT THE AUTHOR

HELEN YGLESIAS is the author of two previous novels, *How She Died*, which was a Houghton Mifflin Literary Fellowship novel, and *Family Feeling;* and a nonfiction work entitled *Starting*. Her stories, articles and reviews have appeared in *The New Yorker, Harper's Magazine, The Nation* and *The New York Times*, among other publications. She has been literary editor of *The Nation* and has taught creative writing at Columbia University and at the University of Iowa's Program in Creative Writing. Helen Yglesias is a member of the well-known family of writers which includes her sons, Rafael Yglesias and Lewis Cole, and her husband, Jose Yglesias.

DATE DUE

MAR 2 6 2000		

Demco, Inc. 38-293